SHROUDED SKY

BOOK 1 OF THE CHOSEN OF THE SPEARS

SANAN KOLVA

To my parents, for teaching me the love of reading and for always encouraging me. To Ravyn and Eirine for always letting me bounce ideas off you and encouraging me.

1

Hide the night and burn the day
The silent stars to quench
Dreamers' paths are closed again
To still the seeking heart

Between heartbeats, birds and insects all fell abruptly silent. Lyan froze, and in the sudden stillness, he heard hooves on the packed dirt trail. He crouched, and the ferns and brambles shifted, concealing him without snagging his shirt or tangling in his red hair.

Peering between the leaves, Lyan saw a coal-black horse on the trail. It bore neither tack nor rider. Its coat gleamed in the patches of sunlight that filtered to the forest floor. The horse paused, nostrils flaring as it looked from side to side. Lyan's breath caught in his throat when he saw its glowing red eyes and glimpsed the tips of fangs in its mouth.

That's a monster, not a horse. What is a pooka doing in Eilidh Wood?

The pooka snorted, tossing its head as if catching an unpleasant odor. The absence of bird and insect sounds amplified every noise the monster made.

Goddesses, please protect me from its tricks. Far too often, a pooka's idea of fun was pleasant for no one but itself.

The pooka resumed walking, and Lyan released his breath. The black horse abruptly stopped, looking sharply over its shoulder. Lyan froze in cold fear.

Did it hear me? Did it see me?

A crow burst from a bush near the pooka, shrieking as it took wing. The sound covered the crunch of branches as Lyan fell back, heart thumping against his ribs. The pooka watched the bird until it took roost in a tree, then cast another look around before continuing its trek.

I've never seen a pooka this close to Heartshrine Village. What is it looking for? Lyan edged back from the trail. *I don't want to be alone and away from the protection of the village with that monster roaming. I need to get back, tell Elder Brenhan, and let the hunters know before someone stumbles into its clutches.* He shivered. *Especially before I stumble into its clutches.*

Moving as quietly as he could, Lyan picked his way through the undergrowth. Plants shifted and swayed as Eilidh Wood opened a path for him. Lyan's pulse raced every time he heard a crunch or snap from the direction of the pooka, but when he turned to move deeper into the forest and further from the monster, a bramble blocked his way. Lyan swallowed hard, but didn't attempt to argue with the forest, continuing on the path it gave him.

He jumped at a loud crash from one side. Lyan looked sharply toward the noise, hurrying his steps. He didn't see the source, whether it was the pooka or something else, but it sounded large.

The ground suddenly crumbled underfoot. His head jerked back to his path as he realized he was sliding. In his distraction, he'd strayed to the edge of a ravine, the lip hidden by leafy ferns. Lyan grabbed for a hold as the ground gave way, but the ferns tore loose in his hand. Rocks jabbed him as he half slid, half fell into the ravine. His left foot hooked on a root as he hit the bottom, twisting and sending sharp pain up his leg. Lyan gasped, breath driven from him.

He lay panting on the ravine floor, anxiously listening for sounds that the pooka had come to investigate. He heard only birds and the wind through the branches. Turning his gaze up the steep slope to the trees above, Lyan gave the forest a plaintive look. "Did you *have* to put my path right next to this?"

He closed his eyes a moment, collecting his wits and fighting pain, then pulled himself to the face of the ravine. Finding purchases, he pulled himself upright, then reached up for new grips. His left ankle sent stabs of pain up his leg every time he moved it, but he could still use his right leg to brace himself. Sweat streaked his face as he reached for the next hold. Another painful grab, and his foot found a resting place. He looked up and tried to convince himself that it was not so far to the top. Lyan drew a deep breath and grabbed for the next shallow rock outcropping.

Even as he used it to lever up, the stone shifted under his weight, and he slid back down the slope to land roughly at the bottom. Spears of pain drove through his injured ankle and Lyan cried out as it was jostled to new agony. He lay unmoving for many gasping breaths. With a moan, he finally rolled on his side and tried to discover whether his fall had added any new injuries.

Only bruises, Lyan decided. He sucked in a shuddering breath and looked up at the thick branches of the trees far above him. "Couldn't I get a *little* help?" he asked the forest. "A root to climb? Point someone my way, maybe? And warn the village about the pooka?"

Leaves rustled, though the source could have been merely a passing breeze. Lyan sighed, seeing no immediate aid coming. Eilidh Wood could be fickle, but he trusted the forest not to abandon him. Some sort of help would come, eventually. He could wait. He had little choice but to wait.

When his ankle hurt a little less, he would try to climb again. Lyan rested his head against the rocky ground and closed his eyes, waiting for the sharp edges of pain to pass.

Lyan started from his half-daze at a voice from above. Anxiety flooded him. *Is that the pooka? Did it hear me fall and come to investigate?* He held his breath, straining to hear. A sharp exclamation came in a language he didn't know, but it brimmed with weary frustration. *The birds are still singing, and the insects haven't fallen silent. They wouldn't be announcing themselves if it was the pooka. Does that mean this is some traveler?* He'd expected to be found by someone from Heartshrine Village rather than a stranger, but Eilidh Wood was capricious, and he wouldn't turn down whatever assistance it directed toward him, even if it had turned around some unfortunate stranger and sent him wandering in circles to happen upon Lyan.

"Hello?" he called.

Silence for several moments, then Lyan heard brush crunch and crackle. Someone voiced a startled yelp, and a small cascade of pebbles tumbled down on Lyan as the person caught his balance before falling victim to the ravine. A jabber of words Lyan couldn't understand followed.

Lyan gingerly used the rock wall to pull himself upright, looking up. "Hello? I fell. Can you help?" He was unpracticed in speaking the Trade tongue, and kept his plea to simple words he could remember.

Several voices spoke quickly above, then Lyan saw a silhouette as a man looked down into the ravine. "… you hurt?"

Lyan limped into a pool of sunlight so he could be seen, and nodded. He touched his injured leg, but couldn't remember the word for "ankle". "Hurt leg… foot."

They could be bandits. Sometimes bandits were foolish enough to attempt robbery in Eilidh Wood. But if they helped him, Lyan didn't care what else they did unless they attacked him. And if they did, he trusted the forest to protect him.

More words—a brief argument. Then a coil of knotted rope thumped down the side of the ravine and a man climbed down. He navigated the descent with confidence. Once on the ground, he studied Lyan before approaching and offering an arm for support. Lyan knew he wasn't a sight to inspire fear. His red hair hung in tangles, his clothes were dirty and ripped, and a tender bruise colored the right side of his jaw. His only weapon was a long hunting knife, and he'd be more likely to cut off his own fingers than stab anyone in a fight.

"Thank you." Lyan accepted the support and limped to the rope. His rescuer stood nearly even with Lyan's height, tall for a human. His blond hair was cropped short and stubble speckled his jaw. He had a warrior's muscles. His clothing was dirty and streaked with dark stains. As close as Lyan was, he could tell the man hadn't bathed in quite a few days.

"Can you climb?" the man asked.

Lyan gripped the rope and nodded. "Yes."

The man gave him a boost, and Lyan pulled himself slowly up the rope, bracing with his good foot as he went. His hands ached, and he longed to ask whoever stood above to pull him up, but the need to maintain some shreds of dignity drove him on. Also, he couldn't assemble a coherent sentence in the Trade tongue to make his plea. As Lyan reached the ravine's lip, two men pulled him up and guided him to a fallen log. Lyan sank down with a heartfelt sigh of relief, wiping sweat from his brow and sucking in deep gulps of air.

Once he'd caught his breath and could focus on something other than his ankle, he looked at his rescuers. The travelers numbered six human men, counting the one who climbed from the ravine, and three pack horses. The animals browsed in the undergrowth, and the men watched Lyan with varying degrees of caution.

"Thank you for your aid," he said in the Trade tongue.

The eldest of the group, a man with gray hair and a short gray beard, scowled at Lyan, and the lines on his face implied that the expression was his natural inclination. Turning from Lyan, Gray-hair spoke a few words to the man beside him. The second man was much younger, clean-shaven with golden brown hair. He raised an eyebrow at Gray-hair, dubious about whatever was said, then he spoke to Lyan. The words were too quick for him to follow easily, but he picked out enough to guess the meaning. "…Hurt? Need help? Your home… near?"

Lyan shifted positions, and his ankle screamed in fresh protest, taking his breath away for a moment. He wiped sweat from his forehead and collected scattered thoughts. "Home… not close. Rest now, walk later." The thought of limping back to Heartshrine Village didn't appeal, but he didn't expect strangers to linger. Travelers tended to feel uncomfortable in Eilidh Wood.

Gray-hair spoke sharply in a language Lyan didn't know. The younger man retorted, and his words brought Gray-hair up short. Lyan had assumed Gray-hair was leader, yet he deferred to the younger man, nodding reluctantly. The younger man sighed, then forced a thin, apologetic smile to Lyan. "Cailean Dev'gilla." He indicated himself, speaking the name slowly and clearly.

Lyan mouthed the foreign name, then pointed to himself. "Lyan." Remembering a custom he'd read, he held out his right hand.

Cailean grasped it in greeting, seeming pleased and relieved. He asked a question, but it was too quick, with too many unfamiliar words.

"Sorry. Not good with this tongue," Lyan apologized. Silently, he vowed to learn more of the Trade tongue and rely less on other means of understanding.

Cailean gestured to indicate understanding, and that the question was not important. He turned back to the rest of the men. Lyan winced as he shifted and another stab of pain ran up his leg.

Cailean spoke his name, and Lyan looked up. Another

man approached. He was shorter, with mouse brown hair and a pleasant smile. His eyes glittered with curiosity, and he carried a bag. Cailean nodded to the man. "Shiolto. He… look at your leg."

"Thank you." He was fortunate the men hadn't simply pulled him from the ravine and left him to fend for himself. At least, that was the lack of hospitality his friend Kithr often ascribed to outsiders.

Shiolto crouched beside Lyan. He looked more like a laborer than a doctor, but he was careful in his examination of Lyan's leg, feeling for any broken bones and watching Lyan for reactions. When he touched the ankle, Lyan tensed.

Shiolto paused, then carefully felt around Lyan's ankle. "Here?"

"Yes," Lyan said through clenched teeth.

Shiolto looked over his shoulder and asked a question. Another man handed him a water skin. Shiolto pulled off Lyan's low boot, soaked cloth strips, and wrapped them around the swollen ankle. The water wasn't particularly cold, but it still felt soothing on his skin. Some of his tension eased.

Shiolto offered him the water skin, and Lyan accepted gratefully. He gulped down deep swallows, soothing his dry throat. Splashing water into one hand, he wiped his face and tried to rub away some dirt with a sleeve. A rebellious lock of red hair drooped into his face, and Lyan pushed it back, tucking his hair behind his ears.

Shiolto drew a quick, sharp breath, jerking back. Lyan looked over his shoulder, wondering if something had crept up behind him, but there was only the forest, and Shiolto's wide eyes were firmly fixed on him. Pale, the man edged back from Lyan.

"What?" Lyan asked, confused.

"You… are an elf." Shiolto barely whispered the words, then he repeated them loud enough for his companions to hear. "An *elf!*"

Attentions that had drifted away from Lyan sharply focused back on him as all five of the other men spun. Gray-hair and the blond warrior both reached for their swords. Cailean held a long ornamented spear, while the man who'd brought the water carried a mace. Only one didn't move for a weapon, a shorter, black-haired man who Lyan had barely noticed. He simply studied Lyan with an interest as unsettling as the sudden hostility of the others.

Tree branches creaked and shifted as if disturbed by a strong wind. Birds and insects fell silent. All three horses stopped searching for food, their heads jerking up, ears pricked and eyes searching for danger. Shiolto yelped when a hawthorn near him shook, branches shifting toward him. Above, tree limbs drooped down, dangling vines swinging toward the humans. Not *quite* attacking… yet.

Lyan quickly held up empty hands. "Calm, please! No weapons. No threats!" He directed that at the humans, and prayed to the gods that they would listen. To the forest, he spoke quickly in his own language, trying to diffuse some of the threat in the air. "It's all right. They were startled, that's all. They haven't attacked or hurt me. You sent them to help me from the ravine, and they did. They were just surprised." Though why they would be surprised to meet an elf in Eilidh Wood, Lyan couldn't imagine.

The black-haired man spoke, and though Lyan didn't know the language, the man's voice was calm and his expression serene. The other men glanced at him, and slowly they lowered their weapons. Eilidh Wood, in return, settled. The swaying branches grew still, and the air became less oppressive, though it remained watchful and wary. The humans cast uneasy looks at the trees, and none of them approached Lyan. Gray-hair spoke sharply, to which Cailean shook his head. He said something in a low voice, gesturing at the confining trees with a wary expression.

"You threatened me first," Lyan sighed in Elven. "The

forest reacted to what you began." Not that the men would understand him. "What did you *expect* in Eilidh Wood?"

More sharp looks, and Cailean strode to him, crossing the distance in long steps. The man stood over Lyan, his face drawn and hand clutching his spear in a white-knuckled grip. The trees rustled a warning that Cailean ignored. "Eilidh Wood," he said in the Trade tongue. "This is Eilidh Wood?"

How in Soldarr's axe could someone enter Eilidh Wood and *not* realize where they were? "Yes, this is Eilidh Wood."

Clearly, that was not the answer Cailean hoped for. The man began cursing softly. He spun away from Lyan and stalked to the horses to dig through a bag.

Shiolto cautiously moved toward Lyan with all the tension of a man approaching a venomous snake. The forest judged him less of a threat, and withheld warnings. Lyan offered the water skin toward Shiolto. "Thank you."

Shiolto hesitated, then, with a tight smile, nodded and accepted the skin. He quickly collected the bandages and his bag, then retreated.

Cailean returned carrying a scroll case. Lyan perked up with interest. He couldn't speak many languages, but he could read and write far more. Cailean pulled out a sheet of parchment and unrolled a map on the ground. Crouching, he jabbed a finger at a small forest some days south of Eilidh Wood. "Not here?"

Lyan shook his head and pointed at Eilidh Wood. "No. Here."

Cailean cursed again, shoulders slumping. Studying him, Lyan realized the man was exhausted. His face was lined and his eyes shadowed with weariness. "How?" Cailean sighed quietly.

Cailean didn't seem to expect an answer, but Lyan knew. "No stars."

The man met his eyes, and slowly he nodded. "No stars. Only clouds."

A man could tell directions by the sun, but to navigate with precision, he needed the Guiding Stars—the one unmoving constellation. Lyan looked up automatically, seeing patches of blue sky through the canopy of trees. No stars shone during in the day, but he had as much chance of seeing them during the day as he did at night. For more than a month, clouds had rolled over the sky at sunset, dispersing with dawn. For more than a month, Lyan had been useless to his village, unable to do his duties as an astrologer.

No one listens when I tell them that this isn't right and this is a bad omen. What will it take to make them recognize that I'm right? Even Elder Brenhan dismisses my concerns! Would he listen if strangers told him something is wrong?

Lyan held Cailean's gaze and collected the right words in the Trade tongue. "Cailean, you and others, come. To my home. Guests. Rest."

Cailean inhaled sharply and stiffened in surprise. "All of us, go with you?" He looked warily at the forest. In the initial threat, the brush had shifted to block the paths between trees, hemming them in around the ravine. Eilidh Wood had not lowered those obstructions yet. Cailean looked back at Lyan, assessing limited options. "Guests?" He sounded dubious.

"Guests," Lyan promised. He addressed the trees in Elven. "You don't have to keep them here. If they don't want to come with me, they don't have to."

Wind brushed through the trees, making the leaves rustle like whispering voices. Not words, exactly, but they carried meaning. Lyan glanced toward the ravine, suddenly wondering whether his fall had been as accidental as he thought, or if the forest had planned it to bring him and these humans together. Several thorny branches withdrew, opening a single path. Lyan looked at it, then gave Cailean an apologetic look. "Eilidh Wood wants you to come."

"So I see." Cailean said nothing for a long moment. He

rose and rolled up the map, storing it back in the tube. Then he eyed the three horses.

Gray-hair asked a curt question. Cailean drew a breath, straightened, and issued an order. The men stared at him in shock. Cailean gave another order, more sharply. Shiolto and the other brown-haired man, perhaps Shiolto's brother, jumped to obey. The two men unloaded the baggage from one horse, and Lyan saw the animal wore a riding saddle rather than one designed for packs. The men loaded some packs onto the other two horses, and the rest they carried themselves. Shiolto led the unburdened horse to Lyan.

"Do you ride?" Cailean asked.

Lyan nodded. "Some." He tried to stand, but pain tore through his leg when he moved, and he sagged back with a gasp.

Shiolto exclaimed in concern and rushed to help him, fear momentarily forgotten. With the man's aid, Lyan rose, leaning heavily on Shiolto to keep weight off his injured ankle. By the time he was settled into the saddle, he was pale and damp with sweat. The horse snorted as if it shared concern for his well-being. Lyan patted the brown neck with a shaking hand that might not have offered as much reassurance as he wished.

The men gathered their gear and assembled around Cailean. Cailean looked at the trees again, debating something. Then he hooked his spear through loops on the saddle of Lyan's borrowed mount, leaving the weapon easily within Lyan's reach. Gray-hair spoke in protest, but Cailean silenced him with a look.

He doesn't want to make it appear that I was forced to bring them with me. Belatedly, Lyan considered how this might look to sentries around Heartshrine Village—Lyan scuffed and bruised, surrounded by armed strangers. He immediately thought of several warriors who he hoped were *not* on watch when they arrived, his best friend Kithr among them.

The horse tossed its head uneasily when Lyan urged it

toward the gap in the undergrowth, but advanced. The trees allowed them to pass, and the forest relaxed. Birds and animal sounds gradually returned. Leaves whispered, though Lyan didn't feel a breeze to move them.

"Do not wander," he cautioned.

Cailean snorted in faint amusement and gestured at the thick brush on either side. "Wander *how?*"

Lyan sighed and addressed Eilidh Wood. "You aren't helping to make them comfortable."

Eilidh Wood didn't share its reasons, and it did not change its behavior, making no effort to hide that it expected the humans to follow Lyan. The forest's path brought them to the packed dirt road that was the main route through the forest. They followed it for a time, then Lyan turned deeper into the forest, taking a narrow trail he knew well. It wound through Eilidh Wood, seeming random in its turns, but each one brought Lyan closer to home.

The afternoon sun hung high. The men spoke quietly among themselves in brief burst of conversation that trailed away again. Cailean walked beside Lyan, not usually joining in the talk. Lyan's mind drifted as he tried to focus on something other than the pain radiating from his ankle, and his attention fell away from their path.

An arrow interrupted the murmur of voices and cut through Lyan's thoughts. The quivering black-feathered shaft slammed into a tree trunk only a handspan from Cailean's neck. Lyan drew to an abrupt halt and turned sharply to the trees. "What's the meaning of this?"

"What's the meaning of this?" Kithr repeated from the shelter of the trees. "I should ask you that, Lyan, to bring *Tathrens* to our home." His bow creaked slightly as he drew another arrow.

2

Whispers in green
The shadows dance
Whispers for blood
The war, the lance

Lyan drew a sharp breath. His gaze shifted uneasily to the humans, then back to the trees. "They helped me," he said flatly.

Cailean stepped forward, empty hands held out, and began to speak. Kithr's arrow whistled close enough for the feathers to brush the man's hair when it thumped into the tree. "Stay where you are, Tathren." Cailean froze, the meaning clear even if the words were not.

Lyan walked the horse between Kithr's sentry post and Cailean. "They helped me, Kithr. Stop. They didn't come with intent to harm anyone."

"This place will not be defiled by their presence," Kithr growled.

"Eilidh Wood thinks otherwise. The forest *demanded* they come here with me."

"What need does Eilidh Wood have for the likes of our enemies?" Kithr's voice was sharp and cold.

"We haven't been at war with Tather for sixty years, Kithr! These are not the men you fought. I'm sure I don't know why the forest wants what it wants," Lyan snapped. "That's for Elder Brenhan to say. So either he can come here, or I can bring *my guests* to him."

"Guests? You call these jabbering magpies your guests?" Anger seethed in Kithr's words.

"My guests," Lyan repeated sharply. "Guests who Eilidh Wood insisted should come with me here. Are you going to get the Elder or not?"

A long silence, then Kithr spoke in a voice more calm, if no more warm. "I will speak to Elder Brenhan. But these will not enter our home without his word."

He left without a sound, but Lyan sensed the lessened hostility in the air. He remained still a long moment, collecting himself. Pain made his temper short and words sharp. Finally he turned to face the men he had brought to his home. His eyes met Cailean's.

The spear-wielder spoke quietly, an apology to Lyan. "I am sorr—"

Lyan cut him short with a motion. "You're Tathren?" he asked. Gesturing to the group of them to make himself clear, Lyan repeated, "Tathrens?"

Cailean's expression was unreadable. After a moment, he said, "Yes."

"Gods," sighed Lyan. "Who have I offended to bring this on me?" He massaged his forehead.

"I thought you knew already," Cailean said.

No wonder Lyan's invitation had surprised the men. Lyan straightened and looked over their faces, seeing suspicion and worry on them. "You are my guests," he repeated. "Guests." But if he'd realized they had come from Tather, he would have protested more to Eilidh Wood. Arguing with the forest was usually fruitless, but Lyan would have tried.

The horses shifted uneasily in the silence that followed. The men fidgeted, checking weapons and eyeing the trees nervously. Cailean tried to project calm, but Lyan saw him toying with the folds of his shirt and glancing toward his spear to assure himself it was near. The silence quickly grew uncomfortable. Lyan cast about for some way to lessen it, but found nothing. If Elder Brenhan didn't agree to let the men enter the village, he didn't know what he would do. He couldn't send them away with a pooka loose in the forest, could he?

Finally, after an eternity, leaves crunched and fallen twigs snapped as someone tromped up the path. Kithr shoved aside concealing branches and scowled at them all. The Tathrens started at his arrival despite of the noise he'd purposely made. His bow was slung across his back. His brown hair, tan skin, and brown leathers gave him the illusion of stepping straight out of a tree.

Kithr's gaze fixed on Lyan. "Elder Brenhan wants to see the Tathrens. Bring them." His voice was clipped and controlled, but he couldn't hide the anger in his stance.

"As the Elder and the forest will," Lyan retorted. Biting back sharp words, he added, "Kithr, there's more than just Tathrens in Eilidh Wood. I saw a poo--"

Kithr had already turned away. "Elder Brenhan said to bring the Tathrens. Any other strays following you about can wait on the road."

Lyan's jaw tightened. "I saw a pooka," he said in a low voice. Kithr's lack of reaction confirmed that he was not listening. Lyan turned to the Tathrens and said in Trade, "Follow."

The men hesitated, but Lyan urged the horse forward. Steps crunched as the humans followed. Lyan's mount calmed as Eilidh Wood, satisfied that its will was being done, loomed less forcefully over them. Kithr lingered just ahead of the group, every movement announcing his loathing of permitting Tathrens into Heartshrine Village.

Before they entered the village, they reached the shrine. The five ancient stones, set in a half-circle and each taller than an elf, were older than Heartshrine Village. Some claimed they were older than Eilidh Wood itself, but that was impossible. Eilidh Wood had always been, and it didn't change. The stones depicted images of Soldarr, Feyra, and Tesseia, the three elven gods. In some scenes, they were shown at rest, Feyra and Tesseia dancing while Soldarr played a harp, or hunting, Soldarr carrying a spear and the goddesses with bows. Other scenes depicted them in war, Soldarr in armor, wielding a two-handed axe, Feyra and Tesseia again armed with bows. The faces and forms of their enemies had worn down with time, so they battled monstrous, featureless shapes.

Kithr knelt at the low altar just inside the half-ring of stones. A few offerings lay on the stone—food, crafts, a branch with four tiny green apples nestled among the leaves. Lyan bowed his head from horseback.

Forgive me for not kneeling, he silently prayed. *Please grant me guidance with Cailean and his men. I don't know why you put them in my path or why the forest wishes them here, but I want to do your will and the will of Eilidh Wood. So please, guide me.*

Behind him, the men shifted restlessly, though they held their peace. Only a fool interrupted another's devotions.

Finally Kithr rose. He turned to see if Lyan was ready, then continued without a word. Between the shrine and the village, the trail transformed into a well-worn path wide enough for three men abreast. The oaks, maples, and birches that dominated Eilidh Wood became a diverse mix of trees, though none encroached on the open village commons. Lyan felt eyes on them, and the commons stood empty where normally elves would be gathered to enjoy the sun while they worked. Human strangers rarely found welcome in Heartshrine Village, but usually at least a few elves lingered to trade goods or stories. Tathren strangers could count themselves fortunate not to be met by a volley of arrows.

Kithr stopped and jabbed a finger toward Elder Brenhan's grove. "The Elder is waiting." The maze of hedges sometimes jarred Lyan with its artificial nature, contrasting with the free-growing plants around them. Whenever he tried to pin down the sensation, though, it slid away like water through his fingers, leaving only a vague, lingering unease.

"Would you lead them to him, Kithr?" Lyan asked.

Kithr's eyes narrowed. "And why don't *you?*"

Lyan closed his eyes a moment, drew a deep breath, and tried to speak calmly. "Because Ada has said if someone is injured, they need to see her first thing upon returning. I fell. My ankle's either sprained or broken, and I *hurt.* So would you *please* see my guests to Elder Brenhan?"

"You're hurt?" Kithr stiffened, then looked with sharp suspicion at the Tathrens.

"Gods, Kithr, they didn't push me into the ravine, they pulled me *out!* And they let me ride one of their horses. I'd still be there if they hadn't helped!" Lyan snapped.

"And did they know you were an elf when they did?" Kithr asked tightly.

"Not when they helped me from the ravine. They learned that after. But they didn't try to harm me then either." Lyan held his friend's gaze.

Kithr spat in the dirt, then exhaled sharply. "Fine. Go to Ada. I'll see your Tathrens to the Elder." He looked at Cailean and said something in a language Lyan didn't know.

The Tathrens all jumped when he addressed them. Cailean answered, expression wary. Kithr snorted, satisfied with their discomfiture, and spoke curtly with a gesture to follow him.

"Lyan?" Cailean looked up to him.

"Go with Kithr," Lyan told him. "I come later. After tend leg." He gingerly touched his injured leg.

Cailean nodded, seeming to understand, though his tense stance revealed hesitation to be left alone with Kithr. Kithr waited with obvious impatience, and Cailean finally waved his men to follow. Lyan turned the horse toward Ada's house. Kithr would do as he said, whether he liked it or not. Lyan's wishes he might not follow, but Elder Brenhan's he would not ignore.

The herbalist opened her door when the horse stopped. "Odd friends you found, Lyan," she greeted.

"They helped me and they have been kind," he responded both in his defense and theirs. "I fell."

"So I heard," she said. "As did most of the village. You weren't exactly keeping your voice down."

Lyan flushed red and focused on climbing from the horse. Ada steadied him, and he leaned on her shoulder as she helped him limp inside. The herbalist was shorter than him and old enough to be his mother, but she was stout and strong. Ada guided Lyan to a chair and propped his leg up on a stool. Her touch was gentle as she examined the injured ankle, but Lyan still hissed in pain. She unwound the cloths Shiolto had wrapped. "Did you tend this?" she asked.

Sweat beaded Lyan's brow and his breath was tight. "One of the men did."

"Reasonably sensible, for a human," she allowed. "Not as swollen as it could be, which makes things easier for me." She shook chestnut hair from her face. "I don't feel a break—you might have gotten away with a sprain. Cool compresses to keep the swelling down, and dayseed oil to numb it. Now, for the gods' sake, try not to walk on it more than you have to for a few days, and keep your eyes on the ground for once."

"I was *not* staring at the sky when I fell!" Lyan protested.

She gave him a long, dubious look.

"I wasn't," Lyan repeated.

"So you say," Ada replied, clearly not believing him. She moved to her medicine chest and prepared a tincture of the yellow dayseed oil for him, then applied some to a fresh wrap. "If I tell you to stay in your home for the rest of the day, will you?"

"My guests are speaking to the Elder," Lyan answered. Some tension relaxed from his body as numbness dulled the pain.

Ada scowled, but nodded. "Try not to walk more than you must." She walked into another room. Lyan heard sounds of items being moved, and the herbalist returned with a crutch. "Try this. Tall enough for you?"

Lyan rose gingerly and leaned on the crutch. "I think so."

She nodded. "It should do. Come along, I'll walk you to your house so you can wash up before you see Elder Brenhan."

Outside, the commons remained empty of people, but Cailean's horses had been unsaddled and hobbled, nibbling on grass and shrubs. Ada set a slow pace, and Lyan limped beside her. Lyan's house stood beneath an ash tree, sheltered by its branches. The door swung open at his touch. Ada set the bottle of dayseed oil on the shelf just inside the door, then withdrew.

"Thank you, Ada," Lyan said after her.

"Read the stars for me sometime, and we'll be even," she replied.

Lyan flinched, but only slightly. "Of course. Whatever night the sky is clear."

She didn't seem to notice the qualifier, but everyone in the village asked him to read the stars for them "sometime," yet never sought him out on any night to actually do his duty. He cast a glance out the window, wondering once more why no one else paid attention to the clouds.

The door swung closed behind Ada, and Lyan limped through the main room and into his private chamber. He paused, momentarily perplexed by the sense of something out of place. Then he recognized the addition to the clutter. Books had been piled to one side, clearing space on the table for the saddlebags from Cailean's horses. Kithr must have brought them in. He was one of the few people who Lyan's home would permit to enter this room unaccompanied. Cailean's spear was strapped to a bag atop the pile.

Lyan considered the bags. Snooping would be rude, and bordered on violation of his responsibilities as a host, but curiosity pressed at him, along with a wish to understand Kithr's hate for Tathrens who had been born long after the end of the war. He limped to the table and fumbled with the laces on the top bag.

His hand touched the shaft of Cailean's spear, and Lyan jerked back with a yelp as a sharp jolt ran up his arm. The tingling raced all the way to his shoulder. He shook his arm as if he could dislodge the sensation. Lyan stared at the weapon, then tentatively touched the bag. Nothing bit him when his hand rested on the leather saddlebag, nor when he untied the laces.

It wasn't magic intended to keep out thieves or spies, then. Cautious, Lyan touched the spear a second time. The jolt flew up his arm again. He pulled back quickly, uneasily eyeing the weapon. Finally, he guiltily laced the bag closed. The spear did nothing.

Shaking his still-tingling arm, Lyan limped to the trunk at the end of his bed. It was mostly filled with books—those he considered too rare to cram onto the shelves with the rest of his library. Instead of a book, Lyan drew out a leather pouch. He tipped out an ear cuff made of a silvery metal worked in threads thin as spider webs and shaped to fit along the rim of an elven ear. He'd found it many years ago on a Day of Remembrance. The festival was the one day of the year when the ruins in Eilidh Wood were not forbidden ground, and village youths inevitably spent the day scouring for treasure while the adults told stories. Everyone had some trinket or prize found in the ruins. Some, like the ear cuff, even held magic that no elven crafter could replicate.

Lyan settled the ear cuff on, then stood. The movement sent a stab of pain through his ankle, even with the numbing oil. He winced and bit his lip, then steadied himself. Leaning heavily on the crutch, he limped outside.

Kithr stood leaning against Lyan's ash tree. He offered Lyan an arm, but Lyan shook his head. "I'm all right."

"If white as a birch is 'all right'," Kithr said, voice dry. "How is it?"

"Ada thinks it's just sprained, not broken," Lyan assured him.

"Elder Brenhan wants you to join him when you're able. If you're not, I'll tell him you need rest."

"I'm *fine*, Kithr," Lyan said. "I won't be winning any foot races, but it won't kill me. I can talk to the Elder and my guests." Sometimes he appreciated Kithr's overprotective tendencies, but other times they were just smothering. He limped toward Elder Brenhan's grove. "What did you say to Cailean earlier?"

"Nothing overly insulting," Kithr replied. He saw Lyan's suspicious look and rolled his eyes. "I said they should count themselves lucky that you claim them as guests, Lyan. That's all."

Lyan accepted that answer. Kithr walked with him to the edge of the Elder's grove, but didn't enter. Lyan limped under the arch of interwoven vines and branches. Flowers bloomed along the path's edge and climbing vines wound up the sides of the hedges, filling the air with fragrance. Lyan navigated the maze with the ease of familiarity, making his way to the pool at the center. He heard voices as he turned the corner, and paused.

"Come in, Lyan," Elder Brenhan called.

Lyan bowed "Thank you, Elder."

Elder Brenhan had been elder of Heartshrine Village even when Lyan's parents had been young, but he carried his nearly six hundred years well. If he didn't move quite as spryly as a youth, generations of children had learned not to underestimate his speed or quick wit, which often caught them unprepared. He sat at ease in a chair under the shade of a tree. His white hair was cut short, currently adorned by several green leaves. "Please join us. You have brought a fascinating collection of guests, Lyan." The older elf waved Lyan closer, and he obeyed.

Cailean, Shiolto, and the other four sat on polished oak benches facing the Elder. Cailean quickly shifted to make room and invited Lyan to sit with a gesture. Lyan nodded thanks and looked to Elder Brenhan for permission. The Elder gave him a look of amused exasperation. "Of course you may sit, Lyan. Do you think I would make you stand with a broken ankle?"

"Thank you, Elder," Lyan responded, settling on the bench. "And I don't know. Ada said it isn't broken, just sprained."

Elder Brenhan chuckled and shook his head. "I am corrected. Very well, I will not make you stand with a sprained ankle either." He spoke again, this time in Tathren. "We have been discussing the reasons behind Lord Cailean's journey. How much do you know, Lyan?"

The ear cuff translated the words, and Lyan understood them as easily as if the Elder spoke Elven, but the statement itself startled Lyan. *Lord* Cailean? He knew the title from reading—it referred to a human landowner and a noble, proud and aloof, by reputation. The idea clashed with what he'd seen of the human so far. Lyan recovered from his surprise and focused instead on the elder's question. "Nothing at all, Elder. My mastery of the Trade tongue was barely enough for simple communication."

The Tathrens started and stared at him, and Lyan knew that the ear cuff's magic worked; they understood him just as he did them. Before anyone could question him, he explained. "I didn't expect to meet strangers in the forest, but I have a trinket that translates spoken words."

Cailean relaxed, as if a mystery had been solved. "I didn't think you were playing at not understanding us."

Elder Brenhan cleared his throat, and Lyan returned his attention to him. "Lord Cailean and most of his companions are from Tather, as you doubtless now know. I asked him to wait for your arrival to tell his tale. I know you like to learn about other lands, Lyan." He gestured for Cailean to speak.

Cailean inclined his head in a polite nod. "I am Cailean Dev'gilla, son of Ereskivan Dev'gilla, and Earl of Ihvako." He cast a glance at Lyan. "Ihvako is a province to the west of Sarahu…" He caught Lyan's expression of polite confusion and shook his head with a smile. "It's west of the capital, a prosperous province. My family has held it for many generations. We are one of the ancient families of Tather."

Lyan spoke before he thought about the question. "Then why are you here?"

Gray-hair stiffened and opened his mouth indignantly, about to speak. Cailean held up a hand to forestall him. "It's a fair question, Aikan. My father died several years ago, and I inherited his title and lands. However, Tather still suffers political turmoil from power struggles and infighting. My father had no brothers, but his cousin, Ewart Col'renn, attempted to claim my holdings as his own. When the king denied his petition, Ewart turned to force of arms. He had the money to hire skilled soldiers and mercenaries." His lips twitched in a humorless smile. "If you cannot take it by politics, take it by force. My men fought bravely, but…"

Cailean sighed softly. "Ewart laid siege to the keep. He had us surrounded, and we would have fallen if not for Yion."

The indicated man bowed slightly from his seat, and Lyan recognized him as the calm man, who had seemed unflustered even when the forest threatened them. His speech had a noticeable lilting accent. His skin was darkly tanned, and his features flatter than his companions. His slick black hair was bound in a short topknot. The center of his forehead, between his eyes, seemed to have an oval divot. "I am honored you accepted my humble aid, my lord."

"Yion was among the mercenaries Ewart had hired. When Ewart's forces took the walls of my keep, for gods only know what reason, Yion chose to help me, and led what remained of my forces from the keep by a secret route," Cailean said.

"Where are you from?" Lyan asked Yion curiously.

"A distant land that I am sure you do not know," Yion answered simply.

"We escaped with what we could take, and I sent most of my men to regroup at designated locations. I stayed in hiding near the keep with these companions, waiting to see what Ewart would do." Cailean gazed at the pool, eyes distant. "Ewart scoured the keep in search of something he believed hidden within, a relic my family held. When I realized what he wanted, I knew I had to leave before he discovered me. If he'd found me, I have no doubt he would have done everything in his power to force me to reveal its location.

"I left most of my men behind with orders to protect what they could from Ewart's hired swords and gather strength. With my present companions, I left Tather and traveled east, toward Gramea. Ewart's men pursued us, and we had to leave the roads and take an overland path. I thought we were well south of Eilidh Wood, but obviously, I was wrong. I had no intention of entering this forest."

Lyan's brow furrowed as he listened. He understood why Cailean had been forced to leave his home, but the tale didn't explain why the man had left Tather completely. "Why didn't you stay with your men? Is the thing that Ewart wants hidden somewhere else?"

Cailean opened his mouth, but hesitated.

"Lyan, you're prying," Elder Brenhan chastised, giving him a stern look.

Lyan looked at his hands, abashed. "I'm sorry. I know you didn't intend to enter Eilidh Wood, but thank you for helping me."

Cailean's shoulders had tensed at Lyan's question, but relaxed when neither Lyan nor Elder Brenhan pressed for an answer. "I'm glad we could help."

"Thinking of that, Lyan," said the Elder, "how did you happen to fall? Cailean told me they found you in a ravine. Not watching your feet?"

"I was not looking at the sky!" Lyan protested angrily. It seemed everyone thought him unable to look away from the heavens, no matter that the stars had been shrouded behind clouds for the last month.

Elder Brenhan raised a hand. "Peace, Lyan. I meant no insult, only thinking something must have distracted you from your path."

"Yes," answered Lyan. "I was distracted, but not by the sky." His expression grew serious as he spoke in his own tongue again. "Elder Brenhan, I saw a pooka in the forest."

Elder Brenhan drew up short. Speaking suddenly in Elven again, he demanded, "Are you certain, Lyan? Such monsters haven't been sighted in Eilidh Wood for a hundred years."

"I'm certain," Lyan said firmly. "A black horse. Its eyes glowed red, and I saw fangs. No horse has fangs."

"Did it threaten you?" asked the elder. "What happened?"

Lyan hesitated, trying to find words for the impression he had gotten when he saw the creature. "It... was hunting. Looking for something in particular. I'm not sure it even knew I was there, and I am sure it didn't see me. I fell while avoiding its path." A thought suddenly came to him. Turning to Cailean, he asked, "Did you see a black horse on or near the road? One with no rider."

The man frowned. "No, I don't think so…"

"You speak of the pooka." All heads turned toward the accented voice. Yion met Lyan's eyes. "Is that not so?"

"You saw it," Lyan said.

Cailean Dev'gilla looked at them both with puzzlement. "What are you talking about?"

"They did not see it," Yion said. "Nor did it see us. We were hidden from its sight, though it sensed our presence. But I saw the monster, and knew it for what it was."

"You didn't say anything?" exclaimed Shiolto. "Why not?"

"I did not wish to alert the creature to us. Attracting your attention to it might well have done so. Such creatures are not trifled with."

"But…" Shiolto protested.

"Let it be, Shiolto," interrupted Cailean. Shiolto bowed his head and fell silent. "I wish you'd told us about it, Yion, at least once it was gone and the danger past."

"The danger is not past, my lord," Yion said. "It is only at a distance. And it was only shortly after I felt we were a safe distance from the pooka that we heard Lyan. Since then there has been little opportunity."

Lyan barely stopped himself from asking if it was searching for them, but bit his tongue before he could trample courtesy any further than he already had. He turned to Elder Brenhan instead. "Elder, the appearance of such a creature can't be ignored as easily as clouds at night."

His pointed words earned a sharp look. "Its appearance is indeed concerning," agreed Elder Brenhan, calm tone not matching his displeased expression. "But if, as you say, it's searching for something, then it will leave once the object of its hunt has left Eilidh Wood." He did not look at the Tathrens, but the meaning was clear nonetheless. Cailean's lips pressed together in a thin line, but he said nothing. Lyan's hands clenched. He remained silent, tight-lipped and angry, but not arguing with the Elder in front of outsiders.

Cailean rose. "We have imposed on your hospitality for too long, sir. We should return to our road and leave your people in peace."

"You're my guests," Lyan said. "And it's late. You shouldn't travel Eilidh Wood after dark, and you won't find your way back to the road without a guide." Assuming the forest would *let* them leave.

"Lyan," Elder Brenhan chided.

Lyan turned to glare at him, willing to defy the Elder on this matter. "Eilidh Wood wanted them to come here, and I have named them as my guests. They can stay the night in my home. I owe it to them."

"I don't want to create trouble here," interrupted Cailean. "I'm concerned that staying here would do just that. As much as I appreciate your hospitality, Lyan, I think it would be better if we left as soon as possible."

Surprisingly, Elder Brenhan spoke in agreement with Lyan. "No, Lyan is right. It's too late for you to travel now. The morning will be soon enough. Lyan has named you as his guests; none will trouble you." Though they would certainly trouble Lyan for bringing the Tathrens to Heartshrine Village.

Cailean bowed to both the Elder and Lyan. "Then I accept your generosity gladly. Thank you."

"Elder Brenhan." Lyan rose with the aid of the crutch, winced as pain burned through his leg, and bowed slightly. "If you will excuse us, I should see my guests fed and settled."

"Of course." The Elder rose as well. "I will see you in the morning. Rest well."

"Thank you," responded Cailean. He looked to Lyan. "At your convenience."

"This way." Lyan led the way out of the maze, the Tathrens following closely, as if they worried he might leave them behind. Even Kithr was gone when they left the Elder's hedge. On another day, the late afternoon would have been filled with voices, and the sight of elves walking in groups, talking or returning from hunts. Today, the village was silent and brooding. Lyan glimpsed movement in a tree from the corner of his eye, and knew resentful, angry eyes trained arrows on the Tathren. No shafts flew as Lyan limped home.

"Is it normally so... quiet?" Cailean asked in a hushed voice. He could feel the oppression even if he couldn't see the watchers.

"Not normally," Lyan admitted, trying to keep his voice steady, though the pain from his ankle made it difficult. "We are wary of strangers."

"And doubly so of us," Cailean said. "I'm sorry, Lyan. Our presence here is going to cause trouble for you, isn't it?"

"I doubt anyone's going to pass up the opportunity to tell me I'm a fool, but they'd do that in any case," Lyan responded, an answer aimed more at the watchers than at the Tathren. "I can't see that my giving them one more chance to do so will make much difference."

Cailean frowned, but said, "If you say so."

"I'm sorry for my ill temper. Normally, I'd be a better host. Please, this way. My house is ahead."

"By that tree?" asked one of the men whose name he didn't know, pointing to the tall ash beside Lyan's house.

Lyan nodded. "That's my tree." The men gave him puzzled looks. He hesitated a moment, then explained. "It sprouted when I was born, and will live as long as I do."

They gave the tree second looks. "You're as old as that tree?" asked Shiolto. Then, looking around at the forest, he asked, "Are all these trees... tied to elves?"

Lyan shook his head. "No. Some are simply trees." His gaze moved over the village and saw too many dead trees, too many empty houses. He didn't say anything more, only hurried his pace as much as he could to his house. "I'll prepare food for all of you, and then there's something I'd like to ask you about, Cailean."

"Of course. I will answer if I can," Cailean replied.

Lyan nodded his understanding, and rested his hand on the door. It swung open. "Please, come in."

3

Gift of the stars, the sky has sent
The spear of peace, the spear of war

Warm light glowed from flameless lanterns hung around the large outer room. Lyan cast an embarrassed look at the books piled on the floor, waiting for him to return them to the shelves. Carved wooden chairs lined a table that could seat ten comfortably. On occasion it had done so, though more often Lyan had only one or two visitors at a time consulting him.

"Please, sit," he invited, closing the door and shutting out the hostility of the rest of the village. "I beg your pardon for the mess."

The men hesitantly moved about the room, looking at everything as if it were all unfamiliar. When no one moved to sit, Lyan asked, "You *do* have tables and chairs in Tather, don't you?"

That startled a laugh from Cailean. "Of course. I'm sorry, Lyan. I wasn't sure what to expect of an elven house." He pulled out a chair and settled at the table.

"Are all those books *yours?*" Shiolto asked, pointing at a stack.

"They are. The rest are in the other room. I inherited many from my mentor, and people have given me others, or I've traded for them from the nomads on the Appret Plains."

"You have more?" Cailean's brow rose in surprise while his men took seats. "Your house might rival the library in my keep."

Lyan shifted uncomfortably, not sure how to respond. "Books aren't common in Tather?"

"A farmer doesn't need to read to know when to plant his crops," Gray-hair said. His tone was cool, as if Lyan's collection was a personal affront.

"You are a scholar of your people?" Yion asked, breaking the silence before it grew too uncomfortable. The lamp glow gave his sleek black hair a reddish gleam.

"I'm the astrologer of Heartshrine Village," Lyan answered. He limped to the cupboards and shelves near the hearth and carefully lifted down wooden plates, then mugs.

Shiolto and the other brown-haired man jumped to their feet and hurried over to him. "I can take those!" Shiolto said quickly. "You're hurt."

Lyan stiffened, but a look at Shiolto's concerned face told him the man intended neither insult nor condescension. "You are my guests," he replied. "I should be tending to you. But if you insist…"

Shiolto had taken plates and mugs before Lyan finished. The other man smiled wryly. "He insists. I can take something too."

It wasn't right for his guests to work, but he had the sense that it would bother these two men far more if he refused their help than if he accepted. He had a responsibility to put his guests at ease, too. Lyan indicated a jar of wine. "If you would, take that to the table."

The man's relieved smile said Lyan had made the right

decision. While the men set the table and poured wine, Lyan prepared a platter of smoked venison and bread, and another with cheese, strawberries, and a few handfuls of tart early cherries. Shiolto carried the trays to the table, and Lyan took his seat. All the food had come as gifts. The village always provided for the needs of their astrologer, even when he had no stars to read.

"Please join me in this meal," Lyan invited.

"Thank you." Cailean inclined his head in a nod, but didn't reach for either platter.

No one took food for a long moment that quickly grew awkward. Yion spoke, addressing Lyan. "I believe that in Tather, a meal is begun when the host is served."

Lyan blinked, startled. "In Eilidh Wood, guests are served first." To break the stalemate, he reached out and plucked a strawberry from the platter, setting it on his plate. "There. Please?" How could something as simple as dinner feel so uncomfortable?

In acceptance of Lyan's offered compromise, Cailean slid a piece of venison onto his plate. Lyan waited for his guests to serve themselves, then added food to his own plate. The table was quiet except for the sounds of eating for a time.

Cailean wiped his mouth with the back of his hand. "Thank you for your hospitality, Lyan. I apologize for the trouble we've caused you. I also realize that I have neglected to properly introduce all my men."

"Your help lifting me from the ravine and assisting me home more than covers any trouble, Cailean," Lyan told him.

Gray-hair fixed a glare on Lyan as hostile as any Kithr had given the Tathrens earlier. "*Lord* Cailean, or Earl Dev'gilla."

"Aikan!" Cailean said sharply.

"Yes, my lord?" Aikan responded stiffly.

"Lyan is our host, not my subject. I do not expect him to use honorifics, and neither will you."

Aikan's jaw tightened, but he gave Cailean a slight bow of acknowledgement. The venomous look the man shot Lyan said that he was anything but chastised.

"Aikan Unne is steward of my house," Cailean told Lyan. "Torqual Ferren is one of my guards."

The blond warrior who climbed into the ravine to help Lyan raised his mug of wine in a salute.

Cailean continued. "You met Shiolto Rona earlier. He worked in the stables. His elder brother Dalrian served primarily as a hunter."

Shiolto nodded quickly, and the other brown-haired man, Dalrian, gave Lyan a friendly smile.

"Yion, of course, you know is a mercenary," Cailean concluded.

"An honor, astrologer," Yion greeted.

"I'm pleased to meet you all," Lyan responded.

Cailean set down his mug. "Do you mind if I ask you something?"

"I will answer if I can," Lyan said.

"When we first met, you didn't know we came from Tather, did you?"

Lyan shook his head. "If I had, I would have hesitated more to bring you here, will of the forest or not."

"That guard knew where we were from," Shiolto said. "And either everyone else does, or your people really don't like strangers." He shivered.

"I am sure Kithr told them," Lyan said, feeling a surge of irritation at his friend. "There are others who would have known you for Tathrens on sight as well. Other warriors like Kithr who fought in the war. I was not part of our village's muster."

Cailean raised a questioning eyebrow. "The war? You don't look old enough to have seen the war."

"I'm not a child!" Lyan scowled. "Kithr and I are only a year apart. I would have been called to the battle, but our village astrologer was old and growing frail. I was his only apprentice, so my life was deemed too valuable to risk, and I stayed here. We should never be without an astrologer." He remembered his fierce jealousy that his friends would see the lands and people outside the forest, places he had only read about and longed to visit. Lyan could recall their laughter, the confidence that they would return victors by the next spring.

He remembered the hardened, unlaughing warriors who had returned years later, far fewer, bearing grim trophies and unhealing scars. And he remembered those who never came home.

The men stared at him with varying expressions of disbelief. "Our stories say elves live longer than humans, but you barely look older than me, Lyan," Cailean said. "My father was still in swaddling and my mother wasn't born when the treaty was made official."

"If you were an elf, Cailean, I would think you near to one hundred and fifty years. And I would judge Aikan to be over four hundred."

"Well I am no elf, thank the gods," Aikan snapped.

Lyan barely caught himself before he retorted in kind. Keeping his voice even, he said, "I'm certain it's not so horrible a fate as you think it."

Aikan just scowled at him, unyielding in his dislike of Lyan. He seemed to have made his mind up already about Lyan and felt no interest in entertaining alternatives.

Cailean drained his mug and set it down with a thump of finality. "Thank you for dinner, Lyan. Earlier, you said you wanted to ask me something?"

"Yes, but in private, please." Lyan pushed himself up slowly, wincing as pain jolted through his ankle. He leaned heavily on the crutch, caught his breath, and limped to the door to his inner room.

Aikan's suspicious gaze bore into Lyan's back as Cailean followed him, but not even the older man voiced objections.

Lyan opened the door and admitted Cailean. When he closed it again, all sounds from the outer room were shut out. Even if the Tathrens stood with their ears pressed to the wood, they would not hear the conversation within.

Cailean glanced around the room, but when his gaze settled on the gear stacked on the table, he relaxed visibly. The Tathren walked to the table and rested his hand on the spear as if to reassure himself. Lyan watched him, and sank down in the chair across the table from Cailean. Cailean remained standing, tracing fingers across the shaft of the spear with no indication that magic jolted his hand as it had Lyan's.

The Tathren spoke. "I didn't ask after our horses or gear. I'm glad to see these safely here."

"Kithr brought them in. I don't know what you keep in what bag, or what you might need for the evening," Lyan said.

Cailean waved his free hand in a vague, dismissive gesture. "Nothing we can't live a night without, thanks to your generosity."

"So long as your spear is safe and in your keeping, the rest is secondary?"

Cailean stiffened then and raised his eyes to look at Lyan narrowly. "Why do you say that?"

Kithr claimed that Tathren were violent, dangerous, and untrustworthy. Lyan staked his hope on Cailean not being a fool and not wanting to risk his shelter by harming Lyan. "I know there is magic in that spear. By your reaction, you've been concerned about it since it left your sight." He paused, watching Cailean for reaction.

The human said nothing, face a mask.

Lyan pressed on, giving voice to a guess. "If you're less concerned with the rest of your gear then with that spear, it seems probable that the mysterious relic you're trying to keep out of Ewart's hands is that weapon."

Cailean's hand closed tightly around the shaft of the spear, but he didn't release the straps binding it to the saddlebag, and he didn't attack. "How do you know about its powers?" he asked tightly.

"I don't," Lyan said simply.

The answer caught Cailean by surprise, and he stared at Lyan. "What?"

"I don't know its powers. I know there is magic in the weapon, because when I touched it earlier, it voiced its objection by sending a jolt up my arm. I accepted the warning, and left it alone." He met Cailean's gaze evenly. "However, I think I have a right to know what I have invited into my house."

"And if I decline to tell you?"

"Then there is nothing we can talk about, and you're free to leave." Lyan saw the hardening of Cailean's expression. "Free to leave the room, Lord Dev'gilla. I'm not rescinding my hospitality."

Cailean let out a deep sigh and released the spear to rub his forehead. "Just Cailean, please. A lord without lands and with five loyal men to call his own is barely even a lord in name."

Lyan looked at him with a puzzled expression. "You told the Elder that you had more men in your own land."

"I did, Lyan. And I left them with orders and what dependable commanders I still had, to try to hold a land against a larger force, without staying there myself to argue against Ewart's claim, as any sensible lord would. They don't even have proof that I'm still alive. They may well be dead now, or deserted to Ewart's flag." He closed his eyes a moment. "I left them, knowing I might not have a home to return to, because of this spear." He laid his hand on the spear again and looked at Lyan as if he sought to look into his soul.

"Nothing you say will go beyond this room," Lyan said. "Not even your men in the other room can hear what we say.

What is that spear? Why is it more important than your people or your home?"

Cailean drew a deep breath and exhaled slowly. He released the straps and took the weapon. "This is Solstice, one of the two Spears of the Stars."

Lyan's eyes grew wide, and breath caught in his throat. He would have sworn his heart skipped a beat. He stared at the Spear, color draining from his face. *Gods, what have you brought into my home?*

"What's wrong?" Cailean demanded, watching him.

"You… are Spearbearer of Solstice." Lyan's eyes moved up to Cailean.

"I am."

"Does anyone else in this village know this?" Lyan was amazed that his voice held steady. "Did you speak of it at all?"

"No," Cailean answered. "I said nothing about the Spear until now, not even when we spoke with your elder."

"Don't tell anyone here. Not even Elder Brenhan."

Cailean frowned. "I didn't intend to. Why are you telling me this?"

Lyan stared at him. "You don't know?"

"Know *what*, Lyan?"

"Don't you know? You really… don't…" Lyan saw the look of puzzlement on Cailean's face begin to shift to frustration, and the elf continued before the man could speak. "This Spear… this… one weapon… was at the heart of the war between your land and Eilidh Wood." His friends, his people had gone to war to claim this legendary weapon for the elves. They had bled, killed, died, and, in the end, failed to take the Spear that now lay in his home, protected by only a handful of men and the sacred rules of hospitality. "For the sake of your life, Cailean, tell no elf of Eilidh Wood that you bear the Spear of the Stars."

Cailean gripped Solstice tightly. "And what about you?"

"I'm not giving you much reason to trust me, am I?" Lyan

said quietly. He looked at the Spear, then turned away, eyes drifting over the shelves of books. "I know that Eilidh Wood doesn't have a claim to Solstice. It is the Spear that tradition claims belongs to your people. The Spear that should belong to us is called Equinox. Or… so we claim. Not all the bearers of Equinox have been elves."

"There is a Spearbearer of Equinox? Here, in Eilidh Wood?" Cailean tensed, but his stance implied eagerness, even hope, rather than worry.

Lyan shook his head. "Not in my lifetime. The last bearer of Equinox died long before I was born, and the Spear hasn't been seen since. The way to the Shrine of Equinox is hidden, and if anyone has solved the riddle and set out to find the Spear, they have not returned."

Cailean attention was focused and intense. "You know quite a bit about the Spears of the Stars."

"I'm no expert, nor am I a scholar," Lyan said quickly. His room, littered with books, charts, and scrolls, seemed to refute him. His star chart covered one wall, and stargazing tools crammed every nook not occupied by books. "The skies aren't my only interest, though, and I like to read."

"The elven definition of 'scholar' must be rather different from the Tathren one, if you're no scholar," Cailean said. "The scholars I consulted about the Spears could barely tell me anything I didn't already know about Solstice. As for Equinox, they only knew that the second Spear existed, and that it was lost. I uncovered a few legends on my own that might refer to one or both Spears." He gave Lyan a thin smile. "I didn't consider asking your people."

"We have some legends passed down about the Spears. They appeared, sent from the stars, during the Devastation. By their powers, order was restored and destruction averted."

Cailean nodded. "We have a similar story. Probably the best known one about the Spears, but utterly sparse on details. The next most common tale about the Spears claims that if a mortal can become bearer of both Spears and performs a certain ritual at the right time at the Altar of Heavens, wherever that is, he'll gain power to rival a god—immortality, youth, strength, magic… It sounds overly fanciful to me. If it was true, surely someone would have succeeded by now."

"Someone did," Lyan said. "Only once."

"And became a god?" Cailean asked dubiously.

"He waged war on the gods, Cailean. He fought them, and he very nearly won. Only when the gods, at great cost, severed the bond between him and the Spears were they able to banish Murdo into a prison that could contain him." Lyan's voice dropped and he shivered even saying the name.

"Mur—the Mad God?" Cailean's eyes widened and he dropped into a chair.

"He was a mortal once, before he completed the ritual. Now, even without the Spears, tales say that he's as powerful as any god." *If not stronger.*

"The Mad God. He was a Spearbearer?" Cailean repeated.

"His power came from them," Lyan said. "Your legends don't tell you that?"

The Tathren shook his head. "None that I saw." He shifted uncomfortably. "The Spears were taken from him somehow? I was told only death broke a Spear's connection to its bearer."

"It took the power of the gods to do so," Lyan said. "I doubt any mortal can take Solstice from you."

"Why should they bother, when just murdering me would be easier; is that what you mean?" Cailean laughed sharply. "It's true enough."

"No, not what I meant, but I suppose it is true," Lyan replied. "Ewart wants to claim Solstice for himself?"

"Ewart wants to offer the Spear as a gift to his mas—" Cailean gasped sharply in pain, doubling over in the chair.

"Cailean?" Lyan pushed to his feet, gripping the table for support.

Cailean held up a hand to forestall him. He gulped in deep breaths. "I'm… all right. It will pass… soon."

"What's wrong? I can call our herbalist." Lyan watched the man with concern.

Cailean shook his head. "Not unless your herbalist can unravel magic. I will be all right. It happens when I try to speak of him. Not Ewart. Another."

"Ewart serves someone else? He isn't trying to take the Spear for himself?"

Cailean raised his head, breathing still ragged and pale face damp with sweat. "I don't know what he's been promised, but it's enough to buy his loyalty."

"Do your men know?" Lyan asked, slowly sinking back into his chair.

"No. I can't say his name, or identify him. Even…" Cailean winced and paused to catch his breath. "Even talking around the subject is… difficult."

"And Ewart's lord enspelled you? Couldn't you use the Spear to stop him or break it?"

"I would… rather not try to talk about it." Cailean sagged back in the chair and wiped his brow on his sleeve.

Lyan persisted. "This man is a powerful mage, though?"
Cailean let out a deep breath and nodded.
"And he wants Solstice."

"He wants both Spears." Cailean leaned Solstice against his chair, finally releasing his white-knuckled grip on the weapon. "I know letting even one fall into his hold would be disastrous. I cannot allow that to happen."

"So you and your men are trying to elude him and keep Solstice from his reach." Lyan paused, eyes narrowing. "Or do you intend something more than that?"

"I intend to be sure that neither Spear comes within his grasp," Cailean said.

"So you think *you* can bear both Spears?" Tension raced through Lyan. "No mortal should ever hold that much power again, Cailean." *Soldarr, I know it is our duty to stop anyone who would try to claim both Solstice and Equinox, but please, do not require me to kill guests inside my own home.*

Cailean heard the accusation in Lyan's voice. "I can safeguard it without becoming the bearer of the Spear, Lyan. And if I knew I could entrust it to someone who would not abuse it, I would do so gladly."

"You don't trust the protections already in place to protect the Spear? It has remained safe and hidden for this many years. You think you can do better by removing it from its place?" Lyan retorted.

"I don't know, Lyan. I don't know what protections the Spear has, or if I can safeguard it more effectively than they do." Cailean let out a heavy sigh. His hand strayed to rest on Solstice again. "I just *know* I need to find Equinox. I can't explain it, but ever since we escaped my keep, something keeps telling me that Equinox is the key. Maybe it can break the magic on me. Maybe… maybe it's time for someone to take Equinox again. I don't intend to become Spearbearer of Equinox, but I *do* intend to find it. I found riddles hinting at its location. I also know that more clues can be found in the stars through astrology. Ewart's lord knows that too. He's hidden the night sky behind clouds so he can decipher the riddle before anyone else does. Lyan, he is already looking for Equinox, and I cannot allow him to find it first."

Lyan stiffened. "Your enemy has the power to cloud the night sky? He's responsible for this?" Anger welled up. Reading the signs in the skies was his skill—the most valuable skill he had to offer his people. Being denied it without knowing the cause had rankled. But knowing some mortal was responsible, not the whim of the gods, gave his frustration a target.

"He is," Cailean said. He watched Lyan carefully, then

added, "Any aid you can give me will work toward breaking his power."

Lyan didn't answer immediately. His eyes ran over his shelves, then he pushed to his feet and retrieved a book. He read seven languages fluently, and could struggle through a handful of others. Lyan handed the book to Cailean, who looked at it curiously and opened the leather cover.

"An account of the legend of the Spears of the Stars, and their following separation, starts in the third section," Lyan said. "If you read Rakkonian."

Cailean smiled thinly. "I've heard of the language, and I can think of one or two scholars in Tather who might be able to read it. But I can't." He started to hand the book back to Lyan.

Lyan shook his head. "You can borrow it. I know most of it by memory anyway."

"Are you sure?" Cailean asked. "I don't know when, or even if I'll be able to return it to you."

"If it will help you stop your enemy, then I will consider it a small price if my book doesn't make it back to my keeping," Lyan said. "How much *do* your men know?"

"They know Ewart isn't the only danger on our heels. They know I'm searching for the second Spear. What more they've guessed I don't know." Cailean rubbed weary eyes. "There is far too much I don't know."

Lyan said nothing for a moment, thinking of the untrusting eyes of Cailean's man Aikan, and dreading the thought of returning to face it again. Finally, he gave in to the necessity. "Your companions must wonder what's taking so long. Perhaps we should return to the other room."

"Yes, of course," Cailean agreed, rising.

Lyan stood with more care and a wince. Cailean waited for him and returned to the outer room. The other five men lounged around the table, talking quietly. They all turned when Lyan opened the door and limped out, followed by

Cailean. Lyan found his chair again and joined them in pleasant, if subdued, conversation. He managed to draw out tales of their homes from Shiolto and Dalrian, and Yion told of places he'd traveled as a mercenary. As night settled over Eilidh Wood, Lyan arranged bedding in the outer room for all six men, and made them as comfortable as he could, then retired.

Once sleep finally took hold of his guests, Lyan rose from bed, dressed, and limped outside as quietly as he could. The night air was chill and his ankle throbbed, but he dared hope that this one night, he might be able to see the stars and ask Veil's guidance. He didn't worship the god of divination, but any wise astrologer respected Veil.

The moon glowed through the clouds, a hazy form in a shrouded sky. As Lyan sat wearily onto the edge of the well, a shadow slipped from the darkness and settled beside him. "They're leaving in the morning?"

Lyan was not surprised by Kithr's appearance, silent though he had been. "Yes, they are."

"Good."

"I'm going with them."

"*What*?!" burst Kithr. "You... what... how..." he sputtered.

"I'm going with them," Lyan repeated. "It's not something they asked of me, or even mentioned. But they won't be able to find what they need without help they won't get from words or books."

"You... Lyan, you have no idea what you are talking about! Don't be an idiot! You *can't* go with them! Are you trying to get yourself killed?"

"I know they're Tathrens," Lyan said. "You don't need to remind me."

"Tathren be damned! You don't know how to hold a *staff*, Lyan, much less a real weapon! How do you expect to survive? You're hurt. You can't run, you can't dodge, you can't even *walk* without a crutch. What use are you to anyone like this? What can you possibly offer?"

Lyan glared at Kithr. "Knowledge. *That* is what I can offer them, since no one *here* will listen to me."

Kithr stared at him a moment, mouth open. Then he shook his head. "You can't leave, Lyan. You're the only astrologer in Heartshrine Village."

"Look up, Kithr," Lyan said flatly. "Look at the sky and tell me what you see."

Kithr sighed, rolled his eyes, and, for once, actually looked up. "The moon."

"What else?" asked Lyan.

"Gods, Lyan, I don't know. You're the one who spends all his time looking at the sky. Why don't you tell me?"

"Because I see the same thing you see when I look up: nothing. *Nothing*, Kithr. Just clouds. I *can't* see the stars. It's like this every night. The clouds gather at sunset, just as the first stars come out, and they disperse after dawn, when the stars are hidden again. So what use am I here? I'm useless to everyone, it seems. So why shouldn't I go? At least I can offer *something* to them." His voice was sharp.

"Have you spoken to Elder Brenhan about this?" Kithr asked quietly.

"No," Lyan answered.

"You can't just abandon Heartshrine Village! You have a duty here!"

"What, you really think anyone would notice?" Lyan asked acidly. "Kithr, no one's so much as asked me to read a fortune in all the time the sky's been like this. No one! They don't even notice. And there isn't time to debate this with the Elder. The Tathrens are leaving in the morning."

"Still, Lyan…" Kithr began.

"Elder Brenhan wouldn't listen when I told him there's a pooka in the forest. Why should he listen to my reasons for accompanying Cailean and his men?"

Kithr froze. "There is *what* in the forest? Tell me you didn't just say what I thought I heard." He reached toward his knife and glanced around warily.

"If you thought I said 'a pooka,' then you heard me correctly. You'd already know that if you'd listened to me earlier. I saw it. I think it's stalking Cailean and his companions." The fact that Kithr, at least, listened to him now mollified Lyan slightly. "I fell because I was more concerned with not being seen by it than I was with my path."

"Gods…" breathed Kithr. "And you told the Elder? No, of course you did. But even if it's following the Tathren, how can he permit such a creature to wander our forest? Anyone could fall to its tricks. And you're still planning to go with them?"

Lyan nodded. "I can't let them go alone. Where they must go, they will need a guide, and best that guide be one of our people, who knows the truth and will not pollute a sacred place."

Kithr paled slightly. "Are you sure you know what you are doing, Lyan?"

"I thought at first that I must have offended the gods somehow to be caught in the midst of this madness. But I think this is their will: they want me to join Cailean and his companions. He has a powerful enemy, who has enspelled him to keep him from speaking of it. But his enemy is the one hiding the night sky from me, so he can be the only one to know the truth. How can I not do something, knowing this? Think about it, Kithr. This *is* my duty! I *have* to do something to try to clear the sky so that I *can* do my duty to Heartshrine Village."

"At least *tell* Elder Brenhan, even if only in the morning before you leave," Kithr told him.

Lyan couldn't ignore the concern in Kithr's words. He finally nodded. "I will."

Kithr rose. "If you're going to be leaving with them, go to

bed. Morning will come sooner than you think. Believe me, I know."

Lyan nodded. As Kithr started to walk away, Lyan added, "Kithr? Thanks." Kithr said nothing in reply, but nodded and turned away.

4

As dawn colored the sky, Lyan examined his decision again, and found his resolve unchanged. He needed to accompany Cailean on his search for Equinox. And if Cailean had lied, and intended to lay claim to the second Spear, Lyan had to be ready to… prevent it. He shuddered.

Am I prepared to kill someone? Lyan amended the thought. *Even if I am prepared to do so, can I? I'm no fighter.*

He pushed the question aside, fervently hoping he would never have to face it in earnest. Lyan pulled his infrequently used travel pack from his wardrobe and considered briefly, then tucked two changes of clothes and an oiled cloak inside. His ankle throbbed painfully, reminding him to grab Ada's medicine. After applying it to his swollen ankle, he packed the medicine into an inner pocket of the pack. Lyan scanned his shelves and selected two books he knew referred to the Spears of the Stars. Those joined his clothes. His compass and

astrolabe tempted him, but he knew taking them was foolish—
he couldn't see the stars, and they were too precious to risk
losing. He belted on his long hunting knife, a familiar weight,
though he'd never used the blade in actual combat.

Lyan slid his arms through the straps and settled the pack's
weight onto his back. Leaning on the crutch, he limped into
the main room.

Cailean and his men had piled their packs on one end of
the table and folded the bedding Lyan provided them. Cailean
looked askance at Lyan's pack when he noticed the elf, but he
only nodded in greeting. The rest of the men fell silent at
Lyan's entrance, though conversation had been sparse even
before then.

"Good morning," Lyan greeted. He limped to the
cupboards and surveyed his food. He set out a tray of berries
and a loaf of bread. "Please eat," he invited. Remembering
the previous night, he broke a piece of bread for himself and
chewed on it as he looked back over the shelves.

The people of Heartshrine Village supplied food as their
duty to provide for their astrologer, but most of what they gave
him was meant to be eaten soon. He scooped the three
remaining bundles of smoked meat into his pack, then a sack
with dried fruit. Kithr had given him the meat. On his own,
Lyan could forage, but as a hunter he was an utter failure.

No conversation broke the stillness in the house, only the
shifting and shuffling of men anxious to be on their way. Lyan
brushed crumbs from the counter and asked, "Are you ready?"

Cailean looked his men over. "We're ready." He picked up
Solstice and shouldered his pack.

Lyan stepped outside. The morning was crisp and the
village stood still and quiet. Only Kithr waited for them. The
three packhorses grazed on the grass beside Lyan's house.
Beside Kithr stood another horse, black with chestnut brown
mane and tail. Nickering, the horse trotted up to Lyan and
bumped his nose firmly into Lyan's ribs. Lyan smiled and

scratched the stallion's ears. "Good morning, Shadowstar. Thank you for coming."

Kithr pointedly ignored the Tathrens as he followed the stallion. "Shadowstar showed up a bit ago. I saddled him for you."

Not only had Kithr saddled Shadowstar, Lyan saw, he'd also tied on a bedroll and a bag, which Lyan guessed held supplies. Even when Kithr thought he was wrong, he still looked out for his friend. "Thank you."

Kithr leaned close. "You can't trust Tathrens, Lyan, and you're in no condition to guard your back. Don't be a fool. See them to the edge of Eilidh Wood, come back, and no one will know."

"I've made up my mind, Kithr. I need to do this. Pick up any food people leave for me when I'm gone, please."

Warning was given and answered. Kithr wasted no more breath on argument. He handed Shadowstar's reins to Lyan with a curt nod, then spun on his heels and stalked away. Lyan watched him go with a sense of guilt he couldn't fully explain.

Elder Brenhan emerged from his house and walked to the packhorses. He spoke a few words to Cailean as Lyan limped over with Shadowstar. Lyan's ankle throbbed in spite of Ada's medicine, but it would be rude for him to tower over the Elder by riding. "Good morning, Elder. I will guide Cailean and his companions." He had promised Kithr he would tell the Elder of his intentions, but Elder Brenhan's dismissal of both his concerns and the danger of the pooka still rankled.

Perhaps Elder Brenhan understood the implication behind the simple statement. He had always been adept at reading hidden meanings. He studied Lyan, and nodded. "As you wish, Lyan. Ride with care." To Cailean and his men he said, "I wish you good fortune in your travels. May the gods watch over you."

"Thank you, sir," Cailean responded. "And thanks to you as well, Lyan, for your continued assistance."

Lyan nodded, but guilt pricked at him. *What would Cailean think if he knew I was joining him not simply to help him, but to stop him… even kill him to keep him from taking Equinox?*

He turned away from Cailean and murmured a word to Shadowstar. The stallion compliantly knelt, and Lyan mounted, wincing. At another command, Shadowstar rose. Lyan slung his crutch under his leg. The humans watched with interest, and Shiolto's expression was especially admiring. Shadowstar snorted and tossed his head, enjoying the attention.

Once gear had been secured onto the horses, Lyan nudged Shadowstar with his heels. The stallion led the way from Heartshrine Village. The six humans followed closely behind him. As the forest closed around them, Cailean and his men looked around nervously. Eilidh Wood stood at rest, making no efforts to block their passage or turn them aside.

Shadowstar stopped at the shrine. Lyan bowed his head. *Shining ones, please guide our journey. Please, let Cailean be who he claims, and nothing more. Please let him not be lying about the Spears. Protect us from evil and lead us home safely once again.*

When he finished, Lyan plucked a hair from his head and wound it around a twig he'd brought from his tree, then dropped it to the ground in front of the shrine as an offering. Shadowstar stepped back from the shrine and continued up the path.

Torqual broke the silence. "Is that a shrine?"

"Yes," Lyan answered. "A shrine to the gods of my people."

"I've seen traveler's shrines on roads before, but none as fine as that. Is it very old? What are your temples like?"

"The shrine is older than our village—we take the name Heartshrine Village from it. That's said to be the oldest one in Eilidh Wood." Lyan considered the second question with a slight frown. "We don't have temples. We honor the gods at their shrines."

"What about priests?" Dalrian asked. "Who teaches you about the gods?"

"The village elders. They speak the gods' will and know the wishes of the forest," Lyan told him. "They lead their villages in all such matters."

"Priests, lords, and judges all in one, then," Cailean said. "Or so I've been told."

Lyan nodded, unable to imagine life in Eilidh Wood any other way.

The sun peered over the trees by the time they reached the road. Shadowstar shook off the leaves that clung to him, and pranced for a moment on the packed dirt. Lyan hissed in pain as the movement jarred his ankle, and he gripped the stallion's reins hard. Shadowstar stopped with some reluctance.

"Are you all right?" Shiolto asked.

Lyan nodded quickly. "As long as Shadowstar doesn't do that again, I will be."

"You really shouldn't be riding, Lyan. You hurt yourself just yesterday, and it needs time to heal, or you'll make it worse." Shiolto showed none of the wariness he'd felt about Lyan only yesterday.

"I know," Lyan answered. "But walking would be far worse, and it would slow you down."

"We can find our way from here," Cailean said, concerned. "Shiolto's right; you should return home and rest."

Lyan shook his head sharply. "No. You are going to need my guidance, not just in Eilidh Woods, but when you find the place you're looking for."

Cailean gazed at Lyan, then looked again at the bags on Shadowstar's saddle. "You intend to accompany us?"

"I do," Lyan said.

"And you think you can just decide this with no questions?" Aikan cut in, eyes narrowing in suspicion. "You, a stranger and an *elf*, think you can simply attach yourself to us without a reason and be accepted?"

"Hey, I think it would be great if Lyan came with us," Shiolto interrupted.

Aikan shot him a withering glare. "And what of his motives? Why should an enemy of our people, about whom we know next to nothing, join us, and what does he think he will gain from it?"

Does everyone doubt me? My own people and the humans both? Lyan turned Shadowstar and faced Aikan. "My motives? Is it entirely unthinkable to you that I might want to help? Cailean is looking for something my people consider part of our heritage. So if you must have some ulterior motive to my actions, let it be my wish to ensure that none of you, by accident or intent, defile a place sacred to us."

Cailean shifted uneasily at those words, and glanced around the forest as if the trees might attack. Eilidh Wood remained quiet and at rest.

Lyan continued. "I know what you are trying to find, and I know your people's lore doesn't tell you everything you need to know. Cailean's lack of knowledge in certain areas made that clear. If you expect to succeed, you will need someone well-versed in our lore, and you will not find that outside of Eilidh Wood. However, if you refuse my aid, there's little purpose in my joining with you."

Cailean cut in quickly. "Lyan, I would appreciate your help, if you are sure you want to offer it."

Lyan nodded, but continued to gaze at Aikan, waiting for his reply.

"Lord Cailean has no objections to your joining us, and the decision is his," Aikan said stiffly.

"No," Lyan said firmly, startling them all. "The decision as to whether I travel with you is no one's but mine. And so I ask if you, *any* of you, wish me gone now. I'll tell you what I can and then return home, if you do not wish me as a traveling companion." *And then I'll find Kithr, and have to tell him exactly why*

I was so determined to go with these men. Then convince him to help me follow them rather than just kill them outright.

Cailean opened his mouth, about to protest. Lyan looked him in the eyes, and Cailean held his tongue. Lyan turned his gaze on each man. Yion met his gaze evenly, the only one who did so.

Dalrian finally spoke. "I grew up hearing stories about how elves are cruel and can't be trusted. But…you aren't like those stories. If you want to come with us, I don't mind."

Lyan waited. Shiolto and Torqual nodded in agreement, and Aikan didn't voice further objections. Lyan smiled finally. "Thank you."

From the corner of his eyes he saw the relieved expression on Cailean's face. "Enough talk!" the Tathren lord declared. "We have a ways to go, and, with no offense meant, Lyan, I want to be away from this forest by nightfall."

"I understand," Lyan assured him. He turned Shadowstar and nudged the stallion to a walk.

The six humans and three packhorses followed. The undergrowth around the road was thick and green, mostly hiding the thorns that discouraged travelers from wandering off the path. Lyan watched the road for other travelers, though he didn't expect to see any. Cailean and his men looked all around, tense as they watched for danger.

At midday they stopped for a brief meal. Lyan gladly took the opportunity to stretch his legs and limp around a little on the crutch. He knew he would be sore by evening; he hadn't ridden Shadowstar for some time. Still, he didn't complain when Cailean announced an end to their rest. The forest felt normal right now, but Lyan recalled the uneasy stillness that had preceded the pooka he had seen yesterday. The monster was still somewhere in the forest and, if his guess was right, it hunted Cailean.

"How much further to the edge of the forest?" asked Shiolto as they started walking again.

Lyan looked around, judging their distance. "We should reach it by evening, if we make good time."

"I hope so," Dalrian said fervently. "I feel like we're being watched constantly."

"Only by the forest," Lyan responded, intending to relieve his concern.

Dalrian gave him a thin smile. "I know this is your home, Lyan, but it's more than a little creepy for the rest of us. Lord Cailean's lands don't have forests this dark or deep."

"Yes," Lyan acknowledged without thinking. "Several friends told me how little they liked the woods of your country."

"Yet they made good use of them, from all I have heard," Yion said. "Rumors claim there are still forests in Tather where none will go because they fear elven ambush."

Cailean opened his mouth to rebuke Yion for bringing up the war, but Lyan only nodded somberly. "It's possible. There are some warriors whose fates we never learned. Their trees still live, so they aren't dead, but they never returned home. Perhaps they chose to continue the war alone." Lyan spoke the last softly. Then he turned the conversation back to its beginnings. "But we should reach the edge of Eilidh Wood by evening."

They met no other travelers on the road, elven or otherwise. On occasion Lyan felt eyes follow them when they passed trails to other villages, but so long as travelers kept to the road, no one would challenge them—even if they were Tathrens.

The sun sank low when Lyan said, "We're almost there."

"Are you sure?" Dalrian looked around. "The trees don't look any thinner."

"I'm certain," Lyan assured him. "I know Eilidh Wood."

True to his word, as evening drew near, the forest ended. There was no warning, no thinning of the trees. As if an invisible line had been drawn, Eilidh Wood abruptly stopped.

Beyond lay the gently rolling plains inhabited by the nomadic herders of Appret. The road continued toward the river.

The men breathed audible sighs of relief as they left Eilidh Wood, but Lyan lingered at the forest's edge. He could count on his hands the number he'd left Eilidh Wood for longer than a night. Uncertainty wracked him as he questioned his resolve once again.

"Lyan? Is something wrong?" Cailean asked.

Aikan watched him with narrowed eyes. Lyan could all but hear the gray-haired man waiting for him to lose his nerve and turn back. Lyan straightened in the saddle. "No. I was just saying a prayer before leaving Eilidh Wood."

"Ah. Of course." Cailean waited.

Rather than make a liar of himself, Lyan whispered a swift prayer to Soldarr, then flicked the reins. Shadowstar snorted and looked at him questioningly.

"Yes," Lyan said quietly. "We are leaving Eilidh Wood. I don't know when we will be back."

That seemed not to bother Shadowstar, once assured that his rider truly did intend to leave the shelter of the trees. The humans stood waiting for him, and Lyan murmured an apology as he joined them. Cailean waved it off. "I won't argue with any man about the devotions he pays his gods." He looked up to the sky. Already clouds began to form, gathering as the sun sank lower. "We need to camp soon. It's probably best to do so before we leave the shelter of the forest too far behind."

"Then why do we not camp here?" Yion asked. "The ground is clear, and we may easily build our camp to the side of the road."

"Agreed," Cailean said. "Go to it."

They moved far enough from Eilidh Wood that the trees didn't loom overhead, then the humans began unloading the pack animals. Shadowstar knelt, and Lyan slid to the ground, biting his lip as pain stabbed through his ankle. He untied the crutch and his bags, then watched the Tathrens. They clearly had a routine, and seemed amenable to letting Lyan sit and rest rather than get in their way. He wasn't certain what help he could offer, in any case. Shiolto tended the packhorses and, with Lyan's permission, Shadowstar. Dalrian made a fire and warmed dried meat for an evening meal. Yion paced the camp's perimeter, then settled before the fire, expression calm and even.

The fire's warmth drew Lyan, and he edged to it. He ached everywhere, and the realization that he didn't have a soft bed to sleep on was disheartening. He chewed on the piece of meat Dalrian offered and looked up at the clouded sky.

A chill suddenly ran down his spine. Shadowstar snorted and pawed the ground in warning. Lyan turned sharply, eyes searching the darkness beyond the camp.

"What's wrong?" Cailean asked, taking a reflexive defensive stance with Solstice in hand.

"It's there." Lyan found the figure, barely visible as shadow against darkness.

"What is?"

"The pooka," Lyan said, watching the stranger with the form of a man. "I see it."

"Sharp eyes." The sugared voice drifted into the camp. "Too sharp for a human. Do you know what these are, elf? Do you realize what your companions are?"

"Show yourself!" Cailean demanded.

"You invite me into your camp?" The sickeningly sweet voice drew closer.

"No," Yion said. "Such a creature as you would take too much liberty with such an invitation."

Nevertheless, the pooka approached, stopping just beyond the camp. The monster wore the form of a human. Firelight reflected in its glowing red eyes and highlighted the black hair that hung long and loose. Its clothing looked as soft as if it had been spun from dyed spider silk. Its lips curled in a smile as it addressed Lyan again. "These are *Tathrens*, elf. Did you know that? And did they tell you where they are going? *I* know. Do you?"

"What I know is no business of yours," Lyan countered. He pushed to his feet. "I've heard of a way to bind your kind. I have always wondered if it would work."

The pooka grinned, showing fangs. "By all means, try. *I* invite *you* to do so, elf."

"Little point to it now," Lyan responded. "Why are you following us?"

"You think too highly of yourself," chuckled the pooka. "I care nothing about you or your Tathren 'friends.' I seek one thing only, and it is not a person."

Cailean's grip tightened around his Spear and he took a step forward.

Lyan grabbed his arm. "Do not attack. It can't enter the camp's boundary without invitation. Don't break that boundary."

"But what fun is that?" murmured the pooka's voice, a whisper in Lyan's ear. Lyan glared at the unmoved creature. It smiled, sketched a bow, and turned to leave.

"Who bound you?"

Lyan's question stopped the pooka in its tracks. It spun to face him, anger in its glowing red eyes as it glared at Lyan. "I am a free spirit. I do as I wish!" As suddenly as the pooka had appeared, it was gone.

Silence fell over the camp, tense and strained. Yion finally broke the uneasy stillness. "Was that a wise thing to ask?" he said to Lyan.

"Probably not." Lyan sighed softly. "I'm sorry. I shouldn't have angered it."

"Why did you assume he was bound?" Cailean asked. "And even if he was, did you think he would tell you?"

"It wouldn't have chosen to follow you for no reason, and

to follow with such determination implies that this isn't an idle curiosity. Thus someone or something instructed it to do so. I hoped to find out who." Lyan paused. "And yes, I thought there was a chance it would answer. Pookas are notoriously tricksters. If doing so had suited its whim, it might have answered."

"But he said he was not bound," Shiolto said, puzzled.

"No," corrected Yion, startling them. "It said it is a free spirit. That is a different matter than being bound. A free spirit may be bound yet remain a free spirit. It has no master, though it may be forced to do some mortal's bidding."

"I don't understand the difference," Cailean admitted. "What would happen if he… it were not a free spirit? What would that mean?"

"That," Yion responded, "would mean that its god, whose name I will not utter here, had bound it to serve someone."

"And that would only happen if it had angered its god," Lyan added. He looked uneasily toward the darkness, but didn't say more.

Silence fell over the camp again, and uneasy gazes searched the darkness as the group bedded down, wondering just what might lurk in the darkness.

5

The past in restless memory
The future yet unknown

Lyan shifted restlessly, trying to recapture the elusive thread of sleep. His ankle throbbed with an angry ache, but he was reluctant to disturb everyone else by fumbling in his bag for the dayseed oil. Lumps or small stones poked him through his bedroll. Every noise was strange and unsettling, and someone among the humans had a habit of snoring a few times, then rolling over and noisily smacking his lips.

When he began entertaining fantasies of smothering the snorer with a blanket, Lyan gave up on sleep. Pulling a cover around his shoulders, he edged over to the embers of the fire. A shadow moved and he tensed, first thinking that the pooka had breached the boundary of their camp. Lyan relaxed when Yion crouched near the fire pit, letting the soft glow of the embers illuminate his darkly tan skin.

"It is my turn to keep the watch," Yion said. "I have neither seen nor heard the pooka near enough to threaten us. Your sleep has been unsettled—do thoughts of the monster trouble you?" He spoke in a low voice, pitched to not disturb the others.

Lyan looked at his hands. "I don't know why it would challenge me to try binding it. I don't understand that." He paused, then continued, not sure why he felt comfortable speaking to Yion. "But that isn't the reason I can't sleep. I don't leave my village often, rarely sleeping in the open. In Eilidh Wood, the forest is always watching over me. Out here, it's…empty. The sounds are wrong. The air doesn't smell right."

"You do not frequently depart the forest, then," Yion said.

"I'm the astrologer of Heartshrine Village. I couldn't be gone for long, or there wouldn't be anyone to read fortunes for my village." Lyan's gaze travelled up to the night sky.

Yion tilted his head, following Lyan's movement. "You do not believe the skies will clear and reveal themselves soon?"

"They haven't in the past month. That gives me reason to think the clouds aren't natural. I don't think they will clear. So I can't do anything to serve my village by staying there. I'll be more use to them if I look for the cause of the clouds."

"Do you believe Lord Cailean's journey will lead you to that goal?" Yion turned back to Lyan. The fire's glow cast shadows across his face, and Lyan noticed again the odd, oval-shaped indentation in Yion's forehead.

"I think it will, and I think that Eilidh Wood wants me to take this journey." Lyan shifted, trying to find a comfortable position for his leg. "Where are you from, Yion?"

Yion ran a finger over the indented spot, a motion that seemed unconscious and born of habit. "I am a mercenary and a wanderer, Lyan Stargazer. I have seen much and learned much in my journey. The place I have come from is unimportant—the place I am going is the one that matters. This lesson the gods have taught me."

"Do you know where you are going?" Lyan asked.

"I am going where Lord Cailean leads; for this time, I am

in his service." Yion rose. "If you rest your leg upon your pack when you lie down, it will be less swollen come morning."

Lyan sighed, but crept back to his bedroll. He propped his injured leg up on his bag, shifted until he found a reasonably comfortable spot, and closed his eyes. In his mind, he pictured the night sky free of clouds, and traced patterns among the stars until he finally drifted back to sleep.

When the humans began to stir, Lyan roused. He winced when he sat, and again when he lifted his leg off the bag. Searching through the bag, he found the dayseed oil Ada had given him. The vial could probably last him five or six days if he rationed it, but the herbalist hadn't thought to give him more. She had no more expected him to leave the village than Lyan himself had. He unwound the linen wrap and dribbled oil onto it. His ankle was swollen and tender, and Lyan stopped to catch his breath before rebinding the bandage.

"Can I help?" Shiolto crouched down beside him and gestured at the bandage.

"Please." Lyan gratefully relinquished the wrap to him.

"You know it isn't good for your ankle to be out here riding and moving around," Shiolto told him.

"I know," Lyan said. "But you need my help, and none of you would want to stay in Eilidh Wood for the time it would take me to heal."

"You could hurt yourself even worse if you're not careful." Shiolto tied the bandage to brace Lyan's ankle and handed him boots. He gave Lyan an uncertain smile. "You sound like you know more about where we're going and what we're doing than we do."

Lyan frowned at him. "You're following Cailean, but you don't know where you're going?"

The young man shrugged. "A lowborn man like me

doesn't ask that sort of question. When your lord tells you to go with him, you go. Especially when the other choice is to stay in a keep being overrun by someone you don't want to serve." Shiolto smiled then. "I guess elves must do things differently."

"I think we must," Lyan agreed quietly. He climbed stiffly to his feet with Shiolto's help and limped to the fire. Dalrian offered him a chunk of dry, crumbly bread and a strip of jerky for breakfast.

Cailean studied the plains as he chewed jerky, ignoring the quiet banter in the camp. Finally he spread his cloak over the dew-sprinkled grass and pulled his map from the case, unrolling it on the cloak.

Lyan limped over to study the map. The parchment had seen better days, and constant travel and use had taken their toll. The Tathren lord protected it as best he could, storing it in a scroll case, but the edges were worn and frayed. The scholar in Lyan wanted to immediately put it away until he could properly preserve it and refresh the ink, which had begun to fade. Several of the illustrations around the fringe had lightened to little more than indistinct shapes. Lyan forced his mind away from the map itself to look at the lands it represented. Aikan had joined Cailean, and he scowled sharply at Lyan.

"I thought we were further south, near here," Cailean said, indicating a small forest some days south of Eilidh Wood. "So we're off my intended course."

"I understand your desire to avoid my forest, but it's saved you time in spite of that." Lyan's intrusion earned another glare from Aikan, which he ignored. His finger hovered over the map, avoiding touching the surface and further wearing down the lines. "We're here, or close by. The Dechosyn River runs through the grasslands out of the mountains to the northeast. To find it coming from that forest would have cost you several days, but from where we are, we can reach it tomorrow." Lyan paused. "Unless there's a reason we shouldn't let the river be our guide until the cliffs? The plains people I've met have been pleasant enough, but I don't know if all of them are."

Cailean smiled thinly. "I've no doubt they're respectful enough to your people, Lyan. Unlike my people, your neighbors know better than to aggravate the residents of Eilidh Wood. But I don't know any reason we shouldn't follow the river, as you say."

"It could be that anyone who might take exception to our passing will give it second thoughts with you in our company, Sir Lyan," Aikan said. The words sounded complementary on the surface, but Aikan's voice filled them with barbs, and mockery lurked in his use of "Sir." "As Lord Cailean said, they wouldn't want to make enemies with a people of such long lives and memories as yours, who can hold a grudge for three generations as humans count years."

Cailean shot his steward a sharp look and opened his mouth to speak, but Lyan cut him off, eyes on Aikan. "We hold grudges over events that have happened in our lifetimes. What about humans, who hold grudges over events that happened before they were even born?"

Uncomfortable silence followed his words. Lyan let out a long breath, then spoke again. "Aikan, if I've given you some reason to dislike me, or unknowingly caused offense, I apologize. Some of my people fought in the war. They lost friends, fathers, and brothers. Some simply never returned. If you wish to hold a grudge against those who attacked your homeland, I am sure you have reason to do so. But not all my people fought, not all went to war. I don't know what stories you have been told about elves, but they probably contain as many exaggerations of the truth as the tales I have heard of Tathrens. Realizing this, I propose a truce. I will do my best to avoid bringing up mentions of the war between our peoples if you will do the same. We have a long journey ahead, and it will be easier if we can agree that we are allies, not enemies."

He was no diplomat, and the words sounded flat to his ears. Lyan waited, watching Aikan and hoping they made some impact. The rest of the men watched in silence, shifting uncomfortable and waiting for Aikan's reply. Aikan gazed at him, as if he could pierce Lyan's mind and see the thoughts within. Finally the human spoke.

"As you say, we have a long journey ahead. I accept this 'truce' you offer, elf." He spoke stiffly, and Lyan didn't want to lay wagers on how long a pause in hostilities would last, but he hoped he could have at least a few days free from acerbic comments. He would probably receive stiff formality or cold lack of acknowledgement from Aikan instead. Lyan didn't mind that as much. He'd received that reaction in Heartshrine Village often enough to be accustomed to it.

"We travel up the river, then, as Lyan Stargazer suggests?" Yion said, breaking the silence before it grew heavy again.

Aikan glowered at the mercenary, not liking the reminder that Lyan had suggested their route. Cailean either didn't notice or chose to ignore the response, answering Yion instead. "Yes, we will. Break camp. It's time to move on, before anything comes visiting."

Shadowstar waited patiently for Lyan to climb onto his back. Aikan gave the elf another dark look, and Lyan felt a moment of unexpected gratitude for his injured ankle. The man might have wanted to argue it was insulting for an elf with no titles to ride while a lord walked, but with Lyan's injury, it would have been impossible for him to walk all day even if Shadowstar consented to allow someone else to ride. The stallion tossed his head impatiently and waited for the humans to finish cleaning their campsite and start walking.

Shiolto stood close, ready to offer a hand if needed, but Shadowstar didn't need any help getting Lyan settled in the saddle. As they started walking, the Tathren gave Shadowstar an admiring look. "He's a beautiful horse."

Lyan smiled as Shadowstar tossed his head again and pranced briefly. "He knows it, too. His name is Shadowstar."

"I didn't see any other horses in your village. Is there a stable?" Shiolto seemed an endless, bubbling well of curious questions, and he showed no hesitation in befriending Lyan.

After his brief confrontation with Aikan, Lyan seized that sense of welcome with desperate gratitude. "We don't have stables. We don't keep animals." There was a word he was looking for, but he couldn't quite remember it. "We don't tame animals."

Shiolto's brow furrowed. "You have Shadowstar."

Lyan stroked the stallion's black neck. "The plains are his home. But he likes me, and will usually come if I call for him."

"You don't keep any animals, though?" Torqual asked, the blond man stepping up to walk on Lyan's other side. "You have horses at your call, but you don't keep chickens? Where do you get meat? Eggs?"

"The hunters bring meat. We can find bird nests when we want eggs. It goes against the ways of Eilidh Wood to raise an animal, building its trust, only to kill it for food." Lyan struggled to explain an idea so innate, he couldn't imagine living any other way.

"But with so much hunting going on constantly, through all the forest, you'll deplete the game and there won't be anything left *to* hunt," Torqual argued.

Lyan shook his head. "Eilidh Wood does not let our people starve. The forest can bring game where it needs to be to give us enough. Even when most of our hunters were gone, no one starved." Although the years of the war, when most hunters were gone to fight in Tather, had been lean ones. Lyan stopped himself from saying more, realizing he had almost broken the agreement with Aikan by bringing up the war.

"So, you don't keep any animals at all? Do you plant food, or depend on the forest for *that* too?" Torqual asked.

"We aren't farmers, if that's what you mean. Plants grow where they grow best. We simply have to find those places." Lyan sighed. "I will probably miss the cherries this year. Maybe someone will dry some for me."

"Cherries grow in Eilidh Wood?" Cailean asked with interest. "One of my provinces has a fine orchard. They're known for making an excellent wine from them."

"A large grove grows near Heartshrine Village. We trade the fruit with other villages. Or if it's later in the year, apples, pears, and plums. Those are the things our village is best known for. Aside from the shrine itself, of course."

"The villages in Eilidh Wood trade with each other? Do you use coin?" Cailean asked. "How do you decide value?"

"We save coin for trade with the herders of the Appret Plains, when they shelter for the summers at the edge of Eilidh Wood," Lyan told him. "Within the forest, we barter. Each village is known for a different specialty. Herbs and medicine, cloth, worked metal… fruit."

"Elves who don't know how to domesticate animals know metallurgy?" Aikan scoffed.

Lyan drew his hunting knife and offered it hilt-first to him. "An elf made this."

Aikan scowled, but examined the knife. Finding no fault, he returned it without comment.

"Lyan? Please don't take this wrong, but… elves are kind of strange," Shiolto told him.

Lyan's mouth quirked in a smile. "We're perfectly normal. Everyone else is strange."

Shiolto laughed. Lyan relaxed, more comfortable than he had been at the day's start. Aikan did not accept him, but Shiolto made up for that with his easy cheer.

~

The day's travel passed without incident. Sometimes the hair on the back of Lyan's neck prickled as if he was being watched, but when he looked around, he didn't see anything trailing them. He didn't mention the sensation. They already suspected that the pooka trailed them, and Lyan wasn't sure whether he sensed the monster's presence or only imagined things. Without the comforting presence of Eilidh Wood to watch over him, Lyan felt exposed and uneasy.

Mid-morning the following day, they reached Dechosyn River. The broad river curled a path across the Appret Plains, offering the prime source of water to the grasslands and those that lived on it. Tracks marked the muddy bank: deer, elk, wolves, even a few large cats. And horses. Many horses. Lyan added his own odd track to the mix when they stopped for a rest, limping down to the water's edge and pulling off his boot to let the cold water soothe his throbbing ankle.

Dalrian followed him, and crouched down to examine the tracks. "The horses are shod."

"The herders of the Appret Plains, probably," Lyan said. "We trade with them sometimes." He limped back to Shadowstar and rubbed the stallion's nose. Shadowstar playfully nibbled at his red hair.

"Are you on good terms with them?" Dalrian asked him.

Lyan smiled thinly. "I think we established yesterday that neighbors of Eilidh Wood have reason to keep on good terms with my people."

Dalrian looked startled, then his expression softened. "I know Aikan's stuffy, but he's not a bad fellow. He's just really keen on traditions and doing things the 'right' way. He didn't used to be quite so bad before his wife died a few years back. I heard his family used to be nobles, but they lost their lands and titles in the war, then became vassals to Lord Cailean's family."

"I see." Lyan wasn't completely sure he did. "His family lost their home because of elves."

"Not just their home. They used to be lords, like Lord Cailean, and now someone else has all that and they don't own any land at all." Dalrian pulled off his boots and waded into the river to fill water skins. "He probably blames the elves for that. Lots of stories about elves get told in Tather. Some are the sort you use to scare little children into behaving and not getting out of bed in the middle of the night, but there are others our grandfathers used to tell about being soldiers." He trailed off and turned to face Lyan. "You're not like that, though. Even with all the old stories, I'm glad you're coming with us. Like the gods wanted us to meet you."

Lyan smiled. "Thank you, Dalrian. I appreciate hearing that." He wet a fresh cloth in the cold water and wrapped it around his ankle. The swelling was down a little, and the soak in the river numbed the ache to a dull throb.

Shadowstar knelt at Lyan's signal, and Lyan climbed into the saddle. Dalrian walked with him back to the rest of the group. The human gave Cailean a brief report on the tracks, then Cailean looked to Lyan.

"Ready?"

Lyan nodded. "I am. Thank you for the pause."

The sky overhead was clear and blue, showing no hints of the heavy clouds that would roll in before the first stars came out. Lyan grimaced slightly when he thought of how they would trap heat as summer progressed, making darkness little relief from the oppressive heat. Would thunderstorms brew in those clouds? Would they release rain, or would they jealously withhold water while scorching the dry ground with lightning?

"Is something wrong, Lyan?" Cailean asked.

"No, I'm just watching the sky."

Cailean looked up, then to Lyan. "See something interesting?"

"The clouds at night will make summer's heat worse than usual. We may find the herders gathering at the edge of Eilidh Wood earlier to find shade and relief."

"Earlier? Is that something they normally do?" Cailean asked. "What will your people do?"

"We don't dislike *all* human." Lyan said with a faint smile. "The nomads often spend some of the summer at the forest's edge. We trade with them. And we enforce the truces that are in place when the tribes stand in the shade of Eilidh Wood. We don't tolerate them pursuing their rivalries and tribal grudges in our home, and they know it."

"So, no one is permitted to shed blood in Eilidh Wood except the elves," Aikan said.

Lyan tensed, but reminded himself that he had friends here. He tried to phrase his answer in a way Aikan would understand. "It is our home, and they are guests. If Cailean had as visitors two groups who held old, simmering grudges, would he stand by and do nothing if a fight broke out between them?"

Aikan frowned, but relented. "He would not. And his guests would be remiss to stir up such trouble."

That seemed to settle the matter. Lyan relaxed, realizing he automatically tensed when Aikan spoke. Shadowstar snorted and tossed his head. Lyan reached forward and scratched the stallion's ears.

They followed the river, stopping when darkness fell and the clouds shrouded the sky. Lyan stared up at the glow of the moon that forced its way through the clouds, feeling a twist in his gut. Being cut off from the stars was like having a piece of himself cut away. He was lost and without guidance. Lyan's eyes searched, praying for even the slightest gap in the cover, the twinkle of even one star. He thought he saw one for an instant, a glint for a heartbeat when the shifting clouds opened a momentary crack. But it could have been only his imagination.

By afternoon the next day, Lyan saw a cluster of shapes ahead near the river. As they drew closer, he identified the forms as horses and tents. A rider came from the herders' camp toward them. Cailean brought his band to a halt and waited for the rider to identify himself. Shadowstar stepped up to stand beside Cailean.

The rider's face, tanned like leather, but sporting a young man's stubble, burst into a smile when he recognized Shadowstar, and he slung his bow across his back. "Lyan! Summer rains, is that you? What in the Horselord's name are you doing here?!" He slowed only at the last moment, drawing up before Shadowstar and offering his hand. "Father will be delighted to see you!"

Lyan clasped the offered hand firmly with his own warm smile. He didn't need the earring's magic to understand the language of the plains, or to answer in the same. "Seifer, it's wonderful to see you! These are your tribe's summer grazing lands?"

Seifer nodded. "Aye, though we never expected you to visit." For the first time, he actually looked at Lyan's companions, and a moment of puzzlement touched his gaze when he recognized none of them, and realized they weren't elves.

"I'm traveling with these men," Lyan answered. "We won't be able to stay long, I'm afraid."

Seifer changed to the Trade tongue, and the earring translated for Lyan once again. "Greetings travelers. I welcome you and invite you to share a meal with the Nakhahra tribe. I am Seifer, son of Ohrlan, chief of the Nakhahra."

"We accept your gracious invitation," Cailean answered. "I am Cailean Dev'gilla."

"I'm afraid your name is not known to me, but you've come in Lyan's company. That says enough." He gave Lyan a grin much less formal than his greeting to Cailean had been. "I'll tell Father you're on your way, Lyan."

The grin was infectious with its youthful enthusiasm. Lyan couldn't help but return it. "I'm looking forward to seeing him."

As Seifer galloped back to his tribe, Shiolto spoke. "What do you know, Aikan? You were right, having Lyan with us *is* going to go a long way to giving us a welcome here."

Lyan glanced over his shoulder, and could feel the weight of the glare Aikan gave Shiolto. Shiolto glanced at Lyan, and winked with a grin. Cailean struggled to keep a straight face, and Dalrian managed to turn a half-choked sound into a cough.

6

The voice of the wind,
Ever seeking, ever searching,
Ever wishing to find her home

The families that made up the Nakhahra clan separated during the summer to spread around the area that formed their clan's grazing lands, but any number of hangers-on followed Ohrlan's camp, whether because they lacked the numbers to remain safe away from a group, or in the hopes of currying favor with their clan lord. Lyan recognized most faces in the crowd that gathered as he and Cailean's band reached the edge of the camp. Foremost stood Ohrlan, a weathered, broad-shouldered man with hands that could have crushed Lyan's with hardly an effort. He kept his graying hair cut short, but his beard hung long, braided with strips of colored leather. He could be stern when he chose, but when he saw his guests, Ohrlan burst into a grin that matched his son's.

"Lyan of Eilidh Wood!" he boomed. "Welcome!"

Lyan dismounted, holding to Shadowstar's mane with one

hand to keep his balance. Ohrlan caught him in a crushing embrace that knocked the wind from his lungs. "It's good to see you," Lyan managed when he had enough breath.

Ohrlan stepped back. His hands on Lyan's shoulders kept the elf steady. "I never expected to see you out here! We'll see your dour friend on occasion, or others from your village, when they want to be seen. Sometimes they'll stop for a meal or news. Usually don't cross their paths until we're closer to Eilidh Wood, though." Ohrlan's gaze moved to Cailean and the other men, studying them. His voice dropped low. "I'm thinking there's a story here. Are you with friends, Lyan?"

"I am, by choice," Lyan assured the clan leader.

"Come! You must sit down and rest with us," Ohrlan invited, his voice again carrying for all to hear.

Lyan smiled. "Thank you, Ohrlan." He pulled his crutch from Shadowstar's back. Ohrlan's eyes narrowed, and Lyan answered the question before he could ask. "I was avoiding a monster that intruded into the forest when I fell and hurt my ankle. It'll heal."

"Aye? But why are you leaving your home before it's done so?" Ohrlan asked, voice quiet. He didn't wait for an answer, but resumed his previous enthusiasm, motioned for all of them to follow him.

Grins and warm welcomes greeted Lyan on every side, and he didn't let pain keep him from returning them as he limped after Ohrlan through the village of hide tents. The clan lord's tent was easily the largest. Its utilitarian exterior sheltered the fine goods within—rugs embroidered with gold threads, tapestries depicting places Lyan had never been or tales he knew by heart, golden serving platters and dishes to match. Many of the treasures had been collected by Ohrlan's father, or grandfather, or a further distant ancestor. As a successful clan lord who knew when to raid and when to trade in his own right, Ohrlan had added to the collection. The tent was cluttered but comfortable, and Lyan felt almost as at home in it as he would have in any house in Heartshrine Village. How Ohrlan managed to move everything each time they changed locations, though, had always been a mystery to Lyan.

Ohrlan's wife, Rissa, greeted Lyan with a kiss on his cheek —a welcome traditionally reserved only for family. "Please sit and be comfortable, friends," she said in Trade. "I will bring refreshments."

Cailean bowed. "Thank you, Lady."

Ohrlan settled into his favorite chair. It creaked ominously under his weight, but it always had, and Lyan barely noticed as he sank down on a padded stool. "Yes, yes, sit down. Sorry, I didn't think to ask if you knew our tongue."

"Enough to follow some of what you said," Cailean answered as they all settled in chairs or on the floor, "but I fear I would not do it justice if I tried to speak it."

Rissa brought wine and a platter of bread. Lyan could smell something cooking, and his mouth began to water. Ohrlan sat up straight. "Welcome to my home, friends. I am Ohrlan, lord of the Nakhahra clan, and this is my wife, Rissa. You met my eldest already. I have a handful more running somewhere around the camp like the little hellions they are. No doubt they'll start showing up once the food's ready."

"It's an honor to meet you," Cailean said. "I've heard of your clan, but never had the pleasure of encountering you in person before. I am Cailean Dev'gilla, Earl of Ihvako, and these are my men: Aikan Unne, Torqual Ferren, Dalrian and Shiolto Rona, and Yion."

"Ihvako?" repeated Ohrlan, gaze sharp on Cailean. He glanced at Lyan, then back to Cailean. "You're Tathren?"

Aikan bristled at the suspicion and hint of distaste in Ohrlan's voice. "Are we unwelcome *here* as well as among the elven savages?"

Ohrlan's eyes narrowed as he leaned forward. His voice

was deceptively even. "The elves of Eilidh Wood have been friends to my people for generations. Their wisdom has guided us and without them, my clan would not survive. Friends of theirs are friends of ours. Fortunately, you are among us as friends of Lyan, and I trust him to be able to answer any insults to his people. So if he does not take offense to your words, neither will I."

And if I do take offense, the entire Nakhahra clan takes offense with me. Lyan shifted uncomfortably when Ohrlan looked at him. He wasn't completely sure how he had earned the clan's esteem, but he had. One word from him would bring the wrath of the clan down on Cailean and his men. Lyan shook his head. "Let it be."

Ohrlan nodded curtly, accepting Lyan's judgment. He leaned back in his chair. "You're far from Tather, Earl Dev'gilla, and look to be going further yet. What brings you here?"

Cailean started when the question was asked, tense and cautious. He collected himself. "We are bound for the mountains and to the lands beyond. Iseek an artifact to help my people."

The moment of danger might never have happened for all the signs Ohrlan showed. "Oh? And Lyan is joining you?"

"Lyan generously offered to help me on my search. His aid is most welcome," Cailean answered. He shot a warning glare at Aikan.

To that Ohrlan nodded. "You're more fortunate than you know to have his help. Lyan's wise—heed his advice. I know none who know the old tales better than he does, and in the reading of the stars, he has no equal. He's blessed my family many times. Lyan read the signs for my grandfather's birth, my father's, my own, and those of my children."

Lyan felt a stab of panic. "Rissa isn't expecting again, is she?" He'd read the stars for Ohrlan's family for each of their children since he'd argued his teacher into letting him do so for Ohrlan's grandfather.

Ohrlan laughed. "No such luck yet, Lyan. Not for lack of trying, I assure you!" His face grew serious. "You're thinking of the clouds." Lyan nodded. "Horselord's Turds, I hoped you could see something through that mess that human eyes couldn't."

Lyan shook his head. "No, I can't see the stars."

Ohrlan spat. "Foul magic at work. All the oracles point toward it. When you're in the mountains, watch for a road climbing toward one of the peaks."

"What's there?" Lyan asked.

"A temple and shrine to Toirni, the Thunderer. The path's a narrow thing in the pass; you can miss it if you aren't watching. I sent an offering, but my messengers haven't returned. If you can get there, you might find someone who knows what is keeping the clouds over the sky at night."

Lyan frowned. "Do you think Toirni is doing this?" He knew the god of storms could be fickle, but to hide the sky every night, only at night, without unleashing a storm or other demonstration of anger was abnormal.

To that, Ohrlan only shrugged. "I don't know, Lyan. I just know it's going to get *damned* hot if this keeps up. If he isn't the cause, then I can at least ask him to be the solution."

"I don't believe the clouds to be the doing of a god," Cailean said.

Ohrlan considered him. "Foul magic. But if you think there's a mortal with the power to intrude on the domain of a god and not be struck dead for the impudence, then that's a man I don't want to meet."

Cailean said nothing in reply, whether because he had nothing to say or because the enchantment on him prevented it, Lyan couldn't tell. Yion broke the stillness, voice calm as always. It took Lyan a moment to realize that the mercenary spoke the language of the plains, if with a strange accent. "We are fortunate to have found your camp, Lord Ohrlan. We were unable to resupply at our last stop. With your permission, we should like to purchase provisions for our journey."

Ohrlan looked as surprised as Lyan, but recovered himself in a moment. "Purchase? I couldn't let you to enter the mountains unprepared! Not going to charge you for that."

Yion shook his head. "You are most generous, lord, but it is a matter of pride. My lord Cailean could not take food from the mouths of your people without repaying you."

Cailean listened to the exchange with the expression of someone only understanding half of what he heard, and he didn't argue with Yion as he might have if he actually followed the entire conversation. But Ohrlan relented. "Very well." Lyan saw a twinkle in the clan lord's eye, though, and could only wonder what excess of generosity he would rise to, being denied the opportunity to gift their supplies. Yion bowed graciously, face almost unreadable. But Lyan caught a gleam in the mercenary's eyes, and wondered if that excessive generosity, whatever form it took, had been his goal.

Is Yion manipulating Ohrlan? But Ohrlan gave in far more easily than I'd expect. He's looking for an excuse to lavish gifts. Lyan smiled slightly. To demonstrate generosity to friends was expected; to show generosity to men who could have been enemies was exceptional hospitality, and the Horselord favored those who did so.

The clan lord turned to Lyan, speaking in Trade again. "I'm glad you came with that guardian of yours, Lyan. There're mares in the herd that'd be blessed by his attention."

Lyan smiled. "Shadowstar chooses his own path, Ohrlan. I don't have any say on what he does, especially not in that regard."

Ohrlan chuckled. "Maybe not, but he fathers strong, smart colts."

"Guardian?" Shiolto repeated curiously.

"Aye, as Lyan says, that stallion chooses his own path. The

oracles say he's a guardian spirit, comes and goes as he wants and a curse on the man who thinks he can command 'im. Dunno what I think of that, but that stallion's picked Lyan, and him, or one identical to him, has come and gone on these plains for as long as our stories know."

"I'm afraid I'll be asking him to travel far from the plains he calls home," Lyan said.

"No man has claim to him, Lyan," Ohrlan repeated. "If he's decided to go with you, then he's going with you however far it is."

The arrival of a pack of youths cut short further discussion. Five children descended on Lyan, crying with delight and excitement. "Lyan! Tell us a story! I want to hear the one about the boy who stole the Horselord's apples. Are you going to read the stars for us? Is Mama going to have another baby? Is that why you're here?" The barrage of questions came too quickly to tell who asked what.

Laughing, he extracted himself from the assault. "Maybe later for stories. No, I'm not here to read the stars. Some other time, perhaps. Don't you need to help your mother with dinner?"

"Lyan is our guest!" Rissa planted hands on her hips, gazing sternly at her brood. "His company honors us. You know all he's done for our clan—treat him with the respect due an elder!"

Lyan almost protested that he didn't mind, but caught himself in time. He knew better than to interrupt a mother chastising her children. Not only that, but the swarm of Ohrlan's offspring constantly wanting him to entertain them grew exhausting.

Rissa put the children to work as she finished preparing dinner. Lap tables were set before each person, then coarse flatbread topped with fresh greens, and finally antelope roasted with garlic. Ohrlan broke out a bottle of his best wine, filling golden goblets with the rich ruby drink. Conversations lagged as they ate. Lyan had the sense that Cailean and his men felt out of place here, speaking as courtesy demanded but little more.

"It'll be good for you to get out and see the world, Lyan!" Ohrlan announced once the plates had been cleared. "Bring home some new ideas for your people."

"Eilidh Wood does just fine doing things as we always have," Lyan told him. The idea of trying to change anything of their way of life sent a strange chill down his spine and made his stomach knot.

Ohrlan snorted. "Lyan, I have never understood how every single one of you can read a book, yet your people can't even figure out how to domesticate animals." He roughly scratched the ears of one of the herding dogs, come in to beg scraps.

Lyan shrugged. "We don't need them."

"Or grow crops," the nomad continued.

"Neither do you," Lyan countered. "And the Elder has his grove."

"Most of your people are hunters because it's the only way you keep enough food in your village to survive, you depend on trade with us for anything else you need, and you live in trees! We don't plant because we have to keep the herds moving. You elves already live in one place. Clear some ground, plant some crops, keep a few goats and chickens." Ohrlan leaned back, making the chair groan. "Mad God's Pits, Lyan, the people of Eilidh Wood barely qualify as civilized by most people's counts, yet *every single one* of you can *read*!"

"We're civilized!" Lyan said sharply. "And what's so strange about being able to read?"

The nomad shook his head. "Get out and see the world, Lyan. Maybe then you'll understand." He waved a hand. "Or maybe not. Your people do things their own way, and it seems to work for them, though gods only know how."

Lyan sighed. "We live by the ways of Eilidh Wood, Ohrlan. The forest doesn't change."

"Aye…I cannot argue that," Ohrlan agreed.

As the sun set, clouds rolled over the sky. A shiver ran down Lyan's spine. Without trees to obscure the sight, the unnatural speed of the shrouding was all the starker. He eagerly welcomed the distractions Ohrlan's camp offered. The nomads built a bonfire and gathered to dance and sing. Cailean and Aikan hung back, watching from a little distance, but Shiolto, Dalrian, and Torqual joined Lyan in the ring around the fire. He didn't know where Yion went.

The clan's young men, those who stood on the line between youth and adult, stripped off their shirts and danced around the fire to a beat set by the clapping hands and stomping feet of the rest of the clan. The tempo steadily grew faster and faster as the dancers tried to outlast each other. The number dwindled under stumbling steps and the rapidly pounding beat. By the time only Ohrlan's son Seifer and another young man remained, the beat thundered like the hooves of a hundred galloping horses. Sheens of sweat gleamed on both dancers. Lyan thought the beat could go no faster, and his hands ached from keeping up with it. Abruptly, at a signal from one of the women, the tempo changed, slowing sharply back to the starting beat. Both Seifer and his rival stumbled. Seifer kept his feet, barely, but the other young man fell, tumbling to the dirt and finally bringing the challenge to an end.

The loser shook his head wryly, grinning as he slowly sat up, panting for breath. "Good round."

Seifer bent over, bracing hands on his knees as he panted. "Good round. You almost had me."

"Hah! The day I can outdance an elf-blessed son of

Ohrlan will be the day my feet sprout wings!" The other dancer grinned, and accepted the hand Seifer offered. The dancers withdrew to waiting jugs of water to cool off.

"Lyan, will you sing for us?" Ohrlan asked.

"If you wish it, I will. But I'm not nearly as skilled as most of my people," Lyan answered. "You should hear Kithr—he was once considered most likely to become Keeper of Tales, and he puts me to shame."

"Maybe so," Ohrlan laughed. "But we can never convince him to prove it!"

Lyan sang a pair of songs he knew to be favorites among the Nakhahra clan. The first was a light-hearted tale of a young man trying to impress a girl, each effort growing more and more outrageous. Slightly off-key voices rose to join Lyan's on each chorus, and one man swung his wife in a dance around the fire. At the end of the song, he bowed to everyone, as if to claim he was the subject of the song. His wife laughed and hit him in the shoulder, telling him to watch himself.

The second song changed the mood. Lyan sang it only on rare occasions, the tale of the wind, lonely, sweeping across the plains, forever seeking a home. The thundering hooves of horses wove through the song, with the echoes of voices. It was a song of the nomads... a song sung in tribute to the people around him. When the last words faded away into the darkness, Lyan glimpsed several people wiping tears from their eyes.

Ohrlan rested a hand on his shoulder. "I've not heard that in many years, Lyan, and never so beautifully sung. Thank you. I couldn't have asked a finer gift from you."

"It was my honor," Lyan said quietly, unwilling to raise his voice and break the stillness over the camp.

Gradually, people drifted to their tents to sleep. Lyan watched the bonfire burn down to smoldering coals. Ohrlan had prepared sleeping arrangements for his guests, but something kept Lyan from following the Tathrens when they retired. He looked up to the shrouded sky, then to the ground once more. *I should lie down. There's nothing to see here. Why am I still sitting here?*

A small hand tugged on his sleeve. Lyan looked down to see Dhee, second-youngest of Ohrlan's daughters. The little girl looked up at Lyan in the faint light from the fire with all the intensity of a five-year-old. "Lyan?"

He smiled at her, though she might not have been able to see it. "Yes, Dhee?"

"Are you gonna make the stars come back?"

He blinked. "Um…"

"I heard Daddy and Mama talking. They said nobody's ever known you to be so far away from the scary forest, and they're worried 'cause you're with people they don't know, and they don't know why. But I do. You're going to go make the stars come back, aren't you?"

"I don't know if I can, Dhee."

"Of course you can," she said, confident voice making it clear that, in her mind at least, the matter was settled. Lyan had left Eilidh Wood to make the stars come back, he would succeed, and all would be right in the world again.

Lyan smiled, knowing she couldn't see the sadness hiding in his expression. "I'll do my best."

"Daddy says if it gets too hot, we're going to have to go to the edge of the scary forest a lot earlier in the summer." She sighed. "And you're not gonna be there, are you?"

"Probably not," Lyan allowed. "But there will be other people there. Singers and storytellers…"

Dhee looked up at him. "Yeah… but none of them will play with us. They just tell us to go away."

It was, unfortunately, true. Elves always collected at the edge of the woods when the plains dwellers began to gather in the shade offered by Eilidh Wood, but few of them actively sought opportunities to interact with the nomadic clans as Lyan had. "I'm sorry I won't be there this year."

Dhee hugged his leg tightly. "You gotta come back, okay? I... I'll get really mad at you if you don't." She sniffled.

Lyan patted her head gently. "I'll be careful, I promise. Now... I think you should be in bed, shouldn't you?"

"So should you," she countered.

Lyan chuckled softly. "All right, then we better both go to bed, before your mother scolds us."

Dhee reluctantly released his leg and handed Lyan his crutch. The little girl escorted Lyan to his pallet, then scampered off to her own bed. Lyan lay down and closed his eyes, imagining patterns in the sky. *Make the stars come back.* He thought of Dhee and her simple faith in him. *I'll find a way. If there is a way, I'll find it.*

Flatbread and warm mare's milk made the morning meal, and if Cailean and Aikan both gave the food dubious looks when their hosts weren't looking, Lyan had no such reservations. While he ate, Dhee clung to one of his legs, and her little sister Asta, barely old enough to toddle about, attached herself to his other.

Lyan smiled down at them. "I seem to have gained a couple volunteers to accompany me."

Rissa gave her daughters a scolding look. "Let Lyan eat in peace! He's going to leave soon."

Little Asta shook her head and buried her face against Lyan's leg, clinging all the more. Dhee tried to give Lyan a serious look. "You better come back again. I'm gonna marry you when I grow up."

Lyan raised an eyebrow at that, and Ohrlan laughed. "My, my, my. Ever popular with the girls, Lyan! I recall my own sister making such a declaration when she wasn't much older than Dhee." The clan leader plucked up his children and dangled them in the air. Both girls squealed in delight. "Best escape while you can, Lyan. Dhee might try to carry through with it!"

Lyan swallowed the last of his milk and smiled. "Thank you for your hospitality, Ohrlan."

Ohrlan set the girls down and shooed them off to play, then clasped Lyan's arm. "It's an honor to have you here, Lyan. I don't know where you're going, and I'm not going to ask why, but wherever you're headed, travel safely, and watch your back. Now come, I have gifts for your companions!" He gestured for Cailean and his men to join them, sweeping them all outside.

The packhorses had been groomed, their burdens repacked, with the additional supplies loaded on as well. Shadowstar stood proud, saddled and awaiting Lyan while he watched over the six additional horses that had been added to his herd. Lyan glanced back at Ohrlan, and saw the clan lord gazing proudly at the animals. "Lord Cailean, it wouldn't be right for me to let you leave without gifts of friendship. Allow me to present to you some of the finest horses from my own herd. None are a match for Lyan's guardian, I fear, but you'll find them strong and clever."

"This is too fine a gift," Cailean protested.

The Tathren's reaction pleased Ohrlan. "You're bound for the mountains. You'll not want to make that crossing on foot. I insist. I could not permit my guests to leave my home like footsore beggars. A gift of friendship."

"Your generosity, your hospitality is beyond words." Cailean bowed deeply. "I am honored and humbled by it."

Ohrlan beamed. "It is we who are honored to have you as our guests with Lyan. We will not soon forget this day." As the clan lord walked Cailean to the horses, Lyan caught the words Ohrlan spoke in a low voice intended for Cailean's ears only.

"And if you allow any harm to come to Lyan, we will not soon forget *that*, either."

Cailean bowed again, and answered in a normal volume. "Neither will I forget your kindness, your hospitality, or your words."

"May the Horselord watch over you, wherever you go," Ohrlan said. "I expect to hear the whole story when you return, Lyan!"

7

Hope in the night
Dream for the day
Of shadow and light
And unbroken way

Not even Aikan leveled criticism at Lyan in regard to the Nakhahra clan or Ohrlan. The horses were as fine as Ohrlan had promised, and Shadowstar welcomed their company with an ease he'd not shown in regard to the Tathren packhorses. Judging from the coloring of two of the horses, Lyan suspected Shadowstar had fathered some, if not all, the horses Ohrlan had gifted to Cailean. The packhorses were loaded with supplies, and an air of security lightened spirits.

Lyan cast a look over his shoulder, though the tents were now lost from sight. *Ohrlan's worried about me. He knows about the war and how most of Eilidh Wood feels about Tathrens, and I couldn't tell him why I'm going with Cailean. If he knows anything about the Spears, it would come through legends. He wouldn't understand why it matters so much that Cailean carries Solstice, and why I must be sure he does not claim Equinox.*

"Lyan?" called Cailean.

Lyan jerked from his thoughts, irrationally afraid that Cailean knew their direction. "Yes?"

"The clan lord, Ohrlan, mentioned a temple to Toirni the Thunderer in the mountains. Do you think we should find it?"

Lyan recalled the map, though he was surprised Cailean would ask his advice on their route. "We have to cross the mountains, and from what Ohrlan said, the road to the temple branches from the road that goes through the pass. It shouldn't be far out of our way. The priests might know what's causing the clouds at night." That matter was one Lyan desperately wanted answered. "And perhaps you can learn more about your enemy."

He saw Cailean's mouth tighten, and the Tathren lord nodded in agreement.

"What do you think foreign priests would know of Ewart?" Torqual interrupted.

Cailean's men don't know that anyone else is involved. "Unless Ewart has powerful magic, someone else must be involved to hide the sky at night, and I am convinced that these events are related."

"Magic?" Torqual spat derisively. "That's for old women and fools too weak to make an honest living with a blade."

Lyan raised an eyebrow. "I'm sure the warrior-mages of Queresh would disagree with you. As might some heroes from your own legends."

Torqual simply snorted, dismissing Lyan's words. Shiolto, however, asked, "Do you use magic, Lyan?"

He shook his head. "No, I don't have any magic, or none that's shown itself. There aren't many in our village who do. Elder Brenhan, of course, can ask the gods to grant blessings, and several villages near ours have craftsmen who know the art of imbuing items with power. Some have gifts with animals, or the skill to influence plants. I don't know if you'd call that magic or not."

"I would!" Shiolto said. "What else would you call it? So, by 'influencing plants', do you mean doing things like making plants attack people? Or to give a place a really uncomfortable feeling? There are a few places I've been near where I just got the sense that I wasn't welcome, and I shouldn't try to enter."

Lyan had been thinking of his cousin, who'd been able to convince plants to flower out of season, or to produce fruit even in winter. Another who'd never come home from the war. "It could be used that way, yes," he said quietly.

An uncomfortable silence settled over the group. Aikan gave Lyan a suspicious look, as if the talk of magic made him doubt Lyan's honesty once again and the Tathren was waiting to see if Lyan suddenly sprouted horns and began spewing fire. Lyan sighed silently and turned his attention to the land.

The Dechosyn River guided them across the plains to the mountains that shadowed the distant horizon. A hawk circled overhead, diving abruptly in pursuit of prey. Behind them lay only more grassland, spotted occasionally with horses or other animals.

Two evenings after their parting with Ohrlan, as they settled around the camp, a shiver ran down Lyan's back. The horses shifted uneasily and tossed their heads. Lyan looked around warily, feeling eyes on him. He caught the glint of red glow, and thought he saw a black horse in the growing darkness.

"Lyan, dinner," Dalrian called.

Lyan didn't move, caught in the creature's gaze.

"What's wrong?" Cailean moved to his side and looked around.

Lyan shivered, blinking and breaking contact with the glowing eyes. "The pooka's near."

Cailean tensed, gripping the shaft of his Spear. "Where?"

The shadow was gone. Lyan shook his head. "I'm not sure. It's close, though. I saw it for a moment."

Cailean helped him stand. "We'll be careful."

Lyan cast a final look to where he'd seen the creature, but found nothing.

A voice whispered in his ear, soft and sickeningly sweet. *"You see me when I want you to see me, elf. When I don't wish you to, you'll never know how close I am, and you have no power to hold me. I am a free spirit."*

Lyan tensed and looked around sharply.

Cailean looked at him. "Lyan?"

"I… thought I heard something. It's… sorry."

"Aww, poor little elf," the pooka's voice whispered. *"Don't you trust your Tathren companions? How many of their ears do you think I whisper in? How many of them listen to what I can tell them about you? Oh, I know… maybe they think you're really here to kill the Spearbearer and take his Spear. After all, that's what the war was about, isn't it?"*

Lyan gritted his teeth and ignored the sugary voice. He managed a smile when he sat by the fire and accepted a plate.

"Lyan says the pooka's close tonight," Cailean said. "Watch yourselves, and don't leave camp."

A chuckle in Lyan's ear. *"You really think I am the worst of your troubles?"*

Then the presence was gone. The horses calmed, but Lyan didn't relax. *What does it want? Why is it following us, and by whose will? What does it know?*

When he lay down to sleep, Lyan tried to shut out the memory of the pooka's whispers, but they crept back all the same. *What if Kithr's right and I can't trust Cailean and his men? What if Cailean lied about why he wants both Spears, or how he gained Solstice? What if he does gain both Spears? What if they turn on me before we find Equinox? What if they really are as deceptive and treacherous as Kithr says their forefathers were?*

He shuddered and opened his eyes, looking automatically

to the shrouded sky. Whatever answers the stars might have offered remained hidden behind the clouds.

Cailean isn't responsible for the clouds. I'm sure of that. How he could be so certain, Lyan didn't know, but he didn't believe the bearer of a Spear of the Stars would conceal the skies. *Someone else has done this, and they've taken my skills from me. If Cailean is fighting him, then I'll take my chances with these Tathrens. Even if they don't trust me any more than Kithr trusts them.*

Lyan closed his eyes again, and resolutely pushed the thoughts from his mind. Sleep eventually found him.

Three more days brought them to the base of the cliffs and to the first indication of a road they'd seen since leaving Eilidh Wood. The river curved away, and they parted ways with that guide to follow the packed dirt trail. Lyan heard the faintest distant rumble of falling water, and tried to imagine the river pouring down the sheer cliff face. He'd heard others describe the waterfall, as they had described the mountains to him, but mere words could not encompass the reality of the massive walls of stone before them. Craning his head back, he glimpsed white snow on the distant peaks, so high they seemed to pierce the sky.

Dalrian considered the road. "This looks nice. Someone maintains this road. It'll be easier than crossing between Tather and Eldonnar, and it looks like the pass isn't as high, either."

"Eldonnar?" Lyan asked.

"Country south of Tather. A mountain range much higher than these forms the border." Dalrian grinned at Lyan's expression. "Oh, never been through mountains before?"

Lyan shook his head, trying to think of mountains taller than these. He almost said more, but hesitated to admit that he'd never been so far from home before.

"Enough dallying—you can tell Lyan whatever stories you're thinking of while we ride," Cailean interrupted.

"Sorry, Lord Cailean." Dalrian scrambled into the saddle.

"I know *about* mountains," Lyan protested. "I just haven't *seen* them before." Shadowstar followed Cailean's horse.

Despite an attempt to rein in curiosity, Lyan soon caught himself asking about their surroundings—the plants, the animals, the rocks themselves. Dalrian, Shiolto, and even Cailean attempted to answer his boundless store of questions. But when Lyan began asking why the rocks were formed the way they were, Cailean burst out laughing.

"Lyan, for all I know, a dragon flew too low and dragged its claws across the ground!"

The scholar in Lyan objected to the idea. "That would be far too large a dragon for this area to support, for its claws to leave marks like these…"

The Tathrens stared at him incredulously for a moment, then Dalrian and Shiolto both began laughing, joined a moment later by Torqual. Yion smiled, and even Aikan's lips twitched in what might have been amusement at Lyan's serious tone.

"It would appear, Lord Cailean, that Lyan finds your theory to be flawed," Yion said.

Lyan flushed, embarrassed. "I didn't mean…"

"Maybe it was a couple of dragons!" Shiolto put in.

"That's--" Lyan began to protest.

"Only if they came with chisels and hammers," Aikan cut in.

"What?" Cailean asked.

Aikan pointed at the face of a rock, carved with two arrows. One pointed in the direction they'd come from, labeled "Appret Plains". The other pointed up the trail, and it bore the marker "Kamael".

Relieved to have a change of subject, and surprisingly grateful to Aikan for providing it, Lyan said, "That's good to see. We won't want to go all the way to Kamael, but it's the right direction."

For the rest of the day, Lyan struggled to keep questions to himself. He had a sneaking suspicion that if he did let any slip out, the answer he got would have something to do with dragons.

～

The road continued to climb when they set out the next morning. Lyan watched for indications of the path to the temple, storing away questions to ask the priests if he got the chance. His ankle ached, but not as badly as it had. Distracted, he almost didn't notice when Shadowstar slowed to match the other horses. Lyan blinked when he realized they'd stopped, and he looked to Cailean.

The Tathren lord eyed the rocks around them warily. "Too quiet." His eyes narrowed. "Show yourselves!"

A man in nondescript leather tunic and breeches stepped from behind a rock ahead. He carried a bow, an arrow held to the string but pointed at the ground. "Lord Cailean Dev'gilla, Earl of Ihvako?"

"I am. Who are you, and what business do you have with me?"

The man smiled, displaying yellowed teeth. "It's about time! You're late. Very rude, to be late to such an important meeting."

Cailean frowned, one hand moving toward Solstice. "What 'meeting' would that be?"

"What meeting?" repeated the man. He grinned. "Why, your meeting with Death, of course!" With a cackle, he dove behind the rock as the twang of bowstrings hummed in the air.

Lyan's eyes grew wide as the volley of arrows soared

toward them. Cailean raised Solstice over his head with a shout Lyan couldn't understand.

Magic rippled through the air around them. Arrows clattered off an unseen barrier. Cailean sagged in the saddle, then straightened. "You want to send me to Death's domain? Then come and try!"

8

The fickle winds, the raging storm
The touch of Toirni's hand

S hadowstar snorted and pawed the ground. Lyan gripped the stallion's mane as his mind conjured visions of Shadowstar rearing and charging, and of himself tumbling to the rocky ground. "Don't," he whispered. "Please."

Shadowstar only closed ranks with the other horses, snorting and tossing his head as the arrows ceased flying. No one emerged to accept Cailean's challenge. Lyan looked at his companions' tense expressions, watching them ready weapons, and felt helplessly exposed.

Cailean leveled the Spear at the rock the man had sheltered behind. "I said come and try, if you think you can kill me. Or do I have to make you show yourselves?"

Another arrow clattered harmlessly off the unseen barrier. Cailean pointed Solstice in the direction the arrow had come from and whispered a word. A boulder shuddered and cracked, splitting up the center in a tortured groan. Someone yelped a curse, scrambling back as his shelter crumbled into a shower of rock shards. The human glared at them. His clothes were patched and dirty. He held a bow, but his quiver had spilled in his haste, leaving him with only an arrow in hand. He tossed bow and arrow aside, drawing a short sword in their place. From the rocks on either side of the road, Lyan heard bows being dropped and weapons drawn. Echoes made their numbers uncertain, but Lyan didn't like the implication of their odds.

"A man for the direct route, then? That's a fancy toy you have, but it won't save you." The leader of the ambush stepped from hiding.

"Stay close, Lyan Stargazer," Yion said quietly, stepping his horse up beside Shadowstar. "And draw your knife, lest they think you a sorcerer and target you for it."

Lyan drew the hunting knife Kithr had given him long ago. He'd never even killed an animal with it, but he tried to hold it as if he knew how to defend himself. Shadowstar snorted again, pawing the ground. Anyone attacking Lyan would have far more to worry about from the stallion than they would from Lyan's inadequate skill with a blade.

The sun beat down on them as Cailean and his men waited for their ambushers to make the first move. The ambushers, in turn, waited, the majority of their numbers still hidden behind the rocks on either side of the road. Sweat trickled down Lyan's face.

Cailean suddenly swept Solstice in a slash through the air toward the stones on their right. A tremor shook the ground, and stones trembled, then rocked loose. Lyan watched them move against nature, rolling up the slope rather than tumbling toward their group. Someone screamed, accompanied by a sickening crunch of bone being crushed. Another yelled in alarm, and half a dozen men scrambled up the slope and to the sides to escape the boulders. One stumbled, and his scream was cut short by the stone that rolled over him. Two men worked their way around the rocks and toward the road. The other three kept running.

"You think you can kill me?" Cailean shouted. "Well?"

"Lord Cailean!" Dalrian warned sharply.

From the other side, a group of seven abandoned their hiding places and rushed toward them, weapons raised to attack. Cailean cursed, and the magic faltered. The boulders crunched to a stop, just enough magic lingering to hold them in place. Torqual spun his horse to meet the first ambushers with a clash of blades, face expressionless.

The leader of the ambushers darted forward, aiming a cut not at Cailean, but at the horse the Tathren lord rode. The horse shied back, taking only a shallow slash, and reared. The attacking man narrowly avoided the iron-shod hooves. Cailean fought to keep his saddle and almost lost hold of Solstice. The tensing of Shadowstar's body gave Lyan enough warning to cling tightly to his mane before the stallion leapt forward, pivoted, and lashed out with rear hooves, connecting with one man and barely missing the leader. Cailean got his horse under control and regained his seat. As if the Spear weighed more than he could lift, Cailean could not seem to level Solstice, but the Tathren still drove it into a man in a filthy fur jerkin.

Shadowstar stepped up by Cailean, and the Tathren's mount calmed. Cailean glanced at Lyan. With no breath to spare for words, he simply nodded to Lyan and cast a look to his men. Three ambushers lay bleeding on the ground before Torqual, who had dismounted to fight on foot. Dalrian and Shiolto fought together from horseback. Aikan, to the other side of Cailean, held a man at bay until Cailean stabbed the attacker. A man lunged toward Lyan, to be cut down by Yion, who had remained close.

Shadowstar turned again and lashed out with his rear hooves, sending another man flying back into the rocks. He didn't get up again.

The leader of the ambush backed away, seeing men falling and rethinking the odds. Cailean's face dripped with sweat, and he looked on the verge of falling from the saddle. His hands shook when he raised Solstice and pointed it at the man, but his voice held steady. "Did you think it would be so easy to kill me?" Behind him, another man fell with a choked cry to Torqual's merciless sword, leaving only two fighting Dalrian and Shiolto. Cailean's gaze remained fixed on the leader. "Who sent you?"

The man grinned, showing yellow teeth again. "You ought to know I won't answer that."

"Tell me!" Cailean demanded. The Spear glowed in his hand.

"Wouldn't if I could."

Cailean gripped the Spear tight enough that his knuckles were white. "Who paid you to kill me? What did they tell you? How much is my life worth?"

"Told you—not telling." The man's mouth twisted in a wicked smile. "Enough to make it worth trying again." He turned and bolted.

Yion moved, and the man staggered as something struck him in the back. Cailean swayed in the saddle and turned to look at the mercenary.

"Your pardon, Lord Cailean. He seemed uninclined to be helpful, and I thought it better to have him dead than allow him to attack us a second time."

"He's dead?" Cailean asked.

"If he is not, he will be momentarily." Yion tucked a throwing star into his baldric.

"Good." Cailean steadied himself and straightened. "Dalrian, Shiolto, Torqual?"

"The ambushers are dead," Torqual answered, emotionless about the men he'd just killed.

Cailean nodded. "Anyone hurt?"

"Nothing life-threatening," Shiolto said. "Are you all right, Lord Cailean?"

"I'll be… Aikan…"

Whatever Cailean intended to say was lost when he slumped forward. Aikan barely caught him in time to keep Cailean on his horse. Solstice fell from Cailean's limp hand to the ground. Lyan cast an anxious glance at the rocks on the hillside, but the magic still held them in spite of Cailean's collapse.

"Lord Cailean?" Shiolto jumped to the ground and dashed over. "What's wrong?"

"He needs rest," Aikan said sharply. "He's not injured."

"Are you sure?" Shiolto asked anxiously.

"Yes." Aikan's voice forbade further questions. "Ride with him, Shiolto, and keep him ahorse."

Shiolto radiated anxiety as he swung onto Cailean's horse. Aikan steadied Cailean until Shiolto was settled, then dismounted and picked up Solstice. His face gave no indication he felt any touch of the magic that had warned Lyan when he'd made contact with Solstice. Aikan slipped the Spear into its straps on Cailean's saddle.

Torqual carefully climbed down the slope he'd ascended. "The three who ran lost their footing and fell. I didn't climb down to check, but they likely didn't survive."

"Get the bodies off the road," Aikan ordered. Finally, he turned to Lyan. "How far to the temple?"

"I don't know, exactly," Lyan admitted, startled that Aikan spoke to him at all. He looked at the unconscious Cailean, and hazarded, "Not far."

"Good," Aikan said shortly. "Lead the way as soon as they're done."

The bodies were given neither burial nor prayers as they were dragged from the road and thrown to the rocks. Lyan realized he still clutched his knife, and sheathed it with exaggerated care, hands shaking. The Tathrens seemed not bothered, as if fighting and killing were part of normal life for them.

Kithr would call me a fool and remind me that I didn't do anything in that fight. All I did was watch and hang on.

Cailean's men climbed into their saddles and waited for Lyan to lead. He urged Shadowstar up the road. The other horses followed close behind, their riders wary. The sun beat down, oppressively hot. Sweat trickled down the back of Lyan's neck.

Yion drew up beside Shadowstar. "This was your first time in battle, was it not?"

Lyan nodded.

"You did well."

Lyan turned. "I didn't *do* anything. Shadowstar did, but I just... didn't do anything."

"You did not panic. You did not flee. You kept on your horse in spite of his attacks. I have seen many do far worse, faced with battle for the first time. You did well."

"If you say so," Lyan said. But Yion's words made him feel a little less like a coward and a handicap to his companions.

The sun crept another handspan across the sky before Lyan spotted a narrow trail winding away from the main road. "This way," he said with confidence he didn't feel. Cailean hadn't stirred at all, and Lyan worried. Hundreds of questions clamored through his mind, but he kept them confined, struggling to stay focused. *Soldarr, please let me be right about this path.*

The narrow trail wasn't as steep as Lyan had feared. Shadowstar climbed with the confidently air of a horse knowing a stable and food awaited at the end. The other horses sensed the unspoken promise in Shadowstar's step, and perked up. Lyan scratched the stallion's ears.

"I hope you're right, Shadowstar."

Shadowstar tossed his head, dismissing any concerns that he might be wrong. Lyan smiled a little. His ankle throbbed and his entire body ached. The Tathrens looked little better, their wary attention faded to exhaustion. The trail continued to climb up a series of switchbacks. Lyan began to wonder if it would ever end, or if they would climb forever in search of a destination that didn't exist. The sun threw long shadows across the mountains.

Shadowstar nickered, and Lyan raised his eyes to find they had reached the trail's end. Ahead of them, across a stretch of green grass, stood a carved and polished stone structure. Pillars rose, forming the impression of walls, capped with heads in the forms of clouds, but no roof covered the center of the temple and the altar. Priests of the god of storms had to accept that their duties required them to be exposed to the elements in weather when most people wouldn't consider venturing outside. Beyond the temple, however, Lyan saw several buildings and a stable area.

"Welcome, travelers."

Lyan turned and found a short woman approaching them, carrying a bucket of water. Her tunic bore the symbol of a lightning bolt across her heart. Graying hair hung in a tight braid, and she walked with a slight limp, but gave them a pleasant smile.

"Thank you," Lyan said.

The priestess looked over their group, though her gaze lingered longest on Lyan. "Have you come to pay your respects to Lord Toirni?"

"We come with questions we hope he will answer," Lyan answered. "And to ask a place to rest. We were attacked on the road."

The priestess's face darkened, and she nodded. "I hope the brigands paid for their attack."

"They did," Aikan said. "But my lord needs time to recover."

"Come with me." The priestess led them around the temple toward the buildings. "Garreth! We have guests!"

A young man, also with the lightning bolt embroidered on his tunic, emerged and hurried to them. "I'll take your horses, sirs."

Lyan climbed stiffly to the ground and took his crutch from Shadowstar's saddle. The stallion sniffed at the younger priest, Garreth, and snorted into his hair, deeming him acceptable. Dalrian helped Shiolto lift Cailean down, and they carried him between them. Aikan took Cailean's bag, with Solstice, from the horse, but left the rest of the baggage in Garreth's care.

"I am Rhonir," the elder priestess said, "and my son is Garreth. We've served this temple for the last five years, and will continue for many more, Toirni willing."

"I am Aikan Unne, vassal to my lord Cailean Dev'gilla." Aikan indicated Cailean. "The rest of his men: Dalrian and Shiolto, Torqual, and Yion. And lately joined us is Lyan."

"We rarely receive visitors from Eilidh Wood," Rhonir said. "Please follow me. I'll show you a place you can rest and recover."

Rhonir led them into a guesthouse. By the time Cailean was settled in a bed, without stirring once, the priestess had prepared soup and bread for the rest of them. The simple meal tasted as good as a midsummer feast to Lyan.

"I'll prepare baths, if any of you wish one. The water will be cold, but clean. I know you have come with questions, but whatever troubles your travels have brought, you all need a good night's sleep. Questions shall wait until morning." Rhonir looked around the table, looking for any objections from her guests. Finding none, she nodded in satisfaction.

"A bath, whether warm or cold, would be welcome," Aikan said.

"Of course."

Lyan also accepted the offer. The water was as cold as Rhonir had warned, and he had no desire to linger once he was clean, but by the time he'd scrubbed off the dirt of their travels, the sky was dark. Lyan looked up as he walked from the bathhouse back toward the guest quarters. Even here in the mountains, the clouds shrouded the skies. Eyes upturned, he nearly ran into Rhonir.

"I'm sorry!" he apologized quickly, barely catching himself.

The priestess steadied him. "No harm done. You were looking to the skies?"

Lyan flushed, embarrassed and hearing the voices of his people, chiding him for not watching his feet. "I'm sorry. It gets me in trouble."

"You want to ask the Thunderer about the clouds that hide the night."

Lyan started slightly, but nodded. "Yes."

He saw Rhonir look up as well. "I will ask him in my prayers tonight. Perhaps he will send an answer I may share with you in the morning."

"Thank you."

Lyan found his way to the guest quarters without further incident. His companions had already picked out beds among the rows of pallets. Lyan chose an empty one, lay down, and quickly sank into sleep.

He woke when someone stirred in the early morning, before dawn. Lyan opened one eye sleepily to see Cailean rousing. Aikan rose and moved to his side.

"Huh… where…?" Cailean started to ask.

"Shh," Aikan said softly enough that Lyan could barely hear him. "We arrived at the temple of Toirni and are guests on the temple's grounds."

Cailean relaxed, laying back. "Everyone's safe?"

"Yes. Lyan led the way here. How are you feeling, Lord Cailean?"

"My head's pounding."

"You were reckless, my lord. Using the Spear drains you, and there was no promise that more weren't waiting."

"What other choice did I have, Aikan? I could use Solstice, or I could watch my loyal few be cut down."

"Every time I see you use it, it seems to weaken you more, my lord. Please… be careful."

Cailean nodded, eyes sinking closed again. "Just tired…"

"Rest, my lord. I'll wake you when we break fast."

Lyan closed his eye and pretended he was still asleep and hadn't heard the hushed conversation. His mind rushed with questions he longed to ask, about Solstice, about its powers, and, most worrying, why it weakened Cailean to use the Spear.

That's not right. Everything I know says it shouldn't do that. So why…?

9

Restless dreams, like falling rain
Pouring down in shattered light

Rain pattered on the roof, filling the room with a gentle, soothing sound and dampening the air. Lyan crawled out from under his covers and poured water into the basin beside his pallet to wash his face. The Tathrens stirred sleepily as he dressed, but didn't rouse. Leaning on his crutch, Lyan limped to the doorway and looked over the temple grounds. Water pooled on the stone-paved paths, making them slick as river stones in a streambed. At the altar, Rhonir and Garreth knelt in prayer, soaked robes clinging to their bodies. The mountains were lost in clouds that hung so close Lyan was sure he could reach out and touch them. The air smelled of rain and the rich odor of evergreens. Birds trilled, and he glimpsed a flock of sparrows hopping through puddles and snatching worms off the paving stones. A chill wind rippled through the misty clouds and tossed at Lyan's unbelted tunic. He shivered and retreated inside, feeling the damp chill sinking into his clothes and preferring the stuffy warmth of the guest quarters.

His bags lay beside his pallet. Lyan sat on the bed and opened one bag to pull out a book. Light in the room was too dim to read, but he flipped through the pages to pass the time quietly.

Torqual was the first Tathren to rise. The blond warrior grunted a greeting in Lyan's direction when he washed, then walked outside despite the rain. Shiolto and Dalrian rolled from their beds soon after. Shiolto blinked blearily at Lyan.

"Kind of dark, isn't it?"

Lyan looked up. "It is," he allowed. "But I didn't want to wake anyone."

"Does it have pictures?" Shiolto asked.

Lyan smiled. "A few."

"Oh." Shiolto rubbed his eyes and opened his mouth in a wide yawn as he stretched. "It's raining? I'd make a bad priest of Toirni. I hate working in the rain."

"It's true. He grumbles like a grouchy bear," Dalrian added.

Lyan smiled and returned the book to his bag. "I'm sure they have other, dryer duties as well."

Torqual stepped back inside, water dripping from his hair. "The priests made breakfast for us. Hurry up, or it'll get cold."

Aikan must not have been deeply asleep if he had been asleep at all. At Torqual's announcement, the older man stiffly sat up. He caught himself against the wall when he stood, straightening with a slowness that spoke of aches and pains. "Go. I'll wake Lord Cailean, and we will join you shortly."

Shiolto combed fingers through his hair and followed his brother and Torqual out. Yion drifted after them. Lyan hesitated, wanting to ask questions of Cailean. When he didn't leave, though, Aikan fixed a dark, pointed look at him. Lyan took his crutch and limped toward the door to escape the venomous glare, but he paused before venturing outside.

"Aikan, have I done something to offend you?"

"If you mean beyond inviting yourself unasked into my

lord's mission and ignoring even the most basic courtesies owed to a noble, no," Aikan said curtly. "Go to breakfast."

"Treating a man not of our people as an equal *is* the greatest courtesy an elf of Eilidh Wood can give," Lyan said, sharpness creeping into his voice. He swallowed back the rest of his words. *And protecting Equinox is the greatest duty any elf of Eilidh Wood can perform, whether or not he is "invited" by those who seek the Spear.*

The rain had let up to a misty drizzle. Lyan took his chances with the slick stones over the muddy grass, and cautiously picked his way to the other building. As he approached, the smell of food wafted out to him, and his stomach growled.

Garreth opened the door when Lyan reached the threshold. "Welcome. I've made porridge and warmed smoked sausages. Help yourself." The young priest wore clean, dry robes, though his hair was still wet. He led Lyan through the outer room and into the dining area.

"It smells wonderful," Lyan told him. He spooned porridge from the kettle into a waiting wooden bowl and took several links of sausage. "Where did you get the sausage?" It had a familiar scent.

"A gift from one of the nomad clans."

Lyan had just settled on a bench at the long wooden table, and looked up quickly. "Ohrlan's men did arrive here, then?"

"Yes, and they departed some days ago with Lord Toirni's promise of rains." The young priest's face darkened. "They didn't make it home, did they?"

Lyan shook his head. "No."

"I see… I'll tell Rhonir. They could have fallen prey to bandits such as the men who attacked you, or worse."

"The men who attacked us weren't bandits." Torqual speared another sausage link. "I won't dignify them with the title of assassins, but they were hired killers sent after my lord."

"At least they're the ones who are dead, not us." Dalrian said around a mouthful of porridge. "Thank you for the food. Appreciate your help."

Garreth smiled. "It's the least we can do. Rhonir will join us when she completes the morning devotions. She hopes Lord Toirni will grant her wisdom to answer your questions."

Lyan was finishing his porridge when Cailean entered, followed by Aikan. Torqual, Shiolto, and Dalrian jumped to their feet. Lyan wondered if he was committing yet another offense to Aikan by not joining them. Weariness clung to Cailean like a cloak, and dark shadows ringed his eyes, but he smiled.

"Good morning. And sit down! Finish your meals!"

They settled back into their seats uncertainly. "Are you all right, Lord Cailean?" Shiolto asked.

Cailean scooped food into his bowl, taking one sausage and leaving the last one for Aikan. He sat down across from Lyan before answering. "Don't worry. I'll be fine. I must have caught a hit to the head in the fight. I certainly have the aching skull for it." Cailean gingerly rubbed his temples before turning to Lyan. "Aikan told me you led us safely here to the temple. Thank you, Lyan."

"It was as much Shadowstar's doing as mine," Lyan admitted. He gazed at Cailean across the table, aching to ask why the Tathren lord lied to his men. Cailean had come through the battle unscathed, and his collapse was connected to Solstice, no other source. Lyan opened his mouth, looking for the right words.

The opportunity slipped from him as Rhonir entered. Lyan let out a long breath and turned. Water dripped from the priestess's thin hair and mud smeared her robes where she'd been kneeling. She smiled at her guests, energized and refreshed by the storm where most people would have looked cold and miserable.

"A blessed morning to you all, friends," Rhonir greeted

warmly. "Welcome especially to you, Lord Cailean. I fear you were not awake for your arrival last night. I am Rhonir and my son is Garreth, priests of the Thunderer. I hope you are recovered from your ordeal yesterday."

"I'm much recovered, thank you. My men have told me of your hospitality. Thank you, and thank Toirni that we arrived here safely."

While the Tathrens ate, Garreth spoke rapidly in a hushed voice to his mother. Rhonir's expression grew serious, and she nodded several times. Once Cailean had finished eating, Rhonir took a seat at the head of the table.

"You've come here with questions, as well as with news that the Nakhahra clansmen who came here never returned to their people."

"The clan lord who directed us to find this temple hadn't heard from the men he sent out," Cailean said. "Were you able to give them any answers?"

"These unnatural clouds aren't my lord's work, nor do they obey his command to disperse," Rhonir said, expression grave.

"Did Lord Toirni tell you who or what *is* causing the clouds?" Lyan asked, attention firmly diverted from concerns about Cailean.

If anything, the priestess's face grew more serious. "A mortal wields these powers, though no mortal, even the strongest mage, should have the strength to defy the will of a god. This foul magic has been granted by Murdo, the Mad God, empowering one of his servants to do his will."

A collective gasp rose around the table at the Mad God's name. Garreth's hands moved in a sign of protection against evil. Lyan swallowed hard, staring at the priestess as ice ran through his veins.

"The Mad God? Why?" Cailean asked in a strained voice.

"The Mad God is eternally fighting to break free of his prison. My lord believes the stars hold signs for those who can read them, guiding them toward a weapon of power. In the hands of a follower of Murdo, this weapon can weaken that prison, bringing him closer to the freedom he desires," Rhonir answered grimly. She looked down the table at her guests, and her gaze settled on Cailean. "My lord also believes the Mad God has sent agents to hunt you."

Cailean tensed. "I… don't know if my enemy follows the Mad God. If he does, then the situation is worse than I imagined."

"Perhaps, perhaps not," Rhonir said. "My lord says you carry an item of power. The Mad God not only wants to claim what you hold, he also fears what you can do with its power." Seeing Cailean's wary expression, the priestess added, "My lord has not told me what you possess, only that you have something the Mad God wants and fears. If he cannot take it by craft, he'll try to use force. For all his madness, he is cunning—he will try to draw you into his service one way or another, Lord Cailean. Be wary. More than that, I don't know." She turned her gaze to Lyan. "Has my answer been any help to you, Lyan?"

"It… it has," Lyan said quietly.

Murdo… the Mad God wants to reclaim the Spears of the Stars. He wants to use them to break free. This isn't just about some mortal wanting the power of the Spears to become a god. This is about an evil so powerful that it nearly destroyed our world, trying unleashed itself on the world again.

If Equinox, if the Spear of my people, fell into the hands of a servant of Murdo…

Lyan shivered at the thought.

"Is there anything more you, or your lord, can tell me that will help me keep his agents from finding the weapon the Mad God seeks?" Cailean asked.

Rhonir shook her head. "It will only be found by those who know where to look. That's the only additional wisdom I can offer to you, Lord Cailean. That, and the knowledge that time is short."

Cailean bowed his head in a nod. "Thank you." He stood. "I have no proper gifts to offer to Toirni." He drew a handful of coins from his purse. "This meager offering is insufficient, but I ask that you accept it."

Rhonir accepted the coins. "Protect yourself and the thing entrusted to you from Murdo, and that will be gift enough."

Cailean bowed. "As you said, time is short. We should be on our way."

"Garreth, ready their horses," Rhonir ordered. The young man hurried to obey.

Cailean nodded to his men, and they followed Garreth out to pack their bags. Cailean lingered by the door while Lyan got to his feet and limped after them more slowly. Rhonir withdrew into another room, leaving Cailean and Lyan alone. Cailean stopped Lyan with a hand on his shoulder before Lyan went outside.

"All right, Lyan, what do you want to ask me?"

Lyan started. "What?"

"You've been avoiding saying something since I came in for breakfast. What is it?"

"You weren't injured in the battle. You collapsed because Solstice drained your strength. Why did you lie to your men? And why did the Spear do that?"

Cailean grimaced. "Exactly the questions I didn't want to hear."

"I've read everything I can find about the Spears of the Stars, Cailean. That should not happen to a rightful bearer of the Spear. Using Solstice should not weaken you, if you really *are* its rightful bearer."

Cailean's eyes narrowed at the thinly veiled accusation. "The Spear didn't drain my strength, Lyan. Using it weakens me, but not because of the Spear itself."

Lyan frowned, reading Cailean's face. After a moment, he guessed. "The curse laid on you."

Cailean nodded. "He couldn't take the Spear from me, and he couldn't use his powers on the Spear itself. But he could enspell me. Any time I use Solstice, that spell wraps itself around me, like a giant serpent wrapping itself around me, squeezing tighter and tighter."

"But why don't you tell…"

Cailean shook his head. "They know little about the Spear, Lyan. They're safer not knowing. Aikan knows a little more, and he knows something of the enchantment. But I'm not going to risk the lives of my loyal men by forcing this knowledge on them."

"I don't understand why not," Lyan protested. "If they know, they can help you more."

Cailean shook his head again. "No, Lyan. Solstice is my burden to bear, and these are my people to protect."

"You shouldn't lie to them," Lyan said quietly.

Cailean's eyes narrowed. "Lyan, you do not understand. I know what I need to do to keep my people safe. This is my duty and my decision. Leave it be."

Cailean stepped aside, and Lyan limped outside. Shiolto met him near the guest house, carrying Lyan's bags.

"Here, it didn't look like you'd taken out anything but that book, and you put it back in the bag."

"Thanks." Lyan forced himself to smile and pretend that Cailean's words hadn't stung. He accepted the bags and waited for Garreth to bring the horses.

Shadowstar found him shortly. The stallion knelt for Lyan to tie his bags in place, then climb into the saddle. When he was settled, Lyan searched through his belongings until he found a small pouch he'd packed in a side pocket. When Rhonir came to bid them farewell, Lyan gave the pouch to her.

"This is my offering of thanks to Toirni."

"Lord Cailean already provided..." Rhonir began, starting to hand the pouch back.

Lyan shook his head. "Cailean isn't my lord... and this is thanks not only for everything your lord has given us, but also for the rains he's promised to Ohrlan's clan."

Rhonir opened the pouch, and tilted out the smoky blue gem inside. Her breath caught and her eyes widened. "A storm sapphire?"

"I received it as a gift many years ago. I believe a jewel holding a fragment of the essence of the storm belongs here, with the lord of storms."

Rhonir's eyes sank shut. Her quiet voice grew deeper and masculine, resonating with power. "Thank you, Lyan of Eilidh Wood. I will remember your gift."

A strange shiver ran up Lyan's spine, and he bowed as low as he could manage on horseback. "Lord Toirni... I... I am honored."

The moment passed, and if Rhonir was aware that she had served as her god's mouthpiece, she gave no indication. The two priests bid the party farewell and offered their hopes for safe travels as the Tathrens mounted.

The winding trail back to the main path felt like a shorter trip than it had climbing up, even though the horses had to take more care for their footing. Lyan kept the few questions that came to mind to himself, watching the trail and taking a little time to admire the breathtaking view. Clouds still hung over the mountains, but when he looked down, he could see the land spreading out in all directions. Trees clustered up to the edges of sheer cliff faces, and clung with determination to the narrowest ledges. Lyan glimpsed water splashing down in small waterfalls running from the snowcapped peaks. They reached the main road at midday. Lyan was just starting to feel at ease when a mocking voice crept into his mind.

"You're still traveling with the Tathrens, hmm? Silly little elf. You really have no idea what trouble you're getting yourself into, do you?

Would you like to know? Why don't I tell you a secret? Ah, here's one… wouldn't you like to know which of them told those men where to find and attack you?"

Lyan stiffened and glanced around as a cold shiver ran down his spine. *"I don't need your lies."*

"Lies?" The pooka's laughter filled his mind. *"Why should I lie, when the truth is so much better than any lies I could invent? No, little elf, you're not so fortunate that I have to invent tales to tell you."*

"Get out of my head!"

"I come and I go as I will, little elf. You have no power over a free spirit." A final laugh, then silence.

10

*Whispers in the forest
Games in the rain*

L yan drew a deep breath, savoring the scents of the trees that covered the land below them in an endless expanse of green. The wind was light but steady on the wide overlook, carrying teasing hints of familiar smells. Patches of mist hung among the trees in the cool morning air.

"That's a whole lot of trees," Dalrian said in quiet awe. "What's it called, Lord Cailean?"

Cailean spread his map out over a flat rock. Lyan winced at the rough treatment of the parchment and limped over to look.

"The Forests of Cossette," Cailean answered, indicating the symbols that marked a forest at least five times the size of Eilidh Wood. The road clung tenaciously to the edge of the forest, never daring to venture into its depths. "It's all claimed as a part of the country of Agathon, but I don't know that anyone actually controls the forest."

"Who's Cossette? And it all looks like one forest. Are there more of them?" Shiolto asked.

Cailean turned to Lyan, clearly expecting him to have an answer. Lyan gave an uncertain shrug. "I've read they used to be five distinct forests, but they've grown together over time. No one's sure who or what Cossette was. Maybe a ruler, but also maybe a god or a powerful spirit."

Shiolto blinked. "If it was a god, wouldn't someone know?"

Again Lyan shrugged. "If Cossette is a god, he or she doesn't seem to be concerned with receiving the worship of mortals."

"I understand that the name was given to the forests before the Devastation," Yion added. "It seems likely that knowledge of Cossette was lost, as much of the knowledge from those days was." Lyan looked at the mercenary in surprise. Yion smiled, but did not elaborate on how he came upon such information.

"Before the… that's… a long time," Shiolto said, growing quiet.

"Thousands of years," Yion agreed evenly.

Cailean cleared his throat pointedly. "We don't have thousands of years to stare at trees."

Lyan looked back at the map. "The road doesn't go through the forest."

"Most likely, it connects the villages along the edge of the forest with Kamael." Cailean indicated a city on the edge of a long lake.

"But we don't want to go to Kamael," Lyan said. "Even the road moves away from your path after a few turns." He tapped the map.

Aikan made a disgusted sound. "No doubt you think we should abandon the roads altogether and go traipsing through the heart of the forest like your kind."

Lyan stiffened at the scorn in Aikan's voice. Without looking from the map, keeping his voice as even and forcibly polite as he could, he said, "Eilidh Wood is filled with roads and paths, sir, as much as any land. If visitors lack the skill or cleverness to recognize them, then they shouldn't be straying from the main road."

Cailean cleared his throat, this time a more sharply annoyed sound. Aikan bit back whatever response leapt to his lips, and Lyan flushed as if he'd been scolded. The Tathren lord gazed at the map. "You think we should leave the main road and venture through the forest, Lyan?"

"I think we should take the most direct route east possible." Lyan thought of the men who had attacked them, then of the pooka's whispers. "If we leave the road, it will also be harder for someone to arrange another ambush against us."

The humans shifted uneasily, not sure whether to take Lyan's words as an accusation. Lyan looked from the map to the forest, longing for the comfort and security of trees overhead again.

"So, instead of bandits, you would throw us to the wolves, wild cats, and whatever monsters lurk in those shadows," Aikan snapped.

"I would save us well over a month's ride out of our way to go around the Forests of Cossette!" Lyan retorted.

"Enough!" Cailean cut in, rubbing his temples. "Enough. Stop bickering and just give me a moment to think." He stalked away from the group.

Aikan glared at Lyan, then followed Cailean. Lyan could have listened to the older man's words if he tried, but instead he looked back at the mountains that stood between him and his home.

What am I doing here? Why didn't I listen to Kithr?

"My lord, why are you letting this *elf* dictate our path?" Aikan burst, forgetting to lower his voice. Frustration and distrust colored his tone.

Lyan wasn't the only one to hear the words. "What's your grief against Lyan?" Shiolto interrupted, scowling at Aikan.

"He hasn't done anything but help us, even when he has no reason to."

"Stop!" Cailean ordered, whirling to face them all. "I will not have my every decision questioned! We are following Lyan's advice and going through the forest. If you don't like that, stay here." His eyes smoldered with anger.

Aikan nodded stiffly. "As you will, my lord."

Lyan wondered, even hoped those words meant Aikan was refusing to go further, but after a moment he recognized them as grudging acceptance of the decision instead.

Dalrian and Shiolto scrambled to the horses, quick to keep their heads down and avoid attracting their lord's attention. Torqual was less anxious in his movements, seeming assured that Cailean's ire was aimed at Aikan. Aikan accepted the reins of his horse when Shiolto handed them to him and swung stiffly into the saddle. He didn't deign even to look at Lyan.

Shadowstar nuzzled Lyan's shoulder. He rubbed the stallion's nose. Shadowstar knelt, and Lyan climbed into the saddle with only a few aches of protest. His ankle throbbed less severely than it had, though he knew it would feel worse by the end of the day. He was rationing his remaining dayseed oil, using it only when his ankle hurt enough to keep him from sleeping.

They rode with little conversation, following the road down the switchbacks that snaked along the slope and carried them from the mountains. Cailean led, his stiff back telling of anger. Lyan hung back with Shiolto and Dalrian, finding the brothers more comfortable company.

He didn't sense anything following them, but he was all too aware that the pooka seemed able to hide when it wished to, as it seemed able to whisper in his ear whenever it wished to.

What's to say it isn't responsible for those men finding us? I'm letting it fool me. He rubbed his eyes. *It's foolish to start suspecting Cailean's men when there's a more obvious answer.*

The thought didn't put him at ease, but it at least lessened his worry about his companions. *Though if anyone is upset to be leaving the road, it's Aikan.*

Cailean called a halt sometime after midday. Lyan looked down to the trees, hating the agonizingly slow speed at which they rode. He knew the horses couldn't go faster without risk of injuring themselves, but that knowledge didn't ease his desire. Torqual watched him and chuckled.

"The trees aren't going anywhere. They'll still be there when we get there."

"I know, but I would rather be there *now*," Lyan said.

Dalrian offered him a strip of jerky, and Lyan sat on the ground, chewing on it and stretching his legs. Shiolto tended the horses. Cailean called Aikan over and walked a little way from the rest of the group. Lyan pulled off his boot and massaged his ankle, surreptitiously watching Cailean and Aikan. Cailean didn't look as angry as earlier, but still irate, and Aikan's jaw was set in a stubborn scowl. Listening, Lyan could catch their words.

"I do not trust him or his motives, my lord," Aikan said. "I do not know how he has bewitched you into accepting him, but I will not do so."

"I am under no enchantment of elven making!" Cailean snapped. "And like it or not, he can help us." He fixed a glower on Aikan. "Ahebban's hammer, none of us know what to expect from an elf, or how one will act. Especially one who's been insulted. But I *do* expect better from *you*, Aikan. Is *this* how a steward should represent me and my people?"

At that, Aikan did finally lower his eyes. Lyan looked quickly away from the two men. Their conversation wasn't intended to be overheard, especially not by him. Cailean's implied question about how Lyan might retaliate if insulted stung, but at the same time, Lyan took guilty satisfaction in hearing Aikan being chastised.

Cailean walked a little further away, and Aikan followed him, taking both men beyond Lyan's hearing. When they returned, neither offered any explanation for the departure, and Cailean declared the rest to be at an end. Lyan kept an eye on Aikan, but the older man chose to ignore him entirely.

They continued down the road. As if coming to greet them, the forest extended up the slopes, creating a gradual entrance with none of the abrupt sense of borders presented by Eilidh Wood. Lyan found himself waiting for the sense of the forest to wrap around him, as Eilidh always did, and found the absence disconcerting.

Torqual made a sound of satisfaction. "Better to be around trees that don't watch you."

That's what's wrong: it isn't welcoming me like Eilidh Wood does. This forest neither welcomes nor rejects me. It's indifferent to my presence.

His companions welcomed that indifference, even as it bothered Lyan. He tried not to let his face show his feelings.

"As a human can grow accustomed to the awareness of an elven woods, so, I expect, can an elf grow accustomed to the quiet of an untouched forest."

Lyan started and turned. Yion rode beside him, and Lyan hadn't even noticed the mercenary until he'd spoken. "It's strange. Like… it lacks a spirit."

"The spirit of the place is here. Think instead that it sleeps. The forest sleeps, and it is at peace. Best we pass quietly, and not wake it."

As evening neared, the road brought them to a village. Lyan saw signs of their trade in the axes and saws outside huts, and in the planks and logs piled ready for transport. One old woman sat outside her house, carving images into the wooden block in her hand. She didn't look up as they passed, though Lyan peered curiously at her work. A bored-looking young man offered to take their horses when Cailean stopped at the largest building in the village, marked by a sign too faded for Lyan to read.

"You have rooms open for a night?" Cailean asked.

"Yah," the stablehand agreed. "Gonna stay? Ya want I take yer horses inna barn?"

"Yes." Cailean pulled his bags from the saddle and swung down, handing over the reins. Seeing the rest of the Tathrens doing the same, Lyan followed their lead and limped after them into the building.

Inside, tables filled a large room that smelled of beer, greasy food, and years of wood smoke soaked into the walls. Cailean spoke to the man at the bar, haggling before paying and indicating for the rest to follow. Aikan scowled in distaste when he saw the state of the room, but he said nothing about the smell of stale beer or the utilitarian row of straw pallets. Lyan was sure he saw one of the pallets move, and tried not to wonder what vermin made its home there.

Cailean looked around as well, grimaced, and said quietly, "I think I'll sleep on the floor."

"It could be worse," Dalrian said.

Torqual gave him a dubious look. "Oh?"

"We don't have to share it with anyone other than the vermin. It's at least been cleaned since the last time a drunk lost his dinner in here. And that load of timber outside says they have trade, which makes it less likely that they'll try to rob us in our sleep."

"So very encouraging," Torqual muttered. He glanced over at Lyan. "You have something to wrap around your head? The first time someone sees those ears... well, you never know what they might think."

Lyan frowned, puzzled for a moment. "What... oh." He had automatically assumed people here would treat him with the same respect and welcome that the nomads of the plains did, but Torqual's words implied that their reaction was more likely to resemble the one he'd gotten from the Tathrens on their first realization of his race.

He dug into one of his bags and found a bandana. It was an imperfect solution, but it covered the points of his ears to Torqual's satisfaction. *I'm a long way from home.*

Lyan had never visited a human tavern before, though Kithr had described them to him. Compared to Kithr's descriptions, this one seemed mild—no open brawls, gambling, or whores. Not that the places Kithr had been would have attracted the best patrons. The locals eyed the travelers cautiously, but all the same, several men made room at a table when they noticed Lyan leaning on his crutch. Lyan thanked them as Cailean's group settled at the table.

"Couldn't leave a fellow standing around like that," one man chuckled, gesturing at the crutch. "What'd you do?"

"A bad fall," Lyan said. "Sprained, but not broken, at least."

"Lucky fellow, then." The man launched into a story about his brother who had broken both legs falling out of a tree.

Once the story wrapped up, the other man asked, "You all going far?"

"Heading to Kamael," Cailean said.

The man nodded. "Who isn't, these days? My sister and her husband own the tavern a couple villages down in Great Oak. Good, clean place. You should stay there when you go."

Cailean nodded. "Thanks. I'll look for it."

A barmaid brought them mutton stew and mugs of beer for dinner. Lyan couldn't say much for either except that the meal filled his stomach. Dalrian, Shiolto, and Torqual relaxed and exchanged stories with the men around their table. Lyan listened and watched. He tried not to wince when someone burst into an off-key rendition of some song he didn't recognize.

Cailean leaned over to him. "You should sing something."

Lyan shook his head. "I'd rather not."

"Why not? It'd be a lot better than listening to this."

Lyan looked Cailean in the eyes. "Cailean, how well do you want us to be remembered here?"

Cailean just frowned. "I don't know what you mean."

"A group of men on their way to the city is unremarkable. But an elf singing in the tavern? You think anyone here would forget that anytime soon?"

Cailean considered, then nodded. "I see your point. Still, it would be better than listening to this." He winced. "Oh dear gods save us, Shiolto is going to sing…"

Shiolto and Dalrian took it upon themselves to teach the local men some new drinking songs. Lyan rather wished they hadn't. For every man in the tavern who could carry a tune, there were two who couldn't, and at least one more who compensated for lack of skill with volume. Shiolto, unfortunately, fell into the latter category.

By the time things finally quieted, and they retired to their room, exhaustion sent Lyan onto one of the straw pallets without caring what vermin shared his sleeping space. He woke briefly when something crawled up his leg. He kicked it off, then drifted back to sleep.

With morning, they left the village. Only after they had gone a little way down the road did Cailean say, "After spending a night there, I can honestly say I'm looking forward to sleeping in the forest instead of under a roof for a while."

"In that, I must agree with you, Lord Cailean," Aikan said. Dark circles around his eyes told of poor sleep.

The first half of the day, they kept to the road. But when the road turned south, they continued eastward. The thick canopy of trees kept the undergrowth thin. The horses snatched bites of leaves as they pushed through the brush at the edge of the road. Lyan cast a look upward, though the trees hid the sky from view, and whispered a prayer to Soldarr that he'd made a wise suggestion, and that this was the best path.

∾

Five days of riding passed without incident. Dalrian hunted, usually catching game birds, and once a deer which fed them several meals. Lyan enjoyed the respite from the pooka's whispers and wondered if their change of course might have thrown the creature off their trail. He doubted it could be so simple, but the wish persisted.

On the sixth day, the clouds opened up and rain poured down on them with all the cold fury of a determined storm. Lyan could only hope someone benefited from the downpour, because he was wet and miserable. They searched for shelter, and finally cobbled together a makeshift roof from branches when nothing better presented itself. Horses and riders huddled together in shared misery. No one spoke much. Lyan didn't trust himself not to say something stupid and spark an argument with Aikan.

The rain relented sometime during the night. Lyan drifted in and out of sleep. Finally, when morning's light had only just begun to creep into the forest, he gave up on rest, pulled himself from the warm cluster of damp bodies, and limped outside. He drew a deep breath of the cool air, a welcome relief from the stuffy shelter.

Leaving the others to sleep and trusting that they could find his tracks easily enough in the soft ground if they looked for him, Lyan moved a little way from the shelter, looking for someplace where he could see the sky. Finding a clearing, he gazed up at the deep blue sky.

"Too easily distracted, little elf. Where are your Tathren friends now?"

He started and turned sharply, nearly falling as he looked back the way he'd come. A figure with the appearance of a human male smirked at him. Its eyes glowed red as it slowly, deliberately stepped toward him, each step making its long cape billow dramatically behind it.

"Are you really all alone out here, little elf? Just you… and me."

Lyan took several steps back, fear crawling up his spine.

"Nothing to say? How strange… you always seem to have so much to say to me other times. Or are you only brave when you're safely hidden behind wards?"

Lyan swallowed hard, eyes fixed on the pooka. "Why are you here, *monster*?"

"Why don't we play a little game, elf? You say you know how to catch me. So, you try. You try to catch me, and I'll try to catch you. Whoever wins gets what they want from the loser."

"And if I don't want to play?" Lyan asked, backing up another step.

The pooka grinned. "Then I win by default." The eyes glittered. "I'll tell you what—I'll give you a head start, because you're hurt. I'll count to fifty."

Lyan stood frozen to the spot. The pooka closed its eyes, and began counting. "One. Two. Three." It opened one eye and smirked. "Time to start running, little elf. Four. Five."

Lyan turned and hobbled as fast as he could from the clearing.

11

Echoes in the forest,
Hiding secrets in the shadows

Heart pounding, breath coming in short, sharp gasps, Lyan stumbled through the underbrush and slipped on a patch of mud. He flung out a hand to catch himself against a tree, scraping his palm against the rough bark. His feet continued to slide despite his efforts, and Lyan stumbled. One leg smacked a protruding root, promising to leave an ugly bruise. Mud and moisture slid into his boots as he struggled upright again, clutching his crutch desperately in one hand and grasping at the tree's bark with the other.

He cast a look to the sky, searching for the sun to orient himself even as he instinctively sought reassurance from the forest around him. In Eilidh Wood, the branches overhead would have shifted a little and parted to show him the sky. Here, they ignored him, just as the trees gave no heed to his struggles and made no effort to ease his path. Lyan guessed his direction from the light through the leaves and turned himself toward Cailean's camp. If he could get there before the pooka finished counting down his "head start," he'd be safe. Or at least, safer than he was.

After several stumbling steps, he stopped short. *I was just here. That's where I fell. But that should be behind me. How can I be going in circles?* Cold, hard panic rose.

A taunting voice drifted on the still air. "Tsk tsk… you don't think I'm going to make it *that* easy for you, do you? This game is just between you and me, little elf."

Lyan's head whipped around, searching for the source of the voice, but the whisper had been distant. *It's playing with me. It's confusing my senses, keeping me from getting back to camp. I have to get far enough from it that it can't keep turning me around. I don't know what the pooka wants from me, but I know I don't want it to catch me.*

Turning away from the direction he thought Cailean's camp lay, Lyan stumbled and staggered between the trees, fighting for footing on the slick leaves that coated the ground. He leaned against a tree to catch his breath, trying to let his racing heart slow and his head clear. *I have to somehow beat the pooka at its game. I know how to bind it, but I don't know if I can. It isn't going to stand still and let me cut off its hair. If this were Eilidh, the forest might help me.* He looked around and shivered, feeling the indifferent emptiness around him. *But this is not Eilidh Wood.*

Lyan pushed away from the tree. His ankle throbbed and his skinned hand stung. He cast a look over his shoulder before limping on. Had the count reached fifty yet? Would the pooka really give him that long?

Yes, I think it will. If only because it will amuse the monster to do so.

He felt into belt pouches for anything that could help. His hunting knife hung in easy reach, but he didn't have any of the tokens traditionally offered to the elven gods to call their attention to him in the absence of a shrine. "Please guide me," he whispered to any power that might be listening. "Please…" He didn't want to raise his voice. He had no idea how far he was from Cailean's camp, but a shout was far more likely to draw the pooka than to summon aid. Even if he called Shadowstar, the stallion would draw the pooka toward him.

"Fifty."

Lyan jumped at the whisper in his mind, biting his lip hard to hold back a yelp of surprise as he looked around wildly. Something rustled the undergrowth to his left, and panic surged back full-force. Heart pounding, Lyan didn't wait to identify the source. He tripped, caught himself, and almost managed to run. The half-formed ideas that had flitted through his mind fled in the burst of fear. Wet branches slapped his face and grabbed at clothes as he pushed through tangles of brush. His crutch caught in the growth for a moment. Lyan jerked it free, nearly falling backwards and crying in pain as agony jarred through his leg.

Whatever lurked behind him, Lyan didn't hear it following, though the blood pounding in his ears muffled other sounds. Driven by fear, he kept moving and grasped at scattered thoughts. *I have to get back to the camp. I have to find shelter, somewhere to hide, somewhere I can defend... How in Soldarr's Axe can I catch and bind a pooka alone?*

"Come out, come out, wherever you are."

Lyan winced as the mocking voice echoed in his mind. His jaw tightened. *Come and find me.* The thought was sheer bravado he didn't dare voice aloud.

He looked to the sky again, turning in the direction he thought the camp should be. The sun hung higher in the sky than he expected, telling him that his sense of time was as unreliable around the pooka as his sense of direction. The oaks and maples all began to look alike, but he did notice when his stumbling feet found a clear path and his crutch thumped against flat stones instead of mud, forcing his attention back to his surroundings.

A road? Here? It's old, overgrown. Those stones, were they part of a wall? His spirits rose. *Can I find shelter here?*

Piles of stone lined the path's edges, overgrown with vines

and moss. Lyan sensed something familiar. Not from the forest, but from the stones. They held an air that vaguely reminded him of the ancient ruins within Eilidh Wood. This place held the same feeling of someplace ageless and forgotten.

A collapsed pile of rocks towered over him, blocking the path. Lyan stopped and stared at it, feeling vaguely betrayed, as if the ruins had dangled hope before him, then jerked it away. If he'd been fit and his ankle uninjured, he might have tried to climb the obstacle, even as unstable as it looked, but Lyan knew better than to try.

He glimpsed deep shadows behind the vines and stepped closer, hoping a passage might hide behind them. As he approached, something shifted and crackled in that dark space. Lyan froze, grabbing for his knife as he backed away, tensely awaiting the pooka's taunts.

Until that moment, he'd all but forgotten that he was in an unfamiliar land, wild, inhabited by more creatures than such passing travelers as elves, humans, or pookas. That realization abruptly returned as a bear pushed through the vines, revealing a cave or tunnel hidden by the growth. The animal gazed at Lyan, growling a low rumble. Its fur was black as charcoal, except around its face, where white streaks curled around its snout, under its eyes, and down its cheeks in strange patterns. A stiff ruff of dark brown ran down its back.

"I'm sorry!" Lyan said quickly as if it might understand him. He took another step back. "I won't bother you. I'm just trying to find my way back to my companions."

The bear growled as it stepped into the open, then reared up on its hind legs to score deep claw marks into the nearest tree. Lyan swallowed hard and continued to back away.

"I won't bother you. Please pardon my intrusion." He shook his head with a strained, thin laugh. "I hope my fate isn't limited to being caught by the pooka or eaten by a bear."

The bear dropped back on all fours and watched Lyan

intently. He didn't want to turn his back on it, but he couldn't keep walking backwards either. His foot hit a root and he barely kept his balance, flailing a moment until he steadied. The bear made a loud chuffing sound, almost a laugh, then trundled back into the web of vines.

Lyan leaned against a tree, heart thudding painfully in his chest. *Where am I? What is this place? Can I use it? Could I trick the pooka into there, lure it to the bear? Would the bear attack it?*

He hesitated, then drew his knife and cut a piece of cloth from his shirt. Limping cautiously to the collapsed wall, he snagged the scrap on the jagged edge of a rock. A low growl warned him that the bear remained nearby. His attempt at misdirection in place, Lyan turned away from the wall, leaving the questionable stability of the sunken paving stones for the muddy forest floor.

It felt like far too short a time when he heard the pooka's voice again. *"In a hurry, little elf? Leaving bits and pieces behind? Ah... are you still trying to get back to your Tathren friends? Are you sure they haven't left without you by now? You've been gone all morning. Maybe they think you've abandoned them."*

That thought hit Lyan like a punch to the gut. The idea that Cailean and his men might already be gone, that they might not have waited for him and there might be no camp for him to return to was more than he could bear. He tried to shove it away, but the doubt had been planted, and it refused to heed his instruction. *Please, if any gods are listening, don't let Cailean have left without me.* If his companions had been elves, he wouldn't have doubted them for a moment. But what did he really know about the Tathrens? Exhaustion and fear pressed close. *Please don't let me be alone.*

A bear's angry roar suddenly shook the forest, booming even from the distance and frightening songbirds from the trees. Lyan's breath caught. "Forgive me for using you as a distraction without asking your permission," he said in apology to the distant bear. "But... you are all I had."

"You dare!" There was nothing silky or teasing in the pooka's voice when it smashed into Lyan's mind, only incredulous fury. He stumbled and fell to the muddy ground. He tried to pick himself up, flinching at the voice screaming in his head. *"You DARE draw me HERE?! You will pay for this! Do not think I will let you escape unpunished, elf."*

The venom of the reaction caught Lyan unprepared. Fear filled his veins with a cold deeper than the chill that sank through his clothes and numbed his limbs. In the back of his mind, he wondered how laying the false trail could be such a dire trespass. The forefront of his thoughts, though, focused purely on survival. Struggling to his feet, he fought against the pain that jarred through his sprained ankle with each hurried step. Something large crashed through the brush in the distance, something that no longer cared what heard it coming. Something very, very angry.

The canopy overhead was thinner, permitting the undergrowth to flourish. The profusion of plants gave the illusion of level ground, and Lyan realized too late that the slight downward slant grew more pronounced. His feet slipped on the loose and muddy ground, and before he could steady himself, he was sliding down the slope. He swung his crutch out, trying to brace it on something, anything. It hooked on a shrub for a moment, but the jerk tore it from Lyan's sweat-damp hands. He grabbed desperately for the crutch, but only reached a handful of leaves that tore from their branch when he caught them. Branches whipped at his face as rocks and roots battered him. Lyan tumble to a stop in a mess of brambles at the bottom. Every bit of his body throbbed with pain. He gasped for breath. Something trickled down his face. Lyan wiped at it, and found blood. His forehead stung when he touched the gash.

'Are you trying to hide, little elf? I'm going to get bored if this is the best you can do. And you really won't like the games I play when I get

bored." The pooka's taunting voice was icy cold, heavy with threat.

Moving hurt. Every ragged, gasping breath hurt. Lyan whimpered when he rolled over and dragged himself to the nearest tree. He clung to the bark and pulled himself upright, barely caring about the added damage to his bleeding palms. An effort to put weight on his sprained ankle drew a sharp gasp of pain. Lyan closed his eyes, then pushed away from the tree and hobbled to the next one. Running was beyond his strength, but stubborn, exhausted determination forced him to keep trying to stay ahead of his pursuer.

"Shadowstar, find me if you can," he whispered. He had little hope that the stallion would reach him before the pooka, but Lyan knew no other way he could find his way back to Cailean's camp now.

His stumbling, painful progress was accompanied only by chirping birds. He didn't hear any sounds of pursuit.

Would Cailean leave without me? Are they looking for me? Do they think I abandoned them? What will I do if I'm alone here?

Lyan slumped against a massive tree and closed his eyes, drawing deep breaths. *I have to rest. Just for a little while.*

The birds fell silent. Lyan's heart beat faster as fear found a new reserve of strength. Brush crackled as something moved nearby. Lyan held his breath.

"I know you're close. You can't run forever, elf. Where do you think you'll go? Your Tathren friends aren't coming to your rescue." The pooka's voice drew closer. Lyan bit his lip and wished he could quiet the beating of his heart as leaves rustled on the other side of the tree he pressed himself against. "Come out and play, elf."

Soldarr, Feyra, Tesseia, if you have ever looked on me with favor or pity, I beg you, protect me now.

In the stillness, a bowstring hummed. Lyan flinched as he heard an arrow thump into the tree trunk. He opened his eyes, but no shaft quivered next to his head.

The pooka voiced a startled sound of pain. Lyan felt the vibration of another arrow thumping into the tree trunk, accompanied by scrambling movement from the pooka. Lyan edged around the trunk to watch the monster shapeshift into a black horse and break into a run. Another arrow flew after it, and both vanished into the undergrowth. Lyan stared after the pooka in dull, exhausted disbelief. Then he turned to look at the arrows buried into the trunk.

A few strands of black hair dangled from one of the distinctive raven-feathered arrows. "Kithr…?" Lyan tried to make sense of what he saw.

A growled curse answered him from the shadows of the trees. "I missed. I *never* miss."

"Kithr? What… what are you doing here?" Lyan kept trying to make everything make sense, but his mind refused to cooperate.

His grim-faced friend stepped away from a tree. Kithr's tan skin was daubed with mud, and his typical brown leathers were meant to blend with the trees. Even his brown hair could be mistaken for moss in a way Lyan's red never would. He slung his bow as he walked to Lyan. When he offered a shoulder, Lyan leaned against it gratefully, gripping Kithr's arm with overpowering relief. *I'm not alone.*

"You're bleeding. How badly are you hurt?" Kithr demanded.

Lyan raised a trembling hand to wipe his forehead, smearing sticky, half-dried blood. "Scraped up. Nothing broken. I lost my crutch somewhere…"

"I know. I found it." Kithr helped Lyan to the tree where he'd set his ambush. Kithr untangled the crutch from the brush and handed it to Lyan. "The tracks looked like a rough fall. You're sure you didn't break anything?"

"As sure as I can be." Lyan freed his arm from Kithr's shoulder and leaned heavily on the crutch. "Going to be black and blue, though."

"Sit down," Kithr told him.

Lyan shook his head. "If I do, I don't think I'll be able to get up again." He closed his eyes, letting tumbling thoughts collect. Opening them again, he looked at Kithr. "You've been following us."

Kithr snorted. "Seed and spark, Lyan, do you think I would let you wander off alone with *Tathrens*?"

"As angry as you were when I told you I was leaving, yes," Lyan answered.

Kithr's eyes narrowed. "Did I or did I not promise that I would watch over you and keep you safe?"

"When you were twenty-three," Lyan said wearily.

Kithr's gaze was sharp. "Do you think a hundred and twenty years would break that promise?"

I think that you're not the idealistic boy who made that promise any longer. And I think it wouldn't be the first time you've forgotten a promise made on impulse.

When Lyan didn't answer, Kithr shook his head and retrieved arrows from the tree trunk. Lyan watched him and spoke quickly. "Don't lose those hairs!"

Kithr caught the pooka's black hairs and brought them to Lyan. "They're no use to me. Keep them."

Lyan tucked the hairs into a pouch. He could finally draw a steady breath, and his hands only shook a little. "When were you going to tell me that you followed us?" *I knew I sensed something following us on the plains. Could that have been Kithr?*

"I was waiting for a chance when you were alone." Kithr scowled darkly, voice grim. "In case you haven't noticed, those Tathrens watch you like wolves watch an injured buck, and they never leave you completely alone." He made a gesture at the forest. "I intended to tell you when you left the camp this morning, but that rotting shape-shifting trickster reached you first. You took off, and after that I had a rotted time trying to follow either of you."

"The pooka was confusing the trails," Lyan said. "I was trying to get to the camp."

Kithr raised a dubious eyebrow. "I wouldn't have guessed that. You succeeded in going almost completely the opposite direction. And I thought you were finally showing some good sense and leaving them behind."

"Leaving Shadowstar and my gear?" Lyan countered. He pushed away from his tree, wincing as movement woke pain. "I need to get back to them."

Kithr stepped in his path, voice sharp. "*You* need to go home and forget this idiocy, Lyan. You don't owe those humans a rotted thing."

"It's not about owing them," Lyan said tersely, limping around Kithr. "It's about my responsibilities." *It's about the Spears of the Stars.*

Kithr grabbed his arm, stopping him. "Responsibilities? To who? Heartshrine Village? What about your responsibilities as an astrologer? What do *Tathrens* offer to *that* responsibility?"

"A responsibility that you and everyone else in the village happily ignores or scoffs at given any chance?" Lyan snapped. "I told you, the stars are hidden by clouds every night. And there are greater responsibilities for an elf of Eilidh Wood." This wasn't a conversation he wanted to have, not here, not now.

"Like *what?*" Kithr retorted. "And *you* can fulfill them? An injured ankle, no weapons skills, and less sense than the gods gave a rabbit, what are *you* going to do?"

It was too much. Something snapped, and the relief Lyan had felt at seeing Kithr twisted into outrage. "I am not some half-wit child in need of a tender!" he snapped, hands clenching into fists.

Kithr jerked back, confusion and surprise in his face. "What? What's that supposed to mean? I never said you were."

"Didn't you? You've questioned every single thing I've done since Cailean and his men pulled me out of a crevice in Eilidh Wood! You doubt everything I say, you dismiss things that I say are important, and you treat me like I'm helpless and stupid. I can take care of myself! I don't need your help!"

"Don't you?" Kithr demanded. "So I suppose you had some brilliant plan for dealing with that pooka? You had everything under control? Then you fooled me *very* well, Lyan. Or were you counting on the *Tathrens* to help you?"

His chipped and cracked nails bit into skinned, raw palms. Lyan jerked away from Kithr. "At least the Tathrens don't treat me like I'm too stupid to understand them. At least they actually *listen* to me, and care that I might know something that will help them!"

It was hard to storm away effectively when every bone in his body hurt, or when he clung to the crutch to remain upright, but Lyan managed to spin away from Kithr and push himself into motion without tripping over the roots and branches littering the ground. He didn't look back at Kithr's blankly astonished face.

"Lyan. Lyan! Come back here!" Kithr demanded.

"Leave me alone! Go home, Kithr. I don't need your help." The words came sharp and bitter. Lyan's eyes stung, and he viciously denied that the tears were anything but a reaction to pain.

He didn't hear Kithr follow him. When Shadowstar found him, Lyan was too exhausted to be alarmed at the sounds of a horse moving through the brush. The stallion knelt and tolerated Lyan's awkward crawl onto his back. Lyan barely managed to secure his crutch, then slumped against Shadowstar's neck and closed his eyes.

"Take me to camp," he whispered.

The ride passed in a dull fog of pain. When Shadowstar stopped, he raised his head and blinked until his eyes cleared. A flurry of noises resolved into voices around him, and he realized that Shadowstar had done as he had asked, and that the humans gathered around the stallion.

"Lyan! Where have you been?!" Cailean demanded angrily the moment Shadowstar stood still. "What in Saiboti's Blade were you thinking to wander off without a word?"

Lyan clung to Shadowstar's mane, shivering, light-headed, and struggling through the dazed fog filling his head. He waited for the tirade to continue. When it didn't, he raised his head and turned toward Cailean. "I'm... sorry," he managed when it seemed some answer must be expected from him.

Cailean stared at him as if Lyan had sprouted horns. "What happened to you, Lyan?" His voice changed from angry to anxious and worried. "Come on, get down and sit by the fire. It's small, but it will warm you a little."

Hands lifted Lyan down to the ground and carried him to the sputtering campfire. Flakes of drying mud fell from his clothes and skin. Lyan shivered and huddled before the source of warmth. Yion wrapped a cloak over his shoulders and filled a mug with steaming water.

"Answer Lord Cailean's question, Lyan." Aikan's icy voice drew him from the daze.

"Leave him be, Aikan," Cailean said sharply. "He's injured."

Lyan lifted his head and pulled Yion's cloak tighter around himself. "Everyone was asleep. I wanted to see the sky. Needed fresh air. I wasn't going far." He raised a shaking hand toward the clearing.

"Saw your tracks go there," Dalrian said. "But it looked like something else came through there, and then everything got muddled. I tried to follow, but..." He made a helpless gesture.

Lyan started to speak, then hesitated.

"What happened, Lyan? You didn't get covered in mud, scraped up, and looking about to topple over at any moment just looking at the sky," Cailean pressed.

Lyan shivered and finally answered. "The pooka. It… followed me."

"The creature is near?" Yion asked, the first time Lyan had heard worry in his voice.

"It toyed with me." Lyan stared into the fire. "It chased me. It even gave me a head start, but it didn't expect to lose me. I barely escaped it long enough to call Shadowstar…"

"You didn't call for help?" Cailean demanded.

"It blocked the path back to the camp and it confused the trail. After I'd gotten a little ways from it, calling out would have told it where I was. It would have found me before you could."

Yion mixed leaves in the mug, then handed it to Lyan. "Drink with care—it's hot."

Lyan clutched the mug, letting the warmth soak into his skin. He took a cautious sip, and the liquid nearly burned his mouth. He blew on the surface of the drink before venturing another sip.

Cailean rested a hand gently on his shoulder, but pulled back when Lyan flinched. "Next time, Lyan, wake someone. Don't go out alone."

"I'm sorry for the trouble I've caused you."

"We were worried," Cailean said. "I'm glad you're safe now. Just… try not to do something like that again, all right? You're safer with us."

Am I? Lyan gulped down the drink, feeling the warmth spreading through him. "We should keep going, before it comes back."

"Not until you've changed clothes and dried off!" Shiolto said.

"But…," Lyan began.

"A sick elf will slow us far more than the delay for you to clean up will," Aikan said sharply—the closest he'd ever come to expressing concern for Lyan's well-being.

Lyan didn't have the strength to argue if he'd wanted to.

With Shiolto's help, he hobbled into the shelter and found clean clothes. Shiolto helped him peel his boots off, and tears of pain ran down Lyan's face as they worked the boot from his swollen, throbbing sprained ankle. Shiolto wrapped his ankle carefully.

"Let me see your hands, Lyan."

"They're just scraped up." Lyan winced and reached for the clean shirt. He blinked and shook his head as his vision swam. "Shiolto?"

"Yes?"

"What did Yion give me to drink?"

"Uh, I thought it was some kind of tea. Why? What's wrong?"

"I'm feeling really… lightheaded…" Lyan wavered.

Shiolto caught his shoulder with a look of alarm. "Lyan?" He turned sharply. "Yion? What did you give him?"

"The stargazer should rest," Yion answered calmly. "I helped him do so."

"You *drugged* him?"

Lyan didn't hear Yion's reply. A last, fleeting thought ran through his mind as sleep claimed him.

Maybe Kithr was right after all…

1 2

Lord of the sky, come down;
We call on you.
Lord Nachyne, hear our plea!
Sweep down with wings of vengeance!

Arguing voices rose and fell, dragging Lyan toward groggy awareness. He had a vague sense that the argument had been going on for some time, and he wanted nothing more than to tell them all to be quiet and let him sleep in peace. Words eluded him, and he rolled over with an inarticulate mumble, pulling the blanket up over his head.

The movement sent pain stabbing through every abused muscle. "Spark and rot…"

"Quiet! He's waking," someone said. The arguing cut off sharply. Steps moved toward him. "Lyan?"

"Leave me alone."

"Lyan." He identified the voice as Cailean's, the tone a blend of concern and unease.

Lyan squeezed his eyes more tightly shut. A hand touched his shoulder, and he jerked away, taking a blind swing at the source. He made a glancing connection, drawing a startled curse from Cailean and a sharp sound of alarm from Aikan.

"My lord, keep away from him! We have no idea what an elf might do."

"Go to rot, Aikan!" Lyan snapped. "Leave me alone!"

Quick, shuffling movements of someone moving away from him. Lyan painfully put his back toward the sounds, hating every ache that ran through him. He heard someone else step toward him, then stop.

"Let him be, Shiolto," Cailean ordered.

"But…"

Cailean lowered his voice to what he probably thought Lyan would not hear. "He's angry. He has reason to be, I acknowledge. But Aikan is right—we don't know what an angry elf can or will do."

"He's not some—" Shiolto cut off, then repeated himself in a lower, but still angry voice. "He's not some wild animal, Lord Cailean! He's Lyan!"

"Sure he is, but we haven't seen him mad at us before," Torqual said. "The warriors in his village were ready to kill us if we moved wrong. That's what elves are supposed to be like."

Lyan's jaw tightened as he bit back words he wanted to release. *This is what you think of me?*

"And Lyan isn't like that," Dalrian argued. "He's been helping us!"

"So he says," Aikan muttered.

"Enough." Cailean's voice was resigned rather than angry. "We've already argued this for too long. Yes, Dalrian, Lyan has been helping us. And we have broken faith with him. Let him be."

Let me be? Are you going to pretend nothing happened? Hope that when I decide to get up, I don't try to murder someone? Lyan's throat tightened. *Kithr must not have followed me. He would have killed them for this. Then gloated at me about being right.*

He tried to find sleep, but he was far too aware of the humans and their wary watch of him. Lyan's blood pounded in his ears and his hands clenched into fists under the blanket. *What have I done to even make them think I'm like that? They talk like I'm some sort of rabid animal, or one of the Mad God's demons!*

Finally, Lyan stopped even pretending to sleep. He shoved away the blanket and sat up, wincing as every stiff muscle cried in protest.

All other movement in the camp stopped dead when he sat up. The humans watched him, other tasks forgotten. Lyan glared at them. "If you're waiting for me to sprout fangs and spew fire, go rot."

Still no one moved, poised like frightened rabbits ready to bolt for cover. Shiolto broke the stillness, offering a tentative, uncertain smile. "Are… you feeling all right, Lyan? Do you want something to eat?"

His mouth was dry and his stomach empty, but Lyan's answer was sharp and curt. "No. I don't want your food."

Shiolto's smile faltered, and he cast a quick, helpless glance around in search of anything he could offer to make peace.

"Yes, because we are so likely to poison the pot we all eat from," Aikan snapped. The older man snatched up a wooden bowl and scooped a glob of thick slop into it. He pointedly ate a bite, then dropped the bowl to the trampled grass beside Lyan.

Lyan just as pointedly ignored the bowl in favor of glaring up at Aikan. "I don't want your food." He tried to stand. Aching muscles rebelled, and his arms buckled before he could get his good leg under him.

Aikan moved more spryly than his grey hair suggested, catching Lyan and pulling him to his feet. His scowl did not relent any more than Lyan's did, and the Tathren released Lyan the heartbeat he seemed steady. Shiolto scrambled over to give Lyan his crutch.

Lyan leaned heavily on the crutch. His ankle throbbed angrily, another pain to torment him. Sweat beaded his forehead in spite of the cool morning air. A dull throb pulsed through his skull, low but persistent, and now that he was upright, he was less sure why he had been so certain he wanted to be on his feet.

"How are you, Lyan?" Cailean asked.

"How do I look?" Lyan snapped.

"You look like you're on the verge of attacking whoever's in reach," Cailean said plainly. "Are you?"

Lyan's jaw tightened and he gripped the crutch's handbar fiercely. "No, I'm not. I'm not going to attack you and your men. Never mind that *your* men—"

"Lord Cailean had no knowledge of my actions until they were done," Yion cut in, voice calm and even. "It was done by my hand and my decision alone, Lyan Stargazer." The mercenary gazed at Lyan from across the small campfire.

"Why?" Lyan demanded. *I thought I could trust you.*

All eyes turned to Yion, as if the mercenary had not explained his reasons to them during Lyan's unconsciousness and they too awaited his answer.

If the anger in Lyan's voice or the stares of his companions troubled him, Yion did not show it. "Because of the pooka. You said that the monster pursued you and toyed with you. Knowing the treacherous nature of such creatures, I feared it might have succeeded in wrapping its power around you, then removing your memory of the act."

"You think I lied and couldn't have gotten away from it on my own." Lyan glared at the black-haired mercenary.

"I would have done the same to any who reported being so close to the monster, even had it been Lord Cailean," Yion said. "The risk of giving it entrance to our camp is too great to leave to chance and fortune."

"You would not dare do such a thing to Lord Cailean!" Aikan said sharply.

Yion gazed at him mildly. "I dared risk our companion's anger to ensure our protection. You think I would not do the same with any who might be under the monster's spell?" He returned his attention to Lyan. "Fortunately, my fears were without merit. You are untouched by the pooka's magic."

Lyan waited. "And?"

"I learned no more than that, Lyan. I could determine whether or not its power had influenced you. I have no ability to see visions of your encounter with the monster."

"What, that's all?" Dalrian said when Yion added nothing more. "You aren't even going to apologize?"

"I regret that the act was necessary. I would not have done differently, though," Yion replied.

"How can you *say* that?" Dalrian burst.

Lyan didn't listen to the answer. He turned his back to the humans and hobbled to Shadowstar. The stallion stood with the rest of the horses. Lyan's saddle and bags lay near his hooves. Most of the rest of the gear was packed as well, only the bare essentials remaining in the camp. Lyan cast a look at the sky, and guessed he had woken a little after sunrise, which meant he had been unconscious for nearly half the previous day and the entire night.

Shadowstar nuzzled his shoulder in greeting. Lyan patted the stallion's nose, then rested his head against Shadowstar's neck. He willed the ear cuff not to translate the words he spoke into the horse's mane. "Maybe Kithr's right. Maybe I can't trust them, and I should not be here. But I can't leave them to find the Spear unguarded, and I can't just kill them, even if I wanted to. Am I doing the right thing, Shadowstar?"

The stallion gave a quiet snort and nuzzled him again.

Steps approached across the damp ground. Lyan stiffened but did not turn. Cailean cleared his throat.

"What?" Lyan said curtly.

"Are you going to leave?" Cailean asked. "Return to Eilidh Wood?"

Lyan snorted. "Much as I'm sure some people hope I will, no." He turned to face Cailean, leaning against Shadowstar for support.

The Tathren lord looked at him with an expression of concern, and his earlier wariness was not evident. "I don't know who you think wants you gone, but I do not."

"You didn't sound so confident earlier," Lyan snapped.

Cailean gave him a baffled look. "When?"

"Lowering your voices means you aren't shouting. It doesn't mean I can't hear you."

Cailean's breath caught as he understood. "I…apologize for our words, Lyan." He almost said more, but caught the words and left the apology as it was.

"I suppose that as one of those terrible, frightening elves, I'm a disappointment," Lyan said bitterly. "No grand tales of battles to tell—instead I get chased around the forest by a pooka, and when I elude it and return to camp, I don't even show the sense to question what my apparent allies offer me to drink."

"Lyan, I did not know Yion was drugging you. If I had, I would have forbidden it," Cailean said.

"So you aren't responsible for the actions of your men?" Lyan asked coolly. "I thought lords were supposed to be accountable for the things done by those who serve them. Or does that only matter when they do something you can take credit for?" The words were brash and rude, but he hurt too much to speak with tact.

Cailean straightened indignantly. "What—" He stopped, drew a deep breath, and collected himself. "Are you saying you want to settle this offense between you and me rather than between you and Yion?"

Lyan hesitated. His first impulse was to say yes, but he wasn't certain what he would be agreeing to. "I… don't know," he said finally. "What does that mean?"

Cailean made a sound of frustration. "It means… Mad

God's Pits, if you don't understand what that means, I doubt I can explain it, Lyan."

"Does it mean I blame you for every rotted thing your men do? Because if that's what it means, no."

"No, that's not what it means. It means… it means that you and I would agree on a response that satisfies the offense, and I will be responsible for seeing it done."

Lyan rubbed his temples. Cailean's speech was too formal—he understood the words, but their meaning hid behind a wall of polite obfuscation. He gave a short, sharp shake of his head. "What would you do if I was a Tathren rather than one of those horrible, terrifying elves?"

Cailean winced at the self-deprecating description. "If you were Tathren, Lyan, we wouldn't need to have this conversation at all. How we resolved it would depend on whether I outranked you or not and what relationship existed between us before the incident. A formal apology, a payment of money or goods perhaps if we were near equals. If you outranked me, you might demand the flogging or even execution of the man responsible. *Those* would be possible responses, if you were Tathren, and I knew your rank compared to my own. But you are *not* Tathren, and I can't even tell if elves *have* ranks among themselves. You certainly don't have nobles as I know them. How would *your* people settle it if we were all elves instead?"

He hadn't expected the question to be returned. Lyan was still struggling with the idea that a single act could be punished by a range of responses that ran from an apology to an execution. "We… bring serious disputes to the Elder of the village and he judges them," he said after a moment.

Cailean raised an eyebrow. "Is that what you would do?"

Lyan paused, then shook his head. "I would tell Kithr, and he would collect some friends to go settle the matter with the person responsible." His eyes narrowed. "And if we were in Eilidh Wood, and you were elves, no one would be likely to raise a complaint about someone avenging an insult to the village astrologer."

"That is a position of importance?" Cailean asked.

"Of course it is! I read our fortunes from the stars," Lyan said. "And the rest of the village makes sure I don't have to worry about hunting, clothes, or food."

Cailean let out a long breath. "You're not in Eilidh Wood, to settle it your way. I'm not in Tather, to settle it as I know or draw on the resources of my home. So how do we resolve this, Lyan? How do we make peace? You're the one who was wronged. What do you require to make things right between us?" He paused. "I need your help, Lyan. What can I, what can we offer you to make amends?"

His eyes and voice were sincere. Lyan didn't want to give up his anger and frustration, but his pride demanded that he not act like a toddler throwing a tantrum. His answer was simple and direct. "Trust."

The single word gave Cailean long pause. "Trust? We do--" He stopped, perhaps recalling the conversation he hadn't meant for Lyan to hear. "Trust. That is… easier to promise than to enforce."

"I'm not some demon from the Mad God's prison. I'm not going to transform into a warrior. And I'm not going to purposefully lead you from your path, Cailean. So is it *really* too much to ask to be treated as an equal instead of as some unpredictable, possibly dangerous creature?"

Surprise crossed Cailean's face, then shame as he looked away. "I'm sorry." There was nothing stiff or formal about the quiet apology. "I could say we are raised on stories of elves as vicious savages, but that doesn't excuse anything. Especially not when the least learned of my men have been the most able to look past those tales." He set his shoulders and met Lyan's eyes again. "I will try. I will probably not always be successful, and for that I apologize now."

Lyan nodded, accepting the words. Shadowstar patiently

supported him as he considered his words. Their conversation was anything but private, and he knew Cailean's men could hear most of it. He lowered his voice, forcing Cailean to lean closer to hear him. "There's one more thing I would ask from you, Cailean."

"What is it?" Cailean asked.

"That you not lie to me."

Cailean stiffened, his expression indignant.

Lyan raised a hand to forestall the Tathren's protests. "I *know* you have lied to your own men about the Spear and the curse on you. I don't understand why, and I want, I need to be able to trust that you will tell me the truth. And if that means that instead of answering something, you tell me that you aren't going to answer it, fine. Just don't lie."

Cailean slowly nodded. "I agree. I will not intentionally lie to you." He held his right hand to Lyan. "Will you accept this agreement to make peace between us?"

The words had the formality of an official and binding contract. *Kithr would call me a fool for making any accord with a Tathren.* Lyan grasped Cailean's hand in defiance of his friend. "I will."

"Then may Ahebban, Watcher on the Walls, bear witness to all I have promised, and may he hold me accountable should I fall short of my word," Cailean said solemnly.

"May it be so," Lyan said quietly, finding nothing else to say. He knew little about the Tathren divinities, but an oath sworn by any god was to be respected. He released Cailean's hand. "We've lost a day of travel already. We shouldn't waste this one as well."

"The time wasn't wasted. My men set snares, caught some rabbits." Cailean looked Lyan over with concern. "Are you fit to ride?"

"I don't want to stay here," Lyan answered. His aching body warned that he would regret a day of riding, but the need to put distance between himself and the pooka overwhelmed that objection.

While they had spoken, Cailean's men had finished breaking camp. At a word from Cailean, Shiolto and Dalrian saddled the horses. Shiolto hesitated before offering to saddle Shadowstar, but when Lyan didn't snap at him, the Tathren relaxed.

Once everyone mounted, Shadowstar took the lead. Lyan tensed when the stallion entered the clearing where he had watched the sky. He looked over his shoulder, but saw only the Tathrens. He half expected to see the pooka smirking at him. A shiver ran down his spine, and he stared down at Shadowstar's mane rather than looking to the sky.

Uneasy silence hung over the group. Lyan felt the sidelong glances the Tathrens continued to cast at him, and they only emphasized his isolation among them, regardless of Cailean's promises. He didn't break the silence, sure that if he opened his mouth, he would regret the words that came out.

Once the trees closed around them again, Lyan cast suspicious glares at the indifferent trees, as if they would carry his thoughts to Kithr. He didn't feel the prickling sense of being followed or spied on, but he doubted Kithr would relent. *I don't need your help, Kithr. I've chosen to follow these Tathrens and I can care for myself. Go home. Leave me alone. I don't need your condescending sneers or your efforts to teach this "innocent" about war.*

An involuntary shudder ran through him, and Lyan gripped Shadowstar's reins tightly, forcing away a memory of Kithr's idea of a "lesson" before it could take form.

"Are you all right, Lyan?" Shiolto asked immediately in concern.

"Fine," he hissed through clenched teeth. "It's nothing. I'm fine."

"All right….," Shiolto said reluctantly. Lyan tensed, ready to argue, but Shiolto didn't press the matter, giving him no opportunity.

The day passed. Lyan rode and brooded. Such sights as the forest offered, he barely noticed except to listen for threats or the sense of being watched. Dalrian, Torqual, and Yion took turns riding point. Shiolto sometimes rode near Lyan, other times Cailean did. Both made occasional efforts to draw him into conversation, with little success, and eventually left him to his stubborn silence.

When a horse stepped up beside Shadowstar, Lyan expected one of the two men to be the rider. He glanced over, then scowled coolly at Yion. The mercenary met the look with his usual placid expression. "Peace, Lyan."

"What do you want?"

"The others believe I should offer you apologies. However, if I were to do so, I would be speaking falsely, and that would do disservice to us both. In its place, then, I offer explanation, should you wish to hear it."

Lyan's jaw tightened. "You didn't think I could have escaped from the pooka regardless of what I said."

"Lyan Stargazer, we both know that the monster has taken special interest in you, beyond the interest it seems to have in Lord Cailean. It toyed with you, and you acknowledged that it did not expect you to slip from its grasp, while your explanation of how you did so was…vague. If it had a chance, do you think the pooka would pass up an opportunity to deceive you or use you to further its goals, whatever those may be?" Yion asked.

"It didn't get that chance." Lyan avoided the implied question about how he had eluded the pooka.

"No," Yion agreed. "This time it did not. But if it had, would you not rather know?"

"What would *you* have done if it had?" Lyan snapped.

"I would have sought a way to break any hold it held on you, and asked my god for aid. Sending you into sleep assured that if the monster's power had enchanted you, and it had left hidden protections to prevent any from freeing you, you would not be forced to fight us against your will. Whether or not you approve of the method, Lyan, drugging you was the safest way for both you and us."

Lyan scowled and didn't reply.

Yion spoke more quietly. "Should it ease your mind any, I chose my actions by what I knew I must do, not what I wished to do."

"So you did what you had to do, and I should just accept it and not feel like my trust was abused." Lyan gazed into the forest ahead.

"You should do as you believe is correct," Yion answered. "But if you lay blame, lay it to the correct person."

Lyan didn't take his eyes from the forest and didn't answer. He hated to admit that he couldn't argue with Yion's reasoning. Rather than whine like a petulant child, Lyan said nothing. Yion let his horse fall back, leaving him to his thoughts.

A distant crackling in the brush made him recall the bear he'd encountered. Lyan thought back on the pooka's unexpected outrage. *"You dare draw me here."* That's what it said. *What were those ruins, and why was the pooka so angry? What does it know that I don't?* He closed his eyes with a silent, thin laugh. *What does it know that I don't? A great many thing, I suspect. Especially about what in the gods' names is really going on.*

When evening neared, they made camp. Lyan could barely slide from saddle, every muscle hurting. Dalrian jumped to help him limp from Shadowstar to a clear patch of ground, and Shiolto brought Lyan's saddlebags. Lyan was too tired, sore, and aware of his injuries to offer any protests that he could manage without help. While the Tathrens set camp, he found the flask of dayseed oil, eased off his boot, and applied the last of the numbing oil to his swollen ankle.

Dalrian made some sort of mash for dinner. Lyan's

stomach twisted and growled, fiercely reminding him that he had refused the morning meal. He waited until the Tathrens had served themselves and begun eating before he did the same.

"How are our supplies?" Cailean asked around a mouthful of food.

"Torqual's set snares, sir, so with luck we'll have a little meat in the morning. We're trying not to use all the grain we bought on the plains—the horses need it more than us. It could get thin if we're here for too long," Dalrian answered. "Then we'll be slowed down to forage and hunt."

"Do what you can," Cailean told him. "Lyan, if you see plants you know are safe to eat, point them out."

Lyan's head jerked up when he heard his name. He took a moment to make sense of the words, then nodded. "I will."

After dinner, he crawled to his bedroll. Aching and exhausted, Lyan closed his eyes as clouds blotted out the few glimpses of the sky not obscured by the trees. Sleep found him quickly.

By morning's dawn, Lyan's anger had relented, and he greeted his Tathren companions pleasantly enough. His tone didn't gush with enthusiasm, but neither did it drip venom. Shiolto returned the greeting warmly, and tension in the camp eased. Rabbit meat accompanied the leftover mash, telling of success in the snares. With better spirits, they ate, broke camp, and began riding once more. Lyan felt no less stiff than the previous day, but some aches had eased.

They had ridden most of the morning when Dalrian, riding point, halted his horse and jumped down to study the ground. "Tracks, Lord Cailean," he announced. "About a day old—an unshod horse."

Lyan tensed sharply, fear running down his spine. "Just one?" *It's ahead of us? And leaving tracks where we can find them?*

Dalrian nodded to him. "Just one. And… there's blood."

That drew everyone's attention. "Blood?" Torqual repeated. "The pooka's injured?"

"I don't know for sure if it is the pooka. It could be a normal horse…though this isn't good land for wild horses." Dalrian turned to Lyan. "Do you think the pooka could be hurt?"

All eyes settled on Lyan and he shifted uncomfortably. "I don't know. I used several tricks to avoid it, and it could have been injured by one of them." *Did the bear attack it? Is that why it was so angry at me? Or did Kithr's arrows find their mark after all?* He forced a thin smile. "I didn't want to stay close enough to check for myself."

That earned several uneasy laughs. Cailean frowned down at the ground. "Can you follow the trail?"

"Lord Cailean?" Dalrian asked.

"Can you track it?"

"Yes," Dalrian answered hesitantly. "But—"

"If this is the pooka, and it's wounded, I have questions to ask it," Cailean said coolly.

"My lord, I don't think--" Aikan began.

"Track it, Dalrian," Cailean ordered.

"Yes sir." Dalrian obeyed, though both his tone and stance said he would prefer to do otherwise.

Lyan shivered. The memory of the pooka's silky, mocking voice echoed in his thoughts. Injured, the monster could be all the more dangerous. And if it was not injured, if it was willing to spill its own blood to bait a trap…. He licked dry lips. "It could be luring us into a place of its choosing."

"I am tired of jumping at every shadow. If this is a trap, so be it. We will find it or fight our way out as a group. And if not, I *will* have answers," Cailean said.

Lyan bit his lip and touched the hunting knife hanging from his belt, assuring himself of its presence. He drew a deep breath and tried to draw confidence from Cailean's words. *I know how to bind it. If it's injured, there is a chance we can do so.* His hands clenched in fists. *Don't underestimate this "little elf," monster.*

At times, Lyan caught glimpses of the trail Dalrian followed—hoof prints in ground that had still been wet the previous day, broken branches, dark stains he guessed to be blood spotting leaves. He eyed the forest warily, alert for the prickling sensation of warning. Shadowstar tossed his head in response to Lyan's unease, but otherwise showed little concern.

Abruptly, the trees stopped, forming a wide clearing that opened as sharply as if they had come to the edge of Eilidh Wood. All the horses halted at the edge of the trees, not setting hoof inside the clearing. Ferns and grass covered the ground, but a path of bare dirt cut through them, packed ground without so much as a tuft of moss intruding on it. Lyan's eyes followed the path to the middle of the clearing, where a building of dark stone loomed.

Plants and vines massed near the base of the building, but not one touched the structure. Sunlight gleamed off the two worn, polished stone steps that led to an open doorway wide enough to admit three riders abreast. A column rose on either side of the doorway, carved of silver-colored stone and shaped in the forms of dragons, their heads looking down to the doorway and their mouths open as if poised to devour any who entered. A relief ran above the doorway and appeared to ring the building, but Lyan couldn't pick out the details from the clearing's edge. Sounds of the forest ended with the trees, creating an unsettling bubble of stillness.

"What is this?" Dalrian asked uncertainly.

"Does the trail lead in?" Lyan feared the answer, but his voice held mostly steady.

"Um... I... think so. But the tracks look like a man's footprints going down the path, and he was stumbling on his way in." He motioned at dark spots on the bare dirt, then looked at the building. "Do you know what this is?"

"The horses don't like it." Shiolto rubbed his mount's neck as the horse shifted and stomped uneasily.

Cailean swung down to the ground without a word and freed Solstice. Lyan cast a helpless look to the others, then let himself down from Shadowstar's back. By the time he had his crutch and followed, Cailean was halfway across the clearing. Behind him, he heard the rest of the group hurrying after.

The Tathren lord climbed the steps without hesitation. Lyan watched the carved dragons apprehensively, but they did not come to life or strike out. Cailean stopped sharply just beyond the threshold, stance wary. Lyan limped after him, pausing to run fingers over four long gouges rent in a stone as tall as the full length of his arm, thinking them suspiciously like those that claws would leave. Claws the length of his hand.

"Lyan, what is this?" Cailean asked, voice tight.

Lyan turned his eyes to the open interior of the building. He swallowed hard and forced out words. "This is a temple."

The sanctuary could have held dozens of men. Or more than one dragon. Chips and scratches both old and new marked the stone floor. No priests emerged to greet them or ask their business. There were no chairs or benches for suppliants, no furniture aside from a low stone altar. Lyan glimpsed some object left on the block as an offering. Behind the altar, two golden statues towered over them. To the left side of the altar, the image of a dragon sat, its wings folded against its body, its eyes gleaming gemstones that glowed with an inner light. Every scale was formed in perfect detail. Its head rested on its forelegs, but it seemed to smirk slightly, watching the mortals who dared to intrude with contemptuous amusement. The figure that stood on the right side of the altar nearly touched the ceiling, and his spread wings shrouded that side of the room. His form looked mostly human but for the massive leathery wings like a bat or a dragon, the long claws tipping his fingers and toes, and the feline tail that wound down along one leg. The cold smile on the god's face reflected the expression of the dragon, and left Lyan unsure if he smiled down on his worshipers, or if he mocked them. Behind the statues, Lyan glimpsed two dark doorways.

"A temple?" Cailean repeated. "Not to any god I know."

The rest of the Tathrens clustered behind them, staring. Lyan limped into the sanctuary. He knew the answer, finally understanding why the pooka had come here. "This is a temple to Nachyne, the god of monsters."

He heard sharp intakes of breath around him. "The god… of monsters?" Cailean repeated, turning slowly to cast wary looks at the two entryways leading deeper into the temple.

"Put up your weapons," Lyan said quietly, though the thought of being unprotected here frightened him. From the look Cailean gave him, Lyan wasn't the only one who disliked the idea. "Please. This is a temple, a sanctuary to anyone…or anything that enters. We should be safe as long as we abide by that." He met Cailean's gaze. "But if you threaten another here… if you break that law of sanctuary…."

Cailean closed his eyes and slowly let out a long breath before nodding. "I would invite divine retribution." He spat an angry curse and paced.

Lyan limped to the altar, curiosity drawing him to see what had been offered to Nachyne. Only the recognition that it was a gift to the god stopped him from sweeping it from sight before the Tathrens noticed it. The raven-feathered arrow was snapped in half, and blood stained the length of the wooden shaft.

Kithr didn't miss after all. Lyan glanced down to the floor and saw bloodspots leading into one of the doorways. He shivered, certain he did not imagine feeling hostile eyes on him.

"We shouldn't linger here," he said.

"Agreed," Yion said. "Even with sanctuary, we are unwelcome to those who worship here."

"Or to whatever's taken shelter here." Cailean scowled angrily at the darkness.

"My lord, for once I must agree with the elf," Aikan said. "If the monster is here, then let it stay here."

Lyan looked up at the statue's face, at the smile that was nearly a sneer, and wondered how it looked to the worshipers. Did their god smile down on them? Did that expression mock them? Did it offer promise of punishment to those who stood against them?

"Pardon our intrusion, Lord Nachyne," he said quietly.

Something moved—a half-seen motion from one doorway. Lyan didn't turn to look. He followed the Tathrens back into the sun, wondering if he'd only imagined the baleful glow of red eyes watching them leave.

13

Dark as night, black as dreams
Distant voice speaks with foul promise

"Monsters really have their own god?" Dalrian asked, breaking the stillness that lay over the camp. Fat dripped from one of the spits of meat he tended, making the fire hiss and pop. They had left the temple as far behind them as half a day's steady ride could, but at the mention of monsters, uneasy eyes searched the shadows their campfire cast into the forest.

"They do," Yion answered. "And like any god, he is not to be taken lightly."

"Do you know much about him, Yion?" Shiolto sat at the fire and looked at the mercenary with interest, like a child asking for a story.

Yion shrugged. "Less, I should think, than Lyan does."

Eyes turned to Lyan, but he was sore and tired. "Go ahead."

"Very well. Please correct me if I speak in error. The lord of monsters is called Nachyne."

"That statue in the temple looked like a man with wings,"

Torqual interrupted. "Not nearly as monstrous as the dragon."

"Both statues depicted Nachyne, Torqual," Lyan said. "The man and the dragon were both images of the god."

Yion nodded. "Such are the forms he is said to prefer, though he has been known to take other shapes. Those of his domain most often see him in dragon form, but when he deals with other gods or, rarely, mortals, he takes the form of the man."

"Why?" Shiolto asked. "Why take any form other than a monster?"

"For the sake of courtesy. It would be… rude for him not to," Yion said.

Torqual barked a laugh. "Rude? He's a god! Who in the Fell Blades does a god worry about being rude to?"

"Other gods," Yion answered evenly. "But to continue about Nachyne, unlike some other gods, I know of only one tryst between him and a mortal woman. He has few dealings with mortals."

Shiolto groaned. "If there's a temple devoted to him, does that mean there are *more* monsters around here? The pooka's bad enough!"

"I think we might be free from the pooka for a little while," Lyan said.

His quiet voice drew gazes back to him. "Something you neglected to mention?" Aikan demanded.

Lyan thought of the blood and the arrow. "The blood we saw was no deceit. It's hurt." He didn't flinch from Aikan's gaze. "The pooka is hurt seriously enough that rather than continue to harass us, it fled and found the one place where it knows it will be safe, but where we are also safe from it under the rules of sanctuary. If it had taken shelter anywhere else, I might think it was trying to mislead us, but if it was laying a trap, it wouldn't have chosen a location where it couldn't attack us."

"It was bleeding pretty badly," Dalrian added in Lyan's support. He checked the meat. "Dinner's ready."

Lyan let Dalrian carve a healthy slice of rabbit meat into his bowl, but he didn't take a bite until after his companions began eating. As he chewed the meat, he recalled the sensation of being watched inside the temple. What other monsters lurked there? Would they seek to avenge the injury done to the pooka?

He rubbed his forehead. He hurt through and through, and regardless of whether anyone had felt some need to drug him tonight, he was exhausted and ready to sleep.

"Lyan, if the pooka stays at the temple until it heals, how long do you think it will take it to find us again?" Cailean's question caught him before he could retreat to his bedroll.

"I don't know." Lyan tried not to snap, recognizing that Cailean was trying to include him, asking his opinion and advice. "I don't know how long it takes a monster to heal, and I'm not sure how it continues to find us. But when it does, it'll be more careful and less eager to play with us." *With me.*

"It's been *playing*?" Torqual repeated.

"The nature of a pooka is to be a trickster," Lyan told him. "Whatever its purpose is, it's been carrying that purpose out in the manner that most entertains it—at our expense. I suspect that will not continue once it recovers."

"Then it's become more dangerous," Aikan concluded.

Lyan wasn't certain if he heard an accusatory note in Aikan's voice or only imagined it. "No more dangerous than if it infiltrated our group. Probably less so, because we know to be on guard."

"How was the monster injured?" Torqual asked.

"I'm not sure," Lyan lied. "I didn't see what happened."

"Do you think the pooka will blame you?" Cailean asked.

Lyan thought of the glaring eyes from the darkness and shivered. "Yes, I do."

Cailean nodded, brushing a lock of hair from his face. "All

right. If anyone sees *any* sign the pooka is nearby, or you so much as suspect it might be, speak up immediately. Understood? I don't want Lyan or anyone else falling into its clutches."

Grim nods answered him.

"Good. Now get some sleep. Tomorrow, I want to put as much distance from this place as we can."

In his dreams, Lyan ran through a forest that, without warning, became endless stone halls. Casting a look over his shoulder, he glimpsed a looming shape with glowing red eyes stalking him, waiting for him to trip and fall. Lyan's lungs burned and his body ached, exhausted, but he couldn't stop. Even as he stumbled, Lyan heard a voice laughing at him. Not the pooka's voice, but one he didn't know.

"You can't escape, no matter how far you run. You know I'll find you. There is no escape."

Lyan tripped and fell, tumbling into darkness, knowing that the thing chasing him leapt, and he would feel it tearing into him any moment.

He jerked awake, shaking and shivering, still half in the nightmare. His heart pounded and his breathing was rapid and shallow, sweat beading his forehead. He forced himself to draw a deep breath and let it out slowly.

Words danced at the very edge of his hearing, muffled and hushed. Struggling through the haze of sleep-fogged thoughts, Lyan tried to focus on the sound, though he couldn't tell who spoke, only that the words were in Tathren.

"…pooka failed, my lord… injured. The elf… problems." Silence for a moment. "A temple… god of monsters. No, my lord." Pause. "No, I'm sure."

Lyan peeled open his eyes, but saw only the dark shapes of sleeping men. To one side, someone tossed and groaned restlessly, but he dismissed that as the source of the whispers. The voice seemed to come from another direction. Lyan strained his ears and caught a final "...will report again, my lord." No more whispers followed.

The restless sleeper tossed again. Lyan thought it must be Cailean. He rubbed weary eyes and tried to relax. He wasn't entirely sure if he'd heard that quiet voice at all, or if it lurked as some lingering fragment of his nightmare.

Cailean mumbled something unintelligible and rolled over. Lyan closed his eyes, breathing slowly until his racing heart calmed. He drifted in and out of a doze, but his ankle began to throb and a root dug into the small of his back. Lyan tried without success to find a comfortable position, finally dozing again.

He started awake when Cailean jolted from sleep with a sharp gasp. No one else stirred. Cailean staggered to his feet and stumbled a little ways from his sleeping men. Lyan peered up at the sky, trying to guess how much night remained. No hints of dawn lightened the clouds, but he knew he wouldn't be able to find sleep again soon. Wincing as pain stabbed through his ankle, Lyan rose, pulling one blanket over his shoulders and another across his arm. He found Cailean sitting at the edge of the camp, legs drawn up and head resting on his knees.

Lyan draped the second blanket over Cailean's shoulders. The Tathren lord started and looked toward him, but the human's eyes weren't sharp enough to identify who stood by him. Lyan sank down beside Cailean.

"Who's there?" Cailean asked warily.

"Lyan."

Cailean untensed and nodded. "Thank you. I'm sorry, I must have woken you."

"I wasn't sleeping well," Lyan said. "Nor, it seems, were you."

Cailean gave a short, sharp laugh. "You have a gift for understatement." He shivered. "My pursuer, who would claim the Spear as his own, visited my dreams. He does so sometimes—I haven't seen any pattern to when." Cailean's hands gripped the edges of the blanket and drew it tight around himself. "He mocks me—telling me that I'm a coward running away from him. Something always chases me in the dream, while he laughs."

"This is the mage who cursed you?" Lyan asked. "He can intrude into your dreams?"

Cailean nodded, and shivered again. "He dares me to use Solstice against him, when he knows I can't—not for long enough to stop him. I don't have the strength against… what he did to me."

"The curse."

Cailean just nodded again.

"Cailean, if he can find and follow you, why are you still intent on finding Equinox? If you find it, you save him the work of hunting for it himself."

"I can't use Solstice to fight him—you know why. But that… same reason doesn't apply to Equinox."

Lyan's eyes narrowed. "You told me you did not intend to become the Bearer of Equinox." Under the blanket, his hand moved to the hilt of his knife. *Please, Cailean, do not tell me you lied to me. Do not tell me that you would take both Spears. Please, by all the gods above and below, do not make me have to try to kill you.*

Cailean made a helpless gesture. "I *know* that I need to find Equinox. I think… this may sound mad, but I think Solstice is telling me that. Someone must wield the Spear. I can't fight my enemy like this, Lyan, and I can't run forever. I have to protect my men, and I can't do that if using the one weapon of power I have leaves me as weak and helpless as a toddling child."

"Do you trust them?" Lyan thought of the voice he'd thought he heard. *Aikan, perhaps?*

"With the exception of Yion, they've all served my family for most or all of their lives," Cailean answered. "They've given me no reason not to."

If Equinox comes into the hands of a Tathren—any Tathren—there will be another war. The elves of Eilidh Wood won't accept it. Lyan didn't say anything.

"You've said Equinox is the Spear of the elves. Maybe you'll become the Spearbearer," Cailean said.

"Wha— *me?*" The words startled Lyan from his thoughts.

"I'd trust it in your hands."

Lyan shook his head rapidly in denial. "I'm a star-reader, not a warrior! I wouldn't know what to do with Equinox. And Solstice made it pretty clear that it didn't want me touching it."

"If Equinox should stay with the elves, you're the only elf with us."

"That doesn't make me qualified for it!" Lyan argued. *Kithr, though…* He shook his head angrily, not wanting to think about Kithr or his uninvited, condescending decision to follow Lyan. "The bearer will have to overcome a series of trials to claim the Spear, and I don't have the skill for any sort of trial involving weapons."

Cailean just shook his head. "I'm trying to get *his* voice out of my head. I don't know how to silence it, and I can't argue with what he says. There's too much truth in it. This is a fool's mission, but it's all I know to do."

"I'm sorry. I'm not helping," Lyan apologized.

Cailean closed his eyes. "No, it's not your fault, Lyan. I'm just tired of running, not knowing what's coming, what kind of attack we will face next, or even if some man by the side of the road is really the farmer he appears to be, or an assassin waiting for his chance. I take my allies, whatever strange form they come in—whether a mercenary who for gods only know what reason decided to change sides in the middle of a battle from the obvious winner's side to that of the loser, or an elf old enough to have seen the ravages of the war for himself who chooses to join us to ensure a bunch of fool Tathrens don't defile a sacred treasure of his people. My men follow me, and I can't even tell them why I don't dare use the Spear except when I must."

"Then why are you telling me?" Lyan asked.

Cailean smiled slightly. "Because you aren't Tathren."

"I don't understand."

"That's exactly my point, Lyan. You *don't* understand. You don't know commoners from lords, you don't know the rituals and trappings of court courtesy or politics." Another thin laugh. "You don't know that you're not supposed to criticize or that you're supposed to hide blunt questions under layers of courtesies. Shiolto, Dalrian, Torqual, they're good men, but they're common birth, and they know it as well as I do. Aikan… wouldn't understand all this."

"I still don't understand why you don't tell them the truth." Lyan looked up at the sky, where the moon struggled valiantly to shine through the clouds. "If I could, I'd offer to read your fortune. But…" He gazed at the clouds, and a chilling thought crept over him, as he recalled something the priest had said at the temple of the Thunderer. "Cailean, the mage who cursed and enspelled you, do you know who he serves?"

"Who he…what do you mean?"

"What god does he follow?"

"I don't kn— Lyan, what are you thinking?"

"Priestess Rhonir said the power that created these clouds is the work of a mortal given their power by the Mad God. Does he…serve Murdo?"

Cailean tensed. "I don't know, Lyan. Truly, I don't. But why are you asking now?"

"If this isn't just a mortal wanting power, if this has the hand of the Mad God, the one who cursed you wants the Spears to break the prison that binds Murdo. If *that* is the case…." Lyan looked at Cailean. "If that is the case, then when we find Equinox, we should pray someone among us is able to complete the Trials and bear the Spear, or we will reveal the location of one of the keys to his prison to the Mad God's minions."

Cailean's face paled, but he nodded. "I have to find Equinox—I'm sure of that, Lyan. What happens after that… gods only know." He slowly stood and offered a hand to Lyan. "We should try to rest. I'll consider your words, Lyan. Thank you."

Lyan limped back to his bedroll with Cailean's help. He lay down and tried to find sleep again, but his thoughts continued to churn. Eventually, sometime before dawn, he finally dozed.

Morning came too soon. Lyan forced himself up and moving, wincing as stiff muscles protested. He didn't say much, but the campfire conversation was subdued, and his contributions weren't missed. They broke camp, mounted, and rode deeper into the forest. Lyan took comfort in not feeling any eyes on them, and prayed they would have a few days' peace.

14

Turning, turning, turning
Dancing in the mist
Turning, turning, turning
By wind and water kissed

Lyan rolled his shoulders and stretched, feeling sore muscles protest. After the days of travel, he was sure he should be used to sleeping on the ground, but his body still complained. Shadowstar tossed his head with an amused snort.

"Sure, laugh," he muttered. But he scratched the stallion's ears.

"As if that animal understands you," Aikan scoffed.

"He does better than some people," Lyan responded. Only when he saw the Tathren stiffen did he realize the words could be taken as a slight against Aikan. Lyan tried to salvage what he could while pretending not to notice Aikan's offense at the unintended insult. "Many in my village don't understand my habits or likes. Shadowstar puts up with my oddities without complaint."

"Were you the only young man of your village not sent to war?" Yion asked.

"Not the only one. But there weren't many of us who were forbidden to join," Lyan said. "Why?"

"Such a thing can create a gap between those who share a similar experience and one who has not. Your path differed from that of your age-mates," the mercenary said.

"It always did," Lyan responded. He knew, though, that the difference hadn't always been so drastic. He hadn't been friends with the few other young men of their village who'd been excluded from the muster, and the gap between them had only grown after his mentor's death to old age, when Lyan had taken on the duties of village astrologer. And his friends, when they finally returned, hadn't been the same enthusiastic youths who'd left with the confidence that the war would be over before the first snow fell.

Aikan just snorted derisively. Lyan scratched Shadowstar's ears again. The stallion tossed his head, then snatched a bite of leaves from a bush while he walked. Lyan rubbed his eyes and gazed at the forest.

They followed a stream that, for now, paralleled their route. A flock of quail darted in front of the horses, startled from cover by the noise and not realizing that, had they remained still, they would have gone unnoticed. Aikan's horse started and danced back several steps, but he kept his mount under control. Lyan kept expecting to feel some reaction from the forest itself, but, as Yion had told him when they first entered, the spirit of the Forests of Cossette slept, inattentive to their presence or their passage. Lyan listened to the babble of water through the streambed. The longer he listened, the more he felt as if he heard voices—soft whispers just at the edge of his hearing.

"Something wrong, Lyan?" Shiolto asked.

He almost said no. Then he remembered that his Tathren companions were deaf to the forest's whispers, and he remembered Cailean's instructions to speak if any of them felt something out of the ordinary. "It's probably nothing. But I heard something like faint whispering."

"Whispering voices is not 'probably nothing'." Torqual scowled and reached for his weapon.

"In Eilidh Wood, it would be," Lyan said. "There, I would call it the spirit of the forest. This might be the spirit of Cossette. Or it might be my imagination."

"Spirits." Torqual scowled again. "Give me an enemy I can see and hit over spirits any day. We're not *in* Eilidh Wood anymore, thank the gods."

Lyan let the statement on his home pass, though with an effort. "Not all spirits are harmful. Most would just as well be left alone."

"Good. They can leave me alone, and I'll leave them alone." Torqual gave the trees a suspicious look.

Lyan fervently hoped that he only mistook the sound of water, and hadn't actually heard soft, mocking laughter in response to Torqual's words. He continued to listen, occasionally catching snippets, never loud enough for him to tell if words were actually spoken, only an awareness of sound. As they continued through the day, Lyan heard them less, and by the time the group camped, he'd nearly convinced himself not to worry about it.

Morning came with a chill in the air and a fog over the forest. The horses shifted restlessly while their riders broke camp. Lyan listened, but the babbling water hid any whispering voices.

Cailean shivered as he doused the fire. "This should burn off soon. Keep close."

The fog seemed to rise off the stream, but it grew thicker and heavier than Lyan thought it should. *The spirit of the forest may sleep, but this is a wild land—fey. It has inhabitants who prefer to remain unseen.* He shook his head with a soft snort. *And I'm more worried by a heavy fog than whispering voices.*

"Keep us on the path, if you can?" Lyan said quietly to Shadowstar.

"Lyan? What did you say?" asked Cailean, a vague shape ahead of him.

"Nothing. Talking to Shadowstar," Lyan answered.

He could hear the other horses, but the mist tricked his eyes and made riders into shadows almost indistinguishable from the trees. A cold wind whipped through the fog, stirring it into darting shapes. Lyan stiffened, eyes widening as a chill ran down his spine and he sensed the creeping sensation of someone or something watching him.

"Cailean! Keep everyone close!" Lyan called.

"Lyan?" Cailean's voice sounded distant.

"Keep everyone close!" he repeated. The sounds of other horses came from his right, but he didn't dare try to follow them. He didn't trust his senses not to lead him astray. Confusion and misdirection surrounded him, woven into the fog. But it shouldn't be able to touch Solstice. Cailean and anyone near him should be safe. He hoped.

Lyan shivered as sounds shifted around him and the mist flowed over him like tiny grasping fingers pawing at his clothes. He leaned close against Shadowstar and closing his eyes. *Please don't tell me that I'm caught alone again. Please, please, in Soldarr's name, don't let the pooka be hiding here, waiting for me.*

As if reading his thoughts, Shadowstar snorted. Lyan wrapped his fingers into the stallion's mane. "You're right; I'm not alone. You're here too." Lyan didn't open his eyes. "When you can, Shadowstar, find Cailean or any of his people."

Shadowstar stood still. The mist darted around them, teasing and sending chills through Lyan. Now he could hear the whispers: soft, high-pitched voices singing to the music of wind and water. It felt like an eternity that Shadowstar remained unmoving. Lyan kept his eyes closed and trusted the stallion. When Shadowstar began walking, the movement was so smooth it took Lyan a moment to notice. He didn't know how Shadowstar could step with barely a sound across ground strewn with twigs and leaves, but he was grateful. He clung to the stallion's mane and listened.

"…seems the fey disapprove… my presence, my lord…"

The snatch of voice was swept away by whatever trick of fog and wind had brought it to his ears. Lyan's head jerked up and he looked around quickly, but he heard no more, and saw only the dancing mist.

Who was that? Was that the same voice I heard the other night?

Shadowstar didn't pause. Lyan shivered and hunched down against his mount's neck again, straining to catch any more words. Heavy silence smothered the forest. The mist still swirled around him, but Lyan took confidence from Shadowstar's steady, unhesitating advance.

Finally Shadowstar stopped and snorted, then sneezed. Another horse answered, and Lyan straightened. Peering ahead, he saw a vague shape that could be a horse and rider.

Please, Feyra, whoever this is, let it be anyone other than the person I heard earlier.

"Who's there?" Movement accompanied the sharp, suspicious voice.

I should be more careful what I pray for.… "I *would* have to find you, of all people." The words escaped Lyan before he thought better of them. But, tempting as it was to turn Shadowstar away and try to find someone…*anyone* else, Lyan let Shadowstar approach Aikan's horse.

"What is *that* supposed to mean?" The fog thinned slightly, and Lyan could see the angry scowl on Aikan's face as he drew close.

"It means I'm as delighted to see you as you are to see me, Aikan," Lyan snapped back.

The older Tathren had fared worse in the fog than Lyan. His horse must have stumbled or lost her footing at least once; mud coated her back legs and splattered Aikan's saddlebags and cloak. "Where is Lord Cailean?"

"I don't know," Lyan said.

"You're the one who told him to keep everyone close. I heard you." The distrust in Aikan's tone was unmistakable.

"Do you think I somehow conjured a fog from the air just so I could get lost in it? I was trying to keep everyone else from getting spread across the forest and turned around by fey magic. Sorry, next time I won't help!"

"And I should believe you? I have no idea what benefit this fog would be to you, unless you intended to separate Lord Cailean from his men." Aikan's eyes narrowed. "Or perhaps, just from those of his men not under your sway."

"Under my sway?" Lyan repeated. "What is that supposed to mean?"

Aikan lowered his voice, and Shadowstar stepped closer to the Tathren's horse. "Shiolto and Dalrian are simple men. I can see how they would be deceived by pleasant words and false gestures of friendship. Torqual should know better. And I do not know what elven magic you have used to trick Lord Cailean into trusting you, but I will not fall prey to it."

Lyan stared at him in disbelief before finally finding words. "Tricked? I haven't tricked any of you, especially not Cailean. I have told him the *truth*. Though as intent as you Tathrens are on lying to each other, maybe that *does* look like a trick to you!"

Aikan stiffened sharply, something unreadable flashing across his face. "You… how dare you! You are accusing *me* of lying to my lord?"

"All of you!" Lyan retorted. "You, Cailean, gods only know what lies everyone else tells without a second thought. It's no wonder that Ki…my friends told me to never trust Tathrens!"

Aikan puffed up in furious indignation. "You call Lord Cailean a liar? How *dare* you, elf?!"

"*Truth*, Aikan. I dare to actually say it!"

"And what do you claim Lord Cailean has lied about?" Aikan demanded.

"How about the reason he can't use Solstice without collapsing?" Lyan snapped. "He's lied to his men about it, trying to convince them it isn't related to the Spear. He's lied to *you* about it. You know as well as I do that he didn't hit his head during the ambush in the mountains."

Aikan's face was tense and pale, hand gripping his sword hilt. "What do *you* know of that, elf?"

"I know Cailean told me what he could by his own choice and not through any magic I worked. I know he was cursed and that it happened long before any of you set foot in Eilidh Wood! What I do *not* know is why in rot and ash he continues to conceal this from his own people." Lyan waved his hand in angry frustration.

Aikan's expression darkened in fury, thought the object of his anger was less obvious. His voice was low and tightly controlled when he asked, "If you deny working any enchantments, assuming your words hold any of the truth you claim, what part *do* you have in this matter? What business does an elf of Eilidh Wood have with Lord Cailean?"

"My part?" That wasn't a question Lyan could answer fully to any of the Tathrens, least of all to this one. He chose his truths carefully. "My part is to offer Cailean my knowledge, should he chose to use it, and to be certain that when he finds what he's looking for, neither he nor those with him defile a place revered and held as sacred to my people." He held Aikan's gaze. "Tell me that you at least know Cailean's mission. Or is he keeping *that* from his men as well?"

"Of course I know. Lord Cailean searches for the second Spear, Equinox. And what will you do if you believe that we will 'defile' this place?" Aikan watched him closely.

"Warn you. Try to stop you before the forces that protect the Spear do so." Lyan dared not say more.

Aikan laughed sharply. "With great concern for our well-being, I'm sure. You may, somehow, have convinced Lord Cailean to trust you. I do not and will not. Know that I will be watching you *very* closely."

Lyan drew a deep breath. "I don't care if you like me or not, Aikan. To be honest, I don't like you either. But I won't let that stop me from helping Cailean, because liking or disliking one of you is irrelevant against the Mad—" Lyan cut off as he became aware of eyes on them, surrounding them. His eyes left Aikan to scan the fog-shrouded trees and brush. "I know you're there."

Voices whispered from the fog and shadows in answer. "Only because we let you."

Aikan stiffened, looking from Lyan to the shadowed trees. "What is this?"

Lyan's eyes moved warily, searching for anything he could identify as a solid shape. "The fey."

"Monsters." The single word carried the weight of accusation.

"Yes." Lyan's gaze settled on a shadow that might have been a small figure, but could as easily have been a knot on a tree. "Why are you misleading us? Have we caused you offense?"

"We are the keepers of our god's temple. A wounded dark horse stumbled into our care, cursing the elf who caused him harm. And you ask if you have committed offense?" The laughter was soft, but chill.

"The pooka challenged me to its game. It laid no rules as to what actions were forbidden," Lyan said, the hair prickling on his neck.

"He challenged and you *accepted?*" another voice scoffed.

"Be still!" the first voice ordered. "He issued the challenge to you, elf?"

"The pooka did," Lyan said cautiously, trying to guess whether his answer would make the situation better or worse. "And if there were supposed to be rules, I do not know them."

"He challenged. You accepted. Those *are* the rules." Scorn laced the fey's voice, derision that Lyan did not know something so rudimentary. "He neglected to speak of challenges." The mist shifted and swirled, drifting away from them. "That makes it a matter between you and him, and we will not interfere. Leave, mortals."

Lyan inclined his head in a wary nod. "So, I have committed no offense against you?"

Several short, sharp laughs answered him from the fog. "No offense against *us*, elf. But I doubt the dark horse will be so lenient once he has healed."

The sense of watchful eyes vanished, and with it went the fog. Aikan eyed Lyan suspiciously. "You seem to have an art for drawing unwanted attention, elf."

"The fey are creatures of Nachyne, and from what they said, they attend the god's temple. They certainly would be aware of the pooka, and it's… understandable, I think, that they would be displeased that a monster was wounded in their forest. Now that they know more of the situation, they've lifted the fog. We should try to find Cailean."

"*Lord* Cailean."

Lyan gritted his teeth. "Aikan, is the use of a title so important to you that it's worth trying to continue a war in which neither of us fought? I respect Cailean, but he's not *my* lord." Shadowstar began walking, and Aikan's horse followed.

Aikan said nothing.

Lyan was spared any need to say more. Brush snapped and crackled as something approached, making both of them reach for weapons. Shadowstar, however, nickered a greeting. Ahead of them, a horse answered. Shortly, the brush parted as the horse pushed through, bearing Torqual as its rider.

The guardsman looked from Lyan to Aikan, studying them both. "There you are. The damned fog kept turning me around." He considered them. "As much noise as you two made arguing, I expected to at least see a black eye or two, maybe a few missing teeth."

"Where's Lord Cailean?" Aikan demanded stiffly, unamused by Torqual's quip.

Torqual pointed over his shoulder. "I marked my path. It'll wind some, but it'll get us back to the others. You two are the only ones who wandered off too far. We collected everyone else easily enough."

"Good," Aikan said sharply. "Let's go."

Aikan rode near Torqual, and Lyan followed behind them. Torqual glanced around, then leaned close to Aikan and spoke quietly enough that human ears wouldn't have been able to hear from Lyan's position. "Strange fog. Reminded me of that fog when Lord Cailean's keep was attacked, how quickly it appeared, then vanished after the enemy got in." He paused. "Oh, but wait…you didn't see that, did you? Where *were* you when the attack came, Aikan? I can't seem to remember seeing you anywhere."

Aikan stiffened in the saddle. "What are you…?"

Torqual sneered at him. "Where were you, when all Lord Cailean's loyal men stood on the walls, fighting to protect his life and his home, and shedding their blood for him?"

"How dare you…?"

"So prove me wrong. Tell me where you were. Or should I be glad I found you two when I did, before our elven guide somehow suffered an accident?"

Aikan drew a sharp breath. His mouth opened, but no sound came out.

"I'm watching you, Aikan," Torqual hissed. "Mind your step."

15

Accursed darkness
Hiding its secrets
Beyond sight of the watching heavens

Cailean's weary expression relaxed in relief when he saw Lyan, Aikan, and Torqual. "Thank Cantorelle you're all safe. I heard you tell me to keep everyone close, Lyan, but I couldn't tell where you were. The fog was so thick, I could barely see my own horse. Most of us didn't get too far spread apart, thank the gods." He looked up at the trees. "I don't normally see fog act like that."

Lyan shifted uncomfortably. "I apologize. Fey targeted us, and I'm afraid I am inadvertently at fault for it."

"Fey? What quarrel would they have with us?" Cailean asked, brow furrowing.

"The ones who caused the fog serve as caretakers of Nachyne's temple," Lyan said.

"So they were mad at us because the pooka was hurt?" Shiolto asked.

"It seems so," Aikan said curtly. "However, the pooka failed to mention pertinent details of the situation. Once Lyan informed the monsters more fully, they released the fog." He had regained his composure during the ride, and he and Torqual had exchanged no words since those Lyan had inadvertently overheard. "You sent Torqual to find us, my lord?"

Cailean nodded. "We couldn't find you or Lyan in the immediate area, and neither of you answered when I called. He volunteered."

"The fog was starting to lift by the time I heard them," Torqual said. His expression was serious, but Lyan heard hints of a smirk. "After that, it wasn't hard to find them. Lyan and Aikan had found each other already. I just had to follow the sounds of argument."

Lyan's cheeks burned, and Aikan fixed Torqual with a glare he normally reserved for Lyan alone.

Cailean looked at them and sighed. "Keep your opinions to yourself, Torqual. The fog has cleared and we're wasting time. If we keep this pace, going around the forest might well have been faster after all. The gods seem determined to cast delays in our path."

"Do you think the fog will come back, Lyan?" Dalrian asked.

"I doubt it," Lyan said. "The fey know now the pooka was injured during a game that it initiated, making the matter one between it and me rather than an offense against all monsters." The idea didn't fill him with confidence—"only" the pooka wanting revenge was nothing to be dismissed, even if it was better than having every monster in the forest on his heels.

Shadowstar snorted and stamped a hoof impatiently. The other horses shifted and snorted in response. Lyan forced a small smile. "Shadowstar agrees with you, Cailean. We should continue."

Aikan's scorn settled on Lyan again. "As if that animal knows what anyone says."

"In the fog, when I couldn't trust my senses, I told Shadowstar to find Cailean or any of his men," Lyan responded as they began to ride. "He found you."

Shadowstar set a quick, confident pace through the forest. Lyan let the stallion lead, as much a silent challenge to Aikan as confidence that Shadowstar knew which way to go. It was petty, and Lyan was slightly ashamed of himself. But he couldn't argue with the certainty in Shadowstar's step. A glance over his shoulder found the Tathrens following with no indication that they objected to him taking the lead.

The forest remained still around them, an eerie quiet. Noises sounded too loud to Lyan's ears: the crunch of the horses' hooves, the jingle of metal when Yion's horse tossed her head, the creak of leather as riders shifted in the saddles. Lyan caught himself listening for whispering voices, but heard none.

Who did I hear in the fog? Aikan? Or someone else? Are the gods teasing me? I don't have proof of anything—not even that whoever I've heard is one of my companions.

His thoughts turned to Torqual's thinly veiled accusation to Aikan. *Cailean didn't say anything about being attacked with magic when his home was assaulted. But he hasn't said much about that attack at all. If that's when he was cursed, he might not be able to talk about it.* Lyan recalled the frustration and growing desperation he read in Cailean's weary eyes. *If I know more, maybe I can help him. So far I've created at least as many problems for Cailean as I've solved.*

They took a brief rest at midday, stretching their legs and eating a small meal. Cailean studied his map, but soon stowed it again.

"It says little enough about this forest. Any landmarks we've seen aren't marked on it," Cailean said in answer to Lyan's questioning look.

"I see."

"You've been quiet since the fog lifted, Lyan. Is something on your mind?"

"Many things," Lyan said. "So much has been happening —do you ever have time to stop and think in the midst of this, Cailean?"

Cailean sighed. "Not really. But the things I have to think about, I'd rather not ponder too long. Thinking about my home or worrying about the men who stayed behind will distract me from my responsibility to protect those here with me. The most I can do for the rest is pray, find Equinox as soon as possible…and hope I will have a home to return to."

Lyan nodded in reply, finding nothing to say.

Once they mounted, Shadowstar took the lead without Lyan's urging. Sounds of animal life gradually returned as the sun warmed the forest. Lyan took a deep breath, relaxing.

Shiolto walked his horse up beside Lyan. Lyan greeted him with a smile.

"It's turning out to be a decent day after all," Shiolto said, looking up to the trees. "I didn't think it would, after that start."

"This forest hasn't been the most welcoming," Lyan said. "Perhaps we *should* have gone around."

Shiolto shook his head. "I know it sounds strange, but I'd rather face monsters and weather than be wondering if we're riding into an ambush down the road." He waved a calloused hand at the forest. "Look at this. Who's going to lurk in hiding somewhere in all these trees just on the chance that Lord Cailean might ride past? There's no road, and even if someone knows what direction we're going, they don't know where we are." Shiolto chuckled. "I mean, I'm *here* and I don't know exactly where we are. What could you tell someone? 'Look for the big tree'?"

"Before you reached Eilidh Wood, you were being chased?" Lyan asked.

Shiolto's smile faded. "Ever since we left Lord Cailean's keep. I'd gotten enough horses out when we left, so we started out riding. But two were killed in the first ambush, and another went lame. Lord Cailean decided to use the rest to carry gear, since we couldn't all ride and we could keep a better pace if we didn't have to carry everything on our backs."

"Did Ewart send the men who followed you?"

"I don't know. Probably. I was more worried about them not killing us than who sent them. They were on our heels, less than a quarter of a day behind us, when we reached Eilidh Wood. They would have caught us the next day for sure. It was almost night, but Lord Cailean saw the forest ahead and said we'd push on and try to lose them in it. I don't know if we would have stopped if we had known it was Eilidh Wood—we didn't have anywhere else to go." He paused. "Then again…if we'd actually seen the forest in daylight, I'd have thought twice about entering. No offense meant, Lyan."

"None taken," Lyan said. "Did your pursuers follow you in?"

Shiolto smiled thinly. "They'd have reached the forest when they started in the morning. I don't think they were *that* determined. We haven't seen them since. Most likely, they went around. I hope they lost our trail."

"The men who attacked us in the mountains weren't them, I assume?"

Shiolto shook his head. "No. Those guys looked like hired thugs. Ewart's men are better trained and have nicer gear." He toyed with his reins.

"Can I ask you something, Shiolto?" Lyan asked.

"Sure. What is it, Lyan?"

"When Ewart attacked Cailean's keep, what happened?"

"Why do you want to know?" Shiolto cocked his head to one side, curious.

"I want to understand what happened. I gather bits and pieces from things people say, but not enough to make sense of them." It wasn't a lie, at least.

Shiolto rubbed the ragged stubble on his chin. "Well, I

worked mostly in the stables, so I don't know everything that happened, but I could tell you what I saw."

"Please, do," Lyan said.

Shiolto considered. "Ever seen a keep, Lyan?"

Lyan shook his head. "I've heard descriptions from our warriors. Their fortifications made them unpopular targets. Prolonged sieges aren't our preference."

"I don't think anyone *likes* sieges, whether they're defending or attacking. We had warning Ewart was coming, and had time to stock provisions in Lord Cailean's keep and offer shelter to the villagers who chose to hide inside the walls. I don't know if Ewart expected us to not be prepared, or if he was crazy enough to think Lord Cailean's men would turn sides and support him. When he reached the keep, the gates were shut and the walls lined with defenders. The braggart offered terms of surrender, if you can call them that."

"What were his terms?" Lyan asked.

"If Lord Cailean would surrender the keep, his titles, and everything else he owned, Ewart would let him to walk away with the clothes on his back—maybe. The rest of us would have been expected to stay and serve Ewart." Shiolto spat in the dirt.

"Cailean refused Ewart's terms?" Lyan asked.

"Damned right he refused! I can't imagine that bastard Ewart expected anything else. That's when the siege started. For a while, he seemed content to sit outside and keep us from leaving. He made a few token attacks on the walls, taunting us, letting his men loot the villages around. There wasn't a lot for them to loot, though. Lord Cailean had encouraged people to find somewhere safer. Most of the women and children in the keep left too, including the young woman Dalrian's planning to marry. Lord Cailean put Aikan's daughter in charge of all of them."

"How long was the siege?" Lyan asked.

"That went on seven or eight days. His archers would

shoot at our men on the walls, ours would shoot back." Shiolto paused for a moment. "After five days, though, those clouds started gathering at night. I remember that, because the first night especially we worried Ewart would launch a night attack, with the clouds hiding the moon. There was one night attack, but even that really didn't feel like they put an effort into it. I think Ewart was waiting for something."

"Do you know what?" Lyan asked.

Shiolto shook his head. "I couldn't even guess. Someone else, maybe, who'd promised him help. I kept the horses in good shape, in case Lord Cailean ordered a sally out the gates. But he kept his men inside, even though a lot of them argued that they could take on Ewart's hired soldiers."

"Did Cailean say why?"

"He said that would be what Ewart wanted," Shiolto said. "He said Ewart had to have some larger plan, or he wouldn't have brought the sort of army he did. And the way Ewart kept throwing taunts and insults at the walls, he had to be trying to goad Lord Cailean into sending men onto the field. He acted frustrated when Lord Cailean didn't."

"Then you had a standoff—he was outside, you were inside, he couldn't get in, but you couldn't leave."

Shiolto nodded. "I thought he would try to starve us out. He could have, but it would have taken a long time—we had plenty of stores, and his men had to scavenge." Shiolto's expression darkened. "But that's not how things went."

Lyan's attention was caught, and he waited for Shiolto to continue.

"He kept trying to lure Lord Cailean out for almost half a month. But finally, one morning as sentries took their posts, they reported a lot of activity in Ewart's camp. Someone had arrived, but they didn't get a look at who it was. Seemed someone important. Ewart didn't come out to make his usual challenges, and his men kept quiet, looking over their gear. Then, in the middle of the afternoon, this strange fog started to spread from Ewart's camp." Shiolto shivered. "That fog we got lost in earlier? I liked it a lot better than the one that covered Lord Cailean's keep. That one was cold, and downright unnatural—a sunny day with not a cloud in the sky, then mist covered everything. It spooked the horses, and down in the stables we were running around trying to calm them down and finding the lanterns. It just kept getting darker and darker, and that fog got thicker. That's when I heard sounds of fighting. Ewart's men got up the walls; I still don't know how they managed that in the darkness, or where they hid the scaling ladders. I just know that suddenly I heard shouts all around that we were under attack, and they'd assaulted the walls."

"Where was Cailean?" Lyan asked.

Shiolto shook his head. "I don't know. He hadn't been on the walls the last time I'd looked, so I'd guess he was inside the keep, talking with his advisers. And after the mist rolled in, I don't know where anyone was until Dalrian stumbled into the stables. He'd been in the fighting, because he was hurt. He said he had orders from Lord Cailean to get all the horses we could saddled and ready. Wouldn't stay still long enough to bandage up his injury—he insisted it wasn't bad." Shiolto gave a thin smile. "My brother's always been stubborn like that. He helped saddle the horses. We grabbed our gear and headed into the courtyard. Ewart's men had taken the walls by then. We fought some in the courtyard too, but the fog helped us— they couldn't see through it any better than we could."

"You found Cailean?"

"Yeah, once we got into the keep, he was there. He looked exhausted, leaning on his spear. He must have gotten onto the walls at some point, or else been in the fighting in the rest of the keep. That was the first time I saw Yion—Lord Cailean explained quickly that we couldn't hold the keep against Ewart, and Yion would show us a way out. Nobody was happy about that. We arrived with the horses on the end of an argument between Lord Cailean and the captain of his troops. The captain didn't understand why we couldn't hold the keep." Shiolto paused. "Well, then a ball of fire tore a hole in one of the walls. Lord Cailean just looked at the captain and said, 'Because Ewart's army has magic.' The next ball of fire settled the matter—it took out a good part of the room." Shiolto shuddered. "I wasn't going to argue about running then."

"How many of Cailean's men—?" Lyan started to ask.

"I think…a third of us made it out of the keep, along with the servants and everyone," Shiolto answered. "It was so confused, all I know for sure is that I stuck close to Dalrian, and we both made it out. When Lord Cailean asked for a few volunteers to stay with him while the rest went into hiding, Dalrian and I both stepped forward."

"Where was Aikan? And Torqual?"

"Torqual would have been on the walls, I'm pretty sure. Aikan, I don't know. He was with Lord Cailean when we brought the horses, so I'd assume he stayed close to him. It would be pretty strange to see Lord Cailean without Aikan somewhere nearby."

Lyan nodded automatically. "I see. Thanks, Shiolto."

"I don't know if it helps answer whatever questions you have, Lyan. I wasn't in a spot to see much. Dalrian can probably tell you more, if you want."

Lyan nodded again. "All right."

The clouds began obscuring the stars while Cailean's home was under siege, and sometime after that, someone came to Ewart, then a fog or mist covered Cailean's keep, letting Ewart's men attack. Lyan thought on it. *Who came to Ewart's camp? The one who cursed Cailean? And what happened in the fog?*

Everywhere I look, all I find are more questions.

16

Black and white her hair
Soft and pure, so fair
Standing in silence so deep
Forever secrets to keep

The following days passed in relative peace. At first, everyone rode on edge, anticipating a new attack or another disaster. By the sixth day, they'd finally begun to relax. Lyan couldn't bring himself to feel at ease with Aikan, and the older Tathren alternated between ignoring Lyan and raining disdain on him. The rest of the men, however, treated Lyan as one of their own.

Dalrian often rode sentry during the days, and at camp, quarters were too close to have a private conversation without being obvious. Lyan could not find a good opportunity to ask Dalrian for his account of the attack on Cailean's keep. He kept his questions to himself rather than risk alerting the traitor—if there was one—that he suspected. And if Lyan was wrong, if none of them had betrayed Cailean, he certainly didn't want them to know his suspicions.

Sometime during the sixth day, the sensation of being

watched returned. Lyan was certain it wasn't the pooka and that the monster was still healing. That meant the watching eyes almost certainly belonged to Kithr. Lyan's gaze flickered over the forest, but he could not pick out one grim figure in browns against the trees.

Why are you still following me? Are you just waiting for some excuse to prove that you're right? Waiting for an excuse to kill my companions? Haven't you had enough Tathren blood? Or are you still hunting heads for your collection?

His hands clenched in fists around Shadowstar's reins. Years of pushing the images back had not softened the memory of Kithr's homecoming or the grisly trophies he had presented with such pride. Burying it had only left the memory to fester like an untreated sore, poisoning his friendship with Kithr.

I don't want your war, Kithr. Keep it away from me and my companions.

The forest was thinning noticeably when they stopped for the night. The thought of returning to civilized lands cheered the Tathrens. Lyan didn't like being without the shelter of trees, but even he would be glad to leave the Forests of Cossette behind.

Lyan swung from the saddle, then gasped in pain as the landing jarred through his ankle, sending pain stabbing up his leg.

Yion offered an arm to steady him. "Your injury troubles you? You have not favored your leg as much of late."

Lyan held to Yion's arm and Shadowstar's saddle as he caught his breath and balance. "I've been trying not to limp, but it still hurts. I think I made it worse when I ran from the pooka."

The mercenary nodded gravely. "You may have strained it. Do you have the means to tend it?"

Lyan gave a quick shake of his head. "I used the last of the oil our herbalist gave me."

"I am neither healer nor herbalist, but I know some small plant lore and also the brewing of teas that can dull pain." Yion made a quick gesture of apology. "Without dulling wits as well. But you would be wise to seek Shiolto's aid in tending your ankle. Also, use your crutch when you must walk."

"If I must," Lyan sighed reluctantly. His shoulder ached from the constant pressure of the crutch, and he would rather be done with the need for it.

"Patience," Yion chided gently. "You must heal, or you risk the chance that the ankle may never regain full strength and you will never be rid of crutch or cane." He lifted the crutch from Shadowstar's saddle and handed it to Lyan.

Lyan couldn't deny that easing the weight off his ankle lessened the ache. "Thank you." A glance around the camp showed the rest of the group occupied in preparing for the night. He lowered his voice. "Can I ask you something, Yion?"

"Ask, Lyan Stargazer."

"Why did you join Cailean? If you're a mercenary, it doesn't make sense to leave the side that was winning."

Yion smiled. "In the realm of men, I call myself a mercenary, yes. I hold no man as my liege, and I must claim some trade if I am not to be thought a brigand. So I follow the path of a blade for hire. But I have a lord, and to him alone have I sworn loyalty. I serve my god with all that I am and all I shall ever be. By his direction, I entered Ewart's army and used it as the means to reach Lord Cailean. By the will of my god, I left Ewart's forces and guided Lord Cailean in his escape. By his will, I remain in service to Lord Cailean."

"Then, if your god told you to, you would leave Cailean again?" Lyan asked.

"If such was his will, yes. I do not believe he will wish me to do so until Lord Cailean has completed his quest."

"What god do you follow, Yion?"

"My lord knows what Ewart seeks, and what Lord Cailean

carries. He knows the force that Ewart serves, and has sent me to ensure that Ewart's master does not succeed."

"But who is your god, Yion? What is his name?" Lyan pressed, unwilling to be placated with a vague non-answer.

Yion shook his head. "He does not wish me to reveal that, Lyan. I am sorry."

"Why not?" Lyan asked in irritated frustration.

"I do not know the answer, Lyan; I only know that he tells me this is not the right time." Yion paused a moment, then added gently, "He wishes you to know that he means it as no offense to you and no slight to your people, Lyan."

"I wasn't going to assume it was," Lyan said quickly. "Besides, I think it's just the Tathren gods that find my people an offense and an affront."

Yion paused a moment, considering his words. Then he seemed to discard whatever he had been about to say, and smiled instead. "My lord says that you will know him in the proper time. You have his interest, Lyan of Eilidh Wood."

Lyan gave Yion a thin smile. "I don't know if that should worry me or not."

"I am sure he does not wish the thought to trouble you." Yion smiled. "Sit and rest your ankle. I will care for Shadowstar."

Lyan relinquished the reins and limped toward the fire as his mind turned over the things Yion had said—and those Yion had *not* said. He stopped abruptly and turned back to the mercenary. Yion was unbuckling Shadowstar's saddle, and if Lyan's hasty return surprised him, his expression didn't reveal it.

"Do you need something from Shadowstar?" Yion asked.

"Are you a priest?" The question came out abrupt and rushed.

To that, Yion raised an eyebrow quizzically. "A priest? I am not. I fear I do not have the character to guide men in worship. I serve my lord in a role outside the ranks of his temples.”

“But he speaks to you. Directly to you,” Lyan said, daring Yion to contradict him.

“When it is needed, yes, he does,” Yion answered.

And he thought it was needed just to answer my questions to Yion? Lyan hesitated to voice the question.

“I know my answers do not satisfy, Lyan,” Yion said. “I trust that my lord will make his reasons clear when the time is right.”

“I hope so.” Lyan left Yion tending Shadowstar and limped again to the campfire.

When he settled beside the fire, Cailean gazed at him, then looked toward Yion. “Is everything all right?” His voice implied a fear that Yion had committed another offense against Lyan.

“Yion asked about my ankle,” Lyan answered.

Cailean’s tense shoulders relaxed. “You haven’t spoken to him much recently. I was concerned.”

Lyan shook his head. “He asked about my leg, then I remembered something I wanted to ask him.”

“How *is* your leg?” Shiolto cut in quickly before the opportunity passed.

“It hurts more than usual today,” Lyan admitted. “Do you know any ways to keep the swelling down?”

“I can try.” Shiolto shifted uncomfortably. “I took care of horses, though, not people.”

“You’ve done a fine job so far,” Cailean told him.

Shiolto looked at the ground and mumbled something about doing what he could.

“How are the rest of you?” Lyan asked, sensing Shiolto’s discomfort with the attention.

“Holding lofty dreams of a tavern, a bed, and perhaps a bath once we leave this forest,” Torqual announced, stretching. "Provided that anyone civilized lives on the far side of this gods-forsaken place."

Lyan bit his tongue, but Dalrian laughed and said the words Lyan restrained. "Torqual, if the gods had forsaken this forest, we wouldn't have seen that temple."

Torqual glowered at Dalrian. "Fine, forsaken by every god but the god of monsters."

"Does your map mark any towns, Lord Cailean?" Aikan asked.

Cailean unrolled his map. "It barely shows anything west of the Forests of Cossette. Chances are any small villages or hamlets wouldn't be marked anyway. With a little luck and some guidance from Cantorelle, we can find a road and figure out where we are from there. But I can't promise hot baths or roofs overhead." In a soft voice almost masked by the crackling fire, he added, "I can't even promise that we will find welcome."

"We'll make do with what we get, Lord Cailean," Dalrian said cheerily, not hearing the whispered words. "Dinner's ready."

Yion finished walking a circuit around the edge of camp and joined them around the campfire for dinner. Lyan ate, and thought, and wondered just how much he didn't know about his companions.

By morning, Lyan's ankle was swollen and tender. Shiolto wrapped a cool, damp cloth around it before helping Lyan ease his boot on.

"Try not to walk much if you can help it," Shiolto cautioned.

"I'll try," Lyan promised.

Late in the morning, Lyan caught distant echoes of axes on wood. The sound stirred melancholy in him. The elves of

Eilidh Wood felled trees from time to time as needed, but in his mind, the chop of axes into trees told of funerals, the bodies of elves returned to the forest and the ritual removal of the dead husk of their tree. Swallowing the apprehension that thought brought, Lyan reached into his bag and found the scarf he'd worn in the last town, before they'd entered the Forests of Cossette.

"I hear woodcutters," he said.

The humans looked around with new interest, though the sounds were barely on the edge of Lyan's hearing. "That's good news," Cailean said. "Speak up if you hear anything out of the ordinary."

By the time Lyan had accustomed to the sound and pushed aside his unease, his human companions could hear the distant thuds as well. A little after midday, they found a packed dirt trail, and before the sun had moved another handspan, they arrived at a cluster of seven houses grouped in a hamlet around a communal well. A child playing in the dirt stared at them wide-eyed, then scrambled into a house with a cry of "Papa!"

Cailean gestured for a halt. The horses snorted and stamped their hooves impatiently, sensing that this wasn't a place where they would find stables or fresh feed. A stout man stepped warily from the house, a woodcutter's axe in hand. He studied the mounted strangers, and didn't appear to be put at ease by what he saw.

"Good day," Cailean said in Trade.

The man gave a cautious nod in return. "Sir."

"What is the name of this village? And the nearest town?"

"We call it Redbark." The man gestured at the nearest trees, as if needing to explain the reason for a name that seemed obvious to Lyan. "Nearest town's Bessel-on-the-Ford, a good day's walk. Maybe less without a load for market." He pointed to the only road out of the village, running along the edge of the forest.

"Thank you." Cailean nodded to the man.

"You get lost in the forest? Happens to most who get too far from the edge."

"I imagine so," Cailean agreed. "Again, thank you."

The man continued to eye them all. "You didn't… come *through* the forest, did you? It's a terrible place, filled with all manner of vicious beasts and monsters. Nothing good ever comes out of the depths of that forest."

Cailean shook his head. "We thought to shorten our trip by cutting through the edge, but got turned around."

The lie put the man more at ease, and he relaxed his white-knuckled grip on the axe. "Aye, better to stay out of it altogether. We've lost good men, men who knew the forest, to its tricks. Strangers to it…" He shook his head. "You're lucky to have made it out."

Lyan wanted to ask why the man stayed here if he disliked and distrusted the forest so much, but held his tongue, seeing that his companions didn't act as if the idea were strange. Cailean didn't linger in Redbark, heading for the road. Once they left sight of the village and the sounds of axes had faded again, he consulted the map.

"Bessel-on-the-Ford…" He scanned the parchment carefully, then shook his head. "Not on the map. I need to find someone who knows these lands or can give me a map of them."

"It will make your tale that we only cut through the edge of the forest less credible if you begin asking after maps, Lord Cailean," Aikan cautioned.

"I know. But the way that peasant acted about the idea of anyone going through the forest, I wasn't going to tell him the truth. Further from the forest, it might be less of an issue."

"If he dislikes the forest so much, why does he live there?" Lyan asked.

Aikan's expression said he thought the question foolish. "Where would you suggest he go, if he left his livelihood?

Another village, to do the same thing? Or become an outlaw, until the lord of the land hunts him down like an animal and leaves his body at a crossroad as an example?"

"Oh." Lyan had no other response.

"He won't leave," Cailean said. "But I wouldn't be surprised if some of the 'good men' who he says were 'lost to the forest' were young men who decided to take their chances and find a new life. Do the elves of Eilidh Wood leave their homes and trades?"

"Sometimes, but not often," Lyan said. "We're apprenticed into trades by our aptitudes and interests."

"But how do you keep enough people doing all the jobs that need done?" Shiolto asked in disbelief. "You can't let everyone go around doing whatever they want! That's just chaos." He waved a hand in the air. "If everyone wants to be a warrior, who's going to take care of the horses, or plant the fields, or… or anything else?"

"We don't keep animals, and we don't plant fields," Lyan told him. "The village elders guide us in finding the best uses of our skills. They also see to it that we have the right number of people where they are needed, and that we don't have too many. Sometimes that means you can't follow your first choice, or you have to live in another village where your skills are needed more." Lyan scowled. "It's certainly not chaos."

"It must work well enough for your people," Cailean allowed. "In Tather, most peasant families can't afford to lose a child to some other trade—they need all the hands they can get to continue their own work."

"I see."

"Many never travel further than a day's walk from their home villages in their life," Cailean continued. "And for the most part, they seem content with their lives."

As if they would tell a nobleman if they weren't. Lyan looked over his shoulder as the forest thinned. Even if the humans didn't like the Forests of Cossette, he would miss their shelter, in spite of the monsters that lived within their shadows.

The land remained thinly wooded, though the area around the road was cleared. Lyan kept waiting for the edge of the forest—some firm, solid demarcation of the end, but it didn't come. Unlike Eilidh Wood, the Forests of Cossette were casual about borders, never clearly indicating where the forest ended and the lands beyond began. The group rode at a good pace, and Lyan learned that a group on horses apparently moved quite a bit faster than a man on foot transporting wood to the market. As evening drew close, they came in sight of a town on the bank of a river.

A guard stood at the edge of the road, watching them. "It's late for traveling, strangers."

Cailean nodded. "I hoped we would make it to town in time to find a room and a little dinner."

The guard nodded, gesturing behind him. "You can find that easily enough. You must be strangers to the area. It's not safe to be out at night. There's no telling what will come out of the forest to prey on honest folks."

"A man in one of the hamlets said something similar, about monsters in the forest?" Cailean said.

The guard nodded grimly. "Those poor bastards have to live with that hanging over their heads every day. You best get in and find the inn—no one with sense wants to be out after dark in these parts."

"Thanks." Cailean rode past the guard, who considered each member of their group as they entered the town. The man's gaze lingered on Lyan for a long moment, but stayed equally long on Yion.

"No mention of the forest, if you can help it," Cailean said quietly. "I don't want to attract that sort of attention."

"Yes, Lord Cailean," the Tathrens answered. Lyan nodded silently. He didn't want to find out what sort of attention an elf would receive, either.

The innkeeper expressed surprise at their late arrival, but welcomed the seven travelers. Cailean haggled briefly over the price for room and dinner, settling on a total that satisfied both him and the innkeeper. The evening's collection of patrons had already gathered in the common room. The travelers received curious study when they settled at a table. Shiolto, Dalrian, and Torqual took it upon themselves to mingle with the locals once they'd eaten, perfectly at ease.

A pair of men paused, looking at Lyan, then Yion. "You aren't from around here."

Yion smiled pleasantly. "We are not. I have been hired as a guard to my companion," he nodded toward Lyan, "a traveling scholar."

They looked at Lyan again. "Oh, you're one of those sorts who goes around collecting old stories and such?"

"There's much more to lore than just old stories," Lyan responded, tone mildly chastising. "And there's value to them that should not be ignored." From the corner of his eye, he saw Cailean biting his lip in a valiant effort not to laugh.

"Uh, yeah. Didn't mean any offense," the man said quickly. "I don't know much about that sort of thing—that's for folks with more time and coin than me. You won't find much around here unless you're looking for stories about the forest. You'd have better luck if you head to Dremsen. There's plenty of bookish sorts there, I've heard." The men edged back, fearing they would be caught in a lecture if they lingered.

"Thank you. I'll bear that in mind," Lyan said. "Before you go, though…"

"Uh, yes?"

"Would you know of anyone with a map of the area I might be able to purchase? I find such things useful when explaining the origins of the tales I gather in my travels."

"A map? Well, you might ask my wife's pa, Old Man

Crann. He used to travel a lot, if half his stories are true. Four houses down, look for the painted door."

"Again, thank you."

The two men retreated to the bar. Cailean tried to smother a laugh into a cough. Lyan gave him a questioning look. "What?"

"Sorry," Cailean managed. "Gods, Lyan, I swear you sounded exactly like my tutor would when I wasn't paying attention to his lessons."

"Meaning that it is a tone Lord Cailean is well familiar with from his youth," Aikan said dryly.

Lyan smiled, and let the scholarly tones leave his voice. "Since Yion brought it up, it seemed as good a way as any to ask about maps."

The mercenary nodded. "Traveling scholars are reputed to be odd. It defused suspicion, and I have confidence in Lyan's ability to play the role as needed."

"We'll find out about the map in the morning." Cailean yawned. "I don't know about the rest of you, but I am not going to waste a chance to sleep in a bed tonight."

When Cailean and Aikan climbed the stairs, Lyan followed. The sleeping area was divided into two rooms, one for men and the other for women. A row of beds lined the wall, offering no illusion of privacy. Without complaint, Lyan picked a bed, lay down, and fell asleep.

The morning sun hung just over the horizon when Lyan, accompanied by Cailean and Yion, found the house he'd been directed to the previous night. The design on the door was meant, he though, to be a stylized dragon. Or maybe a bear. The wobbling and jagged lines hinted that an unsteady hand painted the image. Lyan knocked, and heard the shuffle of steps. An older man with thick white hair opened the door and blinked at him.

"Yes? Can I help you?"

"A pair of men at the inn last night told me you might have a map I could buy," Lyan began.

The old man's face warmed with a smile. "Ah, yes, I heard about the traveling scholar. Come in, come in." He waved Lyan, Yion, and Cailean inside.

Lyan felt at home immediately. Scrolls littered the table, and one sagging shelf struggled to hold the books piled on it. The air smelled of dust and parchment, reminding him of his teacher's home, where he had learned astrology.

The old man shuffled some parchments aside to clear space on the table. "Most people around here call me Old Man Crann. I'm no bard, but I'll tell stories when asked."

"My name is Lyan. I've heard you used to travel?"

Crann nodded. "When I was younger. So, you're here to learn about the forest? Or going further?"

"We're heading further west," Lyan told him.

"Further west? You likely heard all the interesting stories about the forest while you've been moving around the edge. I say mosta those stories are utter nonsense. Lotta folk don't care for the place, and make up wild stories to justify themselves. They don't know how to respect the forest or when to leave well enough alone."

"You're not afraid of the forest?" Lyan asked.

"She has her secrets, and it's no business of mine to pry into them. I respect her, and she doesn't bother me. It's simple enough." Crann searched the parchments, finally making a sound of triumph. He unrolled a scroll on the table. "Here it is."

Lyan stood across the table from Crann, looking at the map. The old man rested a gnarled finger on a town. "Here's Bessel-on-the-Ford. Villages aren't marked; they come and go. This road heads to the capital, but if you're going west, you want the other road, here." His finger moved with his words. "Follow it to get to Riedol, or take the south fork at the river if you're bound for Joski. Been years since I gone to either country, but I hear the folk there are decent sorts."

Lyan nodded, studying the map. "But you did travel through those lands?"

Crann chuckled. "When I was young and foolish." He jabbed a point on the map along the border of the countries. "Now here's a story I wager you haven't heard before. No one much lives in these parts, and I got it in my head that the forest and the foothills would make a good spot for a fellow to hide things they didn't want found. Didn't have treasure of my own, mind you, but figured if I could find someone else's… well, I could make myself a rich man. I'd been there a while, and hadn't seen a soul in days. Was walking along a deer track, when suddenly, everything went quiet. I looked around, but didn't see a damned thing, like even the birds had vanished. But I saw a trail I would swear hadn't been there before. I followed it, every step knowing something watched me. For all my looking, though, I never saw a thing, or heard any sound other than my own steps—not even wind in the trees." Crann shivered. "I remember that unnatural silence to this day. All along the trail stood little markers, white stone as high as my knee. The top of each was shaped like a lantern, but there were no lights inside. They looked old, but they weren't worn by weather—can't say why I thought them old. The trail went on and on, don't know how far. Then it just… ended at a gate in a wall of white stone. The growth around the wall was so thick I couldn't have gone around if I'd tried. As I walked up to that gate, I swear to you, a woman appeared out of nowhere.

"She was the most beautiful creature I've ever seen, with smooth, pale skin. Long black hair flowed over her shoulders, with white streaks running through it at the crown of her head. Brown eyes, not a line or blemish on her face, that woman. An elf. She asked who I was, and I couldn't have lied if I'd wanted to. But when I told her my name, she just shook her head.

"'This place is not for you,' she said. 'You aren't worthy to enter this gate.' I tried to argue, but she wouldn't say anything more, except to tell me to leave. I tried to see past that gate, even a glimpse, but I couldn't. I did as she said and turned to leave."

Lyan listened intently in silence.

"I heard a noise behind me, and turned to look. For a moment, I saw a huge black bear with white marks on its face." Crann shook his head. "Next thing I knew, I stood alone, no gate, no path anywhere to be found. I followed my tracks to try to find the spot again, but…" He shook his head again.

"You couldn't find it?" Lyan asked.

"Not a trace. But I swear it's true." Crann scowled fiercely, daring any of them to argue.

Lyan looked at the map. "And you saw this somewhere over here?"

"That's where I was. If that's where this gate was, or if I got caught in some fairy ring and whisked away into their realm.…" The old man shook his head. "All I know is I never found it again. And believe me, I looked! I'll never forget that woman." He let out a long sigh, eyes distant. Finally he rolled the map. "Take this. I won't need it anymore. But if you're going to try to find her, good luck."

Lyan took the map from Crann's trembling hand. "Thank you. Allow me to pay—"

"No, I don't want your money. It's a gift for indulging an old man in his storytelling."

"Thank you." Lyan bowed. "You're very kind. I'm afraid we can't stay."

Crann nodded and waved them toward the door. "Aye, of course. Can't expect young folks like you to listen to me ramble all day. Come back some time, I'll tell you another story."

Lyan's mind whirled as he walked outside. *Could this old man have stumbled on the hiding place of Equinox?*

He almost walked into a woman who was approaching the house. Yion caught his arm and pulled him out of the way before they collided. Lyan stumbled and blinked, wincing as pain stabbed through his ankle. "I'm sorry. Please excuse me."

The woman looked at him. "You're that traveling scholar, aren't you? My husband mentioned he'd met you last night." She looked past them to Crann's house. "I suppose you've been listening to my father's stories, whatever wild tales he told this time. Did he tell you the one about the mysterious elf woman in the forest?"

"Um… yes," Lyan managed in response.

She sighed. "He acts like it's his story. It's not, you know, though he's probably got himself convinced that it is by now. Some traveler came through telling that wild story, and Father adopted it as his own. But you go to any town in these parts, and you'll find some old man who'll tell a version of it."

"How similar are the stories?" Lyan asked immediately.

She shrugged. "Always some path they never saw before, to white gates or walls, and always some elf woman whose beauty they've never seen before or since."

"I see," Lyan said quietly. "Thank you."

"Well, Father's always happier when someone listens to his stories, so thank you, too."

As they walked back to the inn, Cailean said, "I missed something in all that. Why did that story interest you so much, Lyan?"

Lyan started, surprised that Cailean would ask the question. "If that story is true, whether this old man saw it or someone else did…" Lyan shook his head. "The place he described matches everything I know of the place we're looking for, Cailean."

Cailean stopped. "Are you sure, Lyan?"

He reminded himself that Cailean's research on Equinox had been severely limited. "I'm sure. And an elf, Cailean. He saw an elven woman. Why would an elf be so far from Eilidh Wood?"

"That woman said this same story is told by people all over this region."

Lyan nodded. "If the stories were different, then it could be chance, or someone taking a wild tale and adapting it. But they share certain things, as that woman said. *Someone* found this place, once. They spread the tale, but that doesn't mean it isn't true." He was suddenly eager to be on the trail again. "It means we're getting closer." *We really are going the right way. Doesn't Cailean see that, and understand how important this is?*

"If that is the place, all we have to do is reach it alive," Cailean murmured.

Lyan didn't have a chance to decide whether or not to respond. They reached the inn, where the rest of the group waited impatiently.

"Find what you wanted?" Shiolto asked Lyan.

He smiled. "Yes. It was a good stop." He handed the map to Cailean.

The Tathren lord slipped the map into the scroll case with the other one. "Is everything packed?"

Agreement met the question, and Cailean nodded in satisfaction. "Then let's go."

17

Black wings, black birds
Black arrows, red blood

Lyan's thoughts flew far ahead of the horses, toward lands not yet even a shadow on the horizon. He wanted to urge Shadowstar to a gallop, as if they could defy all logic and reach the Shrine of Equinox in a single day. Sensing his rider's excitement, Shadowstar kept a quick walk, head held proud and high.

Lyan's eyes drifted up to the sky while his mind conjured images. He envisioned walls of thick growth lining a narrow path through a forest, as Crann had described. White stone markers lined the path, their tops hollow and a peaked cover resting over the opening. At night, elven glow-lights would shine from within, illuminating the path. At the path's end, a gate stood. Its metal latticework wove in the patterns of thorny rose vines, and an inner door blocked the view of anything beyond the wall and the gate. Lyan tried to picture the woman Crann had described, but his imagination caught a different image from the story, and added a black bear with white markings to stand before the gate.

Lyan frowned, trying without success to dismiss the animal from the scene. *That's the bear I saw in the forest when I was running from the pooka. I'm certain those ruins were not home to Equinox or its shrine, so why am I thinking about that bear?*

"Lyan. Lyan!" Shiolto said in amused exasperation.

"Huh? What?" Lyan started from his thoughts and turned.

"You haven't heard a word I've said, have you?" Shiolto shook his head with a chuckle.

Lyan's face flushed red. "Sorry." He'd been peripherally aware of Shiolto's voice, but hadn't been listening. "What were you saying?"

The young man waved a hand in easy dismissal. "Nothing important. Did that fellow you visited tell a good story?"

Lyan nodded. "He did. A story that points us in the right direction."

"Are we close?" Shiolto's eyes moved over the land as if the Shrine would appear before them at any moment.

"Not as close as I'd like," Lyan told him. "Did you learn anything last night?" Shiolto might well have already told him, but he hadn't been listening. Now that he returned from his daydreaming, Lyan grew aware of how thin the trees had become, and the open space left him feeling exposed and vulnerable. He glanced up at the sky again, then forced his attention to Shiolto as a distraction from his unease.

"Three new drinking songs, a few stories about the forest, and all the gossip about the mayor's daughter running off with a fellow from another town." Shiolto grinned. "That's the big news in town."

"Don't forget the part where some say the fellow was really a forest spirit who seduced her," Dalrian chimed in.

"Or an elf," Torqual added.

"An elf?" Lyan repeated, startled.

"They don't even know what an elf looks like," Shiolto laughed. "I'm pretty sure you weren't out seducing human girls, and I haven't seen any other elves around."

"Um… no, I haven't been seducing anyone," Lyan said, fumbling for words. "We don't tend to leave Eilidh Wood without good reason. Do they really think an elf abducted the girl?"

Torqual laughed. "Most folk think the mayor put that story out in a vain effort to save face. It looks bad to admit his daughter ran off and eloped."

Lyan blinked. "Why?"

"Tarnishes the family name, implies he can't manage his own house. Don't elves ever have matches that parents think are a mistake?" Torqual asked. He seemed honestly interested in the answer.

"Sometimes," Lyan acknowledged. "But if they are old enough to marry, and the Elder doesn't forbid it, they can marry. And if they later find that they cannot live together, they can petition the Elder, who will help them find common ground. If even that fails, he can grant them a separation. That is rare, though," Lyan answered.

"Huh. I'd hope you'd think about it first if you're going to be living with someone for hundreds of years," Torqual commented.

"So would I," Lyan agreed.

Cailean and Aikan rode at the end of the group, hanging back and speaking quietly. Lyan turned his attention away from the banter between Dalrian, Shiolto, and Torqual to try to catch their conversation.

Aikan's voice held concern. "…enough to purchase supplies?"

"Yes, we should," Cailean answered, but his tone held less confidence than his words.

"We still have to return home, my lord," Aikan cautioned.

"I know. I *know*, Aikan. But we needed to make that stop. We're all better for the rest. I'll be careful. We'll have enough, even if it means we don't sleep in beds again until we reach home."

Cailean is a lord, but he's far from home and his funds aren't endless. Lyan wished he could ease even that weight from Cailean, but he had no goods of value to offer for trade, and astrology was useless under the perpetual night clouds.

"The map?" Aikan asked

"A gift. The old man gave it to Lyan."

Silence for a time, then Aikan spoke again, quietly enough that Lyan strained to head him. "Lord Cailean, there is something else I must ask you."

"Ask," Cailean said.

"My lord... is it true that you have been cursed in some way connected to Solstice?"

Cailean drew a short, sharp breath. "What did you say? Who said—Lyan."

"We were... exchanging unpleasantries in the fog, Lord Cailean, and he spoke of it while speaking of trust and lies," Aikan said.

Cailean was silent for a long moment. "I don't want to talk about this, Aikan."

"My lord, this is..."

"I said I don't want to talk about it, and *that* is no lie!" Cailean said sharply.

Lyan felt Cailean's eyes on him, and didn't turn, pretending he hadn't heard the hushed conversation.

Afternoon shadows were growing long when Cailean called a halt. He had said little since the conversation with Aikan, but while his men set camp, Cailean motioned for Lyan to follow him. "A word with you please, Lyan."

Lyan felt anxiety knot in his gut, but limped after Cailean a little way from the rest of the humans. Cailean's jaw was tight and his body tense when he faced Lyan.

"Why did you tell Aikan about the curse?" he demanded in a low, angry voice.

Lyan didn't pretend surprise, or ask how Cailean knew he had heard their conversation. He drew a deep breath and held

Cailean's gaze. "Because I'm not willing to accept the blame for the actions of your enemies, Cailean. What Aikan said to you is the extent of what I said to him."

"Aikan blamed *you*?" Cailean repeated, eyes narrowing.

"He accused me of enspelling and deceiving you, as that was the best explanation he saw for the actions you refuse to explain to him." Lyan's voice was flat.

"Mad God's Pits!" Cailean rubbed his temples. "Aikan is determined to distrust you."

"Yes, he is," Lyan agreed. "I will not tell your secrets to your men, Cailean, but I will defend myself."

Cailean's jaw tightened again, but he answered with a short, sharp nod before turning and walking back to the camp.

By luck or the guidance of the gods, Torqual snared rabbits for their dinner. They were lean, but Shiolto accepted them gladly and set to making stew.

"Don't get caught poaching," Cailean warned.

"They're rabbits, Lord Cailean, not deer. Most aren't going to miss a few rabbits."

"True enough," Cailean allowed. "But be careful."

"Can I see the map, Cailean?" Lyan asked while Shiolto fussed over the stew.

Cailean gave him a long, silent look, then nodded. "Of course." He retrieved it from his scroll case and handed the parchment to Lyan.

Lyan studied the map, fixing it in his mind and picking the route that looked best. "We should keep to the roads for now. That'll be faster."

"*Now* you think we should follow the road instead of wandering through wild forests," Aikan grumbled.

"In spite of everything, going through the Forests of Cossette got us here at least half a month faster than going around would have," Lyan responded.

"And it served to delay the pooka from our trail," Yion added. "A benefit not to be trivialized."

Aikan snorted and said nothing more on the matter.

Cailean looked at the map. "Whichever route you think best, Lyan."

Lyan looked up at him in surprise. He couldn't read Cailean's expression or his tone. *Is he angry at me for telling Aikan about the curse? If he is, why is he letting me decide our route?* Lyan pointed at the road they followed. "We should stay on this road for a few more days, at least." He rolled the map up again and returned it to Cailean.

If Cailean held any lingering displeasure at Lyan, he didn't show it in the morning. The overall mood was pleasant and relaxed. A breeze teased wisps of clouds in the sky, drawing idle patterns. Lyan watched them, thoughts wandering. His attention only nominally stayed on the ride and the road, though he did listen for any words directed toward him.

The road wound through a thicker patch of trees, limiting Lyan's view of the sky. Shadowstar snorted uneasily, and Lyan patted the stallion's neck.

Shadowstar abruptly reared up, whinnying a challenge and catching Lyan unprepared. He tumbled from the saddle and hit the ground hard, knocking the wind from him. He kept wits enough to curl and shield his head with his arms. Shadowstar danced around him, trying to avoid stepping on him, but the other horses crowded close, adding more hooves to threaten him. One clipped Lyan's arm, sending pain tearing up the limb. Shouts, muffled by the ringing in his ears, were too chaotic to understand. Shadowstar lunged away from him, giving Lyan enough space to struggle up.

"Get up! Lyan, get up!" Cailean shouted.

Fighting for breath and trying to clear his pounding head,

Lyan staggered onto his feet. The horses moved and shifted on every side, blocking his view.

An unfamiliar voice ordered, "Take the elf and the one with the spear. Kill the rest."

The words startled Lyan into clarity. Unknown, armed men were locked in combat with his companions. Shadowstar kicked a man who drew too close, but most men avoided the riderless horse and focused on their targets.

Lyan fumbled over the strap securing his hunting knife in the sheath, fingers damp with sweat and clumsy with fear. The movement of the horses raised clouds of dust to sting Lyan's eyes and clog his nose. Someone grabbed his arm. Lyan jerked his knife free and swung wildly. The blade glanced off the man's thick leather jerkin, and the assailant seized Lyan's wrist, twisting his arm. Lyan felt the knife slipping from his grip, and kicked with his good leg, fear dulling the pain of resting his full weight on his injured ankle. His foot connected with the man's knee, and something gave with a sickening crunch. The man screamed and released Lyan, falling back.

A glimpse of movement to the side made Lyan spin around, knife clutched in a sweaty hand. Yion, dismounted, fought two men. A third lay in the dirt at his feet, staining the ground red. The mercenary wielded a blade in either hand, and moved more like a man dancing than fighting.

"Lyan, stay close!" Yion called.

He stumbled toward Yion, but one of the horses backed between them, whinnying in fear. He glimpsed Torqual fighting to control his mount, then Lyan was dodging away from lashing hooves. He stumbled over a stone and fell. Even as he tried to rise, something slammed into Lyan, knocking him back down. He struggled to get out from under the weight.

A hand roughly jerked him to his feet. Lyan had a moment to realize that he didn't recognize the man holding him, then a fist slammed into his stomach. Lyan doubled over, gasping for air. The knife slid from his grip as he was dragged back, too breathless to call for help. He struggled against the hands holding him as they pinned his arms.

The grip released abruptly and the man staggered, hands rising to his neck to grab at the arrow jutting through his throat. Gurgling, the man collapsed. Lyan stumbled forward several steps, coughing and fighting for air. Another arrow intercepted the next man to rush for Lyan, and the assailant fell with barely a cry, a raven-feathered shaft quivering in his eye. Lyan lifted his head. His eyes raked the trees, but he couldn't pick out one grim figure in brown leathers against the trunks of the trees. Lyan scrabbled in the dirt, fingers finally finding the hilt of his knife. He snatched it up and turned back to his companions.

Only Cailean and Dalrian remained mounted. Lyan saw a man coming up behind Yion, and stumbled to intercept the attack, barely feeling the pain in his ankle. His knife deflected the striking blade with a ring of metal on metal and a flash of sparks. The impact vibrated through Lyan's arm and numbed his fingers. Before the attacker could turn to face Lyan, an arrow took the man in the neck. Even in the fighting, Lyan had to admire the skill that went into each precise strike.

"Withdraw!" The order came with no hints of panic, and the ambushers obeyed, disengaging from battle and retreating without a word.

"Lyan, are you all right?" Shiolto rushed toward him.

Lyan heard the hum of the bowstring, and shoved Shiolto aside. The arrow sank into his left arm, and his breath hissed between his teeth.

Fury boiled in his blood. Lyan panted for breath, glare fixed on the trees. "Get...out...here..." he demanded.

Kithr stepped from the trees, bow in hand. He held an arrow at the string, but loosely, pointed at the ground. His eyes met Lyan's. "That was not meant for you, Lyan."

"How dare you...." Lyan stalked toward him, dropping

the knife as his hands clenched into fists. "How dare you, Kithr?"

Kithr's eyes narrowed. "I gave your Tathrens a chance to prove they could keep you safe. They failed. That was a warning. I wouldn't have killed your 'friend'."

Lyan threw all his strength behind the punch. It connected solidly with Kithr's jaw. Kithr staggered back, momentarily dazed. "You have no right!" Lyan shouted.

Kithr raised an arm, taking some of the force of Lyan's next swing. Before he could take a third, someone dragged Lyan back from Kithr. Lyan struggled, and Kithr tensed as if to attack, but Cailean simply said, "Enough, Lyan."

Lyan jerked from Cailean's hold, and Cailean let him go. Lyan glared at Kithr. "You have *no* right to attack my companions, Kithr!"

Kithr spat. "You're welcome for saving your hide again."

"I. Do. Not. Need. Your. Help." Lyan panted for breath. Sweat dripped down his face, and pain pushed through his anger. "Not when your 'help' includes taking aim at anyone *else* who comes to my aid, Tathren or not. Especially not when you take aim at my friends."

He wavered a moment, and Cailean steadied him. "Lyan, sit down." When Lyan shook his head, Cailean pushed, and Lyan found himself on the ground despite his objection.

Kithr stood in silence. His gaze moved from Lyan to the humans.

"Shiolto, care for Lyan," Cailean ordered. He kept one wary eye on Kithr, but only added, "And get a cold rag for his friend."

"Kithr is—" Lyan began.

Cailean's hard look silenced. "He *is* your friend, Lyan. Believe me, whether you think it or not right now, he is."

Kithr glared at Cailean. "I don't need any help from *you*, Tathren. If you harm Lyan, I will kill you."

Lyan's lip curled in anger. "Funny, I don't think Cailean is the one who just put an arrow in my arm."

"You're not the first to tell me that, and I doubt you'll be the last," Cailean answered Kithr, ignoring Lyan's words. "Dalrian, Torqual, clean up this mess. We're stopping here."

Shadows of the past
Ghosts yet to be left behind

Lyan bit his lip hard enough to taste blood, and still couldn't stop a cry of pain as Shiolto extracted the arrow.

"Sorry," Shiolto said quickly, pressing a bandage against the wound. "Hold this."

Lyan held the bandage while the Tathren found something from his pack. "There's nothing for you to be sorry for. *You* didn't loose the arrow."

Shiolto cast a look across the hasty camp, where Kithr glowered at all of them and held a wet rag to his jaw. "Lyan, it was an accident. He was trying to protect you, and erred on the side of caution."

Lyan's fierce, angry look silenced Shiolto. "Don't talk to me about Kithr. Just…don't."

Shiolto glanced away and fell silent. He finished bandaging Lyan's arm, then moved toward Kithr. Kithr's eyes narrowed on the Tathren. Shiolto drew bandages and a handful of herbs from his pack and set them on a stump.

"You're welcome to use those if you need anything."

Kithr didn't reply, but his head moved in a slight nod of acknowledgment. Lyan shot Kithr a dark look and turned his back, rubbing his arm.

"That will not help," Yion told him.

"What won't?" Lyan snapped, looking up. He always expected Yion to be taller than he actually was, and his eyes rested first on the mercenary's black hair before shifting down to meet Yion's gaze.

"Your arm. That will not help, it will only aggravate the wound. It should be allowed rest to heal. Are you hurt otherwise?"

Lyan let his hand fall. "Bruised. You?"

"I have once again escaped serious injury. Our enemies were less fortunate." Yion gestured toward lumps of dirt off the road where he and Dalrian had dug shallow graves and buried the dead. The bare dirt cut a sharp contrast against the carpet of undergrowth and moss covering the ground.

Cailean and Aikan stood aside from the rest, speaking in low voices. Lyan didn't have to hear the words to know Aikan was angry. Cailean didn't raise his voice, and appeared calm about the problem, whatever it was.

Me, no doubt. Aikan is always angry about me.

Finally Cailean shook his head firmly in answer to Aikan. With an angry scowl, the older man turned and walked to the horses. Lyan waited for Cailean to give the word that it was time to ride on. Cailean looked at Lyan, then cast a glance around the area. His gaze settled on Kithr for a long moment. Kithr returned the look with a challenge in his eyes before continuing to clean his weapons and check the fletching of his arrows with exaggerated care.

As Cailean walked toward Lyan, Kithr tensed, eyes narrowing for all that he pretended not to be watching Lyan just as much as Lyan pretended not to be watching him.

Cailean paused beside Lyan. "Can I talk to you for a moment?"

Lyan nodded, shifting his gaze away from Kithr to Cailean. "Of course."

He walked with Cailean to the edge of the trees, where the growth half hid them from sight of Kithr or the rest of the party. Cailean spoke in a low voice, studying Lyan's face. "What's this about, Lyan?"

Lyan's jaw tightened. "What's what about?"

"You know full well what, and who, I mean. Your friend, the one who demonstrated his archery skill at our first meeting by using a spot on a tree an arrow's breadth from my head for target practice. The one who just saved all of our lives, who you're now glaring daggers at. The one who has probably been following us since we left your village."

"The one who was about to send an arrow at Shiolto?" Lyan responded sharply. "Kithr. I didn't ask him to follow me, and I don't need him trying to play nursemaid! If he has something to say, he can say it. If not, he can leave me alone."

"And would you listen to what he might say?" Cailean countered. "I don't blame him for staying where he is when venom all but drips from your glares at him."

"I don't need his help!"

Cailean's hand flashed out, and the slap stung across Lyan's face. "You don't need his help? Well, the rest of us could use it, Lyan! I swore I would tell you the truth. The *truth* is that we could well be dead or captured without his intervention. I saw one of those men dragging you off. Where would *you* be right now without the help you claim not to need? Are you, as you say, an elf older than my grandfather, or are you a spoiled child throwing a tantrum?"

Lyan stared at him, one hand rising to his red cheek. "I am not--"

"Yes, that is exactly what you are acting like, Lyan. I don't know what problem lies between you two, but right now, it doesn't matter to me." Cailean rested his hands on Lyan's shoulders. "This has nothing to do with any lack of skills on your part. You have invaluable knowledge I could never hope to match. Your friend is a warrior, and without that, we're not likely to *reach* our destination so you *can* put your knowledge to use. Tathren, mercenary, elf… I'm in no position to reject any help I can get right now, Lyan. If that damned *pooka* came and offered its help, and if I had some way to guarantee its trustworthiness, I'd accept it. I *cannot* afford to turn away potential allies if we're going to survive. But I can't invite your friend to join us. He would refuse me. He didn't leave his home or follow the descendants of his enemies for *my* sake. Do you understand, Lyan? He isn't here and he didn't save our lives for the sake of me or my men. He's here because of you."

Lyan's jaw tightened. He looked beyond Cailean at the trees. "I didn't ask him to follow me."

"Would you have if you'd wanted to?" Cailean asked. "You dig in your heels like a stubborn bull, Lyan. But you're no warrior. I know that, and so does your friend. He doesn't know me or my men, he doesn't know what we might do, and he knows you don't have the skills to stop six men if we decided to do you harm. I know you want to prove yourself. Believe me, Lyan, I've seen it among my own men often enough to recognize it in you. But this isn't the place for bull-headed stubbornness. Prove yourself by using the knowledge I know you have and the quick wit I've seen. Recognize which fights you should face alone, and which would be better with a friend at your back. A friend who cares enough about you to leave his home when doing so can hold little but dark memories for him. I can't ask your friend to help us, Lyan. Only you can... and you must decide whether or not you will."

Cailean waited a moment for Lyan to respond. When Lyan said nothing, the Tathren gave his shoulder a pat and walked back to his men. Lyan sat down and stared blankly into the trees. Finally he yielded to instincts and turned his eyes up to the deep blue sky. No answers came to him from the heavens, only the patterns of leaves reaching up toward the sun.

A spoiled child. Have I been acting like one? He recalled the fight, remembering his fear, remembering being unable to do anything, not even protect himself. The sound of Kithr's arrows striking home, the overwhelming relief that had filled him when he knew he would be safe. *Kithr rescued me, and I couldn't show him gratitude. Would I have thanked him even if he hadn't loosed an arrow at Shiolto? Or would I have been too selfish, too proud, too certain he was patronizing me to see that without him, I could have been captured, and my companions could be dead?*

Lyan didn't like the answer he found to that question.

Only after some time did he realize he didn't hear the impatient jingles of harnesses or shuffling of feet that told him it was time to stop his distracted skygazing and resume riding. Looking over his shoulder, Lyan saw that Cailean and his men had set up camp. Something cooked over the small fire. Usually their midday meals were small and cold, comprised of dried meat and hard, stale bread eaten at a brief break or in the saddle. Lyan levered to his feet and limped to the fire. His ankle throbbed angrily, aggravated by the day's rough treatment. Shiolto jumped to his feet and offered Lyan an arm. Lyan forced a smile, but shook his head.

"I'll manage. Thank you."

"All right, if you're sure." Shiolto stayed close until Lyan reached the fire.

Dalrian gave him a small smile. "We found some supplies on the men, and one had a nice hank of smoked pork." He nodded at the meat on the skewer.

Lyan looked past the camp, and saw that Kithr now sat silently on a rock, chewing on a strip of tough dried meat. Across the fire, Cailean watched Lyan as if to judge what effect his earlier words might have had, then followed Lyan's gaze. "We'd invite him to join us, but I have the feeling I'd end up with the plate thrown back in my face if I tried."

Lyan bit his lip, then sighed. "Would you give me two plates?"

"No." Yion carved slices of meat and arranged them in trenchers, but didn't hand them to Lyan. "I will bring them to you."

Lyan didn't argue. He limped toward Kithr. Yion followed and set the trenchers beside Kithr's rock. Kithr's eyes silently followed the mercenary. Yion inclined his head in a small nod of greeting, then returned to the fire.

Kithr pushed to his feet, standing eye-to-eye with Lyan and braced for another assault. "These Tathren magpies are untrustworthy fools. I don't care what you think or say; I will not leave you at their mercy." The words came in rushed Elven, intended to cut off Lyan before he had a chance to lash out, whether with words or fists.

Lyan winced as he sat on the grass, and he pulled the earring from his ear, turning the low murmur of voices from Cailean and his men to gibberish. "Could you pass me a plate, Kithr?"

Kithr blinked, then sat and handed him one of the trenchers. Lyan picked out a chunk of meat with his fingers and chewed on it to give himself a moment before he spoke. "I'm sorry, Kithr. Thank you for your help. I should have said that earlier."

Kithr stared at him, at a loss for words. He'd expected another attack—thanks caught him unprepared. "I…"

Lyan chewed and swallowed another bite, then continued. "You have good reasons to worry about me, I know. And knowing what sort of mess we're in, I'm glad to have a friend guarding my back."

Kithr collected his wits. "Someone has to! And don't tell me *they* will." He jerked a hand toward the Tathrens.

"No, they'll be guarding my front, since I have trouble doing that too," Lyan responded mildly.

The second, longer pause from Kithr said he was uncertain what direction this conversation was going, especially after Lyan's earlier outrage. "I don't trust them, Lyan. I don't know what they're planning or where they are going."

"I do," Lyan said. "You might as well eat—the meat isn't going to kill you, and if you were eating the jerky from last winter, the leather of your belt would be easier to chew."

Kithr did take his trencher, though he frowned at it. "I have no desire to eat food brought me by a Tathren."

"Yion isn't Tathren, he's a mercenary. I don't know where he's from."

Kithr frowned at Lyan. "You trust a *mercenary*? That's worse than trusting a Tathren. Where is it you think your lordling is going?"

Lyan hesitated. "You won't like the answer, Kithr. But if I trust too much, then I have to trust you as well, and tell you. His name is Cailean, and he is searching for Equinox."

"*What?*" Kithr jerked to his feet. "By what right does he think to claim Equinox? Some Tathren noble already holds Solstice! You would see *both* in their hands?! Why? So the gods can send us to war again?" He spat. "If they do, at least we'll have a name. The gods didn't see fit to give us one last time, leaving their people in a foreign land to slaughter any man, woman, or child to find the Spear."

Lyan flinched. "No, Kithr, no more of that. This isn't the start of a new war between Eilidh Wood and Tather." He drew a deep breath. "Solstice is the reason Cailean is here. The Spear isn't held by 'some Tathren noble.' It is held by the Dev'gilla family. Such as Cailean Dev'gilla."

Kithr stiffened, looking toward Cailean. "*He* bears…"

"The spear on the bag you brought into my house when the Tathrens arrived, Kithr? That was Solstice. This isn't about Tathrens and elves! Cailean's enemy is hunting for the Spears, and if *he* can claim either one, much less both, the results would be more destruction than anything our people unleashed on Tather. This enemy sent the pooka as one of his minions to stop Cailean. This enemy has the power to completely shroud the night sky and deny me the sight of the stars, Kithr!" Lyan raised his hands in helpless gesture toward the sky. "I'm useless as an astrologer when I can't see the skies. If finding Equinox will help to defeat him and clear the sky..."

"This entire time, you've been traveling in the company of the Tathren Spearbearer, and you *knew* it?" Kithr demanded.

Lyan nodded.

"And you *knew* he was looking for Equinox. You know better than anyone why no mortal should..." Kithr trailed off, eyes widening in sudden understanding. "Of course you do. *This* is why you insisted you had a responsibility to join them. To make sure he doesn't claim Equinox. It is, isn't it?"

Lyan nodded again.

"Fire and rot, Lyan, why didn't you *tell* me?"

Lyan shifted uneasily. "I didn't want you to do something rash like try to kill Cailean."

Kithr opened his mouth indignantly, stopped, and finally found a tight, thin smile. "Not unreasonable, I suppose." He finally took a bite of meat. "So what was your plan?"

"Cailean promised he won't try to claim Equinox for himself, even though he needs *someone* who can use Equinox's powers to help him against his enemy. He asked my help because I know more about Equinox than he does. Maybe more than anyone in Tather does. I intend to hold him to his promise, and..." He stopped, swallowing hard. "And do whatever I must to be sure he doesn't break that promise."

Kithr gazed him gravely. "Lyan, if you had to, do you think you could kill him?"

Lyan looked at his hands. "I don't know, Kithr. I do think... I do think if I had to try, Cailean wouldn't expect an attack from me. I might be able to. I wouldn't be able to stop his men from killing me afterwards, though."

Kithr considered that in silence. To Lyan's relief, his next question changed the topic slightly. "So why would Cailean's enemy hide the stars? How are the stars tied to the Spear?"

"The Shrine of Equinox is hidden," Lyan answered, gladly seizing hold of a familiar and more comfortable topic. "There are supposed to be several ways to find the path to it, but the one mentioned the most in writings is a riddle hidden in the stars. Cailean's enemy hid the night sky to keep anyone from finding the Shrine before he does."

Kithr frowned again. "So we're traveling blind?" He eyed Lyan. "Or do you already know where we're going?"

"Cailean does as well," Lyan protested. "I solved it a long time ago. Or at least I think I did. When I was still an apprentice, I told Monterr how much I wished I could have gone with you and the rest of the muster from our village. He gave me a book about Equinox and its last bearer. The book also talked about the signs in the stars, how they would tell the path and show the way for the next bearer of the Spear. Anyway, I used that and the stars... it was a challenge, but a good one... What is it, Kithr?"

"Repeat that part about 'showing the way for the next bearer'," Kithr said quietly.

Lyan gave him a puzzled look. "That's how the book put it, that 'the signs in the stars will reveal the way for the next Spearbearer to find Equinox'."

"Lyan..." Kithr just looked at him, and Lyan shifted uncomfortably under that intense scrutiny, not sure what Kithr found so significant. But Kithr bit back whatever he was about to say, and instead said, "You should tell your Tathren friend where we're going, then."

Lyan frowned. "What do you mean? Cailean knows—he must know. He's led us this far."

"No, he doesn't. I'm certain. I've been following you this

long, and I've been watching all of them. He believes you know where this group needs to go, and he's careful to watch you whenever the question of route comes up. He's changed direction several times when the path he or his men suggested didn't agree with the one you thought they should take. He seems to have some clues, but nothing more steady than a faint rabbit trail got him as far as Eilidh Wood. He doesn't know where he's going, but he isn't willing to admit that weakness."

"But... You mean... Do you mean this path we're following is entirely my choosing? What if I'm wrong, Kithr?"

"Then he's no worse off than he would have been without you, Lyan. Just a little older. And if you're right, then..." Kithr let his voice trail off.

Cailean doesn't know where we're going. I'm the only one who does. He said I have invaluable knowledge. Does anyone else realize the truth? Is this why Aikan resents me, because I know what Cailean doesn't? He looked at Kithr. *I know where we're going, but I don't have the skills to protect myself. I... need help.*

"Will you help us, Kithr? I don't mean... just me. I mean them too—at least to be civil to them." And, not without some of his earlier anger, he added, "And not let arrows fly at them."

Kithr flinched, and he looked at the bandage on Lyan's arm. "How bad?"

Lyan shook his head. "It could be worse." As if to counter him, pain stabbed through his arm as he shifted the trencher between hands.

"Lyan..." Kithr sighed. "Lyan, I'm sorry. I was wrong. But for what you ask..." His jaw tightened, and he studied each man around the fire. They sensed his gaze, for conversation ceased and they looked toward Kithr. Only Cailean and Yion met Kithr's eyes without flinching away, but their gazes were steady and even. "You'd do better to leave them behind and find the Spear yourself," Kithr said. "But if you won't do that... fine. It's no longer a secret that I'm here, and they should have the sense to know I'm not here for their sakes. I won't taint myself with their company any longer than I have to. But I'll be here all the same. I made you a promise that I would protect you, or did you forget?"

"That was a long time ago," Lyan said. "Even before the war."

Kithr scowled at him. "And? I made a promise; I'm not going to back down from it."

Lyan smiled. "You're as stubborn as I am. But all the same, I'll be more at ease knowing you're watching, whether or not anyone else sees you. However, I'd at least like to introduce you to 'my' Tathrens and assure them that they will only be catching your arrows in their bodies if they turn traitor."

Kithr helped Lyan up. "For no one else would I do this, Lyan. For *no* one else would I let the Tathren Spearbearer live." The cold hate in his voice added weight to his words.

"I know," Lyan said quietly. There was little else he could say.

19

The path to seek
The road to find
Strength to the weak
And those left behind

"Kithr, this is Cailean Dev'gilla, Spearbearer of Solstice," Lyan said, trying to portray calm he didn't feel, standing between his childhood friend and his present companions.

Stiff and tense, Kithr gazed for a long moment at Solstice before turning his eyes to Cailean himself. His head moved in a tight jerk of acknowledgment.

Lyan tensely awaited an outburst from Aikan at the lack of courtesy, but the older man wisely said nothing. To Lyan's greater relief, Kithr and Aikan simply exchanged silent glowers as Lyan continued the introductions. Dalrian and Shiolto received the briefest acknowledgments, while Torqual earned a slightly longer consideration and a nod. Kithr studied Yion with brows furrowing in a frown. He spoke to Lyan in Elven.

"He's not Tathren."

"I told you that earlier," Lyan answered in the same. "And you've been spying on them."

"You did, and I have. But I didn't get a good look at him until now, and thought you were wrong. Something about him feels Tathren, but he's certainly not one by birth."

"He never told me where he's from. But I trust him," Lyan said.

"Bah." Kithr shook his head. "You trust all of them."

"Not *all* of them." Lyan didn't look at Aikan.

"Good." Kithr turned to Cailean and spoke in Tathren. "There, we've met. Enough of the day wasted." The words came harshly from his mouth, proclaiming loathing to even speak the language of his enemies.

"If you and Lyan are ready, we'll press on," Cailean replied, offering no reaction to Kithr's spite.

"Good." Kithr shouldered his bow and strode toward the trees. "I'll be near."

"Kithr. Do you have a mount?" Lyan asked, for the first time wondering how Kithr had kept up with them.

"Ohrlan gave me one," Kithr told him. "With his blessings and relief that you would not be alone with... strangers." With a significant look at the Tathrens, he vanished into the shadows.

The heavy tension eased slightly. With Kithr out of sight, Lyan's companions could pretend, for a little while, that he was gone entirely. Lyan shifted uncomfortably, knowing that if Kithr changed his mind and attacked, the concealment would be far more to his advantage than to the Tathrens'.

Shiolto led Shadowstar to Lyan, thought he did walk so Shadowstar stood between him and the direction Kithr had gone. "Do you need help, Lyan?" He gestured at Lyan's bandaged arm.

"I can manage," Lyan answered. "Thank you."

Shadowstar gazed at Lyan, then knelt unasked. Lyan smiled wryly as he settled into the saddle. "I would have been fine," he told the stallion, patting Shadowstar's neck in the thanks his words didn't offer.

A quiet that was neither calm nor peaceful hung over the group as they rode. Lyan tried not to search the shadows as his companions did. They all knew Kithr followed them, and picking him out from cover would gain nothing but Kithr's ire.

For the first mile, no one rode too close to Lyan. Before the isolation could grow too fierce, though, Cailean's horse stepped up to walk beside Shadowstar. Lyan turned to the Tathren lord. "Thank you."

Cailean interpreted the words as a reference to their earlier conversation. "I only told you what you already knew, Lyan."

"Maybe," Lyan said. "But I wouldn't have listened if Kithr had said the same things."

"Don't make a habit of it. Gods know something is wrong when a Tathren lord has to play peacemaker between two elves of Eilidh Wood." Cailean smiled.

Lyan laughed softly with dark humor. "I know." *Especially when one of those elves sought to kill your ancestor for possession of the Spear you guard.*

"Did you tell him where we're going?"

"I told him why we're going there," Lyan said. "And who you are."

Cailean grimaced. "The look in his eyes told me what he thought of *that.*"

Lyan lowered his voice. "Cailean, *do* you know where the Shrine of Equinox is?"

Cailean's long hesitation was answer in itself. "No, I don't. I know you've assumed I know where we're going, and I've let that misconception continue even when deciding our route. Even Aikan believes it, and wonders why I always follow the suggestions you offer. The truth is, Lyan, once we crossed the plains, we reached the limit of my knowledge of the Shrine's location." A thin smile. "Your friend noticed, I assume?"

"His name is Kithr."

"My apologies. Kithr brought it up?"

"He did, and said I should tell you where we're going."

"He said that?" Cailean's eyebrows rose in surprise. "Do *you* think you should? Knowing that I haven't solved any great mysteries, do you think you should just give the answer to a Tathren who stumbled this far by the gods' fortune and blind luck?"

Lyan smiled faintly. "Does Solstice give you the power to read minds, Cailean?"

"I don't know, Lyan. It would cost too much for me to find out. But I know that if our positions were reversed, and I held such knowledge of an artifact sacred to my people, I would hesitate to tell anyone, even someone I trust."

"Then you'll understand if I don't tell you," Lyan said.

"I understand." Cailean's mouth quirked in a half-grin. "Though if you're willing to share a general idea of our direction, I won't object."

Lyan nodded seriously. "Tonight, when we make camp, if Kithr will join us. I'll give both of you an idea of which way we need to go."

"Thank you."

The rest of the day passed without incident. Once camp was set, Kithr appeared and scowled his way around it. If he found it wanting in any way other than the presence of Tathrens, he chose not to mention the faults, finally sitting with a glare that challenged anyone to object. The Tathrens, for the most part, pretended not to notice him, though Dalrian kept a suspicious eye on him, and Shiolto avoided him.

After dinner, Lyan asked Cailean for the map and motioned for Cailean and Kithr to join him. Kithr scowled at the Tathren lord and positioned himself where he could keep an eye on Cailean and the camp while looking at the map.

"What's this about, Lyan?" Kithr asked.

"I'm following your advice, to a point." Lyan pitched his voice low to keep their conversation as private as possible in the camp. "It will be safer if I'm not the only one with an idea of where we are going."

"So you're going to tell him," Kithr said.

"No," Cailean responded. "Lyan isn't going to tell us where Equinox is hidden."

Kithr frowned.

"If the Shrine is hidden, it's hidden for good reason," Cailean continued. "Lyan has solved the riddle. He knows where the Spear is, but I have not earned that knowledge for myself as he has. Perhaps you have as well, but if that's true, you don't need him to tell you. The meanings of the signs are beyond my skill."

"The stars are Lyan's craft, not mine." Kithr's gaze shifted to Lyan. "What *are* you going to tell us, then?"

Lyan tapped the map. "We are about here, by my guess. We need to continue west toward the border. The road leads through several towns and a larger city, but I think we should avoid them."

"Why?" Cailean asked.

To lessen the chance that Kithr will kill anyone. "The more people who see us, the more who can say which way we went," Lyan answered. "But if you disagree, I'll listen."

Cailean grimaced. "You're right. Though I worry about supplies. We have little time to forage."

"Who's chasing you?" Kithr interrupted.

"Since the end of the war, Tather has fluctuated between uneasy peace and civil war—" Cailean began.

Kithr cut him off. "If Tathrens spent less time talking and more time acting, they could solve that. Simple questions, simple answers. I'm not here to listen to you jabber like a magpie."

"My late father's cousin, Ewart Col'renn, sent them. He serves another lord, and ultimately, Murdo."

Kithr's eyes narrowed at the Mad God's name. "How does he find you?"

"I don't know. Perhaps through magic."

"You don't use Solstice to shield yourself?" Kithr frowned. "The last Bearer did. Otherwise, we would have scryed him out and hunted him down."

"I can't explain my reasons for not using the Spear," Cailean said stiffly. "Lyan can, and since he likely will with or without my leave to do so, he has it."

Kithr raised an eyebrow at Lyan, who kept his answer as short as Kithr preferred, though the sting of Cailean's barb tempted him to elaborate. "A curse on Cailean."

Kithr snorted in scorn. "A Spearbearer who can't use his Spear. How useful."

"If I could, I wouldn't need to find Equinox," Cailean countered flatly.

Lyan cleared his throat pointedly. "Do you want to bicker, or do you want to listen?"

Kithr chose not to answer. Cailean focused on the map. "So we continue west? Old Man Crann mentioned the borderlands between Riedol and Joski. Is that right, or was his location off?"

"That direction, though he was wrong about the specifics," Lyan answered.

Cailean measured distance with a finger. "Half a month more, approximately?"

"That seems a good estimate," Lyan agreed. "What's the state of your funds and supplies, Cailean?"

"Assuming Yion doesn't insist I start paying him, we avoid most places where we can spend money, continue to camp rather than find inns, and can hunt and scavenge for food… I should be able to stretch what I have far enough."

"Left in a hurry without preparing for a long trip," Kithr remarked.

"Ewart attacked," Cailean said, starting to understand what Kithr meant by simple and short answers.

Kithr grunted. "Your men hunt well enough. I hunt. We'll find food." He stood, brushing off his pants. "Anything else?"

Lyan shook his head. "Not for now."

"Good. I'm going to sleep."

Wherever Kithr slept, it was not in the camp. He returned in the morning and dropped a handful of freshly picked plants beside Dalrian. "Put those in the pot tonight. It'll taste better."

"Thanks…" Dalrian eyed the herbs dubiously, but packed them with the supplies, deciding Kithr wouldn't intentionally poison the communal meal.

Kithr kept his contributions and conversations, such as they were, brief, and vanished once the day's ride began. Isolation crept over Lyan to fill the absence. Kithr was near, but didn't want to associate with the Tathrens long enough to ride with them during the day. His presence, however, reminded Cailean and his men that not all elves were as friendly as Lyan. Kithr reminded them of the tales they knew of the war. Lyan sensed their reactions in the hesitations to speak to him, the sense of distance growing between them and him.

He was relieved when Dalrian walked his horse beside Lyan's, and greeted him with a smile. "How's your arm, Lyan?"

Lyan moved his bandaged arm experimentally. "Sore and tender, but it's not troubling me too much if I keep it still."

"Good, glad to hear that." Dalrian paused, his expression growing serious. "Thank you."

"For what?" Lyan asked.

Dalrian hesitated. "Whatever reason was behind it, that

arrow was meant for my brother. You took it for him. I…we owe you for that. Thank you. I'm in your debt. We're just poor men, and don't have much to offer, but if there's anything Shiolto or I can do, Lyan.…"

"Thank you, Dalrian."

"I know Shiolto doesn't blame Kithr. My brother can forgive anyone."

"But you do not," Lyan finished.

Dalrian gave Lyan a thin smile. "I know he's your friend, so… I'll try. But it was more pleasant riding when I didn't know someone was watching my back with a thought to put an arrow between my shoulders."

The words seemed to sum up the mood of the Tathrens. Aikan shot glares at Lyan, holding him responsible for the present situation, but even he showed more caution than outright hostility.

"Do not let it trouble you too much, Lyan," Yion said.

Lyan jumped, turning to the mercenary and wondering when he had taken Dalrian's place. "What?"

"The shift in the mood. Do not let it weigh upon you. As we and your friend adjust to the change, tension will ease."

"I'm that easy to read?" Lyan asked.

"I have been watching you, and am coming to recognize your moods," Yion said.

"I wish Kithr could do so as easily," Lyan muttered.

"Familiarity breeds complacency," Yion told him. "And perhaps you as well are too familiar with him, and do not easily recognize when he does take notice."

Lyan shifted uncomfortably and said nothing. Yion let the matter rest.

Tension eased only slightly over the next two days. They left the road behind as it turned southward, and soon rode once again through wooded lands. Kithr remained aloof, though his contributions to the food pot, both in meat and edible plants, added welcome variety to their meals. Lyan guiltily wished he could add to their provisions as easily, but in Eilidh Wood, his sustenance had been provided by the gifts brought by the rest of the village when he read fortunes for them. Kithr had attempted to take Lyan hunting at times, but usually gave up in frustration when Lyan managed to scare off all the game by distracted skygazing and careless steps.

Even as the tension within the group lessened minutely, Lyan's own anxieties revived. The sense of being followed returned. He never saw anything he could identify, and if the unseen presence belonged to the pooka, it did not announce its presence to Lyan. At times, he thought he saw a hunched humanoid shape crouched in the shadows from the corner of his eye, but when he looked, he saw only a stump, or a strangely shaped patch of brush.

Lyan caught Kithr before his friend withdrew to his separate camp. "Kithr, have you noticed anything following us?"

Kithr frowned. "No. I'd have told you if I had. What do you sense?"

He'd expected Kithr to dismiss his concerns and tell him that he was imagining things, but Kithr gazed at him with serious intensity. Lyan hesitated, then spoke. "It might be the pooka, but I'm not sure. The pooka usually whispers to me if it's near. I thought I saw something crouched in the brush earlier, but...I could have been wrong. It was gone when I looked again."

"Inconvenient that your Tathren friend can't use Solstice to find out," Kithr said.

"He didn't ask to be cursed, Kithr," Lyan responded.

Kithr waved a hand derisively, dismissing Cailean and all Tathrens as he did not dismiss Lyan's concerns. "I'll keep my eyes open. Don't leave the camp alone. Not for any reason. Is that clear?"

"Very clear," Lyan said quietly. "Be careful, Kithr."

"Watch your back." With those words, Kithr left the camp.

~

As they rode the next day, Lyan caught occasional glimpses of Kithr, or heard the muted strike of hoof beats. Kithr's presence did nothing to dispel the sense of the other lurker trailing them. If anything, it grew stronger, until Lyan found himself searching every shadow.

"Lyan?" Cailean asked.

"We're being followed." Lyan's eyes raked the undergrowth.

The Tathrens drew weapons. Cailean's expression darkened. "I'm tired of this—it needs to end *now*. I want to know who, what, where they are. Kithr, are you here?"

"Yes." The cool voice spoke from the trees.

"Take Lyan with you. Aikan, with me. Dalrian and Shiolto together, and Yion with Torqual. Keep together, and call out the moment you find anything. Whatever is there, I want it *found*."

Shadowstar made straight for Kithr, even before Kithr emerged from shelter. His friend waited for Lyan to join him.

"I haven't seen tracks or signs yet, Lyan. They're good, who or whatever they are." His tone held every confidence that Lyan's gut feeling was correct, despite the lack of evidence. Kithr checked the directions the Tathrens split to search. "The watcher must know we're aware of him now. If I were him, I'd move ahead of our group and lie low until we give up the search."

"All right." Lyan waited for Kithr to lead.

Shadowstar moved with a silence Lyan could rarely match

on foot. Kithr dismounted and tied his horse to a branch, searching the ground for tracks. As they moved between the trees, Lyan, on Shadowstar's back, couldn't resist an impulse to look to the sky, as if the blue glow of the heavens could reveal what the shrouded stars could not. He drew a sharp, startled breath.

Kithr turned sharply to him. "What?"

"I saw it. It's not leaving tracks because it's not on the ground, Kithr. It's moving between the trees." He'd only glimpsed the form, but it bounded from slender branch to branch with inhuman ease, balancing on tree limbs he would have sworn were too thin to support it.

Ahead, a branch snapped and something fell to the ground with a crash. Kithr pulled his bow into hand and ran toward the sound. Lyan sprang after him, dismounting when the spindly trees crowded too closely together for Shadowstar to navigate. He scrambled after Kithr. A hunched humanoid shape, dark and ragged, bolted away from them, shaking off the rough landing from its fall. Kithr loosed an arrow, but the other darted aside. Cursing, Kithr pursued, Lyan on his heels.

Something isn't right.

Lyan grabbed Kithr's arm and jerked him to a halt as Kithr's leg hit the trip cord stretched across their path. Something snapped, triggered by the pressure on the rope, but the snare was hastily constructed, and only one side of the net fell from above, missing them.

Kithr spat a curse, looking ahead. He spun Lyan around and all but dragged him back the way they'd come at a run as men emerged from hiding.

A trap. That thing led us into a trap.

Oh shit.

2 0

Fire light, fire bright,
Burning ever through the night

Pain stabbed through Lyan's ankle as he ran alongside Kithr. His heart pounded and he saved his breath rather than ask questions Kithr could no more answer than he could: who, why, how. The ambushers cursed and called to each other, but Lyan couldn't make sense of the words.

Something hit his legs, tangling around them. Lyan fell face-first to the ground. He tried desperately to kick loose of the encumbrance as he spat pine needles and twisted around to see what had hit him.

Three cords with weighted ends wrapped his legs. Lyan's hands shook and his injured arm added its protests as he freed himself and staggered to his feet.

Kithr grabbed for his arm to pull him back into motion, but jerked aside to dodge another set of weighted cords. Something hit Lyan in the back, driving the wind from him and knocking him to his knees.

Traps, ropes to tangle us. No arrows, no blades. They want to capture, not kill. The thought flashed through his mind as he heard the pounding steps of the ambushers closing on him. With all the breath he had, Lyan called, "Kithr! Go!"

Rough hands seized Lyan before he could draw his knife. He kicked and struggled as they pinned him to the ground. A man grunted when Lyan's foot connected with his stomach.

Another voice spoke. "This is the right one? You're sure?"

"Red hair. Yessss." The last word came out in a reptilian hiss.

"The other elf?"

"Unnecessary."

Lyan heard fighting, heard Kithr's enraged shout. He twisted against the men holding him and shouted in Elven, "Kithr! Find Cailean! Find help!"

One ambusher pressed a cloth over Lyan's nose and mouth. Lyan tried to turn away as a pungent, cloying smell filled his senses. His vision swam, then darkness claimed him.

Lyan's mouth was as dry as an empty streambed in midsummer, and his eyes stung with grit. Every muscle ached. When he peeled open his eyes, Lyan saw only darkness. Hot, stuffy air filled his lungs, and coarse cloth hung over his face, rough against his skin. He shook his head to dislodge the obstruction, and instantly regretted the movement. Pain flared to life as spots danced across his vision and blood pounded in his ears. He closed his eyes with a moan that came out muffled. Lyan's parched tongue found a piece of cloth in his mouth, secured so he couldn't spit it out. Fog and pain numbed his thoughts, and the meaning of his maladies eluded his understanding.

Voices drifted through his awareness. "…coming around?"

"Maybe. Think…pretty foggy. How much…use?"

"Enough. Used enough. Never know what tricks…damn elves…Keep him quiet. You saw…whatever he said… other one went berserk."

"Let's move out."

Lyan was lifting roughly, drawing another moan of pain as

his head pounded. He tried to move, but his limbs wouldn't obey his hazy instructions. He was flung over something, and when it shifted under him, his mind fuzzily identified it as a horse. He lay on his stomach across the horse's back, and someone secured his hands and feet to hold him on. His stomach lurched unhappily and Lyan fought nausea.

Leather creaked and metal jingled as someone swung into the saddle, then the horse began moving. The initial walk didn't jostle Lyan too badly, but the animal stepped up to a trot, jarring through his bones with every step. Time passed in a blur of pain and pounding in his skull.

Eventually, the horse stopped and Lyan was dragged down. He tried to move, his thoughts starting to clear despite the throbbing headache. Coarse ropes bound his ankles, and before he could think to pull away, someone tied his hands behind his back. A hood covered his head. Lyan tried to shake the thick cloth away from his nose, but each breath seemed to pull it back. The gag muffled anything he might say even if his mouth had found enough moisture for speech.

He tried to jerk free when his captors dragged him across the ground. They left him sitting against a tree to twist ineffectually at his bonds. Lyan heard the crackle of a fire. The light cast patterns across his hood. He heard at least five horses, maybe more.

"So, this is the elf? Somewhat disappointing—the stories make them sound far more impressive." The coolly amused male voice spoke from across the fire, and Lyan turned toward it. The inflections were similar to Cailean's, and the language was Tathren, but the man's tone was harsher, less cultured.

"The other one was more like the stories, sir—fought like a rabid animal. But Thyis said this one's the one you want." A pause. "We lost Bron to the other elf. Lev and Torr are injured."

Lyan steeled himself to listen and not react. *Kithr. I heard fighting, and I told him to find Cailean. What happened? Was he captured as well?*

"I hope you put down the rabid animal properly," the first man said coolly.

"Of course, sir."

The euphemisms didn't hide the meaning of the words from Lyan. *No. I won't believe that. They couldn't have killed Kithr.*

"Good. Take off the hood. Let's see the elf."

Steps rustled across the grass toward him, then someone jerked the hood away. Lyan drew in a deep breath of fresh air and fixed a glare on the man across the fire from him.

The human's hair, black or dark brown, was cut short and neatly trimmed. A short, pointed beard accentuated the angles of his face, sharpening his features. The firelight glittered in his eyes, and Lyan couldn't guess their color. His clothes were plain, but even in the flickering light, Lyan could tell they were better made than those worn by most brigands. He smiled grimly at Lyan.

"Here we are. Do you understand me, elf?"

Lyan continued to glare silently.

"Mrynn, bring water."

Another man handed him a water skin, but the bearded man shook his head. "To the elf. There's no one near enough to hear him."

"Are you sure, sir?" the man asked. "What about elf magic?"

The bearded man just fixed a pointed look on his underling. Mrynn grunted reluctantly and tugged the gag down from Lyan's mouth. Lyan warily looked from the bearded man to the water skin held to his lips. Thirst won over caution or anger, and he drank.

"My men took no chances once they had you, but I know that drug has an unpleasant way of leaving the victim parched. That's enough, Mrynn."

The water skin was pulled away. Lyan swallowed the last gulp and glowered at the human.

"I have some simple questions, for which your answers will earn you more water. Straightforward enough, I should think. Do you understand me?"

Lyan commanded the earring not to translate his words as he spoke in Elven. "What do you think, ignorant dog?" His words slurred, but he found his voice.

The man turned to another, who bowed and joined him at the fire. "Jaist?"

"I couldn't catch all of that, sir. I believe, though, that he called you an uneducated mongrel."

"Insults already? I see." The man considered, then spoke in Trade. "I said, do you understand me, elf?"

Lyan responded in Rakkonic, an obscure, nearly dead language. "Does your translator understand me *now*?"

"Jaist?"

The translator smiled wryly. "Sir, I don't even know what language that *was*, much less what he said."

"So you do understand us, don't you, elf."

"Sir?" Jaist asked.

"Why would he have answered in a different language if he didn't know you understood when he spoke his own?"

Lyan swore silently, seeing his mistake in the twists of the Tathren's logic.

"So, do we keep playing this game, or are you going to answer me, elf?"

Lyan gave him a wordless glare.

"You really ought to. You see, I have reason to keep you alive. You know something that I want to know. But at the same time, I only have reason to keep you *alive*—keeping you whole is not required. So long as you have eyes, ears, and tongue, the rest is, in the end, extraneous. Fingers, toes, hands...." His gaze met Lyan's, deadly serious. "Do you understand me?"

Lyan read no bluff in those words or on the man's face. He let the earring translate his answer into Trade. "I have answered you twice already. The fault isn't mine if you didn't understand."

"That may be. But I happen to be the undereducated human in the position to say whether or not you are fed, whether or not you can see and speak, and whether or not you are tortured. Consider the benefits of not exploring the limits of my patience."

"And who is this undereducated human who's abducted and now threatens me?" Lyan shot back. *Kithr would be attacking him by now, bonds or not. But Kithr might be… no. Kithr isn't dead, whatever these men think. He will find me.*

"I am Vynzent Col'renn of Tather. I don't expect you to have heard of me, nor do I expect you to use titles; I understand your people put little value in such things."

"At least as far as Tathren nobility goes, no," Lyan said sharply.

"Yet you've been traveling with a Tathren noble, and knowing how stuck on titles his steward is, you couldn't have avoided knowing that Cailean is one," Vynzent responded. "I don't know how Cailean tolerates the insufferable ass."

"Your point?" Lyan's eyes narrowed.

"Cailean is using you to find the lost Spear, Equinox. You know where Equinox will be found."

Lyan stiffened, shifting positions and twisting at his bonds. His lips pressed into a thin line and he said nothing. His fingers were numb, and the ropes bit into his skin.

Vynzent watched him like a bird studying its prey. "You know where to find Equinox," he repeated in a low, dangerous voice. "My spy has been watching you leading my cousin about."

"Cousin," Lyan repeated, cold, hard dread sinking into his gut. "Your father is Ewart."

Vynzent raised an eyebrow. "You're smarter than you look, elf. He is—or so I've been told."

"And you want the Spear for him."

The Tathren's face hardened sharply in anger. "My father will be the *first* I spit upon the Spear's head."

That was not the answer Lyan expected. His mind raced. Could Vynzent somehow be convinced to help them? "Then why Equinox? What do you want with the Spear?"

Vynzent laughed sharply. "Are you testing me, elf? Trying to determine if I am 'worthy' of the Spear, when *you* are *my* prisoner?" He leaned closer to the fire, letting the light dance across his face and add further menace to his cold smile. "My reasons are no business of yours. All you need do is answer my questions."

"You think I would let *you* claim the Spear of *my* people?" Lyan asked coldly, putting aside the thought of trying to sway this man to Cailean's side. "When you will not even tell me your purpose? You have no right, no claim; you've done nothing to solve the riddle or earn the knowledge of Equinox."

"Mrynn."

The man standing to Lyan's side moved, and a heavy foot slammed into Lyan's side. He doubled over with a cry of pain. The man grabbed Lyan's hair and pulled him back upright.

Vynzent shook his head. "I don't expect to have all the answers in one night. Gag and hood him again. We'll move out in the morning."

Lyan tried to turn away when the gag was tied back in place. His guards showed no hesitation to cuff him hard enough to leave his ears ringing in order to stop Lyan's struggles, such as they were. Once they had him gagged and hooded, the men shoved Lyan roughly to the ground and left him. As the fire died down, evening chill crept through his clothes. He curled up and closed his eyes.

~

Morning came as something of a relief. Cold and uncomfortable as Lyan was, sleep had come in snatches. He listened to the humans moving around the camp and building the fire. The warmth finally chased away the shivers that had run through him during the night. Vynzent gave brief, cryptic orders, and Lyan listened, wondering what the instructions meant. Most seemed no more than a word or a name, then someone moving. Lyan smelled food cooking, reminding him that he hadn't eaten.

"This bowl, sir?" a man asked.

"Yes. Take care of it," Vynzent ordered.

Lyan groaned stiffly when rough hands dragged him to a sitting position. Hood then gag were removed and a spoonful of porridge was shoved into his mouth while his eyes struggled to adjust to the light.

"Let me feed myself," he snapped after the first spoonful.

"And free your hands? No, I think not," Vynzent responded. "Eat, elf."

So you expect me to lead you to Equinox, but can't be bothered to learn my name?

After he'd been fed the last of the porridge, the gag and hood returned, and Lyan found himself once more lying across a horse's back. His stomach churned unhappily, but the horses kept to a fast walk, less jarring on his body. Hazy numbness settled over Lyan, and the day passed in and out of a daze in which he slept, or nearly slept. He remembered being let down to the ground once and unbound to relieve himself, but his thoughts remained muddled, leaving him wondering if he'd only dreamed doing so.

By the time they stopped, his head had cleared enough for Lyan to wonder what drug Vynzent had put in his food. Lyan's feet were unbound before he was pulled from the horse, and he stumbled unsteadily in the hold of two captors.

They dragged him to a tree and shoved him back against it. Lyan kicked at the men and was rewarded by a cry of pain and cursing in Tathren.

"Hold him!" someone snapped.

Hands seized Lyan, and he twisted and jerked away from them, kicking at sounds and his best guesses of where his captors stood. Men cursed and swore, hitting him in return. From the cursing and the blows, Lyan guessed it took three of the humans to finally pin him long enough to untie his wrists, twist his arms around the back of the tree trunk, and bind them again. Pain stabbed through his injured arm at the rough treatment. Lyan cursed at them through the gag, struggling.

"The sedative has worn off, sir," someone said unnecessarily.

"So I see," Vynzent replied dryly. "Secure his feet."

The men were prepared for his struggles, and Lyan was exhausted. He still fought, but they had less trouble restraining him and binding his ankles to the tree trunk.

"Well, that was more like the stories I've heard of elves. Don't be surprised if he bites." Vynzent sounded almost amused.

Lyan snarled and strained against his bonds. *Elf or human, you expect anyone to submit to this quietly?*

They left him alone, still gagged and hooded, while setting up camp. Lyan listened. He raised his guess as to the number of men to ten or twelve. Vynzent issued an occasional order, brief words that meant something to his men but not to Lyan. Lyan shifted, testing his bonds, but the ropes bit tightly into his skin. His head throbbed and new bruises were forming from the blows.

Steps approached, then the hood was pulled off. Vynzent stood before Lyan, and met his glare evenly. Lyan resisted the impulse to bite when Vynzent untied the gag—the Tathren would both expect and anticipate the reaction. He'd already said as much. Instead, Lyan looked around the camp, trying to determine where they were. The firelight hindered his night vision, but a few trees sheltered the camp. He couldn't see any other lights in the growing darkness, and the landscape was lost in shadows.

"Where are you taking me?" Lyan demanded.

"We're following an approximation of the route you were leading Cailean. However, you must say if it's the right way to continue."

"If you're so determined to find Equinox, solve the riddle yourself."

"That is difficult these days," Vynzent replied, "with the clouds hiding the night sky. This 'uneducated human' had begun working on it before the skies were hidden."

Did you? How? Cailean barely knew that a riddle existed, much less how to solve it. Where did you learn things he could not?

"So." Vynzent gazed into Lyan's eyes. "How far do we follow this path? To the border lands? Beyond?"

"Follow it as long as you want. You won't find the Spear."

"So stubborn," Vynzent sighed. He unlaced Lyan's shirt, keeping a watchful eye on Lyan should his prisoner try to bite.

Lyan jerked in his bonds. "Get away from me."

"Answer my question." Vynzent waited. When Lyan didn't answer, he jerked Lyan's shirt up, pulling it over his head to hang from his bound arms.

Lyan's heart pounded and he fought fear. Such a simple act, yet it left him exposed, vulnerable, as if a mere piece of cloth could protect him. Vynzent's expression didn't change. "I will ask you one more time, elf. How far do we follow this route?"

Soldarr, Feyra, Tesseia, please help me... Kithr, where are you?
"No." Lyan's voice quavered slightly on that one word.

Vynzent turned. "Ferren."

"Yes sir." A man moved to the fire and drew a brand from it. As he handed it to Vynzent, Lyan realized the object was not a piece of wood, but a metal rod left in the fire to heat to a red hot glow. Vynzent held the rod as if it were a sword and pressed the glowing metal against Lyan's bare chest.

Lyan screamed. The stench of burning flesh filled his nose as he thrashed in his bonds. The burning metal withdrew, and Lyan doubled over, panting for breath. Tears of pain coursed down his face.

Vynzent lifted Lyan's head by the hair. "Answer me, elf."

Lyan closed his eyes and gulped in more gasps of air.

Vynzent waited a moment for an answer. When none came, he again said the name. Lyan flinched, refusing to open his eyes. He jerked away when he felt waves of heat next to his face.

The heat withdrew for a moment, then burning metal pressed against his chest again. Screams tore from Lyan's throat. The ropes cut into his wrists as he struggled to escape the scorching touch. Vynzent held the rod in place a long moment before allowing Lyan relief from the torture.

"More await. Do you want this to continue, elf?"

Lyan moaned.

"No? Then answer me. How far do we follow this route?"

He answered in Elven, voice slurring. "Border."

"Jaist?"

"To the border, he says, sir."

Vynzent released Lyan's head. "There, you see. No need to make this so difficult on yourself."

"Rot in Murdo's Pits before I'll show you the path."

"Jaist?"

"An insult, sir."

Vynzent snorted, a mildly amused sound. He pulled Lyan's shirt back down, covering the blistering burns. He wasn't as cautious as he'd been before, and didn't react quickly enough to avoid Lyan's pain-hazed lunge, biting the human's hand as hard as he could. Vynzent shouted as much from surprise as pain. He struck Lyan with his free hand. The second blow dazed Lyan enough to release his bite. Vynzent stepped back, rubbing his hand.

"Drew blood. Damn. Gag him—carefully."

Bound to a tree, his chest burning like the metal still rested against his skin, Lyan found unconsciousness eluded him. He sank in and out of awareness, and even gagged, he snapped at any movement near him, enough that the sentries skirted around him on their rounds. Morning found him slumped against the tree trunk, somewhere between consciousness and a haze of pain.

Vynzent's face entered his field of vision, snapping Lyan firmly back into awareness. With a snarl, he fought his bonds.

"Hold him still," Vynzent ordered.

Men pinned Lyan back against the tree and untied the gag. Lyan spent more time trying to fight and bite his captor than eating the porridge forced into his mouth, but eventually Vynzent succeeded in feeding him. The men didn't let release Lyan until the gag was securely in place again and Vynzent had moved back.

"Put him on my horse when we set out," Vynzent said.

"Sir, are you sure that's wise?"

"He and I both know I'm responsible for his pain. Should he manage to lash out, it should be at me rather than any of you."

Lyan was in no mood to appreciate any apparent gesture of self-sacrifice from his torturer. The gag muffled his opinion of Vynzent's words.

The drug worked quickly—pain and exhaustion united against Lyan. The agony of his burns dulled. Everything dulled, even his anger, and he managed little more than a glare when Vynzent next paused before him. Vynzent tilted Lyan's head up and peeled open Lyan's drooping eyelids. Satisfied with the glassy glower that met him, the Tathren nodded.

"Hood him and move out."

The burns Vynzent had inflicted didn't stop the men from shoving Lyan across a horse the same way as before. And the drug didn't numb him nearly enough to stop a scream of pain, muffled but not silenced by the gag. Mercifully, unconsciousness followed in the next heartbeats.

Fleeting awareness came and went in snatches and impressions. Jarring pain as the horse moved, though not as severe; he was sitting upright and slumped against the rider before him. His hands were still bound, but his feet were free, allowing him to straddle the horse. The sound of hooves drumming on the ground echoed through his skull, blending into a chaos of noise that chased him even back into unconsciousness.

Lyan didn't struggle when he was lifted down from the horse and bound to another tree. He was aware of being moved only in a distant, disconnected way. When Vynzent pulled off the hood sometime later, Lyan looked at him without expression.

"Do you understand now, elf? Refusing to answer does nothing but cause you unnecessary pain."

Lyan didn't attempt to respond. There didn't seem any point to doing so.

Vynzent pulled the gag from Lyan's mouth. "Once we reach the border, then where?"

Lyan didn't answer. His thoughts flitted briefly over the idea of giving Vynzent what he wanted, but drifted away as quickly.

The fire popped and crackled. "Sir, do you want...." someone began.

Vynzent studied Lyan's face, then shook his head. "It would be pointless right now. He'd barely feel it. Give him water."

Cold water soothed Lyan's parched throat. He couldn't rouse the energy to be interested in anything more than the most basic necessities. Even Vynzent intently studying a map, speaking in a low, worried voice to two other men stirred no more than the faintest wondering of what Vynzent feared.

Lyan woke in pain to the sounds of a camp being hastily broken. Two voices, thick with anxiety, whispered near Lyan.

"We have to feed him!"

"We don't have time!"

"If he's not drugged, who knows what evil magic the elf can work? Sir Vynzent says he must be drugged before we ride!"

"Fine. But if he bites…"

They jerked the hood off. Lyan half opened his eyes and groaned, as if the action had woken him. The two men standing over him looked anxiously over their shoulders. One quickly untied the gag, and the other practically shoved porridge into Lyan's mouth. Lyan's stomach churned, and he turned his head to the side and spat out the overcooked mush.

The man trying to feed Lyan swore. "We don't have time for this."

The other held Lyan's head still as the man with the bowl forced the wretched food into Lyan's mouth, barely giving him a chance to even swallow.

Lyan's stomach rebelled. He barely choked down the last bite before his body made its intent known. Lyan twisted his head to the side and managed not to vomit all over himself. He hadn't thought the porridge could possibly taste worse than it had going down, but he was proven wrong.

The two humans both swore and looked around quickly. "Now what?" one hissed.

"Clean him up and let's go. There's no time!"

They splashed water on Lyan's face and gave him a swallow to wash the taste from his mouth. Then, with hands too hurried to check their work, they replaced gag and hood, then untied him. Lyan cried in pain as they jerked him forward and agony tore through his chest. The men just bound his hands behind his back and pulled Lyan toward the horses.

"What took so long?" Vynzent demanded.

"Sorry, sir," the men said quickly.

"Get him on a horse. We need to move *now*."

Why? What happened? Lyan heard restrained anxiety in Vynzent's voice. *Could he be afraid of Cailean? Are my friends close? Is Kithr coming?*

To the relief of Lyan's still-churning stomach and his burned chest, they left his feet free and allowed him to sit upright on the back of a horse rather than flinging him across the animal on his stomach. Lyan tried to relax a little. He wasn't riding on Vynzent's horse—he could hear the man giving curt orders further ahead. The horses stepped up to a quick trot, then a canter.

The haze didn't come. Enough drugged food managed to stay down to numb Lyan a little, but he was aware of his pain. He was also aware of the hasty work on his bonds, and when he cautiously twisted his hands, he found give in the ropes.

He could only guess how long they rode, but sweat lathered the horse Lyan rode by the time Vynzent slowed the pace. The horse's sides heaved, and Lyan felt sympathy for the animal.

You can't help who owns you. I'm sorry for the extra burden you have to carry. I don't want this any more than you do.

If anyone pursued them, Lyan neither heard nor sensed them. The men on the horses near him sounded less anxious now, although Lyan felt the tension in the man whose horse he shared. He suspected his own presence had more to do with the man's fear than any pursuers did. Lyan shifted, testing the ropes again.

I can get a hand free. That'll have to do. Kithr must be close. He has to be, even with the pace these men are keeping. He promised to protect me. I just can't sense him because of the drugs, or the hood. Lyan tried to calm the knot of fear in his gut. *If I can just get away from these men and give Kithr an opportunity, he'll be able to help me.*

His chest burned as he drew a deep breath, immediately making him doubt the wisdom of his idea.

I have to. Vynzent won't stop. He'll torture me until he gets what he wants, and it will only get worse. No—now is the best chance I will get.

He waited until the horse's sides stopped heaving, then wormed one hand free. From the sounds, Vynzent and his men paid more attention to the land around them than to their supposedly drugged elven captive.

Lyan swung balled fists at the head of the human rider before him. Taken by surprise, the man tumbled from the saddle with a cry of alarm. Lyan jerked off the hood and grabbed hold of the horse's mane, kicking his heels into the animal's sides. With a startled whinny, the horse burst into a run. The reins hung loose and out of reach, but the horse followed the guidance of Lyan's shift in weight as he leaned to one side, bolting away from the road and Vynzent's men. Behind him, alarmed shouts and Vynzent's outraged cursing rose. Lyan leaned close against the horse's neck and worked the gag from his mouth. His mouth was dry, but he whispered to the animal.

"I'm sorry to do this to you. I know you're exhausted, but please, help me a little longer. Please…help me get away from them."

2 1

So sing the reapers:
Men will rise, men will fall.
So sing the reapers:
Lord Murdo takes them all.

The weary horse stumbled, but caught itself. Jarred, Lyan cast a look over his shoulder. He couldn't see his pursuers; the trees grew thick enough to shield them from sight, but he could hear their furious cursing and thundering hooves.

"Shadowstar, I need you," Lyan whispered. He didn't know how far away Shadowstar might be, or how long it would take the stallion to reach him, but his stolen mount couldn't keep this pace for long. He patted the animal's sweaty neck. "I'm sorry to do this to you. Please lead them on as long as you can."

The horse seemed to understand his intent. It slowed near a patch of tall grass. Lyan fell more than jumped off and landed awkwardly, the grass doing little to cushion his landing. The horse ran on. He gasped raggedly for breath as first his chest, then his ankle, then the rest of his body screamed in protest. He crawled to the dubious shelter of a large bush moments before hooves pounded past, men cursing their mounts and their escaped prisoner. Lyan swallowed hard and staggered to his feet. Much as he longed to stay mounted, the exhausted animal wouldn't be able to stay ahead of the humans long enough for Lyan to escape Vynzent. Now they would have to backtrack to find his trail once they discovered he'd abandoned the horse.

The sounds of Vynzent's men grew fainter. Lyan oriented himself by the sun and turned eastward. If Vynzent had not lied about continuing on the route Lyan and his companions followed, east should lead him toward Cailean.

He expected Kithr to appear from the trees at any moment. Lyan followed animal trails, picking around the leafy underbrush, waiting for the sound of his friend's voice, or the prickling sensation that someone watched him.

A scream, shrill and distant, echoed through the forest. Lyan froze in his tracks, heart racing as his head whipped around. He tried to convince himself that the sound had been a bird's screech, but couldn't. There has been something far too human about it.

The trees seemed suddenly too close, the shadows threatening rather than sheltering, and Lyan was far too aware that this forest was as indifferent to him as the Forests of Cossette had been. "Please hurry, Shadowstar. I'm not sure Vynzent is really the worst thing out here. Gods, Kithr, where *are* you?"

The forest lay silent, not even the birds daring to announce themselves. Lyan let out a shaking breath and continued walking. He wanted to run, but his ankle pulsed with pain, and the soft crackle of dry leaves under his feet already sounded too loud to his ears.

The sun crept across the sky, shifting the shadows and warming the land. Lyan paused when he found a stream. Cold water soothed his parched throat and drove back some of his weary daze of pain. Wincing, Lyan peeled up his shirt and washed the blistered burns on his chest. He no longer heard pursuit, but couldn't relax. He had seen the steel determination in Vynzent's eyes, and knew the man would not surrender his elven captive easily.

I have to find Kithr or Cailean. I'd even be glad to see Aikan right now.

The eerie silence persisted as midday passed into afternoon. Several times, Lyan almost called for Kithr, only to stop himself for fear of drawing something less friendly.

He sensed eyes on him. For an instant, Lyan's spirits soared. Then he saw the source: not Kithr, but the spindly creature he and Kithr had chased. The one that had lured them into Vynzent's trap. It crouched on a thick oak branch, watching Lyan with unblinking, disconcertingly human eyes. Lyan had only glimpsed it before, but now he saw the elongated face and mouthful of sharp teeth it exposed when its lips curled back in a savage smile. The creature's mottled brown reptilian hide could have blended into the undergrowth, if it had wanted to hide. Its snout ended in two vertical slits of nostrils. Claws tipped the fingers and toes, digging into the branch. Its clothing consisted only of a loincloth.

Lyan stepped back, and the creature sprang from the branch to another tree, clinging like a lizard to the trunk. It bared fangs at him. "Running not wizzzze, elf."

"Indeed." Vynzent moved from the shadow of the tree the creature had just left. "Not wise at all."

Breath and words both stuck in Lyan's throat. His heart pounded and color fled his face.

"Thyis followed you for days before you even knew he was there. He has a nose to match a bloodhound, with far more cleverness than any mere animal. Did you really think you could slip away from me so easily, elf?" Vynzent's boots crunched through a burst of ferns.

Lyan stepped back. "What is…?"

Vynzent matched him step for step. "Thyis was one of my men once. He angered the wrong person at the wrong time, when I could not protect him. As punishment, my father permitted him to be tortured and twisted into this." Vynzent gestured at the creature watching Lyan's every move. "To the surprise of the man responsible, Thyis retained his loyalty to me rather than mindlessly obeying his torturer."

Lyan took another step back, almost tripping over a root. *That thing is… was human.* "Who did that?"

Vynzent followed. "The mage Porephyn, whose favor my father thinks he can earn. But that is neither here nor now. You've cost me two men to a reaper in the distraction of your foolish escape attempt. Or did you think me the only danger here?"

"Reaper?" Lyan repeated, one hand groping for anything he could use as a weapon. His hunting knife now hung from Vynzent's own belt. *Kithr says Tathrens like to talk too much. If I can keep Vynzent talking, I can delay him, maybe until my friends find me.*

"A demon—a servant of the Mad God." Vynzent's eyes narrowed, though whether in anger or because he suspected Lyan was trying to buy time, Lyan couldn't tell. "Teeth like shards of broken glass and a venom that eats a man from inside. Reapers feed while their prey is still alive. They like to hear the screams."

"Then shouldn't you have more important things to worry about than one elf?" Lyan asked. "Like keeping your men alive?"

"I will find, Equinox, elf," Vynzent said, eyes narrowing as he closed the distance between them.

"Kithr!" Lyan shouted, scrambling back and flinging a handful of sticks and debris at Vynzent.

The Tathren froze, one arm rising as if to ward off an attack. When none came, he smiled coldly. "Are you calling for help, elf? Trying to bring your friend to your aid?" His smile twisted into a sneer. "The other elf won't come. He's dead, bled out somewhere back there. My men left his corpse for the crows."

He's lying. He didn't see Kithr fall. He'd just repeating what his men told him.

"No one's coming to save you. No one."

Lyan licked dry lips. "If you're so sure, what are you running from?" *Kithr, Cailean, Shadowstar, someone, hurry!*

Anger flashed in Vynzent's eyes. "I am not *running*. Not from Cailean, and not from my father, whatever demons Porephyn's magic drives onto my heels."

Keep talking, Lyan begged. *Keep talking, and give me more time.* "So both are chasing you."

"Enough of this. Thyis!"

Lyan hadn't been paying attention to the creature, focused on Vynzent. Weight slammed into his back, claws tearing through his shirt and into skin as the force threw him down. The impact with the ground drove the air from Lyan's lungs, and he could only gasp rather than scream in pain. Thyis growled in his ear, and claws rested on his neck, almost drawing blood.

"Give me one good reason I shouldn't let Thyis hamstring you, elf," Vynzent said.

Lyan sucked in enough breath to answer. "You won't… find Equinox…without…an elf who could…claim it." He didn't know if he was lying or not.

Vynzent scoffed. "An elf must bear the Spear? I doubt that. Before the Spears were divided, Murdo bore both of them."

"Murdo…*was*…both," Lyan panted.

"Murdo is a *god*."

"He was born…half-breed," Lyan managed. He felt blood trickle down his neck as Thyis's claw pierced skin. "Elf and human." His chest burned, and he couldn't tell if the moisture on his skin was sweat, blood, or blisters breaking.

"But even…if not…the guardians won't…let you pass without.…"

"Without an elf fit to bear the Spear?" Vynzent finished. "Then I'll have to be careful not to let you slip away again." Lyan heard the human's steps approaching. "Thyis."

One of the clawed hands withdrew from Lyan's neck. Then a rag pressed over his face, filling his nose with a sickeningly sweet odor before the world spun away into darkness.

A rough jerk made pain flare from his injured shoulder up his arm, then it radiated across to the other shoulder, dragging Lyan to awareness. For once he was neither gagged nor hooded. He'd been stripped to the waist. His arms were bound to a tree branch over his head, and his ankles tethered to a root. Night shrouded the land, and the fire burned painfully bright. He glimpsed the shapes of men moving around the fire, then closed his eyes to slits against the glare.

Kithr didn't come. Why wasn't he there? Why didn't he come? Is it possible that Vynzent's men… Did they really… kill him?

A man spoke. "You aren't going to take one of his feet for running, sir?"

Vynzent answered. "No. If he's telling the truth and we won't find my goal without an elf fit to claim the Spear, I can't take chances with dismemberment."

"How will we know which way to go, then?" someone else asked angrily. "How will we know he's not going to lead us in circles for the reapers to pick us off like Lev and Torr?"

Vynzent answered, standing and lifting an iron from the fire. "I said won't take chances on dismemberment. Other methods of persuasion remain open."

A slap stung across Lyan's face. He forced his eyes open further and focused on Vynzent. "It's time to answer me, elf."

Lyan muttered a response in Elven.

"Jaist?"

"He suggested you attempt something physically impossible, sir," the translator said.

The first time he'd questioned Lyan, Vynzent's air had been almost amused, as if his captive were an entertaining novelty to study. Now, the amusement was gone, and Vynzent's face was cold as ice. "Where is Equinox hidden? Tell me."

Lyan spat in the human's face.

Hot metal pressed against Lyan's bare chest. He screamed and jerked against his bonds. The rope bit into his wrists, another pain atop the first. For a moment, the burning relented, and Vynzent repeated his question. Lyan gasped for breath, and managed an insult in response. Burning metal touched his skin once more. He lost track of how many times. Each blended into the next, never ending. Vynzent issued his demand, then Lyan burned, again and again. He couldn't remember if he answered, if he spoke at all. All he remembered was burning and screaming, endless screaming, long after any words held meaning.

He screamed again in the morning when they cut him down, but the sound was raw and ragged in his throat, and they'd already gagged him. If he cried out when they dragged him onto a horse, Lyan didn't know, awareness already fleeing from the fire that burned in his skin and pursued him into the darkness. Time passed in fleeting snatches of consciousness.

A slap struck his cheek, barely rousing Lyan from darkness. Another slap got a brief fluttering of his eyelids in response. He heard sounds—Vynzent's voice, and a whimper of fear escaped Lyan, his heart beating faster. He cringed in the expectation of pain. The words were nonsense to his ears, heard without understanding. A third slap, and Lyan peeled his eyelids open enough to see the human. He also saw the darkness of night and a fire's glow, far too bright, stabbing pain into his skull. With a moan, he closed his eyes again. The fire wasn't near him, but Lyan was sure he felt its heat.

"You aren't listening to me, elf," Vynzent warned, the first words to really make sense to him. "What did I just say?"

His mouth was dry, his lips swollen. Lyan managed, "Don't know."

"Obviously." Vynzent pushed Lyan's head up and pulled open his eyes. Lyan moaned and tried fruitlessly to turn away. Vynzent released him. "You disappoint me. I'd heard your people were more resilient."

Lyan didn't respond. When neither further questions or further torture seemed likely to follow, he sank back into unconsciousness.

In the morning, Lyan roused to a half-conscious state. Vynzent fed him the drugged porridge and spoke to him, telling him to point out landmarks they needed to find the path. If he would do that, the human would give him…some kind of reward, but Lyan's thoughts were too clouded to understand exactly what was being promised.

The drug dulled his pain. He drifted from awareness for a time. Next time Lyan stirred, his head felt marginally clearer. He was on horseback, slumped against the rider in front of him. His hands were bound, but no hood covered his head. Lyan blinked, then made a sound of pain.

Vynzent spoke, and Lyan realized that the Tathren was the other rider on the horse. "Back in the waking realm, elf? Look around. We're nearing the borderlands between the lands of Riedol and Joski. Find your landmarks."

Landmarks? Did I tell him there were landmarks? Lyan shivered. *What did I tell him? What did I say, what did I do to make the pain stop? What did I say?*

The horses moved at a quick walk. Lyan turned his head

enough to look beyond Vynzent's shoulder. His vision swam, but he could see the other riders.

Where is Shadowstar? I called him…where is he?

As the question worked through Lyan's mind, he knew the answer. Close, Shadowstar was close. Waiting.

Waiting for what? Waiting for me to wake enough to know he's there?

A horse snorted. It might have been the mount of one of Vynzent's men. It might have been Shadowstar agreeing with Lyan.

For a moment, Lyan thought the next sound was only his imagination, a hopeful hallucination—the thump of an arrow. But a man just in his field of vision slumped, then slid limply from the saddle to fall in a heap to the ground. In the frozen moment of surprise that followed, another man toppled from his horse, clawing feebly at the raven-feathered shaft in his back.

Kithr? Please gods, let it be true.

"Ambush!" Vynzent snapped. He dug his heels into his horse, driving the animal into a run.

Other horses followed, and not all belonged to Vynzent's men. Yion shouted a battle cry in an unfamiliar language. Cailean yelled Lyan's name, and an order to attack. But closer, Shadowstar closed on Vynzent's mount, and with the stallion came Kithr, grim as death.

"Die, Tathren scum."

Vynzent cast a look over his shoulder and grimaced, ducking low. "Damn. It seems we must part ways for now, elf."

It was all the warning Lyan received. Vynzent turned his horse sharply, veering from the path into the trees. Lyan felt a shove, then he was falling. The hooves of the Tathren's horse narrowly missed him. With a scream of pain, he hit the ground directly in the path of the charging Shadowstar.

22

Blood and fire
Dream and sleep
Casting higher
Pain to reap

The pounding of hooves on the ground matched the pounding of blood in Lyan's ears, nearly drowning any other sounds. Hooves loomed over him and he curled reflexively in a feeble effort to avoid being trampled. His swimming vision shrank to pinpoints as darkness tried to claim him.

The horse jumped over him and skidded to a stop. The rider dropped to the ground and stumbled to Lyan. Lyan jerked away when hands caught him, struggling and terrified that Vynzent or one of his men intended to drag him with them.

"Lyan. Lyan!" A voice repeated his name urgently, finally reaching him through the confusion of pain and noise. "Lyan, hold still."

"K...." His voice stuck in his throat when he tried to

speak. *Kithr?* Lyan's vision blurred, but he clung desperately to consciousness.

A knife sawed through the cords biding his wrists. "Lyan, do you hear me?"

Lyan sucked in air and focused on the figure crouched on the pine needles beside him. A bloodstained bandanna wrapped Kithr's head. Rips and rusty stains marred his clothes, revealing more bandages underneath. His face was strained, as if every movement cost him pain. "You're…hurt," Lyan managed, his voice a rasping croak.

Kithr gave a quick shake of his head. "I'll heal. They didn't check whether I was playing dead." He put a hand on Lyan's shoulder to sit him up, but his head jerked up sharply when horses gathered around them. "Tell me the bastards are dead."

Cailean answered, voice quivering with rage. "They scattered. Got away."

Lyan raised his head. Shadowstar stood guard over him and Kithr. Torqual circled his horse, sword in hand, watching for enemies. The rest of Cailean's men took up protective positions, and even Aikan's anger was directed away from Lyan. Cailean swung off his horse and stepped toward Lyan, though his gaze stayed on Kithr, and he stopped when Kithr tensed.

"Can you stand, Lyan?" Cailean asked.

Every breath sent fire searing through his chest. Lyan didn't want to move; he just wanted to close his eyes and sink into oblivion. Kithr hooked an arm under him, trying to lift him, and Lyan could feel the pain that the effort cost his friend. Feebly, Lyan moved his legs under him, though they had no strength to support him. Another hand caught his arm. Lyan flinched away, nearly unbalancing Kithr.

"Peace, Lyan," Yion soothed. "Allow me to assist."

The mercenary stood more than a head shorter than Kithr, making an awkward difference in height, but between them, they held Lyan upright. Lyan tried to shift more of his weight from Kithr to Yion. Pain tore through his chest. Color drained from Lyan's face and his breath came in short, ragged gasps as the world again faded around him.

"Lyan?" He couldn't tell who said his name urgently.

He tried to lift his head, but the effort took too much of his failing strength. "Hurts…" A wash of darkness obscured his vision before daylight returned in a gray haze. "Burning." Moisture seeped through his shirt.

Yion's hand touched his forehead, then the mercenary spoke in a firm voice. "Lord Cailean, we cannot pursue. Lyan has suffered more harm than being thrown from a horse."

The words arrested Cailean's attention. He turned sharply to look at Lyan, as if really seeing him for the first time. His expression grew sharply concerned. "How bad? Lyan?"

Lyan bit his lip. If he opened his mouth, he feared only screams would escape.

"Shiolto, see to him," Aikan ordered. "Dalrian, Torqual, find a site to set camp. Lord Cailean, we are *not* pursuing those men."

Cailean's jaw tensed, but he didn't argue. Drawing a deep breath to steady himself, he asked, "How serious? What did they do?"

Ice hung from Kithr's words. "Do you need me to tell you what Tathrens do to elves they capture?"

Lyan gripped a handful of Kithr's shirt. "Not… Cailean's…fault."

"I know," Kithr growled. "That's why he's still alive."

Shiolto rushed to them, clutching a saddlebag. His gaze traveled down Lyan's damp shirt, the cloth clinging to blistered, burned skin. "Lyan should lie down until we find a camp."

Lyan clung more tightly to his supporters and jerked his head in a quick refusal. "Not… yet. Stop now, won't get back up." He closed his eyes. "Water?"

Someone held a skin to his mouth. Lyan gulped lukewarm water and focused only on staying upright and staying conscious, fearing that if he gave in to the darkness, he would wake to find that he had only dreamed his rescue, and Vynzent still held him prisoner.

"Lord Cailean, this way." Torqual returned. "We found water. Dalrian's clearing a campsite."

Yion and Kithr carried Lyan between them. Kithr let Yion carry most of Lyan's weight, and Lyan's thoughts caught on the realization that whatever Kithr claimed, he was hurt more seriously than he wanted to admit.

Dalrian had hacked away the larger underbrush in their chosen campsite and piled it to one side when Yion and Kithr brought Lyan. Shiolto picked a spot under the shade of an oak tree and quickly swept away debris before spreading bedrolls to make a pallet. Yion eased Lyan onto the blankets, then unlaced Lyan's shirt and began to carefully peel it off. The cloth stuck against the burns, and Lyan gasped in pain.

"Cold water. Soak bandages." Shiolto's voice was tight.

Kithr silently did as Shiolto directed. Cool cloths bathed Lyan's chest, waking fresh pain. Lyan gave a sharp cry as someone carefully worked his shirt loose, then began washing his chest.

"I'm sorry!" Shiolto apologized quickly. "Gods, Lyan, I'm so sorry. I know this hurts, but we have to clean them."

Kithr's calloused hand took hold of Lyan's, and Lyan gripped it as if his life depended on it. After an eternity of agony, cool, wet bandages covered his chest, finally offering relief to the burning. Lyan finally lapsed into something near sleep.

Feet rustled the leaves and crunched on dry needles as someone approached. Lyan's eyes snapped open and he flinched back before he identified Yion. The mercenary waited until he was certain Lyan recognized him, then offered a tin mug.

"Drink, Lyan."

Lyan turned away. "No drugs." His voice, raw from screaming, rasped in his throat.

"It will numb the pain, not leave you unaware." Yion offered the mug again.

"No. No drugs. No," he repeated.

A hand touched his arm. Lyan tensed, but no restraint followed. Kithr crouched beside him. "If you won't drink whatever foul brew he's made, you can try this." He held out a small, unfamiliar metal flask. When Kithr opened it, Lyan smelled the pungent odor of strong alcohol.

Lyan's nose wrinkled at the odor, but he nodded. Kithr helped him sit and held the flask to his mouth. Kithr allowed him one deep gulp, and it burned all the way down Lyan's throat, but the fire wasn't as harsh as the one burning in his chest.

"It's strong. One drink should be plenty for you," Kithr said. "Now rest, Lyan."

Lyan gripped Kithr's arm as tightly as he could and spoke in Elven. "No more drugs. Don't let them drug me."

Kithr didn't have to know the details to hear the desperation in Lyan's voice. "No one will drug you, I promise. I won't allow it." The soothing tone sounded strange coming from Kithr. He took one of Lyan's hands in his own. "You're safe, Lyan. Rest. You're safe." Lyan closed his eyes, but his restless doze was haunted by dreams. Every time he stirred, he found Kithr still at his side, calming him, and he still clung to Kithr's hand.

Sharp pain finally roused Lyan. Drawing a deep breath brought tears of pain to his eyes, but his head was clearer. Vynzent's drug had worn off. He no longer clutched Kithr's hand, but his friend sat close by. Shadows shrouded the forest floor, and Lyan smelled food and a fire. The odor of wood smoke sent a shudder down his spine. Bracing his hands on the ground, Lyan tried to sit. Fresh pain assailed him, drawing a breathless gasp.

Kithr gently pushed him back down with a hand on his shoulder. "Lay still, Lyan."

Lyan sank back, trembling with pain and weakness. "How bad?"

Kithr hesitated, then said, "Bad enough." He paused again, and his voice dropped low. "Who did this, Lyan? Why?"

"Equinox." Lyan clutched a blanket. "The leader of those men… he wants the Spear. He knew I knew where to look." Lyan's voice trailed off. "Kithr… he said you were dead, that his men killed you."

"Dead? At the hands of Tathren? Hah!" Kithr waves a hand to dismiss the idea.

"You're hurt," Lyan persisted. Kithr had changed from his blood-stained shirt, but that didn't hide the lines on his face or the exhaustion in his eyes.

"I'll heal. It's nothing your horse-tender friend couldn't patch up enough to keep me on a horse."

"Shiolto," Lyan corrected.

The look Kithr gave him said the correction was unnecessary. "I know his name."

Steps approached, then Cailean quietly asked, "Is he awake?"

"I'm awake," Lyan answered. He tried to put some strength into his voice, but it sounded faint and frail to his ears.

Kithr scowled at Cailean, but not as fiercely or as deeply as he had in the past. Cailean crouched beside Lyan opposite Kithr and searched for something to say. "You're… you look like you got some rest."

"Is everyone all right?" Lyan asked.

Cailean glanced at Kithr before he answered. "We have some cuts and scrapes, but nothing serious. When you two didn't return, Shadowstar led us to Kithr, and we followed the trail from there." The quick, dismissive way he spoke did more to raise Lyan's suspicions that a great deal was being left out of the story than it did to reassure him. Cailean's face was serious. "I didn't get a good look at the men, but some of them seemed familiar, and Kithr is convinced they were Tathrens. Did they say anything about who sent them, Lyan? Were they Ewart's men?"

"Ewart's son. Vynzent." Lyan shuddered.

Cailean stiffened. "Ewart's bastard? He led those men? You're sure, Lyan? I didn't think he walked in his father's steps." Cailean shook his head angrily. "Watcher's Beard, if I had known he was involved…"

"He wants Equinox for himself," Lyan said. "Not for anyone else, god or man."

Kithr locked eyes with Cailean. "You know this man."

Cailean's mouth twisted in distaste and anger. "Not well, it seems. I've had few dealings with him, mostly when we were both much younger. What does *he* want with Equinox?"

"Power," Lyan said. "And to kill his father."

Kithr's mouth tightened to the thin line. "The world would be better for everyone if Tathrens confined themselves to just killing each other."

"We have a tendency to do so, except when some other land decides to attack us," Cailean countered coolly.

"Is there food?" Lyan interrupted. His stomach was unsure about eating, but he could feel a fight brewing and seized at any distraction.

Cailean looked over his shoulder. "It's almost ready. Do you think you can eat something?"

"I think so. As long as…" He shook his head. "I think so." *As long as it isn't porridge.* Lyan drew as deep a breath as he could, and pain raced through his chest. "Cailean… Tomorrow. We should keep going."

"What?" both Cailean and Kithr burst in protest.

"You're in no shape—" Cailean began.

"Absolutely not!" Kithr said. "Are you trying to kill yourself?"

"We must," Lyan insisted. "We don't have time to wait."

"No. You can't ride. We're not leaving." Kithr glowered at him.

"We must," Lyan repeated. "You don't understand…"

"What don't I understand?" Kithr demanded. "That you think you can somehow stay on a horse in this condition, or that you won't make this worse, or fall ill?"

Lyan's voice dropped to a whisper, for only Kithr and Cailean to hear. "Vynzent… wanted to know where to find Equinox. This… he did this to get answers." He shuddered, closing his eyes. "And I don't know what I told him. I don't *know*! If I told him… if he knows… if he…" He trailed off as another wash of pain hit.

"Lyan." Cailean said his name firmly. "*Lyan*. You *cannot* ride, not yet. You have to trust us. Vynzent will not find Equinox."

Kithr stood silently. Lyan opened his eyes and looked at him, seeing his friend tense with barely restrained rage. Lyan said his name softly.

"I'll get you something to eat," Kithr responded, turning sharply and walking to the fire.

Lyan watched him, saw Kithr's tense, hunched shoulders. "Cailean, how badly… is Kithr hurt?" he asked quietly.

Cailean hesitated before answering. "Worse than he'll admit. He was unconscious and bleeding when Shadowstar found him. He'd been following the men who took you, and it had to be sheer will that carried him as far as he got. When he woke in our company, the situation was… tense." For the first time, Lyan noticed fading bruises on Cailean's face. The

Tathren offered a small shrug. "Despite being weak from loss of blood, he made an impressive effort to kill someone."

Kithr spoke sharply from the fire, words not directed toward Lyan or Cailean. "What is that?" Yion answered quietly, and Lyan couldn't distinguish his words over the crackle of the fire. Kithr's response, however, was clear. "Then eat it yourself. No drugs for Lyan. Not in his food, not in his drink, none."

Cailean looked toward the confrontation at the fire, then quietly said, "Yion is trying to help you, Lyan."

He shuddered. "I know, but… I can't…"

"Why?"

Lyan closed his eyes. "Vynzent… He kept me drugged, except when he… wanted answers."

Cailean inhaled sharply and cursed, then raised his voice. "Yion. Do as Lyan wants."

Lyan shivered, but opened his eyes. "Thank you."

Cailean touched his shoulder. "Rest, Lyan. You're safe here."

But we have to keep going. We can't stay here. What did I tell Vynzent? How much does he know? I won't… I can't let him reach Equinox.

Kithr helped him sit and eat the stew—thick, with enough meat and flavor that it bore no resemblance to porridge.

"Why am I so weak?" Lyan whispered. "I can hardly lift my arms. While… while he still had me captive, I didn't feel so…" He searched for the right word.

"Fear brings its own strength, Lyan," Kithr answered in Elven. "But that can only last so long, and it carries a price."

"We have to keep going. In the morning."

Kithr didn't say anything except simply, "Sleep if you can."

～

Lyan woke screaming, struggling and clawing at the air. He felt the hood covering his face, blocking his sight and stealing his breath. He felt the ropes biting into his wrists. Felt the sear of hot metal against his skin.

Someone stilled his thrashing limbs long enough to pull the tangled blankets off him. The shock of cold air on his skin drove back some of the burning from the nightmare, and the release from tangled blankets, a result of his own tossing, calmed the fear of restraint. Lyan swallowed down the last screams and huddled on the ground, shaking. It hurt almost more than he could stand. A hand touched his shoulder, and Lyan flinched.

"Shh, you're safe. Lyan, you're safe, I promise. No one's going to hurt you."

Kithr. His tremors eased. He wanted to believe Kithr. "You promise?" Lyan whispered.

"I promise." Kithr draped a blanket over Lyan's shoulders, then, after a moment of hesitation, sat beside him and wrapped an arm around Lyan.

Lyan clutched the blanket around himself and leaned against Kithr. His heart still pounded as if it would burst from his chest, but gradually, safe under his friend's watchful guard, he calmed. Sleep eventually found him again, and he didn't dream.

Lyan woke to voices. Cailean asked, "How long until we can risk traveling?"

Shiolto answered. "Four or five days at the earliest, as long as he rests and doesn't get sick."

No. We can't wait that long.

Cailean paced, worried. "I don't like staying here so long. Something else lurks out here. You remember the two corpses we found?"

"Hard to forget those, sir," Shiolto answered with a shudder in his voice. "But Lord Cailean, even that doesn't change the truth. Lyan's not fit to travel, and if he refuses any drugs, he'll be in too much pain to do anything."

"He has reasons for not wanting to be drugged," Cailean said.

Kithr interrupted, his tone making every word sound like a profanity. "I know a better way to be sure this Vynzent does not reach our goal before us. Or ever."

"No," Cailean said sharply. "It's debatable whether you're in any better condition than Lyan. You cannot take on Vynzent and his men and succeed."

"He deserves a slow, painful death for what he's done."

Lyan forced his eyes open. Kithr glared at Cailean. He held his bow, quiver slung over his shoulder, and wore unremarkable brown leathers, as if he were going hunting.

"No," Lyan protested, but his voice was faint and weak. "Kithr, no…"

Kithr chose not to hear him. "I suggest you move out of my way, Tathren."

Cailean didn't break eye contact with Kithr. "Dalrian, Torqual, go with him."

"I do not need your help." Kithr's voice was low and dangerous.

"I won't let you go alone," Cailean said. "And what about Lyan?"

"Are you implying that you will not protect him?" Kithr's eyes narrowed.

"I am saying that you are finding it very convenient to suddenly start trusting us to guard your friend now, when you wouldn't have done so yesterday, because you want to go kill someone."

Kithr's hands clenched in fists and trembled with fury, but he restrained himself from punching Cailean. Without another word, he stormed past the Tathren lord.

"Kithr, don't," Lyan called weakly. Kithr didn't stop. "Shadowstar!"

The stallion stepped up behind Kithr, leaned out, and closed his teeth firmly onto the back of Kithr's shirt. Kithr jerked to a stop with a curse. Shadowstar took a step back, then another, tugging Kithr with him.

Kithr tried futilely to free his shirt. "Fine. Fine! Shadowstar, that's enough!"

Shadowstar released Kithr. With a scowl at the stallion, Kithr stalked to Lyan.

"Don't go after him on your own, Kithr," Lyan pleaded.

Kithr scowled again. "I wasn't going to be *alone*. I was going to have two *Tathrens* with me, one of whom dreams of putting a knife in my back for aiming an arrow at his brother," he snapped in Elven.

"And you… would have left them behind… at the first chance," Lyan responded. "Please, Kithr, don't."

"You're not fit to travel, you don't want him finding the Spear, but you won't accept a solution that involves ripping out his heart and shoving it down his throat for torturing you?" Kithr demanded.

"This isn't… your fault, Kithr," Lyan said.

"I can end this, Lyan."

"That thing that spied on us. It'll smell you coming. He'll know you're there, Kithr, and if he catches you…"

"What would he do to me that I haven't already faced at the hands of Tathrens?" Kithr said coldly. "What could he do that I haven't already endured?"

Lyan thought of Vynzent's cold eyes and shuddered. He hated the answer that came, and he hated himself for saying it, for using it to manipulate Kithr. "He could tell you, in every detail, exactly what he did to me."

Kithr froze, hands clenching again into fists. A tremor of rage ran through him.

"He could… he would, Kithr," Lyan whispered. "And if he caught you, how would you keep your promise?"

Kithr drew a short, angry breath, then cursed. He forced his hands to unclench. "You need something to eat."

"Kithr."

Kithr turned away from him. "I'm staying. Leave you in the care of Tathrens and a mercenary? What was I thinking?"

As a victory, it felt bitter. Lyan ate the food Kithr brought him, wondering if he shouldn't let Yion drug him as Vynzent had and allow his companions continue with him in a semi-conscious haze where the pain wasn't so fierce.

Shiolto changed Lyan's bandages, applying a salve to the burns and refreshing the cool cloths. The pain eased enough that Lyan slept again.

He woke with a start and a whimper of pain and fear, gulping air. Lyan's eyes opened to slits, and he froze, breath catching. A man who looked far too much like Vynzent sat on a blanket near him, running a hand over his chin and the several days of unshaved brown stubble that sprouted on it. He turned toward Lyan, and the movement banished the shadows accentuating the family resemblance between Cailean and Vynzent. Cailean's brow wrinkled in concern.

"Are you awake, Lyan? Can I get you anything?" Cailean's voice was less harsh than Vynzent's, helping to banish the comparison from Lyan's thoughts.

Lyan blinked to clear his eyes. "Water?" The word scratched in his throat.

"Of course." Cailean eased him up, one arm behind Lyan's back to support him, and he held the water skin when Lyan couldn't keep it steady. Lyan found himself waiting for an expression of disapproval from Aikan, but if the older man thought Cailean acted beneath his station, he kept any objections private.

"Where's Kithr?" Lyan glanced around the camp, not

seeing his friend.

"Ignoring all advice against the idea, he went hunting. Hunting for food," Cailean quickly clarified. "He rode Shadowstar, and issued any number of unnecessary threats of bodily harm should I allow harm to come to you in his absence."

Lyan managed a small smile, hearing exasperated humor in Cailean's voice. "Shadowstar will make sure he comes back." *And Kithr knows I can call Shadowstar if I need him.*

"How are you?" Cailean asked.

"Tired," Lyan answered. "Everyone else?"

"Worried, but as well as can be expected under the circumstance." Cailean paused, and his voice grew quieter. "Lyan, I recognize that you probably don't want to talk about this, but can you tell me anything more about Vynzent? How he found us? How much he knows?"

Lyan tensed. "I don't know. He didn't say, except that his creature spied on us."

"Names?" Cailean persisted. "Things you overheard?"

"The spy was called Thyis. His translator was Jaist." Lyan closed his eyes for a moment, knowing this wasn't the information Cailean sought. "Reapers. A reaper killed two men when I tried to escape."

Cailean tensed, gripping Solstice. "You're sure?"

"Vynzent was sure. He… wanted to be sure I wouldn't try to run again."

Cailean winced. "I only know one mage who has both the power and inclination to summon demons from the Mad God's prison. Ewart's master. If he set reapers after Vynzent, the rift between father and son is greater than I knew."

"Porephyn," Lyan said.

Cailean stiffened as if a bolt of lightning had struck him.

"That's the mage's name, isn't it?" Lyan asked.

Cailean's lips barely moved, forming an almost soundless "Yes."

"Vynzent said his name." Lyan tried not to think on the circumstances of that conversation. "That's all I know."

"If I'd known for sure Vynzent was against Ewart, I might have offered him an alliance," Cailean said. "But not now. Not after this. I may not need more enemies, but I will not ally myself with anyone who tortures my friends."

"I thought at first he might be convinced," Lyan said. "Vynzent proved that idea wrong."

Cailean let out a breath. "Gods, Lyan... I'm sorry. I should have kept you safe, stopped this from happening. Kithr blames himself for your capture, but there must have been something... or some way we could have reached you sooner." He turned away, looking toward the stream. "The truth is, I was afraid we wouldn't find you. We kept losing the trail, and Kithr could barely stay in the saddle. Until your stallion suddenly found some path invisible to the rest of us, I was praying to every god I knew to help us reach you."

"I called Shadowstar when I tried to escape." Part of Lyan wanted to cry out how desperately he had depended on his friends finding him before Vynzent, but he held the words back. The guilt in Cailean's eyes said the Tathren already knew. "I couldn't call him before then. When he wasn't questioning me, Vynzent kept me gagged."

"You needed our help. We should have been closer; we should have been able to aid you when you tried to get away from him. Lyan... I'm sorry."

Lyan shook his head, thinking back. "Vynzent was running from the reaper. His horses were exhausted, and mine carried double. It couldn't have outrun the others. I took a fool's chance, but I had to try." He bit his lip and drew as deep a breath as he could bear. "Cailean, it isn't your fault. Not Kithr's either. At least... I gave you time to catch up. I knew you would find me."

"I wish I could have been so sure," Cailean whispered. He rose and left Lyan to rest.

Guardians speak
In whispering words
"Be not weak,
The Trials begin."

"So, little elf, how will you run now?"

Lyan drew a sharp breath and tried to stand. But he sat on the ground, wrists bound around the trunk of a tree behind him, surrounded by fire on all sides. The pooka, in human form, stood before him, smirking. Lyan tensed, pulling at the ropes restraining him. "Get away from me."

"Your protectors haven't done a good job, have they? Just look at you. And to think, you might still be there if I hadn't given that reaper a little help in finding its prey." The pooka grimaced in distaste. "Disgusting thing."

Lyan's eyes narrowed. "Then why work with it?"

The pooka hit him, a stinging slap across Lyan's face. "I did not ask to be forced to serve with the likes of that perversion, elf."

Lyan twisted, and somehow freed a hand from his bonds.

He struggled to his feet. "You are bound to serve a mortal master, then."

The pooka's mouth twisted in an angry snarl. "You think you can bind a free spirit, little elf?"

"Why did you lead reapers to their prey, when they're Murdo's servants?"

The pooka bared its teeth, then calmed and smiled viciously. "It's no fun to catch someone who's already caught. Where's the game in that? I was disappointed, though. You didn't give those Tathrens nearly the chase you did me. You didn't even make it interesting." The pooka leaned close, voice dropping to a whisper. "If you'd really tried, I might have joined the fun. I wonder how well that Tathren could have followed you if I'd removed his twisted little hunter-beast."

"Why?" Lyan demanded. Had the pooka been following him? It had watched his attempt to escape, but had neither helped nor hindered? How long had it been watching him in uncharacteristic silence?

The pooka grinned wickedly. "You seem to believe I am bound to serve some mortal. Even if I am, that mortal most certainly is not Vynzent Col'renn. And my claim on you comes before his—I want no one stealing what I've chosen."

Lyan's expression darkened. He looked around slowly, and saw nothing beyond the fires surrounding him. "Get out of my head. My life and my mind are not your playthings."

"Make me." The pooka gestured, and the fires around them flared up in jets of flame.

"I said *get out!*" Lyan shoved at the presence in his mind, felt resistance, and forced past it. The fires died, snuffed out without a trace, throwing everything into darkness. His bonds vanished. Lyan lunged forward, and his hand found the pooka's hair as the other moved aside. Lyan seized hold.

The pooka made a sound of surprise, with the slightest hint of alarm, before slithering free of Lyan's grasp. "*As you wish then, little elf....*"

The presence vanished as suddenly as the fires had, leaving Lyan alone in the darkness of his dreams.

He woke with a cry, agony tearing through his chest. Someone crouched over him, and Lyan jerked back.

"It's all right, it's all right, Lyan," Shiolto said quickly. "I'm sorry. I need to change the bandages."

Lyan panted for breath, finally forcing bleary eyes to focus. He didn't know how long he'd slept, and the light in the sky had a strange tint to it that wasn't quite right. He closed his eyes again, blinking several times to clear them, and the sky seemed a little closer to its normal color when he looked again. Shiolto watched him, face worried. When he caught Lyan watching him, the Tathren forced a reassuring smile.

"You were sleeping pretty restlessly. I was worried. Are you all right?"

"The pooka's near," Lyan answered. "At least... I think it is."

Shiolto stiffened looking around sharply. "It's back? I'll warn the others."

"I might... I might just have been dreaming," Lyan said, second-guessing himself. "Is Kithr back?"

"He's back and resting. He brought a deer."

"I am awake," Kithr interrupted. Lyan turned and saw his friend sitting up. Kithr's face was lined and his eyes shadowed as he looked at Lyan. "What did you say about the pooka?"

Kithr spoke his question loud enough to draw the attention of the others. Shiolto finished bandaging Lyan's burns and helped him sit. With all eyes on him, Lyan again questioned his impressions. But if the pooka were near, he didn't dare ignore the threat it posed.

"I think the pooka has found us again," he said finally.

Cailean nodded soberly. "It was too much to hope it would stay away. It's healed enough to be on the hunt again, then. Is it targeting you again, Lyan?"

He considered the pooka's words. "I… think so. But it's also angry at Vynzent for… trying to steal its chosen prey."

"So it's still playing games," Torqual said.

"A pooka will always play games," Kithr said coolly. "That is the nature of the creature." He looked at Lyan. "The pooka was injured?"

Lyan just nodded. Torqual, however, studied Kithr and spoke. "Yes, it was injured. And my guess is that your hand wounded it, Kithr."

"Torqual?" Dalrian asked. "Why do you say that?"

"In the temple to the god of monsters, I saw a blood-stained arrow on the altar. It looked a lot like those in Kithr's quiver. As he has followed us since we left the elven forest, don't you think he's helped Lyan before?" It was the most Lyan had heard the taciturn soldier say at once.

"Three arrows," Kithr answered. "One missed. One barely skimmed it. I thought the third missed as well." He eyed Lyan. "You didn't tell them."

"You didn't want them to know you were following," Lyan said with a thin smile, "and I didn't want to explain my childish outburst at you in the forest. No, I didn't tell them."

"Lyan was remarkably vague regarding his evasion of the pooka," Aikan said coldly, accusation in his voice as he gazed at the elves.

"Regardless, the monster is shadowing us again," Cailean interrupted. "And Lyan's in no shape to be facing it. Keep your eyes open."

Cailean's men cast wary glances around, nodding in agreement. Kithr looked at Lyan, crouched down beside him, and spoke in Elven.

"You're sure?"

"No." Lyan looked at his hands. "I'm not sure at all. I might have just dreamed it was talking to me. But it might not have been just a dream, and…" He took a deep breath and spoke softly. "I'm afraid, Kithr. We shouldn't stay here."

Kithr rested a hand on his shoulder. "I know, but we can't keep moving yet. You look like you'll pass out if you stand up, Lyan. Riding? No, not yet." Kithr held up a hand. "I know you want to argue, but no. You're not ready to ride."

Lyan bit back his protests and said nothing.

"Have you eaten anything? You're probably hungry." Kithr rose painfully and moved toward the fire.

"I'm not really…" Lyan started to say, but Kithr wasn't listening. Lyan watched his friend and remembered what Cailean had said—Kithr was injured as well. *Is he more worried that I won't be able to stay in the saddle, or that he won't?*

Kithr brought hot stew with thick chunks of meat. Lyan forced himself to eat, though he wasn't sure whether food would stay down. When he'd eaten all he could manage, Lyan handed the bowl back to Kithr.

Kithr frowned at him. "You should finish this, Lyan."

He shook his head. "Maybe later. I'm not very hungry. Have you eaten?"

"Yes, I have. And I have rested, and I have let your friend check my injuries." Kithr scowled, as if reading Lyan's mind. Then he sighed. "Try to rest, Lyan. And trust me. We'll leave once you're fit to ride."

Lyan lay down, but didn't sleep. He didn't want to dream any more. Kithr sat near the fire and checked the fletching on his arrows. Cailean paced for a time, deep in thought. Shiolto and Dalrian diced, and Torqual joined them after a little while. Aikan read a small leather-bound book. Yion paced the camp's perimeter before coming around to Lyan. Seeing Lyan awake, Yion sat down beside him.

"Might I join you for a little time?" the mercenary asked.

"I don't mind." Lyan realized he hadn't seen much of Yion since immediately after his rescue.

"How do you fare, Lyan?"

"I feel like I'm going to be sick, and I hurt," he answered honestly.

"I have herbs that will settle your stomach," Yion offered. "Not a drug—medicine."

Lyan shook his head. "Not right now. Thank you, Yion. I just… would rather not."

"Your captor kept you drugged. Is that so?"

Lyan nodded.

Yion bowed his head in a nod. "I apologize for attempting to force the same on you, Lyan."

"You didn't know," Lyan said quietly. "And I was in no state to be explaining coherently. I know… you meant it to help, Yion." He drew as deep a breath as he could. "What's wrong?"

If the question surprised Yion, he didn't show it. "The same thought troubles me that troubles the others. We failed to keep harm from you, though we know your skills are those of a scholar and not a warrior. We could not protect you, nor could we free you before harm came to you."

"I don't blame any of you for this, Yion," Lyan said.

"That may be so, Lyan. But as you may learn some day, that rarely stops those who feel they should have done more from blaming themselves."

"I know. But I don't blame you." Lyan hesitated, then said, "I think… I'll try your medicine." It was the best he could offer, for now, as proof that he meant his words.

Yion gave him a look of surprise. "If you are sure."

Lyan gave him a thin smile. "I'll trust you that it doesn't do more than you say."

"You may find sleep comes more easily with the lessening of some small part of your discomfort. But the herbs themselves should not cause you to sleep." Yion stood. "I have no wish to dull your wits with the pooka nearby."

Lyan expected the tea to be bitter, but Yion sweetened it—it tasted like honey. The drink did settle Lyan's churning stomach. He rested, and ate a little dinner with his companions as evening fell, then slept again.

~

Lyan woke with the certainty that something stood over him. He knew Cailean's men kept watch, and Kithr's bedroll lay next to Lyan's. He knew nothing should be able to slip into the camp unnoticed. He listened, and heard only the sounds of sleeping people around him. His dread wouldn't be pushed aside so easily, though. Lyan forced open heavy eyelids, heart pounding with the terror that he would see Vynzent leering down at him, or Thyis smirking from some perch.

Moonlight glowed through the clouds to cast faint illumination over the camp. Lyan's mouth opened, and he blinked several times. The form standing over him didn't change. Of all the possibilities his sleep-fogged mind had conjured, a bear had not been among them. The distilled moonlight illuminated the white marks on the bear's face, so close that Lyan could almost understand the shapes of the runes he saw. He felt the bear's hot breath wash over his skin and smelled scents of the forest. Lyan's eyes darted over the rest of the camp, wondering how his companions could be asleep—and how whoever kept watch could have failed to notice a bear enter the camp. He drew a breath to wake the others.

The bear raised a paw and touched it to his chest. It wasn't a blow; it wasn't even a heavy pressure, but the pain it woke drove Lyan's breath away in a gasp as color drained from his face. The bear lifted its paw away and Lyan panted.

He sucked in enough air to gasp, "I'm not... to call out. I get... the idea..."

That seemed the proper response. The bear rested its paw on the ground once more and gazed at Lyan with intelligent brown eyes.

"Am I dreaming?" Lyan managed, trying to catch his breath.

The bear cocked its head to one side in an attitude of

amusement. A voice spoke in his mind in Elven, female and musical, like the song of wind through chimes. *"What do you think?"*

"I think it's the best explanation I have for there being a bear in the middle of camp without anyone else noticing it," Lyan responded. His burning chest argued against this being a dream, but he waited for a response.

"I don't want them to wake," she said. *"And the protections on this camp are meant only to keep out those who would enter with harmful intent."*

"You…" Lyan struggled for words. "I… I've seen you before. In the Forests of Cossette, when the pooka chased me."

"Yes."

"Why… are you here?"

Her eyes were pools of darkness in her face. *"You fought to protect Equinox from one who would claim it unjustly and abuse its power. You continued to fight, even in torture, though you knew the cost."*

Lyan shuddered, closing his eyes. His voice shook. "Fought? I couldn't do anything. I couldn't escape him, even when I had a chance. How can you say I fought, when… when I don't even know what I told him." Fear and shame made his voice crack.

"You told him nothing. Nothing more than he already knew, nothing that will guide him to the Spear."

He opened his eyes and looked at her with desperate hope. "Is that true?"

The bear gazed at him solemnly. *"I swear by my life that I speak the truth."*

Lyan believed her. "Thank you."

"Why do you thank me? I should thank you, for you endured the Trial of Fire and emerged victorious."

He didn't feel victorious. Pain burned though his body and fear lurked in his mind. "Did I?"

"If you were granted one boon for a reward, what would you ask?"

"I would ask to be fit to ride," Lyan answered quietly.

She cocked her head to one side. "*Nothing more?*"

"I haven't earned a reward," he said. "But we can't move on while I'm hurt. My friends won't leave without me, and even if I didn't tell Vynzent anything of use, we don't have time to wait until I've healed." His conscience pricked him, and Lyan suddenly added, "No, there is something else."

She waited.

"If I could be granted a request, I would ask that both Kithr and I be fit to ride. I know he's hurt too, and he won't tell me how badly, but… I can't leave him behind, either."

She gazed deep into his eyes, and Lyan felt as if she looked into his soul, as if he would be swallowed up if he looked too long into her eyes. "*You are determined to find Equinox. But do you know why you seek the Spear? Do you know what reason drives you?*"

Lyan didn't answer.

She continued. "*You must know this before you continue: the Trials will test you in ways you do not dream. They will drive you beyond what you believe your limits to be. They must, because the Spearbearer must have the strength to endure even greater trials.*"

"What happens to those who fail Equinox's Trials?" Lyan whispered.

"*Those who reach the shrine but fail the Trials remain there, forever bound in service to Equinox.*"

"Forever?" Lyan repeated.

"*Forever, undying, never free. Knowing this, are you willing to continue?*"

He drew a deep breath. "Yes."

She nodded, solemn, but pleased. "*Then as you have asked, Lyan, stargazer of Eilidh Wood, I will grant you this boon.*" Warmth flowed over Lyan like the gentle run of a sun-warmed stream, easing his pain and lulling him toward sleep. He struggled to keep his eyes open as the bear turned and walked away from him. She paused before the edge of the camp and looked back at him. Lyan swore he saw amusement glitter in her eyes. *"And Lyan, in regards to you using me to distract the pooka without asking my leave? Your apology is accepted."*

2 4

Gods and mortals,
Bears and blades,
Secrets and silence

Awareness drew Lyan from the comfortable laziness of a deep, restful sleep. He blinked away sleep with dawn's light glowing in the sky. When he drew a deep breath, nothing hurt. Pushing up on one elbow, Lyan looked around the sleeping camp.

"Who's on watch?" Even his voice was steadier.

"Me." Dalrian hurried toward him anxiously. "Do you need anything? Should I wake Shiolto?"

Lyan shook his head. "No, I'm all right. I just wanted to ask if you heard anything strange last night. Large animals?"

Dalrian gave him a bemused look. "It was quiet all my watch, and Shiolto was before me. He'd have mentioned if he heard anything. We're all watching for the pooka. Do you think it was around last night?"

"Not the pooka, but I heard something. No one else woke up, though," Lyan answered. He recalled the bear and her words. *She didn't want anyone else to witness her visit, and had the power to ensure it.*

"A large animal? I'll check for tracks once the others wake," Dalrian promised. If he suspected Lyan had only dreamed the sounds, he hid it well. "Your color's better, and you slept hard during my watch. I'm pretty sure that's good."

Lyan smiled. "Thanks, Dalrian. I'm feeling much better today."

Dalrian resumed his patrol. Lyan turned his gaze to the sky and wondered if he'd only dreamed the bear. Looking to the ground beside his pallet, he sucked in a sharp, startled breath. A single, deliberate, distinct print marked the dew-damp dirt. Lyan ran his finger over the massive paw print, feeling the impression and knowing it was real. He saw no other tracks, approaching or departing.

Slowly, he sat. The previous day, doing so would have left him breathless and shaking with pain. His chest ached, the bandages too tight and restricting his breathing. Lyan picked at them, trying to loosen Shiolto's careful work. Beside him, Kithr roused.

"Lyan? What's wrong?" Sleep fogged Kithr's voice.

"The bandages are too tight," Lyan told him.

"Leave them alone," Kithr told him in Elven, half-opening one eye. Seeing that Lyan wasn't listening, he heaved an aggravated sigh and sat. "Stop. At least let me do that before you make something worse."

Lyan relinquished his efforts to untie the bandages to Kithr, watching his friend carefully. "How are you feeling?"

Kithr stretched, winced, and rolled his shoulders. "A little stiff, otherwise fine. Slept well."

"Did you hear anything strange in the night?"

Kithr frowned. "No. Why?"

Lyan pointed to the bear print.

Kithr rubbed his eyes and looked past Lyan to the ground. His entire body stiffened and his eyes opened wide. "Soldarr's axe! A bear? In the camp?" He turned sharply to Lyan. "What is this?"

"Help me take off these bandages, and we can decide if I've lost my mind," Lyan said quietly.

Kithr tore his gaze from the track with an effort and unwrapped the stiff, stained bandages. He froze again. "Lyan…" Kithr's tone said he questioned his own sanity.

Lyan looked down at the new pink skin on his chest. He hadn't wanted to see his chest before, and Shiolto had made every effort to shield the sight from him. Lyan could only guess how severe his injuries had been. He ran a finger over a thin, faded scar where one of the most painful burns had been. Not even discomfort remained.

"Lyan, what in rot and ashes happened?" Kithr demanded in a whisper.

Lyan licked dry lips. "Last night, some being entered our camp in the form of a bear. It… she spoke to me, and she…" He looked at his chest, then at Kithr. "She healed me, Kithr. And unless I'm mistaken, she healed you too."

Kithr started, as if in his focus on Lyan, he'd forgotten his own injuries. He suspiciously lifted the side of his shirt, and Lyan saw a bloody bandage wrapped around Kithr's ribs. Kithr pulled down an edge of the bandage, then looked sharply at Lyan. "What did you do, Lyan? Did you make some sort of bargain with this creature?"

"No. No, I didn't." Lyan cast his thoughts back, and couldn't remember anything he'd said that could be considered making a bargain. "I… think she was one of the Guardians of Equinox."

Kithr tensed. "What did she say, Lyan?"

Cailean stirred and lifted his head as Kithr forgot to keep his voice low. "What's wrong?" the Tathren lord asked, bleary-eyed.

"She said I had endured the Trial of Fire and asked what

reward I desired. I said that I wanted for you and I to both be fit to ride," Lyan told Kithr.

"Lyan? Kithr? What's wrong?" Cailean crawled from his bedroll, rubbing his eyes.

"I'm fine, Cailean," Lyan answered.

Cailean looked at him, blinked and rubbed his eyes, and looked from Lyan to the bandages on the ground, and back to Lyan. Lingering traces of sleep fell away. "Maybe you are, but there's no way in the gods' names you *should* be." His gaze was as sharp as Kithr's. "What happened?"

The rest of the party was starting to rouse. Lyan held up a hand to Cailean. "Could I wait until everyone is awake, so I don't have to repeat myself? Please?"

"There *will* be an explanation, I hope," Cailean said.

Lyan nodded. "As best I can give one. But first, I'm… very hungry." His stomach twisted and growled, as if wanting to make up for all missed meals immediately.

Cailean gave him a curt nod, displeased to be dismissed. The Tathren lord stirred the fire to life. Kithr still watched Lyan, expression unreadable. Lyan waited for his friend to speak.

"The Trial of Fire," Kithr said in Elven.

Lyan nodded silently.

"Not *a* trial. *The* Trial."

"Yes," Lyan confirmed quietly.

"A guardian of Equinox rewarded you for succeeding in the Trial of Fire." Kithr seemed determined to force Lyan to say the words again himself.

"I *know*, Kithr!" Lyan burst.

Kithr let out a deep breath. When he spoke again, his voice was deceptively calm. "At least you won't have to worry about your Tathren trying to claim both Spears."

Lyan opened his mouth, stopped, and tried again. "Kithr, I didn't leave Eilidh Wood with the intention—"

"Didn't you?" Kithr cut in. "You wanted to find Equinox. First seeds, Lyan, who wouldn't? And you know where to go; you've figured out whatever riddle you claim is written in the stars. You said it yourself, Lyan: the signs are there to guide the next Bearer to the Spear. Now a Guardian of Equinox says you've completed one of the Trials. What do *you* think that means?"

"What are Kithr and Lyan arguing about?" Shiolto asked from across the camp.

"Perhaps they discuss who ought to have noticed the bear that left her print beside Lyan," Yion answered, mild tone at odd with his words. "I know the question of how I could have failed to observe such an entrance weighs on my thoughts."

"A bear?" Shiolto repeated in consternation. "When? I didn't hear anything on my watch." He looked to his brother, then Torqual. Both shook their heads.

"A bear, at the side of the elf, and he's without further injury?" Aikan scowled fiercely, as if Lyan were somehow to blame for something again.

Lyan seized the chance to avoid Kithr's pointed words. "Yes, a bear entered our camp last night. Or rather...." He hesitated a moment, then trusted his instincts. "A Guardian of Equinox in the form of a bear entered our camp last night."

Cailean turned from the fire. "That's not an explanation, Lyan."

Lyan drew a deep breath that the previous day would have left him trembling in pain. "She said I hadn't revealed anything to Vynzent when he questioned me. She asked what I wanted as a reward for fighting to protect the Spear from someone unworthy of it."

"What did you tell her?" Shiolto asked, eyes wide.

"I asked to be fit to ride." Lyan slowly stood and faced his companions. Twinges of pain ran through his ankle, but he could stand without assistance. "And she healed me."

Sharp intakes of breath met his words and the sight of his healed chest.

Aikan, inexplicably, looked outraged. "And to which of the elven gods is the bear sacred?"

Lyan looked at Aikan in confusion, bewildered by the question. "What?"

Kithr, however, smirked and rose. "To none of our gods. The bear is only a sacred animal to your *Tathren* god Ahebban, Watcher on the Walls." With the smile of one knowingly stirring up trouble, he added, "Perhaps he hates elves less than you think."

Aikan sprang to his feet in outrage. "You dare!"

"I dare what, Tathren? Say what I see?" Kithr retorted.

"Do not insult our gods, elf!" Aikan snapped.

Kithr laughed scornfully. "An animal sacred to one of your gods entered our camp, prevented anyone but Lyan from knowing it was there, healed him, and left. So tell me, how am *I* insulting your gods?"

"She was a guardian of the Spear of the Stars," Lyan interrupted, desperately trying to head off a fistfight between Kithr and Aikan. "The Tathren gods have no more wish to see the Mad God free than the elven gods, do they?" He turned to Kithr and added in Elven, "Don't bait him, Kithr. We're on the same side."

"If you say so," Kithr responded in the same.

Lyan looked back at Aikan. The man trembled with anger, hands clenched into fists. *Are we on the same side, Aikan? Or are you the traitor among us?*

Lyan's stomach growled loudly, breaking the tension as no words could have. Dalrian chuckled. "I guess healing that fast makes a person hungry."

"Starving," Lyan acknowledged wryly.

"At least some troubles have simple answers." Cailean filled a bowl with the previous night's stew and handed it to Lyan.

He accepted the food and devoured it with a vengeance. When Lyan had scraped the bowl clean and licked the last scraps from his fingers, Cailean refilled the bowl. From Aikan's fierce scowl, filling bowls and serving food were improper activities for a lord, and Shiolto scrambled to take Cailean's place. While his companions broke their fasts, Lyan finished off his second helping. He resisted the urge to ask for a third, though the emptiness in his stomach hardly felt any lessened.

Kithr ate with equal vigor, though he made an effort to be less obvious about it. Shiolto asked him something, and Kithr shook his head in answer. Shiolto frowned, and Kithr shook his head again with a characteristic glower. "I'm fine, Tathren, and I can deal with my own bandages."

"Just because Lyan's healed doesn't mean you have to start acting like we're enemies, Kithr!" Shiolto said, exasperated. "I'm trying to help."

"It's unnecessary," Kithr responded. He scowled, then relented. "What Lyan neglected to mention is that he not only asked for his own healing, but mine as well."

Aikan glowered at both elves. "Don't try to claim Lord Ahebban's hand was involved in healing an elf who attacked and pillaged our land. Call that bear another of the spirits that seem drawn to Lyan—its work was certainly not that of a servant of our gods." He turned to Cailean. "However, with Lyan's recovery, it appears that our greatest obstacle to continuing is resolved, my lord. We should ride today."

As Lyan helped pack the camp, he discovered new aches, and stiffness that slowly worked out as he moved. His ankle complained, but the discomfort paled compared to the pain he no longer felt.

Whether you came here by the will of a Tathren god or by some other, thank you for your help, Lady.

Shadowstar nuzzled Lyan, and he scratched the stallion's ears. "And thank you as well, Shadowstar. Thank you for watching over Kithr and for finding me."

By late morning, birds sang from the spindly branches of tall, slender trees, and small animals rustled and darted through the lush undergrowth as Lyan, Kithr, and the Tathrens took to the trail again. Calling the path they followed a road was overly generous to the track of packed dirt, barely wide enough for two riders abreast. The trees crowded together, as if fearing to be alone, and some reached branches out to hang over the trail.

"This isn't the only road, is it?" Lyan asked.

Cailean, ahead of him, turned in the saddle and shook his head. "There's a main road, but Vynzent avoided it like his life depended on it—and it probably did. For now, I'm following his example. We might meet bandits lurking away from the road, but I think we're better off taking our chances with any such encounters than we are on the road."

Lyan frowned. "Why?"

Shiolto answered. "While we were on your trail, we met some people. They were pretty tattered, and one said soldiers attacked their village. They didn't know who the men were, but when they found a patrol of their own soldiers on the main road and asked for help, the soldiers demanded they surrender any valuables as a 'war tax.' When they said they'd lost everything, the men threatened them, looted what little they had, and took one of the young women before driving them away. Those folk warned us against going anywhere near the main road. Gods only know what soldiers looking for trouble would do if they ran into armed men."

"At that point, we couldn't have afforded the time we would have lost to an encounter with soldiers, and I can't afford to pay whatever taxes they want," Cailean added. "I don't want to get caught up in whatever trouble brews here. We're half a day's good ride from the border, by my reading of your map, and whatever ill wind blows through this area, I want to put it behind us."

Lyan nodded in understanding. He tried to get his bearings, but he felt disoriented, lacking any good sense of their location. He promised himself a look at the map once they stopped, but for now he had to trust Cailean's judgment.

Kithr's horse walked beside Shadowstar. Lyan turned to his friend and spoke in Elven. "Are you going to stay with the group?"

Kithr nodded. "For today, at least. As the Spearbearer said, there are strange things in the air, and I'm not going to test my luck against the pooka, wherever it's hiding, or against whatever else might lurk near." He eyed Lyan, then finally said, "I didn't thank you."

"For what?" Lyan asked.

"For asking your mysterious guardian bear to heal me. Thanks."

Lyan shifted uncomfortably. "Kithr, I didn't accompany Cailean with the thought of trying to claim Equinox. I didn't think beyond… the reason I told you."

Kithr sighed. "That doesn't surprise me, knowing you. Fires, you can be such a mooncalf sometimes, Lyan."

"I know," Lyan acknowledged. "Though I thought my cousin was the only person who called me that." He watched a red-breasted bird jump from branch to branch, scolding them. "Do you think that bear was actually a servant of Ahebban? I didn't know Tathren gods have sacred animals."

"Some do, some don't," Kithr replied. "As for Ahebban, don't you know more about him than that?"

"I know the names of some of the Tathren gods, and he's their leader," Lyan answered. "And that he's said to have a grudge against Soldarr."

"According to Tathrens, Ahebban hates elves with a passion, and it goes back to a fight between him and Soldarr," Kithr replied. "Don't ask me why they fought; I don't know. Ahebban supposedly protects those walled fortresses Tathrens like so much. And yes, bears are sacred to him. Tathrens won't hunt bears." Kithr's eyes glittered maliciously. "We, on the other hand, made a point of doing so at every opportunity while in Tather."

"And that's why Aikan was so offended when you suggested Ahebban sent the bear," Lyan said, understanding.

"The old man's easy to rile. He's probably right, and the Tathren gods had nothing to do with the bear."

"What other Tathren gods have sacred animals?"

"Why not ask the Tathrens? You seem to have a few around here." Kithr continued despite his words. "The main ones I know of are Saiboti, Erskine, and Kessel. Saiboti is their god of war… or warriors, I was never sure which. His animal is the hound, and he's brother to Ahebban. Erskine is god of the fields, and the cat is sacred to him. As for Kessel, her animal is the crane, but I couldn't tell you what she's goddess of. The rest of their gods aren't associated with animals."

"Don't the Tathrens have more goddesses?" Lyan asked.

"Not many of importance that I know of. The Tathren gods seem to prefer mortal women, to judge from their legends. Most of their heroes are either children or descendants of one or another of their gods."

Lyan ducked under a low branch. "So are some of ours, Kithr."

"True, but Eilidh Wood hasn't seen any children of divine origins since Tesseia threatened to castrate Soldarr next time he lay with a mortal woman," Kithr said.

Lyan smiled slightly, though both the irreverence and the thought made him wince.

The day passed quietly, and when they stopped for the night, Cailean pulled out the map before Lyan had to ask. Lyan spent the evening light studying the parchment. Was it coincidence that strange, sinister events were unfolding so near the hidden Shrine of Equinox? Or was it a sign of Murdo's hand seeking to close around one of the Spears?

As darkness settled across the sky, Lyan gazed up in the

continuous, faint hope that he would find stars. The clouds gathered, snuffing out the slim hope. Lyan rolled the map, returned it to the scroll case, and lay down to sleep.

What Trials do I have to endure to clear the skies and give me back the stars?

2 5

Seek the path
For it opens to those who search
Seek the way
For at the end lies the truth

Two days after Lyan's healing when they stopped for the night, Torqual paced restlessly around the camp. The Tathren paused, then spun and fixed his gaze on Kithr.

"Spar with me."

Kithr started, eyes narrowing suspiciously. "Why?"

"I need someone to train with before I lose any more of my skills."

Lyan looked up from study of the map. He rarely heard Torqual say much.

Kithr made no move to stand. "Then ask one of your own people."

"They aren't soldiers," Torqual retorted. "They won't challenge me. And I want to see if the stories do justice to the skills of elven warriors."

Kithr couldn't ignore that challenge. He rose. "Practice staves or bare blades, Tathren?"

Torqual smiled as he retrieved a pair of staves he'd been whittling during the day's ride. Each was about the length of a sword. Lyan rolled up the map and set it aside to watch. The exchange between Torqual and Kithr had drawn attention from the others as well. Shiolto and Dalrian pulled packs aside, clearing a space for Kithr and Torqual.

"Try not to break any bones," Cailean warned.

"I'll be careful not to hurt him too much, Lord Cailean," Torqual replied.

Kithr smirked, amused rather than insulted. "Worry about your own bones, not mine."

Torqual returned the smirk and offered Kithr his choice of weapons. Kithr weighed both in his hands and took one. Elf and Tathren faced each other, settling into fighting stances. Kithr took the offensive first with a series of quick attacks. Torqual blocked and parried, but Lyan, watching carefully, knew Kithr's stave made contact with skin more than once. In a real battle, Kithr would have intended those to draw blood, weakening and distracting his opponent. In this fight, they would leave bruises. Lyan well remember the bruises he'd carried anytime Kithr had convinced him to spar.

Torqual had more skill than Lyan ever would, and shifted from defending to attacking. Kithr, in turn, blocked many blows, but Lyan suspected both combatants would have their share of bruises to show.

Torqual and Kithr separated, each taking a step back. Neither appeared winded, and a moment later, wooden staves clattered again as they resumed the battle.

Kithr lunged and swung not at Torqual, but at the other's weapon, intending to strike it out of Torqual's hand. Torqual twisted aside, avoiding the attack and tripping Kithr. Kithr landed hard, the wind knocked from him, and Torqual touched the tip of his stave to Kithr's chest.

Defeat was unfamiliar to Kithr, and his eyes burned with anger as he glared at Torqual. Finally, though, he nodded in acceptance of the Tathren's victory, though his eyes narrowed. "You expected that."

"Using the same tactics repeatedly only works until your opponent learns how to counter them." Torqual offered Kithr a hand up. "You fight the same way your people did three of our generations ago. We've had some time to learn them."

Kithr took the offered hand and let Torqual pull him up. As he stood, Kithr's off hand scooped up his stave and used it to give Torqual a quick, though not too forceful, jab in the gut. "In that case, you ought to remember this as well."

Torqual winced and coughed. "The old saying about never approaching a dead elf until you're sure he's dead?"

Kithr got his feet under him and smirked. "Vynzent's men remembered it well enough, to my disappointment."

"I'm not familiar with this saying…." Lyan said, trailing off in a questioning tone.

Kithr looked to him. "A half-dead warrior is one who's still half alive. And one who's half alive is one who keeps a dagger close to take down any Tathren foolish enough to come close."

"I heard one old soldier say he wouldn't go near the body of any elf, ever. Not even one clearly in advanced states of decay, for fear that somehow, the elf would still have enough life left to kill him," Torqual added.

Kithr tossed the stave back into his main hand and took another jab at Torqual. Torqual barely blocked it. "Seems I'm out of practice, Tathren. Another bout?"

"I should hope so," Torqual replied. "I haven't even worked up a sweat."

Lyan pulled his gaze from the sparring and unrolled the map again, trying to focus despite the clattering staves. He snuck glances back at the mock battle, though. Kithr adopted a less aggressive strategy, letting Torqual attack him while he studied his opponent's style. They sparred for several minutes before the Tathren grew overconfident, and Kithr found an opening, dodging one attack and spinning around behind Torqual to slap the stave against the human's exposed back.

Torqual grunted, but smiled. "We're even, then."

"Dinner's ready, whenever you two are done trying to hit each other," Shiolto called.

"Hmm." Kithr tossed his stave to Torqual, who caught it easily. "You aren't bad, for a Tathren."

"And you're not bad, for an old man," Torqual responded. He set the staves with his weapons and speared one of the game birds roasting over the fire with his long knife.

Lyan had smelled the birds cooking, and quickly stowed the map again. Dalrian handed him a bird still on its spit. Lyan accepted it with a word of thanks, grateful for the reprieve from stew and hard bricks of bread. He peeled away the blackened skin to reach the hot, juicy meat, nearly scalding his fingers in the process. Lyan ate the bird straight off the spit, imitating his companions, and picked meat from the bones with his fingers. Only Aikan made a token effort to use his belt knife to cut the meat, and even he soon used fingers instead.

Lyan wiped greasy fingers on his tunic after stripping the last scraps from his bird. Everyone welcomed the variety as much as he did, to judge from the lack of conversation as they all devoted their attention to the meal.

"This tastes wonderful," Cailean said around a mouthful.

"Thank Yion," Dalrian said. "He caught the birds."

"Fortune smiled on my hunt," Yion responded. "I saw few tracks other than those of the birds—deer, for the most part, and no tracks of men."

Cailean nodded, wiping his mouth on his sleeve, then he turned to Lyan. "Does the map indicate any settlements nearby?"

"One a day's ride south, and several along the river," Lyan said, wiping his fingers clean again. "But those are the closest I saw on the map—which seems strange, not to have some closer to the border."

"That depends on how well the neighboring countries get along," Cailean said. "There might be villages not on the map, but hopefully we can avoid most encounters. I'd rather not meet anyone who could identify us or the direction we traveled."

"Because of the things those people said about soldiers, sir?" Shiolto asked.

"Because I like the idea of having a few days when nothing's actively trying to kill, harass, or imprison us," Cailean said with a wry smile. "Even if Torqual seems to think a little calm will make him forget all his fighting skills."

Torqual sniffed. "Few of the men we've fought thus far had enough skill to be called warriors." He nodded toward Kithr. "An opponent with more finesse and less reliance on brute force will be welcome for training."

Kithr picked his teeth with a bone, listening. He was the closest to looking relaxed as Lyan had seen him around the Tathrens. Tossing aside the bone, he leaned back on his elbows. "Who are your best trackers? If you want to avoid people, you'll want more than one scout, using the men most familiar with this terrain. Lyan, what are we going to be seeing?"

"We're bound west by northwest, through forests and mountains," Lyan said.

"In that case, you're probably the best suited among us, Kithr," Cailean said. "Dalrian is also skilled in tracking."

"I am not familiar with this area, Lord Cailean, but I have some skill in the tactic Kithr speaks of," Yion said.

"Of course," Kithr muttered under his breath in Elven. "The mercenary."

"Kithr, would you organize the scouts as you think best?" Cailean asked.

Kithr cast Cailean a surprised look.

Cailean continued. "You have the most experience in this area. Since you brought up the subject, I assume you have something in mind already."

Dalrian didn't look happy with the idea. Yion remained unperturbed. Kithr studied both, then nodded. "Tomorrow. Three scouts should suffice for this group."

~

The following morning, Kithr instructed Dalrian to ride behind the group and watch for anything on their trail while he and Yion rode ahead and to either side of the party. Lyan didn't hear most of the instructions, but he did catch Kithr's final warning.

"Don't go too far back. Remember that the pooka's watching us."

The day passed without incident. Kithr rotated the scouts during the ride. The few times Lyan saw him before they made camp, Kithr was scowling.

Once everyone settled into camp, Cailean asked, "Anything to report?"

"No tracks," Kithr said. He looked to Dalrian. "You're too loud."

Dalrian jumped to his feet, insulted. "What?"

"Every time you changed posts, any spies nearby could have heard you—even humans. Work on it. You do tolerably once you're in place."

Dalrian glared, face red with anger at the curt dismissal of his skills. "So it isn't enough for an elf that I can track a deer across a forest without it knowing I'm there? What exactly *do* you expect, then?"

"That could be enough if you were the hunter. But right now, you're not the hunter, Tathren. You're not stalking the deer, you *are* the deer. Stop telling the hunter where you are."

Dalrian blinked, startled by Kithr's answer. Finally he sat back down without saying anything.

Lyan waited for Kithr to issue some criticism at Yion as well, but he didn't, instead sitting down beside Lyan with a tired sound.

"Sparring with Torqual tonight?' Lyan asked in Elven.

Kithr shook his head. "No. I've had enough of Tathrens and their carelessness for one day. It's obvious Dalrian has never stalked anything smarter than an animal." Kithr's gaze moved to Yion and he scowled. "And just as obvious that the mercenary knows exactly what he's doing."

"Kithr, why do you dislike Yion?"

"He knows how to hunt a man, and how to hide from one. He knows herbs, he knows drugs, and I would wager my bow he knows poisons. You say he wouldn't tell you where he came from. I don't like the implications. On top of that, he's a *mercenary*." Kithr said the word with at least as much venom as he would say "Tathren". "A soldier or warrior fights for loyalty to his lord, or country, or for a cause. A mercenary has no loyalty, no reason for being on the battlefield except for money. He makes a business out of killing people he has no grudge against. No reason not to change sides." Kithr gazed at Lyan. "Didn't you tell me Yion changed sides once already?"

"From the side that was winning to that of the loser," Lyan said. "Doesn't sound like the decision of someone just looking for money."

"It makes his motives all the more suspicious," Kithr said, "and leaves a sensible person wondering what he's hiding."

"I do so appreciate your confidence in my ability to judge character," Lyan muttered.

"You've been sheltered, Lyan. You've lived in Eilidh Wood; you don't know the world beyond it except by your books and the stories that the horse tenders of the plains tell. I listen to you, though I might not agree with your judgments."

Lyan gave him a dubious look.

"I do. After all, I'm here, aren't I?"

"Yes, I guess I can't argue with that."

Kithr chuckled softly. "You worry about getting us where we're going. Leave worrying about what might not want us to get there to me."

~

They continued northwest for three more days. A few times, one of the scouts saw signs of people, encountering isolated shacks, and once a village wedged between a rock face and the trees. At Cailean's instructions, they avoided the habitations, skirting around them and keeping to the forest. Kithr didn't find any signs that they were being followed, and the pooka, if it still lingered on their trail, remained unusually silent.

On the fourth day, Lyan couldn't shake the feeling that something watched them. Shadowstar was calm, though Lyan's restlessness and unease carried to the stallion. The massive hardwood trees could practically hide a village in their branches, and Lyan found himself looking up often, searching the branches high overhead for signs of movement.

His preoccupation didn't go unnoticed. Aikan snorted in scornful humor. "For all that it is called the Spear of the Stars, elf, I doubt Equinox is going to drop from the sky onto us."

Lyan started and looked at the man. "That's not... I just..."

"What's wrong, Lyan?" Cailean asked.

"I feel like something's watching us, but I don't know what, or from where. If it were on the ground, Kithr, Yion, or Dalrian ought to have found some sign."

Cailean reached for Solstice. "Something spying on us again? Something hostile?"

"I don't know," Lyan admitted.

"So helpful," Aikan scoffed.

In the face of Aikan's mockery, Lyan held back his doubts

as to whether he was imagining the watcher or not. He straightened in the saddle. "We're getting close to the sanctuary of Equinox. More than likely, one of the guardians is watching us."

"A bear, no doubt, that somehow leaves no tracks," Aikan countered.

"She leaves tracks if she chooses to. Perhaps she doesn't want to reveal herself to someone who doubts her existence," Lyan said coolly.

"Perhaps she enjoys listening to the banter of mortals," whispered a familiar female voice in Lyan's mind. *"Call your friends close, Lyan of Eilidh Wood. The path will not reveal itself to them, only to you, and if you follow it without them, they will not find it."*

Lyan drew a sharp breath and pulled Shadowstar to a stop.

"Lyan?" Cailean asked.

Lyan raised his voice a little. "Kithr, Yion, Dalrian, gather up."

The scouts converged on their position quickly. "What's wrong?" Kithr demanded.

"We're close," Lyan said. "We need to stay together now, or some of you might miss the path when it reveals itself."

Surprise and disbelief crossed the faces of Cailean's men. "You mean… we're *all* going to see this place where the Spear is?" Shiolto asked.

Lyan frowned. "Why wouldn't you?"

"In this sort of story, just a few people actually get to see places like that—you know, the lords and nobles and heroes, not the stable hands and the like." Shiolto glanced at the others and was met with nods of agreement. Even Aikan looked taken aback at the idea.

Lyan gazed at his companions and spoke bluntly. "Yes, you're all going to see it. But don't think that it means you'll be able to find it again. Even if you know exactly where the path reveals itself to us, you won't be able to locate it a second time. The power of Equinox protects the Shrine, and the Spear decides who it will reveal the path to. It shows the way to those worthy to take the Trials—those worthy to claim the Spear. Don't think I'll allow you free access to a place sacred to my people, any more than you would give the same to Kithr and me."

Silence met his words. Lyan flicked the reins, and Shadowstar started walking. Lyan's pulse pounded, whether at the thought of seeing the shrine, or in fear he hesitated to name after issuing such a statement to his companions.

He heard the other horses following. Birds chirped in the trees, and a breeze stirred the branches, showering down a cascade of leaves. Lyan closed his eyes, envisioning the path. A narrow track, barely noticeable at first, almost an animal trail, leading through the forest. It would widen gradually, and the magic at work would be subtle, beyond the recognition of most people. Most wouldn't even realize they were on a path until they began to pass the low-lying light posts—white stone markers lining the path, their tops hollow and a peaked cover resting over the opening.

Shadowstar snorted and tossed his head, and Lyan opened his eyes. His breath caught a moment as he realized that the stallion was expressing appreciation for the solid path under his hooves—narrow enough to be an animal trail, but, Lyan knew in his heart, a trail made by no mortal power.

"This is it," he whispered.

"This is what?" Cailean asked.

"This is the path that will lead us to the Spear," Yion said, his voice calm, but hushed, tone reverent.

"We'll see the light posts soon," Lyan said, "though it's too early in the day for them to be glowing."

The path widened, as he knew it would, and Kithr walked his horse up beside Lyan. Lyan glanced at his friend, and read nervous tension in Kithr's face.

"Don't worry; it'll be all right," Lyan said in Elven.

Kithr glanced at him. "Trials, Lyan. More Trials. Of course I worry." He paused. "And… by the gods, you are leading us to a place of legend, Lyan. You are bringing us to the Shrine of Equinox."

Lyan looked at his hands, sharply overwhelmed by the thought. He didn't speak, even when the light posts began to appear, and the Tathrens exclaimed in surprise. He didn't say anything until, abruptly, the path ended at a closed gate of silver metal, wrought in a lattice too tight for even a child to squeeze through. A wall of white stone stretched to either side of the gate, and the trees and foliage off the path wove into an impenetrable barrier, leaving them nowhere to go but back the way they had come… or forward, through the gate.

A single figure stood before the gate, as Lyan knew she would: a bear with fur as black as night, a stiff ruff of dark brown fur running down her back and silver runes on her face. Before their eyes, she rose on her hind legs, her form melting and shifting like water, becoming an elven woman. Her hair, long and black, flowed over her shoulders. At the crown of her head, white streaks ran through her hair. Her brown eyes fixed on Lyan, and she spoke in a musical voice.

"We have been waiting for you. Welcome, Lyan of Eilidh Wood."

2 6

White stone, temple walls
Mist and dreams, forgotten halls

Lyan climbed down from Shadowstar and bowed deeply to the woman. "Lady, we ask your permission to enter this sacred shrine."

She gazed at Lyan, then studied the other members of the group. Her eyes lingered on each man just long enough to elicit uncomfortable shifting. Even Kithr self-consciously rubbed his cheek as if to wipe away dust.

When the woman spoke, Lyan understood her without needing the earring to translate, but he couldn't say what language she used. "Enter under the protection of Equinox, but know that you enter as guests, not as claimants to the Spear, aside from the one among you who is worthy to take the Trials."

Lyan's companions glanced at each other uncertainly. Shiolto ventured a question. "Um… what… does that mean, Lady?"

She smiled at him. "It means you will not be allowed free access to the whole of the shrine. The Guardians will tell you if you are not allowed to enter an area. Heed them—the consequences of ignoring their warnings will be swift and bloody. In addition, you must leave your weapons with the gatekeeper."

"All of us?" Cailean asked warily.

"All but you and Lyan, Spearbearer Cailean. Solstice remains in your keeping."

Cailean's shoulders relaxed slightly, then his brow creased in a frown. "You know who I am?"

"This is home to Equinox, brother to Solstice, Spearbearer Cailean. We Guardians of the Shrine make it our business to know who bears your Spear." She turned, resting her hand against the gate. It swung open. She stepped over the threshold, beckoning them to follow.

Lyan entered first, leading Shadowstar. Magic tingled over his skin as he walked through the gate. Mist curled and pooled around his feet. To either side, white walls rose to form a straight path, leading from the outer gate to the inner, nearly identical to the first. Pale stones paved the walkway, lined on either side by broad-leafed plants that Lyan didn't recognize. The large flower buds at the ends of the stems hung lazily, as if sleeping. Lyan looked around and realized with consternation that the woman was gone and he hadn't even noticed her departure. Before the inner gate sat an elf dressed in a long brown robe. A woven headband restrained short reddish-brown hair. He looked nearly the age Lyan's father would have been, were he still alive. The gatekeeper greeted Lyan with a smile, rising from his stool.

"You are free to pass. Your companions can do the same once they have left their weapons here."

"Do you mind if I wait for them?" Lyan asked.

"That's up to you," the gatekeeper answered.

Lyan started to move to the side, but before he stepped from the paved path, the gatekeeper caught his arm.

"It'd be better to wait at the gate. The space will be

crowded, and the dragontooth flowers wake with too much activity around them."

Lyan started and edged away from the broad-leafed plants, seeing one of the flower buds closest to him bob, as if sensing his presence. "Dragontooth flowers?" he repeated. He'd heard of the carnivorous plants before, but had never seen one.

"Not all who seeks Equinox come under the banner of peace," the gatekeeper replied, a glitter in his eyes.

Lyan looked again at the entryway, realizing how it confined and restricted the flow of any group trying to enter. He nodded and walked past the gatekeeper to the edge of the gate as his companions approached. Kithr came first. He scowled, but handed over bow and quiver, then his knives. The gatekeeper accepted the weapons, giving the bow a look of admiration, then cast a critical look over Kithr. With a nod, he gave Kithr permission to pass. Cailean followed. The Tathren noble kept Solstice, but offered over his belt knife, and he too was permitted to pass.

The rest of the Tathrens sorted themselves into some ranking Lyan didn't try to understand. Aikan came after Cailean. He considered the elven gatekeeper suspiciously, but surrendered his weapons. Torqual followed, and he unloaded sword, the practice staves from his bag, and a smaller blade. The gatekeeper simply gazed at him, waiting. Torqual gazed back, and neither moved or spoke. Torqual broke eye contact first, muttering under his breath, then rolled up his sleeve to unbuckle a dagger sheath strapped to his arm. The gatekeeper looked him over critically, then said, "The earring as well."

Torqual started. "What? Why?"

"Torqual, do as he says," Cailean ordered.

"Fine." Torqual pulled the ring from his ear with ill grace, slapping it into the gatekeeper's palm.

"You may pass," the gatekeeper told him mildly.

Dalrian and Shiolto entered without mishap. Yion, the last to enter, laid one saddlebag at the gatekeeper's feet, then divested himself of an impressive collection of throwing stars, knives, his sword, and some weapons Lyan couldn't identify.

"These are all the weapons in my possession that I can remove," Yion said, awaiting the gatekeeper's judgment.

The gatekeeper considered Yion for a long moment. His only comment, however, was, "Interesting. You may pass."

Yion bowed. "Thank you."

"I expect to get everything back when I leave," Torqual said sharply. He shifted from one foot to the other, discomfited to be unarmed in an unfamiliar situation. Lyan could see the same unease in Kithr, though Kithr was less obvious about it.

"You will," the gatekeeper said, unperturbed. "When you leave."

The mist that swirled between the gates dissipated within the shrine itself. Lyan looked around slowly, stepping aside to let his friends and companions in. Stone-paved paths lined with fluted pillars wound through a lush garden of unfamiliar plants. Buildings of white stone, like the outer wall, looked as if they had grown from the ground as naturally as the plants. Though trees hid some of the shrine from sight, Lyan counted five smaller structures at a glance, and one larger building. Pillars supported the roof of the larger building, creating a covered porch beyond the walls. He thought carvings decorated the walls, but without getting closer, he couldn't see what the images depicted.

The black-haired woman waited for them, and she smiled. "Once again, welcome to the Shrine of Equinox. It's been some time since we last had visitors. I am Venycia, a Guardian of the Spear. All who reside here are Guardians of the Spear."

"All?" Torqual looked around, not seeing anyone else. "Are there many here?"

"More than you may think. We all have duties to perform —duties essential to the protection and preservation of this place. You will meet some of the others during your stay. Now come, rest from your journey. Leave your mounts here. They'll be tended."

Lyan rubbed Shadowstar's nose. "Behave yourself, okay?"

The stallion gave an amused snort and nuzzled Lyan's hair. Lyan smiled, then followed Venycia. She led them into a smaller building, and Lyan realized the designation of "smaller" was deceptive. The building stood two stories tall, the first floor comprised of a single open room furnished as a gathering area. The long table could have easily seated three times their number, and around the edge of the room, padded chairs circled smaller tables for relaxed conversations, or games, or reading. A staircase led upstairs, the banister carved from a rich brown wood.

"This will be your dwelling area for as long as you are our guests," Venycia said. "Bedchambers are upstairs, and also a study with a small library, if you are interested. We will provide meals, any necessities, and such amenities as we can offer to you. Is there anything I can offer at the moment?"

Aikan looked at Cailean, then shot a venomous look at Lyan. He spoke to Venycia. "When we set out in search of Equinox, it was with the intent for my lord Cailean to seek the Spear. Your words so far have implied that the only person *you* consider worthy to claim Equinox is this… stargazing elf."

At Aikan's words, Lyan tensed. He opened his mouth, but stopped his words before they came. Before he could say that he could not allow Cailean to claim Equinox.

Venycia answered. "Spearbearer Cailean is not and never will be permitted to take the Trials to claim Equinox."

Lyan let out a breath he didn't remember holding, relief washing over him with the realization that he did not bear sole responsibility for stopping Cailean from taking the Trials.

Aikan stiffened, and Cailean looked startled and taken aback. "Why not?" Aikan demanded.

"Because he bears Solstice," she answered. "That alone is reason enough. There has only been one time when a mortal claimed both Spears, and there will never be another, so long as even one Guardian of the Spear remains alive. We will not allow it to happen again."

"Murdo," Cailean said quietly.

Venycia nodded. "He claimed both Spears of the Stars. That power unleashed his madness, and released chaos unlike any this world had known since the Devastation, destruction on a scale beyond any mortal's comprehension. Entire lands were swallowed by the seas, and new ones dredged from the ocean floor. Thousands died. The gods themselves fought him to contain his madness. They succeeded, at great cost, but such forces should never be unleashed again. Even a mortal of strong heart and spirit can fall to the darker desires of his soul. It is no insult against you, Spearbearer Cailean. It is the way things must be. It is the way Solstice and Equinox have told us it must be."

Cailean nodded in reluctant acceptance. Aikan, however, wasn't satisfied. "So instead of Lord Cailean, you'll give that power to *him*?" He glowered at Lyan.

Kithr sneered. "Tell me, Tathren, would you rather see it in *my* hands?"

"We wouldn't be here without Lyan," Cailean said. "It's that simple, Aikan. Lyan solved the riddle to reveal the Shrine's location, not me. Once we left Eilidh Wood, we reached the extent of my knowledge. You asked me repeatedly why I let him choose our route, and now you have the answer: he knew where to go, and I didn't."

"Lyan has already completed one Trial," Venycia said in the following pause. "Two more await him." She turned to Lyan. "Tomorrow, they will begin. Choose three companions. They will aid you in the Trials at certain points. Or, if you choose unwisely, they will hinder you when you need them most. Choose now."

Lyan opened his mouth, on the verge of protesting the abrupt demand, but he caught himself. He drew a deep breath, then let it out, trying to calm his automatic, nervous reaction. Three companions. The first two were easy. "Kithr. Cailean." Lyan hesitated, looking at each of his companions. *I have to pick one more. Why does it have to be three? If it were only two, or even one, I know who I would choose.*

Aikan scowled at him. Torqual watched Lyan with interest. Shiolto and Dalrian looked uneasy, not sure whether to hope they were or were not picked. Yion just smiled, serene.

Who do I trust most, of all of them?

"One more," Venycia prompted.

"Yion." Lyan said the name quickly, before he could change his mind. "Kithr, Cailean, and Yion."

"Very well." She nodded, then walked to the door. "I hope you will all make use of the time you have to rest and relax from your journey. You are free to walk the grounds, and will be told if you are not allowed in a place."

Lyan let out a deep breath. Whether he'd made the right choices or not, it was done. Yion walked to him and rested a hand on Lyan's shoulder.

"You honor me with your trust, Lyan Stargazer. I pray that I prove worthy of it."

Lyan laughed nervously. "I think I'll be doing a lot of praying tonight myself." He looked to Kithr. "Kithr… can we talk for a bit?"

"Of course." Kithr followed Lyan outside.

They followed a path that wandered among plants Lyan had only read of in books. Lyan searched for the right words, and Kithr waited for him to speak. "There are…a few things you should know about the Trials."

Kithr gazed at him. "I'm sure there are any number of

things I should know about them. Which ones are you going to tell me?"

"I've passed the Trial of Fire. I believe that's the only one in which my life and health were in danger. The Trials are meant to challenge more than the physical abilities of the candidate."

"I hear a 'but', Lyan." Kithr's eyes narrowed. "If not death, what becomes of the people who fail the Trials?"

"They stay here," Lyan answered. "They… are bound to serve Equinox, and they stay here. They *are* the Guardians of the Spear."

"For the rest of their lives."

"Kithr, all the Guardians at this shrine—they are people who came here seeking to claim Equinox. Now their lives are bound to the Spear, and unless some other force kills them, they will live for as long as Equinox exists."

Kithr was silent for a long moment. Finally, he spoke. "You still intend to do this, Lyan?"

Lyan nodded, bracing for an argument.

Kithr let out a breath, then said, "Well, you've already completed one Trial. No sense in quitting now."

"Thank you, Kithr."

Kithr snorted. "As if you need my permission or my blessing. Just prove that all those years you've spent with your nose in a book and your head in the clouds have been worth it."

Lyan smiled. "I can do that."

"Good, because there's no way I'm making a trip home with only a bunch of Tathrens."

They walked in silence for a while, Lyan listening to the birds and looking at the plants, and Kithr keeping his thoughts to himself. They returned to the building just in time for dinner. A pair of humans, one man and one woman, brought covered trays. The table had been set with places for each of them, and the Tathrens were already seated. Lyan realized that his seat was at the head of the table, and he slipped into the chair self-consciously. The servers smiled at him.

"Enjoy."

The meat was hot, the greens steamed and still crisp. Lyan didn't try to identify the dishes—they were hot, and they were good, and that, for once, was more than enough to satisfy him. He couldn't dismiss the possibility that he might have all the time in the world to learn what they were after tomorrow.

After the meal, Lyan went upstairs and found the library. He tried to read, but his tumbling thoughts wouldn't let him focus. Finally, he opened the window and leaned outside, taking deep breaths of the evening air.

He heard voices below, and cocked his head to listen when he caught Venycia's words. "Lyan spoke to you."

Kithr answered. "I just want to know this: do you believe he can succeed in the Trials?"

"I would not have revealed my presence to him if I didn't believe he could become Bearer of Equinox, Kithr."

"And if he doesn't succeed, you get a stargazer and scholar to keep—and I know Lyan is very, very good at both." Suspicion colored Kithr's voice.

"Equinox does not collect followers the way some mortals collect baubles, Kithr. The Spears are the only weapons a mortal can hope to wield with any chance of standing against the Mad God. What use is Equinox's power if it only remains here, unused? What use would Equinox have for challengers who are unfit to succeed in the Trials? If Lyan succeeds, we will rejoice. If he does not, we will grieve, but we will welcome him as a brother."

"If Lyan doesn't succeed, I will take the Trials," Kithr said. Lyan started, taken aback by the words.

A long pause, then Venycia spoke. "If that is your intent, we will not stop you. But unlike Lyan, your chance of success in the Trials is, at best, slim."

"I know," Kithr said simply.

"I see…." she murmured. "That choice is yours, Kithr of Eilidh Wood, but if entry to the Guardians is what you seek, the Trials are not necessary. You can become a Guardian by choice, so long as Equinox accepts you. If you are so determined to remain at his side, I wish more friends as devoted as you existed in this world. Lyan will need them."

Four seals to wake
Three to aid
Two fates
One

A light rain fell over the shrine. Lyan stood outside in the predawn morning, the mist of rain settling on his clothes and hair. Shivers ran down his spine, though the rain was almost warm, and he shifted nervously from one foot to the other.

Kithr, Cailean, and Yion stood behind Lyan. Before him, Venycia and a gray-haired human man named Waldros studied him. Lyan sensed other shapes in the shadows and mist, but couldn't pick out forms.

"Who challenges the Trials of Equinox?" Waldros asked in a deep, clear voice.

"I do," Lyan answered.

"Your name?"

"I am Lyan, astrologer of Heartshrine Village of Eilidh Wood."

"By what right do you think yourself worthy of the Spear?"

"I solved the riddle in the stars, discovering the path and following it here," Lyan said.

Waldros's eyes narrowed. "You are neither the first nor the last to do so. Merely solving a riddle proves nothing. Why do you seek Equinox?"

During the night, Lyan had devised an answer to that question—a tale of selfless purity and devotion. He drew breath to recite the words he'd practiced, but let it out, leaving the words unspoken. He wouldn't begin his Trials with a lie. "You've heard every answer a person could give to that question before. I seek Equinox to prove myself. To show my home, my friends, and myself that I'm more than just a foolish stargazer." Behind Lyan, Kithr made a sound of protest, which both Lyan and Waldros ignored. Lyan glanced to the sky, and rain brushed his face. "To use the Spear's power to clear the clouds that cover the night and hide the stars." He looked back to Waldros. "But ultimately, I seek the Spear to aid and protect my friends and my home."

Waldros watched him, expression stony, leaving Lyan with the sense that his answer didn't satisfy the human, though he didn't know why. Waldros gave Lyan no clues. "Should you succeed and become the Spearbearer, you will bear the Spear for life. No other will be able to use it or take it from you, and you cannot pass the Spear to another, whether mortal or god. The powers, responsibilities, and burdens of Equinox fall solely on the Spearbearer, and to no other."

"I understand," Lyan responded.

"Many say that, few actually do. Are you determined to follow this path, accepting the results, for good or ill, Lyan of Eilidh Wood? Are you prepared?"

"I am ready."

Waldros smiled darkly. "I doubt that."

Behind Lyan, Kithr shifted, uneasy and suspicious.

Venycia looked past Lyan to his chosen companions. "For each potential claimant to Equinox, the Trials differ. Equinox has decreed that during Lyan's Trials, he shall have aid. There will come points in his Trials when he will need your help, and there will be other times when you cannot aid him, even if he calls out to you. Each of you holds a key to his success or failure."

"We do, Lady?" Cailean asked uneasily.

"Lyan has chosen you as his companions. Whether he has chosen wisely or foolishly will be seen." Venycia gestured, and three robed figures emerged from the mist. "These Guardians will guide you to your place and explain the rules you must follow. If you do not heed your instructions, you will be working against your friend."

Kithr set a hand on Lyan's shoulder. "Be careful, Lyan."

"You too," Lyan told him. "I'll... see you later."

"Gods be with you, Lyan," Cailean said, following his guide.

Lyan nodded.

Yion smiled, as calm and confident as ever. "Do not fear. That which is meant to be shall be."

"Are you ready, Lyan?" Venycia asked. "This is your final opportunity to turn back."

Lyan drew a deep breath. "I've already begun the Trials with fire and... Vynzent. I'm as ready as I can be."

"So be it," Waldros said coolly. Mist rose thicker around Lyan, seeping from the ground. "Around the shrine lie four seals of protection. Find each and speak the words to activate them. Beware, though...for each true seal, there are dozens of imitations, waiting to trap intruders. Also be aware, nothing forbids another would-be claimant from challenging their own Trials while you are attempting to complete yours."

His voice faded as the mist swallowed Lyan. Lyan opened his mouth, a question on his lips, but no sound came. He saw nothing but the swirling white that muted all noise.

Am I alone?

His pulse quickened and his muscles tensed. Lyan drew quick, shallow breaths as fear crawled up his spine.

The pooka isn't here, and neither is Vynzent.

He closed his eyes a moment to steady himself. When he opened them, Lyan stared in confusion. The mist was gone, and he stood in a field of wildflowers of every color. Turning, he found no sign of paths, buildings, or people. Lyan turned his eyes upward, and a thrill of disbelief filled him. Though the sun shone, for the first time in months, he saw stars.

Lyan stared at the sky, searching for familiar constellations, but found none of the patterns he sought. He shook his head, confused, squinting at the glints of light. His stomach tightened as he realized how fiercely he wanted to read the signs. "Have I offended you, Veil?" he asked toward the god of divination. "Is this meant to torment me? Why show me the stars if they don't *say* anything?"

He rubbed his temples, closed his eyes, and drew a deep breath. *Is this even Veil's doing? The Trials are meant to test me. Is this a test of my fears? Isolate me, take away my guides, and see what I will do? Or is there something else? Why give me stars that carry no signs?*

Opening his eyes, Lyan looked again to the sky. Struggling not to seek constellations he knew, he searched for other patterns to the glints of light. He found lines, straight and true, the brightest stars spanning the sky like the compass on a map. Lyan let out his breath in a shaky laugh. "A guide waiting for me to see it."

He rose and walked in the direction the compass's needle seemed to point. His gaze constantly returned to the sky, drinking in the single constellation that filled the sky. He didn't see an end to the field, but Lyan stepped over an unseen line and magic seized him. Shaking off vertigo, he looked around.

Forest surrounded him on all sides. Turning his gaze up, Lyan saw just enough of the sky between the spreading oak branches to orient himself by the compass needle. As he walked, the forest closed around him. Lyan shivered, feeling it watching him. Unlike Eilidh Wood, this forest did not welcome him.

He stopped and knelt on the mossy ground. "Please forgive my intrusion. I seek only to be allowed to pass and find the seal as part of my Trial."

Branches rustled above him, angry sounds. Lyan remained kneeling. "I have come in peace and ask your permission to continue."

A vine slithered across his legs, and another dropped down like a snake to wind over his shoulders and loop loosely around his neck. Lyan flinched.

A voice whispered in his ear. "Why should I let you to pass?"

"I'm not your enemy, nor am I an enemy of Equinox. I have challenged the Trials to bear the Spear against the minions of Murdo."

"Brave words," the other whispered scornfully. "Very well. Answer one question to my satisfaction, and I'll let you pass." The vine at Lyan's neck shifted. "Who am I?"

For a moment, Lyan knew blank terror at a question he couldn't answer. He licked dry lips and spoke. "You are an elf. You are a Guardian of Equinox, and once sought to complete the Trials. You are gifted in the control of plants, and you have bound your spirit to this place. You are this forest, and you are everywhere it is. Your reach is as high as the tallest branches, touching the sky, and as deep as your roots, burrowing through the earth. You should be celebrated and honored in song, but ...I do not know your name."

The forest fell silent around Lyan, nothing moving. The wind whispered one word, one name. "Damasek."

The vine slithered from Lyan's neck. The next moment he yelped in surprise as the vine at his legs jerked him from the ground, dangling him by his ankles. The vine swung Lyan forward, then released him to fly through the air. Another vine caught his arm before he slammed into a tree trunk, swinging and tossing him again. Lyan's stomach lay somewhere near his toes by the fifth toss, and he regretted the light breakfast he'd eaten. He squeezed his eyes shut as he flew toward another tree.

A toss landed him in a net of vines. Lyan had just enough time to orient himself before the net unwove itself, tumbling him to the ground. Laughter echoed through the air, then silence. Lyan lay on the ground, panting, heart racing, before finally crawling unsteadily to his feet.

Before him stood a wooden wall. Niches pocked the wood, and in the nearest Lyan saw a stone plaque. He stepped closer and saw the rune for "north" etched in the stone.

Is this the seal?

He moved to the next niche, and saw an identical plaque.

They can't both be the seal. Waldros said there would be false seals. So how do I find the right one?

He looked more closely at the rune. It wasn't quite right. Something was subtly off about it; a line misplaced, drawn crooked when it should have been straight. Lyan checked the first one again, and found another flaw to that rune.

The real seal shouldn't have any flaws, would it? There must be some way to tell it from the false runes. He looked down the length of the wall, seeing dozens of niches. *If I have to check each of these…*

He walked down the wall, looking inside each niche. At the tenth one, he stopped and stared at the rune. He couldn't find any flaws to it, and Lyan's heart beat faster.

Is this it? It looks right…so why do I have this feeling that it's still not right? Somehow…something still isn't right. This isn't the seal.

He doubted himself even as he kept walking. He had no reason to think the rune was wrong, only his doubts and fears.

No one said I have a time limit. I can go back if I don't find any others that seem right.

Lyan neared the end of the rows of niches, double-guessing himself still, until his eyes fell on the plaque in the next niche. The rune for north marked the stone, but behind it, another rune had been etched, faint and barely visible.

"Truth," Lyan whispered. "Not just north. True north."

He lifted the plaque from its resting place, then hesitated. Waldros had told him to speak words to activate the rune, but hadn't told him what those words were. "How do I…" Lyan licked his dry lips. "Damasek, how do I activate the rune?"

Laughter rippled through the leaves. "How did you find your way to it?"

"The stars—," Lyan began. He turned his eyes up, searched the sky. Squinting, he made out runes around the tip of the compass needle. He sounded them out aloud, and felt the stone in his hand grow warm. The symbols on it glowed as Lyan returned it to its niche. In the sky above, the needle of the compass moved before his eyes, swinging to the left.

Lyan let out his breath. "Thank you." He looked to the trees and bowed. "Thank you, Damasek. Should I leave this shrine, I will not forget you, and your name will live on."

"Who makes me this promise?" whispered the wind.

"I am Lyan of Heartshrine Village in Eilidh Wood."

"It appears, Lyan of Heartshrine Village, that you are supposed to go somewhere." Branches rustled.

Lyan nodded cautiously. "The compass points that way. If this is north, that would be west."

"Of course it is. When the stars guide you, you travel to the reverse of the sun."

Lyan hesitated. He could see the vines lingering at the edge of the trees, and couldn't see any way to leave but back through the forest. "If you would be willing to allow me passage through the forest again…?"

The vines snatched hold of him again before he had any chance to protest, tossing Lyan into the air and flinging him through the forest with apparent carelessness. He never actually collided with anything, though, and the vines never grabbed him too roughly. When they lowered him to the ground, Lyan staggered drunkenly and tried to steady himself.

A laugh lingered in the air as Lyan straightened. He rubbed his forehead, giving himself a moment to settle, then he looked to the stars once more. Damasek had set him down facing in the direction of the compass needle. Lyan stepped forward, and immediately felt the vertigo of magic.

The forest vanished into swamp. Lyan took a step forward, feet sinking into mud. The smell of decay hit his nose in a burst. He grimaced and looked around for dry ground, feeling moisture seeping into his boots. Sloshing toward an island in the muck, he soaked boots and trousers thoroughly. With a sigh, Lyan climbed onto the solid ground and tried to get his bearings.

"West…I'm trying to go west."

A line of the islands ran south-west from the one he stood on, but to go straight west… Lyan looked from the sky to the swamp, and sighed again. That, of course, led straight through the center of the murky, filthy water. Even as he watched, something slithered through the water, leaving ripples in its wake and making Lyan doubt the wisdom of sharing the water with the wildlife. He drew a deep breath, then gagged on the smell and covered his mouth.

He walked around the little island, pushing aside a large bramble at the western side, and stopped in surprise. Hidden by the growth, where he wouldn't have seen it from any other angle, a small rowboat was tied to a stake in the ground. Lyan looked at it uncertainly, but there was no indication that it had an owner, or that it had any purpose except to allow him to cross the water without swimming. He untied it from the stake and cautiously stepped inside, nearly spilling into the water before he caught his balance and sat down.

The boat swayed precariously when Lyan shifted around to pick up the oars, but didn't tip over in spite of his fears.

Lyan pulled the edge of his shirt up to cover his nose and dipped the oars into the water.

I can do this… I'll be all right. Nothing's going to jump from the water and try to eat me.

I hope…

2 8

Call the four corners
Cage the waters
Bind the wind
Lay bare the secrets of the earth

Murky water splashed into the boat as Lyan struggled with the oars. He had given up trying to keep his face covered, and each breath filled his nose with odors of damp and decay, though they hit him less sharply than they had at first. Keeping the boat moving dominated most of Lyan's attention. He had no experience with rowing or with boats, but his efforts kept him marginally drier than walking through the murk would. The rowboat moved through the water as much in spite of his efforts as because of them. After some futile time, Lyan dragged the oars into the boat and let it drift where it wished. He couldn't see the sky through the canopy of the trees, making the flow of water his best available guide.

I didn't think this was the right sort of land to have a swamp. Is this an illusion? Or some magic inherent to the Shrine? Lyan grimaced at his boots, soaked with swamp water. The chill and the odors both argued against illusion. *Am I even still within the Shrine?*

To his left, something splashed in the water. Lyan's head jerked toward the sound, but he saw only large ripples in the water. Insects droned around him, and the largest dragonfly he'd ever seen zipped past Lyan's face. He fell back, and the boat rocked precariously. Lyan hissed in pain as a splinter jabbed into his hand when he sat up again.

Splinters fled from his thoughts when the boat rocked more violently and something scraped across the underside. Lyan snatched one of the oars as a makeshift weapon, blood pounding. Water splashed over the sides of the boat as it continued to rock sharply. The boat was moving faster, as if pulled or carried by something under the water. Lyan peered over the edge, but couldn't see into the silty depths.

"I don't know if I have to ask before anyone can help, but…can I have some help?" Lyan asked. Someone had to be watching his progress. The Guardians wouldn't have left him completely alone. Lyan clung to that belief as tightly as he did the oar in his hands.

The boat seemed to sink lower in the water for a moment, losing momentum. A solid thump as the prow hit something stopped forward progress and sent Lyan falling forward to land in the stinking water filling the boat's bottom. Spitting the foul taste from his mouth, he edged to the prow and cautiously poked the oar into the water. It met muddy resistance immediately. Lyan tested the surrounding water, finding it to be little more than ankle deep.

Lyan let the oar clatter into the bottom of the boat and warily climbed out. Nothing surged from the muck to attack him or investigate. His feet sank into the mud, and cold water chilled his feet immediately. Lyan slogged to the trunk of a massive tree, climbing the roots for solid ground. Finding a relatively straight piece of deadwood, he claimed it as a walking stick. Using it to test the ground as he walked, Lyan pressed on, keeping to the tree roots as much as possible. They didn't prove as reliable a pathway as he wished, often being slick and slimy enough to send him sliding back into the water.

Searching the path ahead with his walking stick, Lyan felt a thump as he hit something solid. Startled, he probed in the water. The mud gave way to a level and solid surface. Lyan stepped forward until the mud no longer sucked at his boots. Pushing up a sleeve, he reached into the water and felt the ground. His fingers picked out the shapes of stones, cut and shaped to form a road. Cobblestones. He straightened, wiping his hand dry on his shirt. A paved path, here?

Lyan followed the cobbled path, grateful for the relief from the mud even as he mulled over the puzzle of the path's presence. A little further on, shapes he had thought were rocks or fallen trees resolved into crumbling stone walls. The path finally climbed above the water's surface, to lead straight to the remnants of a gate, though only the shape of the doorway remained, an arch of stone. Lyan cast a quick look to the sky, but the trees still hid it. He walked through the arch and into a ruin.

The path split, one turning to the left, the other going straight for a short way, leading through another archway. Lyan looked to the left, curiosity urging him to explore the ruins before returning to his task. The desire was overwhelming, turning him toward the left-hand path.

It couldn't hurt just to look.

He shifted his grip on his walking stick, then hissed in pain as the movement dug a new splinter deep into his hand. "Ow! First seeds!"

His words broke the stillness that muffled the ruin like a blanket. Lyan tried to bite out the splinter, but it was wedged tight and he only succeeded in filling his mouth with the foul taste of the swamp. Lyan turned back toward the arch, his desire to explore suppressed by his desire to be out of this place. As he moved toward the arch, Lyan felt resistance, as if he was trying to slog through thick mud again. Staggering several steps, he caught hold of the edge of the arch to pull himself in.

The resistance vanished when he stumbled through the arch, and Lyan found himself in an alley, the path running straight with a tall wall on either side. And in the walls, he saw niches again, once more with runes etched on tablets. Lyan panted in relief and searched the runes.

What am I looking for this time? His head swam as he tried to pick one rune over another, and the longer he stared at them, the less sense they made. *I might as well just grab any one of them. I have no idea what I'm supposed to know about this place to help me chose correctly. Maybe I really should go back and explore.*

In his heart, he was sure that wasn't the right answer, but no other solution presented itself. Lyan sank down on the ground and rested his head on his arms with a weary sigh. *Feyra and Tesseia, please help me. Give me guidance and direction. I don't know what to do.*

No words of divine wisdom answered him, but Lyan felt himself calming. Either he would chose correctly, or he was not meant for this honor. He pushed up from the wall, closed his eyes, and walked a handful of steps, then reached into the nearest niche. He pulled out the stone within and looked up to the sky to read the signs on the needle of the compass of stars. The tablet in his hand grew warm, and when it glowed, Lyan glimpsed the word "impulse" before it faded. He replaced the tablet, heart pounding again, wondering if he'd made the right choice. He stepped back through the arch toward the split in the path. Before he reached the second path, magic snatched him away and his surroundings changed once more.

He stood in darkness. Lyan groped blindly, and his searching hands hit stone. He hissed in pain as he skinned his palm. His breath sounded loud, and the air was still, smelling of dust and rock. Lyan tried to get his bearings, but found little to orient him. His eyes played tricks on him, creating ghost images of light or color where none existed, and the only sounds he heard came from his own making. No stars offered their guidance here.

Lyan felt his way along the wall of what he guessed to be a cave. When he raised a hand over his head, his fingers brushed the ceiling, and if he kept one hand on the wall nearest him, he sometimes could touch the other wall. Hoping that meant he was not going to walk in an endless circle, he moved slowly, tripping or stumbling over unseen obstructions and desperately praying he would not sprain his ankle again. Uncertainty clung to him, making him question what he was expected to do here, and how he was going to do it.

"Is anyone here?" Lyan called. He heard no one, but his movements could obscure other sounds.

No voice answered him, but he heard movement. Lyan advanced cautiously, then paused to rub his eyes, uncertain whether he actually glimpsed light or if his eyes played tricks again. As he approached, the light held steady, and he began to see details, shadows and shapes around him. The source of illumination proved to be a lantern sitting on a wooden table, casting light around a small chamber in the cave. Beside the table stood a figure in a hooded robe, face hidden in shadow.

Lyan paused, then approached cautiously. "Hello."

The robed figure's head moved in a nod.

"Can you help me find what I need to find here?" Lyan asked, trying to draw more response.

Again, the figure nodded silently.

Well, I shouldn't expect the Guardians to make this easy. Lyan let out a breath. "Where do I need to go?"

The other picked up the lantern and motioned for Lyan to follow. As the passage narrowed again, the robed figure took a staff that rested against the wall. Then the light caught it, and Lyan realized it was not a staff, but a spear.

"Cailean?" he asked.

The other paused, turned toward him, and nodded.

"So, there must be some reason you aren't saying anything."

Agreement again.

"All right. I'll follow you, then."

Cailean led Lyan, holding the lantern so it would illuminate the path for both of them. Lyan wanted to ask him where they were, and why, but he could already guess that Cailean wouldn't, or for some reason couldn't, answer.

The walls curved away from them. Cailean continued forward. Lyan looked to either side, searching for a sense of where he was and where the walls went.

Abruptly, the light went out. Lyan froze, looking all around for any glimmer of illumination. "Cailean?"

He heard something crunch and grind against the stone, and felt vibrations through the floor as if something had been rolled away. Light returned, coming from the center of the chamber. Lyan let out a breath of relief when he saw the robed figure next to it, then felt the breath stick in his throat when he realized Cailean was no longer alone. He counted seven robed, hooded figures, and as he approached, each beckoned him to follow. Each of them held a spear, and in the dim light, Lyan couldn't tell them apart.

I can't follow them all. Which one is Cailean, and how do I tell? Lyan stopped before the line of hooded figures. Their heights were all similar enough that he couldn't judge by that, and the robes obscured the shapes of the bodies so thoroughly that Lyan wasn't sure whether they were male or female.

Only one of those spears can be Solstice, though.

Lyan reached out, his finger's brushing the spear of the figure nearest him. No jolt or tingle ran up his arm, and he turned to the next. At the fifth robed form, Lyan touched the spear and jerked back quickly as the warning tingle of magic raced through his hand. The figure shifted from one foot to the other as if unsure what to think of Lyan's reaction.

Lyan nodded to him. "Lead on," he invited.

He wasn't sure whether he actually sensed relief in Cailean's movements, or if he simply projected his own feelings. All of the robed figures took lanterns, turned, and walked out different passages. Lyan clung close to Cailean and they walked in silence until they reached the next chamber. Cailean offered Lyan the lantern and gestured toward the far wall. Lyan took the light with a nod of thanks and found rows of niches carved into the stone.

The tablets within did not bear symbols representing south, as he had expected they would. Instead, the runes formed simple statements, or single words. Lyan picked up one, gazed at it, and nodded.

"Trust."

The stone glowed briefly in his hand, and Lyan slid it back into its niche. "Well, that's this one, I hope," Lyan said.

Cailean let out a relieved breath and pushed back the hood. "And that means I can speak again." The lantern light caught the quirk of the Tathren's smile. "I had no idea how you were supposed to figure out who to follow when no one could speak to you."

Lyan rubbed his fingers on his shirt as if he could wipe away the sting of Solstice's touch. "No one else carried Solstice."

Cailean cocked his head to one side. "How could you tell, though?

Lyan rubbed his fingers again. "Solstice doesn't seem to like me touching it. Stings a little. None of the other spears did that, so I knew which was Solstice."

"Are you all right?" Cailean asked, concerned.

Lyan nodded. "Yes. I'm fine." He let out a long breath. "So what next, do you know? Can you keep helping me?

"I don't know," Cailean said. "But if I can, and you want, I'll help you as much as I can."

"Thank you." Lyan gave the Tathren a tight smile. "I'd much rather have friends by my side."

"I can understand that," Cailean agreed. "Which way from here?"

Lyan pointed at the tunnel they had come through. "Back the way we came," he said with more confidence than he felt. He heard Cailean's steps behind him, but only for a moment. Magic caught Lyan once again.

When the world settled, Lyan stood in a grassland much like where he had begun. He turned around slowly. "Cailean? Are you here?"

He saw no sign of the Tathren Spearbearer. *I'm alone again.* Lyan shivered, then resigned himself to the solitude.

He heard water running nearby, prompting his mouth and throat to complain of their plight. The hope of a cool drink was too much to pass up, and Lyan found the stream, pushing aside the reeds and water plants that half-choked the streambed. Water had never tasted so good. He washed his face and combed back his red hair with wet fingers now muddy from the dust of the cave.

Refreshed and as ready as he could be to find the last rune, Lyan looked to the sky. The stars were distant and faded, sunlight drowning their lights. He searched for "east". The faint symbol led him away from the stream, across the plains. No visible rise broke the landscape. Lyan scooped up another drink, splashed water over his face, and followed the stars' guidance.

The empty blue sky above and the open plains around him left Lyan feeling exposed and uneasy. *I don't like being alone out here. I rarely mind solitude at home…what's so different?*

Wind rattled tall stalks of dry grass, making Lyan jump and sending his heart pounding until he identified the source of the sound. He tried to laugh off his nervousness, but it wouldn't be completely banished.

In Eilidh Wood, I'm never really alone. The forest always watches over me. And in Eilidh Wood, nothing is trying to hunt me down.

Lyan rubbed his eyes. "Why am I thinking about this now? I need to stay focused."

Focus became a greater challenge the longer he walked the endless grassland. The sun beat down on him, and he was exhausted, with no idea how far he had traveled since the beginning of this Trial. Lyan's mind continued to wander back to thoughts of home—whether daydreams of shade and cool streams, or wishing for the sense he had taken for granted, the knowledge that the forest protected and guarded him. He still checked the sky to keep his path straight, but looking to the stars was as natural as breathing.

It's hard to believe that all this started because of the pooka, before it even knew about me. I'm here, challenging the Trials of Equinox, because I fell when I wasn't watching my feet. With a faint smile, Lyan looked down to the ground.

He yelped in surprise and stumbled back a step. Somehow, in all his distraction and looking to the sky, Lyan had missed noticing the gaping chasm running down the center of the plains. A few more steps and his feet would have met empty air. From a distance, the tall grass hid the presence of the chasm, giving an illusion of unbroken land. This close, Lyan had no excuse for not noticing it. He peered over the edge as far as he dared, and knew if he'd fallen, he would not have survived.

A better, stronger climber than Lyan might have been able to find hand and footholds to pick a way down into the depths, but he knew that without help—or rope, at the very least—he couldn't continue east.

Lyan sat down with a tired sigh, a sense of defeat start to creep over him. "I can't climb that. So that leaves…what? Did I miss something, some clue I should have noticed? I could have walked past anything while I wasn't paying attention…." He looked to the sky. "Maybe there's a spot where I can cross. Which way, though? Am I even going the right way?"

The stars had nearly faded from sight. The only symbol

Lyan could make out with any certainty pointed him up the north side of the chasm. With no other clues visible and no other ideas, Lyan turned to his left and followed the edge of the crack in the earth. The chasm ran so straight, he could imagine a god dragging a blade across the ground, readying to strike at some enemy.

What enemy, though? Murdo, perhaps?

Catching his mind wandering once more, Lyan shook his head and tried to shake off the distraction. His legs ached, and his stomach grumbled in complaint, hunger and weariness both growing stronger the longer he trudged on. Looking ahead, Lyan saw a shape that looked like a rock near the chasm's edge.

I'll take a little rest when I reach that. Just have to get to that rock, then I can sit down for a bit.

He forced one foot to continually follow the other, determined to reach this goal before resting. His heart lifted and a little energy returned when Lyan drew close enough to see that someone sat on the rock, waiting. He recognized Kithr immediately. Kithr turned and saw him, but didn't get up, waiting for Lyan to reach the rock. Finally, Lyan arrived, sinking down to sit near the base of the rock.

Kithr stood and smiled slightly, taking any sting from his words. "You took your time getting here."

"Sorry." Lyan let out a relieved sigh. If Kithr was here, it felt safe to assume he was on the right path.

"No, don't tell me," Kithr said. "You looked up."

"I have *not* been staring at the stars the whole time," Lyan responded with mock indignation. "And besides, that was the only guide I had to tell me which way to go."

Kithr waved dismissively. "You're lucky I didn't come looking for you."

"If you've been waiting long, I'm a little surprised that you didn't," Lyan admitted.

"My instructions were pretty clear that I needed to wait

right here. But honestly, the reason was more that I didn't know which direction you would be coming from."

"But now that I'm here, you can help, right?"

"That is why you picked me, isn't it?" Kithr responded. He paced. "How many of these things do you need to find, Lyan?"

"This is the last one," Lyan told him. "Four runes that I have to activate. So… do I have to get down there to find it?" He motioned to the chasm.

Kithr looked dubiously over the edge. "They gave me some rope, and I think it would be long enough for you to reach the bottom, if you actually want down there."

"I don't really *want* to, no, but it seems likely to be the place where I would find the rune." Lyan looked at Kithr curiously. "Unless it isn't actually down there?"

Kithr shrugged, though the effort to not say anything showed in his expression.

"Kithr, do you know where I will find the rune I need to activate?" Lyan asked.

"Yes, I do, Lyan."

He made a guess. "Then, could I have it, please?"

Kithr picked up a tablet from the rock where he'd been sitting. "Venycia gave it to me, saying it was 'the best way to keep your Trial fair', whatever that means."

Lyan looked back to the chasm. "Probably it means this tablet normally is someplace I would not be able to get to." He took the tablet from Kithr and looked at it carefully. Not being able to compare it to any other tablets left him uneasy. No extra symbols adorned this tablet, only the rune for "east".

Soldarr, Feyra, Tesseia, please protect me. Let this be the right rune, and not a deception.

Lyan chanted the mantra to activate the rune, and felt it grow warm in his hands. When beams of light burst from the tablet, Lyan stumbled back quickly, releasing it. The tablet didn't fall, but hovered in the air, beams from it running north, south, and west.

"Lyan, what's going on?" Kithr asked warily, reaching to his belt in search of a weapon that wasn't there.

"I…think it's okay…." Lyan said uncertainly. "I think, at least, that the four runes are linking to each other. And if I've activated the right ones, then I should have succeeded at this Trial." He had no guesses as to what would happen if he had chosen incorrectly.

A secondary light grew to the side of the floating tablet, forming a doorway. Lyan stepped toward it. Kithr raised an arm across his path.

"I'll go first, Lyan. You don't know where this will take you."

Lyan pushed Kithr's arm aside. "No…this time, I need to go first, Kithr. This is my Trial, and I'm going to accept the outcome, whether I succeed or not." Before Kithr could protest, Lyan stepped into the shimmering portal.

He stepped into a courtyard paved with white stones, surrounded by greenery. To his right stood a building Lyan recognized as one of the living quarters of the Shrine of Equinox. A light rain still misted down. Ahead of him stood Venycia and Waldros. Cailean sat on a bench, fidgeting. The Tathren jumped to his feet when he saw Lyan, relief spreading across his face. Kithr appeared beside Lyan a moment later.

Waldros scowled at Lyan, as though doubting that he should have returned. Venycia, however, smiled in welcome, and she spoke first. "You have successfully completed the Trial of Quarters. Congratulations, Lyan of Heartshrine Village."

Waldros's scowl relented slightly, and he nodded. "You have a little time to rest and refresh yourself. In the building to your right, you'll find food and drink. We will fetch you when it is time for your final Trial."

Lyan bowed. "Thank you."

"You did better than I expected, I will grant you that, Lyan of Heartshrine Village. Whether your luck and skills will be enough to bring you through the next Trial remains to be seen," the human said. "Your companions can stay with you while you rest."

Kithr scowled, clearly disliking the man's attitude, but Lyan shook his head to his friend. "Come on Kithr, Cailean. I'm hungry, and more than ready for a little rest. I'm sure I'll need it."

29

Shadows above and earth below
Pillars of the sky
Between them, let all grow
That we may never die

The scent of food started Lyan's stomach growling the moment he entered the building. One end of the central wooden table was set for three, and he made for it with the expectation that Kithr and Cailean would follow. Lyan glanced briefly around the room, but it was nearly identical to the one they had been housed in the first night. His gaze settled on the table spread with platters—fruit, bread, meat, and dishes he couldn't identify. His mouth watered and his stomach continued its vehement assertions that he hadn't eaten in days. Lyan couldn't imagine the three of them making a dent in the wealth of food, but found himself more than willing to try. He grabbed a plate and piled on every food in reach.

Kithr chuckled, but he and Cailean applied themselves to the feast with similar enthusiasm. Conversation was limited to "Pass that my way" or an occasional noise of approval.

Once his gnawing hunger had eased, Lyan passed around a bottle of fruit wine and asked, "Are you both all right? What did you have to do?"

"I'm feeling a little dusty, and glad to be back in daylight again," Cailean answered. "No harm done, though. I went with a Guardian to another building. They gave me the robe and lantern, then Venycia entered. She told me my task would be to act as your guide, but I wouldn't be able to say anything to you during the test." One corner of his mouth twitched in a half-smile. "A requirement enforced by some form of magic. I was trying to answer when you asked me questions."

Lyan nodded in understanding. "Kithr had a similar restriction."

"I won't take it as a reprimand that I talk too much, then," Cailean said.

Kithr snorted. "You're Tathren. Of course you talk too much. So why stop now?" The jab was mild, and he listened to Cailean with interest.

Cailean swirled the fruit wine in his goblet and sipped. "Eskrin's plow, this is a fine vintage." He leaned back in his chair. "Where was I? Oh, restrictions. I had to wear that robe, hood up so you couldn't see my face, and when the others were in the chamber, I was not to do anything to identify myself." He let out a shaky laugh. "I wasn't sure what I would do if you decided to follow one of the others, though. I'm fairly sure that running after you and pulling you back would have been frowned on, though no one said I *couldn't*. And to be honest, I probably would have."

Kithr nodded curtly. "Good. I can see why they didn't expect *me* to play that part. But the process was the same: followed the Guardian, was given instructions about what *not* to do, and left to wait for you." He wiped his plate clean with a piece of bread. "So you must have succeeded so far."

"Venycia said I was successful," Lyan agreed. "I assume that if I'd failed, she would have told me." He tried to make the words sound more confident than he felt. "So only one Trial remains."

Kithr scowled. "To judge by his absence, the mercenary is supposed to help in it."

"Yion might not have been my first choice, but he's proven reliable so far," Cailean said.

"What do you know of your hired soldier, Tathren?" Kithr asked.

"Not much," Cailean admitted. "He discovered an overgrown, long-unused escape tunnel from my keep, and during Ewart's attack, he used it to enter my stronghold on his own, without bringing any of Ewart's men with him. He swore into my service, and led me and all my remaining men out of the keep."

Kithr's eyes narrowed. "And based on *that*, you trusted him?"

"No, I didn't trust him. But I was running out of options. I know Yion knows more than he says about quite a few things, and I don't know why he chose to side with me, or why he still hasn't demanded the payments due a mercenary."

Lyan recalled a conversation with Yion. "He told me he's a mercenary because a man away from his homeland needs to claim some manner of trade, but his path is guided by his god's will."

"His god?" Cailean repeated. "He's never spoken to me about his god."

"He wouldn't tell me which god he follows when I asked," Lyan said. Deciding to change the subject before Kithr and Cailean made him doubt his choice of Yion more than he already did, Lyan asked, "Who would you have chosen, if you had been asked, Cailean?"

"You, Aikan, and…." Cailean thought for a moment. "I'm not sure. Shiolto or Torqual, probably." He smiled. "Not that it matters, since I would never have been allowed to take the Trials to begin with."

"I didn't know about that restriction," Lyan said. "But… it's a relief to know it."

"It wouldn't have changed our coming here," Cailean said, frowning at Lyan's words. "It's just as well that we didn't know."

"Just as well *you* didn't know, perhaps. The knowledge would have made a difference to us." Kithr drained his glass and looked at Lyan. "You should rest. Whatever they expect of you next, you need to be ready."

The thought appealed…except that it meant leaving Kithr and Cailean alone in the same room. "I'll be all right."

"A nap does sound welcome," Cailean said, unsuccessfully stifling a yawn. "Take the chance while you have it. I will do the same." The Tathren lord pushed away from the table and settled in one of the overstuffed chairs, closing his eyes.

Kithr scowled at Lyan and spoke in Elven. "Just because I don't like your Tathren friend doesn't mean I'd attack him in a place of sanctuary while you sleep, Lyan." He pointed to the stairs. "Sleep. Now. I'll keep a watch."

"I'll be all right," Lyan repeated.

"You'll be better with sleep." Kithr crossed his arms and waited.

Lyan relented and climbed the stairs to the upper level. He found pallets in one room and lay down. Worries faded as sleep came.

Something pulled Lyan insistently back to waking, a nagging tug in the back of his mind that wouldn't be still. Sitting, he blinked and looked around the room, but saw no one. Blearily rising, he walked to the window and opened it, hoping fresh air would clear his head.

Mist filled the air with light haze. Lyan closed his eyes and let his head rest on his arms on the sill. The sound of voices made him jerk up, but they came from outside rather than in the room.

Waldros spoke, anger and frustration coloring his words.

"Of course he could tell who to follow! He wasn't going to mistake Solstice for an ordinary spear. Why didn't you put Kithr there and Cailean at the fourth seal?"

"Do you think Lyan would have more difficulty identifying a friend he's known his entire life, Waldros?" Venycia answered. "We could conceal Kithr head to toe in a robe and Lyan would know him by the way he moves. And aside from that, do you honestly think either of us have magic strong enough to force Kithr to remain silent when Lyan asks his aid? Preventing him from volunteering answers before Lyan asked the right questions was challenge enough!"

Lyan pulled back from the window, not wanting either Guardian to see him. *I shouldn't be listening to this.* Despite the thought, he didn't leave his seat by the window. The musical cadence of Venycia's voice held him, and the nagging tug in the back of his mind urged him to stay and listen.

Venycia continued. "Cailean was the better choice to test his intuition, Waldros. Had it been Kithr, the test would have been entirely different."

"And then you gave the final rune to Kithr," Waldros said sharply.

"Lyan overcame the enchantments of distraction and befuddlement to reach that point and find Kithr. Would you have had him sprout wings and fly? Summon one of the great birds from her roost by an untrained and instinctual use of his skill?" Venycia countered.

Waldros made a sound of displeasure. "I know that you fancy red-heads, Venycia, but that doesn't give you an excuse to meddle in his Trials—"

Waldros barely finished the sentence before he gave a grunt of pain to accompany the sound of a fist hitting flesh. Lyan peered out the window, trying to see what had happened, not yet able to make full sense of what he'd just overheard. Waldros stood against a tree, and Venycia glared at him, hands clenched in fists.

"Do you think I would put Equinox in the hands of someone not worthy? *Anyone* not worthy? Do you?"

"I think you're letting yourself become too invested in his success," Waldros said, a hand rising to his jaw.

"And *you* are too invested in an opinion formed too quickly from one answer to one question," Venycia retorted.

The two Guardians locked gazes. Abruptly, both turned. Lyan froze, dread racing like ice through his veins. *They know I'm listening.*

Their gazes did not rise to his window. Venycia and Waldros both looked at something Lyan couldn't see for several long, silent moments, then stepped apart. Waldros spoke first. "Equinox, that's not what I said!" Another long moment of silence, and he reluctantly bowed his head. "As you wish."

Equinox? Are they speaking to the Spear? Is the Spear speaking back to them? Can it do that? Lyan remained unmoved.

Venycia bowed her head as well after another moment. "Very well, if that is your will. I will speak to Sirex and Ude to take our places for the final Trial."

Waldros glanced at Venycia and let out a long breath. "I'm sorry. That was uncalled for on my part."

"Well, perhaps we both have our reasons for wishing his success or lack thereof." She held out a hand to him. "Peace?"

Waldros took it. "Peace. And, it seems we have substitutes to inform of new duties. Apparently, Equinox doesn't believe either of us should be overseeing the end of it."

"Perhaps with good reason," Venycia admitted. "We should see to it."

The two Guardians moved away and vanished into the mist. Lyan stared out after them, head spinning and thoughts tumbling together. He was certain neither Guardian had intended for him to hear them, but he was sure something had. Something that had woken him, and urged him to stay at the window.

Who, though? And why?

He let his head rest on his arms again, resting them on the window sill. Without meaning to, Lyan sank back into a doze.

He woke with a stiff back and sore arms. Moving slowly, Lyan rubbed sleep from his eyes and rolled his shoulders to ease the ache. He found a basin and pitcher of water on a low table near him, which he was sure had not been present when he fell asleep, either the first or the second time.

Mud and dirt still coated his clothes, cracking and flaking as he moved. Lyan wished for a change of clothes and a bath, but he didn't even know where his bags were. He resigned himself to waiting until after the final Trial to wash.

He made his way downstairs. The remains of their meal had been cleared away, and in its place he saw several trays with bread, fruit, and an assortment of small jars. Lyan investigated, and found honey and an assortment of preserves in the jars. Two jugs, one of water and one of wine, completed the refreshments.

Cailean still slept in the chair he'd chosen, one arm wrapped around Solstice. Lyan smiled a little to see that Kithr, despite his words about keeping watch, also slept across the room from Cailean.

Lyan spread honey on a slice of bread and poured himself wine. Though he moved quietly, Kithr roused. His friend blinked and looked around, groggy for a moment, then started to his feet.

"Dammit, I didn't mean to fall asleep."

"It's all right, Kithr. You needed rest too," Lyan said.

Kithr grimaced, but finally nodded. "I suppose. It isn't as if I actually had to *do* anything, though. For all the dire warnings, I expected to do more than sit, waiting and hoping you asked the right questions."

"So part of your instructions was that you had to wait for me to ask about the rune?" Lyan asked, remembering what he'd overheard Venycia saying to Waldros.

Kithr shook his head. "No. Well, yes, it was, but once she handed me that tablet, I *couldn't* say anything about it until you asked." He scowled. "It's…frustrating to know something important and to not be able to say anything about it, even the fact that you know it."

"Cailean probably felt the same way," Lyan said. He sat down and took a drink of wine. "He probably feels that way often, with the curse on him."

Kithr eyed the sleeping Tathren, and finally grunted in response. "I suppose he might."

Lyan ate his bread and tried to relax. But he'd eaten, he'd slept, and still the last Trial loomed before him. He shifted restlessly in his seat.

"What's wrong?" Kithr asked.

Lyan sighed. "Nothing. I just need to remember that the Trials are made up of more than just the obvious parts, and waiting can be as much a piece of the Trial as doing something is."

"Nervous?" Kithr asked.

"Gods, yes!" Lyan whispered. "And terrified."

"That you won't succeed, or that you will?"

"Can I just say 'yes'?" Lyan asked with a half-smile. "I have no idea what to expect of the last Trial."

"You'll be fine," Kithr said, almost dismissively. Lyan recognized it as Kithr's attempt to lighten Lyan's spirits. He paused. "I'm going to hope I'm wrong and you're right about that mercenary."

"I trust Yion," Lyan said.

Kithr filled a goblet with wine and raised it in a toast to Lyan. "To your luck."

Lyan raised his goblet in return, and they both drank.

Cailean finally woke when Venycia entered. The Tathren

shook off sleep, rose, and bowed to the elven woman. She nodded in return and looked to Lyan.

"Are you ready, Lyan?"

"As ready as I can be, Lady."

She smiled warmly, and Lyan felt his heart skip a beat. For that smile, he would face any challenge the Trial cast in his path. "Then come with me. Your friends can follow for a little while. But once the Trial begins, they must wait here."

"Thank you."

Lyan walked with Venycia from the building. He had no idea what time it was. Mist still shrouded the shrine, and the light seemed unchanged. Venycia followed paths past looming trees to a courtyard with a small fountain, the stream of water flowing from the mouth of a bear carved of black stone. There she stopped, turning to face him. Her expression was serious. "My part in your Trial is done, for now. Sirex will lead you to the start of the next part. If Fortune and Equinox favor you, I will see you when you have completed the final Trial."

The elf who had kept charge of the gate at the entrance to the Shrine entered the courtyard, and nodded to all of them. "Follow me when you are ready, Lyan."

Lyan looked over his shoulder to Kithr and Cailean. He searched for words, but found none. Kithr met his gaze and gave him a curt nod. "Be careful."

"Thank you." Lyan nodded to the gatekeeper, Sirex. "I'm ready."

Waldros had scoffed when Lyan had said those words to him, but Sirex only motioned for him to follow. "You solved one riddle to find this shrine," he said as they walked. "You must solve another one now, Lyan."

Automatically, Lyan looked up, but mist shrouded the sky. He tripped over a root, caught himself, and asked, "Another riddle?"

Sirex smiled. "You'll see the stars when you need to. But they will be the only guide you have." He stopped before an arch set between two towering trees. Lyan looked through the arch, and saw darkness. "You have triggered the runes. They have opened this door to you. Beyond it, a scroll waits. You must find it and complete the ritual you began when you activated the runes. The scroll is the means by which you will do that, and the stars are your guide. Once you enter this room, you must find your path. You understand?"

Lyan bowed. "I do." *I must solve the riddle, or I will not find my way out.*

He looked into the darkness, then stepped through the arch. He heard a door close behind him, leaving him in fading twilight, surrounded by the stillness of night.

30

Three stand before you
The middle shall be first
And the first shall be last,
Yet none shall open twice.

Lyan closed his eyes and drew a deep breath. The air smelled like home, like stepping outside on a spring night with the memory of rain still clinging to the trees. Insects chirped and sang, though they fell silent when he moved. Without opening his eyes, he felt the ground and found a soft patch of grass to sit on. Leaning back, he finally opened his eyes to see the heavens, drinking in the sight like a thirsty man given a river of pure water.

He recognized the forms and patterns of the stars, and Lyan pretended he lay in Eilidh Wood, reading fortunes in the heavens for his friends and fellow villagers. He searched for Kithr's signs, and frowned. The constellations didn't have any sense to them, revealing nothing about Kithr's fortunes. A knot settled in Lyan's gut, and he let out a shaky breath.

This isn't the real night sky. It looks like it is, but it's not. It's another piece of the Trial. And to solve a riddle from the stars, the first thing I have to find is the riddle. He rubbed his eyes and refocused his attention.

Calling it a "riddle" was slightly misleading, Lyan knew. Perhaps there was a better word, but astrologers in Eilidh Wood had been using it for too long to easily change. "Puzzle", maybe…but the word was unimportant.

I'm looking for a scroll. So where do I start? I don't know anything about this scroll to know its signs, but it's probably made of parchment, and the constellations for parchments are the Forest and the Field. Then, ink, that would be Soot. What about the Quill…no. No, if this is a magical scroll, I don't want to look for the Quill, I want the Staff. As his thoughts raced, he picked out constellations, looking for a pattern to tell him that he was starting correctly. *That doesn't look quite right, what do I have wrong…. Soot doesn't fit. I have the wrong sign for ink. Take that out, and then…what should take its place? The base isn't complete. So what would be used instead?* He searched for another constellation to complete the foundation. *It looks like it should be something in the western sky, so….*

Lyan shivered abruptly. *Blood. Older than ink, more powerful. More dangerous. For magic, much more powerful.* It wasn't a sign he consulted often. It wasn't one Lyan wished to consult often— blood too often stood for death, sickness, and danger. And now it was one of the bases he had to build on to find direction to the scroll. *A scroll of magic, written with blood.*

From that foundation, Lyan traced a path to each of the four compass points. *From the scroll, north, south, east, and west. That doesn't help me find it, so what's the purpose behind this? Or…do they indicate the purpose of the scroll? The four directions, the four runes I activated earlier. They work together somehow. The runes are the first part in a ritual, perhaps, and the scroll completes it? There's no single symbol for a ritual—what kind of ritual would it be? Not a sacrifice, I don't think, even if the scroll's written in blood. Sealing something in? No. Blocking something out? That could be. And protection. Those two signs are together. So the scroll and the four direction runes are part of a ritual of protection and shielding. What are they protecting?*

The answer seemed obvious: the shrine itself. Lyan started at that thought, and only barely kept from losing the image he was building in his mind. *The Guardians of the Spear are using one of their own rituals of protection on the shrine as my Trial? What happens if I do it incorrectly?*

Yet that single realization, however unsettling, unfolded the puzzle before him. Lyan arranged the pieces until he was sure he knew where he needed to go. Then, he simply stared at the sky for a long moment.

Is this really the right answer? It seems…this is too easy. I'm sure I'm right, but…the Trials are supposed to test me "in ways I can't imagine." Is this really the right answer? It all just fell together, but….

Lyan took a deep breath. No matter how many times he rethought it, he was convinced this was correct.

If I'm wrong, I'll never see Eilidh Wood again. I'll be Lost to my home and my people. And if I'm right… He looked at the sky again. *If I'm right, maybe, just maybe, I will have the power to break the enchantment that hides the sky.*

He climbed to his feet. His stomach growled, leaving Lyan wondering how long he'd lain on the ground looking at the sky. It hadn't felt long to him, but Kithr had often remarked on how easily Lyan lost track of time when stargazing. Temporarily pushing aside hunger, Lyan looked around the night-shrouded forest. He found no trails, but to his left stood three massive trees, each with a closed door set in the trunk.

Lyan looked to the sky once more, searching for any final sign he might have missed. "The middle shall be first, and the first shall be last, and none shall open twice." It was one of the simplest riddles he'd learned as an apprentice, and one he'd never expected to find in his Trial. He let out a breath and opened the door in the center tree, stepping through.

He entered an identical clearing, again facing the three doors. He opened the third door and walked through. Once more, three trees, three doors. Lyan chose the first door, praying he was making the right decision as he stepped through.

Sunlight blinded him. Lyan staggered, raising a hand to shield his eyes with a sound of pain. Blinking rapidly and shaking his head, he saw green grass underfoot. When he raised watering eyes, he saw jagged rocks ahead, jutting from the ground to claw at the sky. Lyan turned around slowly until he saw two curved spines of rock arched to form the illusion of a vaulted doorway over the sun. Still blinking and squinting against the light, Lyan walked toward them, relief lifting a weight from his shoulders.

He kept his eyes turned to the ground often. Sharp, jagged stones littered the ground, lying in wait to trip him. Lyan stumbled even while watching his feet, and one rock ripped a long gash up his pant leg, scoring his skin. He picked himself up carefully and continued toward the arch. He sighed wearily when he found himself at the base of a steep hill. Lyan consoled himself with the thought that it wasn't nearly as steep as the sides of the ravine he'd fallen into when he sprained his ankle, and also that his ankle only occasionally bothered him now.

Panting for breath, sporting scrapes on hands, knees, and legs, Lyan dragged himself onto the top of the hill. Raising his head, he saw what he fervently hoped was his destination: a circle of tall stones. Lyan staggered up and stumbled over to the stones.

In the center of the stone ring, Yion sat cross-legged on the packed dirt, waiting with an air of patience, as if he could as easily have waited for years. Gasping for air, relieved beyond measure, Lyan flopped down on the ground beside him. The mercenary smiled.

"It is good to see you, Lyan Stargazer."

Lyan wiped a hand over his sweaty brow, then smiled in return. "Thanks. I was…getting worried I'd misread something. But if you're here, I must be on the right course.

So…do you have the scroll I need? Or do you have some clue I need to find it?"

"I have it," Yion answered.

Lyan caught his breath and sat up. After a moment, he asked, "Could I have it, please?"

"You had but to ask," Yion said. He drew a plain scroll case from his tunic and offered it to Lyan. Lyan took it gratefully. Before he opened it, Yion spoke again. "I am grateful for your trust, Lyan Stargazer."

Lyan blinked, surprised. "What do you mean?"

Yion made a gesture to encompass the entire situation. "If I had wished to see you fail in these Trials, I could have done something as simple as leave this site, so that when you arrived, no one awaited you. Or I could have replaced the scroll within the case. None would have stopped me, for your choices of companions is as much a part of your Trials as these tasks. More so, perhaps, than even the tasks you have been given to perform. So, I thank you for your trust."

"I…." *I never considered that my friends could intentionally sabotage my Trials.* "Thank you for all you have done, Yion. I know that ultimately, you serve your god, but whatever your final goals are, thank you for your help."

"My god would have me stand with the Spearbearers and guard them. He would see both Solstice and Equinox united against Murdo." Yion gazed at Lyan. "The Mad God rages against the prison that cages him, and his minions and followers in this world stir in ever greater numbers."

Lyan shivered.

"Should you take up Equinox and become Spearbearer, Lyan, I will stand by your side whenever you have need of my aid." Yion spoke with the solemnity of an oath. "And whether you take Equinox or not, I offer my friendship."

"Thank you," Lyan said quietly. He looked at the scroll case in his hands, then opened it and slid the parchment out.

The parchment crackled softly as he carefully unrolled the

aging sheet. Lyan couldn't guess how many times others had done this before him. The Guardians of the Spear must conduct the ritual with regularity to guard the shrine against the Mad God. Lyan drew a deep breath and read the scroll aloud. The script was written in archaic Elven, but the words flowed from Lyan's mouth more easily than they should have. None stuck in his memory, though—by the time he finished reading a line, Lyan couldn't remember what he'd said. Yion didn't interrupt, as calm and peaceful as a statue.

Wind howled to life as Lyan finished the last line. The blast of air slammed into Lyan, throwing him back against a rock. He clutched the scroll, praying that it wouldn't tear and wouldn't be ripped from his hand. Four final words glowing faintly on the scroll where there had only been blank parchment before—the only words on the page that stayed with him. He gasped them into the raging wind.

"Let it be so."

The wind released him abruptly, swirling above the standing stones and no longer buffeting Lyan and Yion within the circle. Lyan panted for breath again, staring up and watching as lines of magic gathered into a cloud over them. Yion helped him to his feet.

"It appears your work here is complete, Lyan Stargazer. We should depart, I believe, that the magic might complete its work uninhibited by our presence."

"Right." Lyan nodded, looking to either side in search of an exit.

Yion gestured, drawing his attention, and Lyan saw a glowing doorway shimmer into being.

"I'll go first," Lyan said.

"Of course." Yion waited for Lyan to step through.

With one final look to the chaotic powers swirling over his head, Lyan stepped through the portal.

Kithr paced. Cailean sat on a bench. Venycia, however, was looking expectantly toward Lyan even before he recognized the clearing he'd appeared in after the last Trial. Venycia's face brightened and her eyes danced with joy. "Welcome back, Lyan."

Kithr spun around, and Cailean jumped to his feet. Kithr grabbed Lyan in a fierce, unexpected embrace. "You worried me, dammit! You've been gone at least a day and a half!"

Lyan coughed, and wondered if Kithr had actually cracked any ribs, or just bruised them. "Sorry. I guess it took longer than I thought."

Kithr released him and stepped back, regaining his composure. "Just don't make a habit of it." He looked past Lyan. "I see the mercenary made it as well."

"Indeed," Yion answered simply.

Cailean embraced Lyan as well. "You're back, Lyan. You did it!"

"I…Yeah…." Lyan looked to Venycia, who still smiled. "Is there… still something else, Lady?"

She shook her head. "Only that you—that all of you come with me."

Kithr scowled at Cailean, who laughed softly and stepped aside to make room for Kithr to walk beside Lyan. Lyan looked at his friends, feeling his breath catch as the realization caught up with him and his heart beat faster with joy. "Kithr, I really…I completed the Trials."

"Of course you did. I never had any doubts." Kithr smiled —a rare, genuine smile untainted by sarcasm or anger.

Lyan stepped forward, following Venycia. For a moment, the world spun, and he felt like he was falling. He stumbled, catching himself against a tree.

"Poor little elf… to come so far and be so close, only to fail now."

Lyan's head jerked up and he looked around sharply as the pooka's voice whispered in his mind. He stood alone on the path. Turning in a slow circle, he didn't see anyone, not even Kithr, who had been at his side. "What do you mean? What are you talking about?"

"Yes, you're all alone. The rest, they've all gone ahead to prepare to welcome the new Spearbearer. And I'll tell you a secret, little elf: it's not you."

"The new…That can't be…How…Did…someone else take the Trials while I…?"

"Poor little elf," the pooka purred. *"Too slow. You took too long, you let someone else beat you. Wouldn't you like to see him? Of course you would, since you're now bound to serve him, forever. You failed."*

Lyan took a step back, shaking his head as the thrill of victory and success turned to disbelief and cold fear. "You're lying. That can't be true. I completed the Trials. I didn't fail!"

Ahead of him, from the direction of the largest building, the one that housed Equinox, steps crunched through the dry leaves. A cold voice spoke, a voice Lyan recognized with terror. "No, you didn't fail. You did everything perfectly—and you led me straight to Equinox."

Lyan's eyes grew wide. "No."

Vynzent smiled, icy eyes trapping Lyan in his gaze as he raised his prize: a Spear the twin to Solstice. "Thanks to you, all my ambitions are finally within my grasp."

31

*Twelve are they who stood
Unbowed before the Deceiver's rage.
Five are they who fell
To free their charge of the Deceiver's cage.
Seven are they who live
Ever watching, ever guarding, until the end of the age*

No. This can't be happening. Lyan couldn't tear his eyes away from Vynzent or the Spear in the Tathren's hands. *Please help me, Soldarr. Not Vynzent. Anyone but him.*

Vynzent walked toward Lyan deliberately, like a cat toying with its prey. His mouth curled in a mocking smile. "No congratulations? Not even acknowledgement of my thanks? How discourteous of you, Lyan. Don't tell me you actually thought *you* were worthy to hold Equinox?"

The words swept over Lyan, but one grabbed him despite the terror sinking fangs into his soul. The voice and the appearance were a perfect match to Vynzent, exactly as Lyan remembered on every point but….

He always called me "elf". He never used my name. He never tried to learn my name.

Lyan took a deep breath, voice trembling and sweat trickling down his brow. "I don't know who you are, but you are not Vynzent Col'renn."

Vynzent stopped, eyes narrowing. "You think not, elf?"

The voice sent chills down his spine, but given a moment's reprieve, Lyan's wits caught up with him, and he answered with more confidence, though his voice shook. "You are not. You can't be Vynzent if you've taken the Trials. The Guardians wouldn't have allowed Vynzent to take the Trials, because he's of the same family line as Cailean. If something happened to Cailean, then Vynzent, gods forbid, could claim Solstice. Therefore, if you hold Equinox, you *are not* Vynzent."

A ripple ran through Vynzent's form, like a stone disturbing the smooth surface of still water. His appearance didn't change, but the voice shifted to a silky purr all too familiar to Lyan. "Then who *am* I, little elf?"

Whoever, whatever you are, you're taking on forms and voices that I fear. Why?

"I don't believe you're the pooka, either," Lyan said.

"Such confidence…" The other's features melted into those the pooka used in human form. He looked at the Spear in his hands, then at Lyan. "And how are you so sure, little elf? You think only an elf can hold Equinox? Or that only a mortal can?"

"I think the pooka which has been taunting me would hesitate to come here," Lyan answered. "I don't believe it could enter without the knowledge of the Guardians of the Spear. In the Forests of Cossette, I stumbled across Venycia in bear form, and tricked the pooka into encountering her. From its reaction to the meeting, I don't think it would risk a second confrontation."

"Venycia." The other smirked. "Pretty, isn't she? You like her. You could give up seeking Equinox, stay at the shrine as a Guardian of the Spear, and have all the time in the world to woo her."

Lyan blinked, taken aback at the sudden change of subject and at the suggestion itself, but more startled at the idea's appeal. Then he shook his head. "What sense would it make for me to come this far to give up, failing to become the bearer of Equinox based only on the daydream that a Guardian of the Spear might like me?"

"Others before you have given up as much with less promise of reward," the other said.

Lyan shook his head again. "How could I expect her to respect me if I did that? No, I won't give up becoming Spearbearer in hopes of pursuing Venycia."

"And if I told you she is fond of you?"

The words brought to mind the argument he'd heard between Venycia and Waldros. An argument that something had wanted him to hear. "Then she wants me to succeed, not give up," Lyan said firmly. "You are certainly *not* the pooka."

The other smiled mischievously, twirling the Spear in his hands. "Then who am I?"

Lyan faltered. *I completed three Trials. Didn't I? The two at the Shrine, though, felt too easy. Venycia said the Trials would test me in ways I would not imagine.* He opened his mouth, closed it, and licked dry lips. His voice came out barely louder than a whisper. "You are Equinox."

The other still smiled. "Not a minion? Not a Guardian of the Spear, dissatisfied with your success and testing you further?"

"Testing me, yes. But you're Equinox, deciding if I'm worth your time."

"Determining if you can tell truth from illusion," corrected the other. "I already knew you were worth my time." He still wore the pooka's features, but his eyes changed. Black orbs studied Lyan, glittered with sparks of light like stars. His voice was serious. "Are you sure you want to follow this path?"

"I keep being asked that." Lyan laughed faintly. "My answer hasn't changed yet, has it?"

"Those who ask have witnessed Spearbearers before you, Lyan of Eilidh Wood. They warn you and question whether you possess the strength to carry this burden. Ignore that warning at your own folly."

"I'm not ignoring it," Lyan protested. "But I'm not changing my mind. I may not know what lies ahead if I take up Equinox, but I'm not backing down."

"Are you prepared to make choices that will affect thousands of people you may never know? Are you prepared to make choices that will affect the people you *do* know and care about? Are you prepared to have others give their lives for you? Are you prepared to sacrifice to save them?"

Lyan shifted uncomfortably at the thought. "How many people are?"

"There are some. Are you one?"

"I...don't know. I don't want anyone to die for my sake. But I... I am prepared to sacrifice to save them."

"Once you become Spearbearer, your life is forever bound to Equinox. There is no turning back, no undoing it. You can decide never to use the Spear in all your life, but you and only you will be Spearbearer, until life finally leaves your body. You will not be just Lyan, astrologer from Heartshrine Village any longer—ever. Some Guardians will rejoice, and others will resent and despise you for succeeding where they failed. Your friends will be unsure how to treat you. Sycophants will seek you out, hoping to flatter their way into your favor. Powerful people will search for you to use the Spear's power for their own ends. But most of all, Lyan, taking Equinox will turn Murdo's eyes onto you. The Mad God *will* hunt you. He will tempt you, and he will try to corrupt you. He will threaten anyone you care about. He will attack you and everything that gives you strength."

Lyan paled, feeling the words pressing down on him.

Finally he spoke, voice soft. "I know. I've seen the attacks on Cailean. I know…I'll be putting everyone around me in danger. But if I don't, who will? I won't turn back now. If you think I'm worthy to be the Spearbearer, then I will carry Equinox."

The other smiled, dispelling the grim mood. "Your mind's made up, then, and no one is going to dissuade you. Good. I look forward to traveling with my brother once more. Here— catch!" He gave the Spear in his hands a final spin and tossed it to Lyan.

Lyan reached out reflexively, hands closing around the gilded shaft. Warmth flowed up his arm, wrapping around him in comfortable, welcoming magic. He opened his mouth, words on his tongue, but he stood alone again.

"Lyan?"

Lyan blinked and opened his eyes, trying to figure out why he was on the ground. He lay on his back, and Kithr looked down at him, worry written on his face.

"Are you awake? Are you all right?"

"Um…yes?" Lyan pushed himself up to a sitting position. Kithr moved back a little, his eyes still filled with concern and caution. Cailean crouched near Lyan, his expression nearly identical to Kithr's. Even Yion's features weren't as placid as usual, which probably meant worry. "What…?"

"You collapsed," Cailean said. "We were walking, and you collapsed. We couldn't wake you, and not even Lady Venycia knew what happened."

"I'll be all right," Lyan said. "I'm sorry."

"You should be!" Kithr found his typical scowl. "What happened?"

"Equinox decided to have a say in the matter of my candidacy," Lyan said. "So… it did. There wasn't much I could have done about that, Kithr."

Venycia, standing to the side, started. "Equinox spoke to you directly?"

Lyan nodded.

"I see…." She gave him a half-smile. "You woke again. I'll take that as a positive sign."

Lyan looked at his empty hands, then at the ground beside him with growing anxiety.

"What's wrong?" Kithr asked.

"It's not here." He looked around, as if the Spear had fallen from his hands.

"What isn't? What are you looking for, Lyan?" Kithr insisted.

"Equinox remains in its resting place, Lyan," Venycia said. "In your vision, the Spear was handed to you?"

"Well…tossed, really," Lyan answered. "I think…Equinox has a sense of humor." With a hand up from Kithr, he got to his feet.

Venycia smiled in wry sympathy. "That it does. To our regret, sometimes."

"Is this a common occurrence, Lady Venycia?" Cailean asked.

She shook her head. "No. It's rare for Equinox to address a candidate directly. Some Spearbearers never fully understand what Lyan now knows: the Spears have awareness. They are more than just items of power."

Cailean shifted uncomfortably. "Both Spears?"

Venycia nodded solemnly. "Yes. Solstice as well as Equinox."

Cailean looked at Solstice and said nothing.

Lyan watched Venycia, and a blush crept up his face as he desperately hoped she didn't know she had been one of the temptations Equinox had offered. He busied himself with brushing off his clothes and trying to look halfway presentable, picking leaves from his hair. "Um…what happens now?"

Venycia smiled at him. Lyan was sure his heart skipped a beat every time she did that. "The Trials are complete, and

Equinox has chosen a new Spearbearer. Now you have an opportunity to bathe, to put on clean clothes, and celebrate. The rest of your companions will join you then. They have been anxious."

"And…Equinox?" Lyan asked, unsure why he felt so anxious to have the Spear in his hands again. Or would it be for the first time? He wasn't even sure of that.

"You will take the Spear at the feast's end, Lyan," she assured him. "Now come—the longer we stand talking, the longer Equinox must wait." Venycia smiled again, then raised her voice slightly, addressing the air. "And you make your choice quite clear, Equinox. But you know what store we place in our celebrations."

The anxious urgency Lyan felt to reach the Spear relented, and he blinked, puzzled. "What was that?"

"Equinox has, without a doubt, chosen you, Lyan," Venycia said. "The Spear is eager to be united with its new bearer." She walked down the path.

Lyan followed, with Kithr, Cailean, and Yion close on his heels. The mist and fog finally began to lift, and the sun peered down on them. Lyan had no idea how many days had passed since he began the Trials, but whatever the day, it appeared to be mid-afternoon. They entered an open area, and were met by other Guardians of the Spear, led by Waldros. The human studied Lyan with less venom than he had previously. Venycia spoke quietly to Waldros, and his eyes widened in surprise. Venycia nodded.

"Well, Lyan of Heartshrine Village, you have surpassed my expectations," Waldros said. "Congratulations." The word sounded sincere.

"Thank you."

"Come with me," Waldros instructed. "Your companions will rejoin you later."

"Wait!" Kithr protested. "Where are you taking Lyan *now*?"

Lyan looked back at Kithr. "Hopefully, to someplace where I can take a bath and change clothes."

"Oh." Kithr stepped back, flushing at his overprotective outburst.

Waldros smiled. "Yes, and you will have a chance to do the same shortly. Rest easy, Kithr of Eilidh Wood; Lyan's Trials are done, and I doubt he's in danger of drowning in the bath."

Kithr scowled at the man. Lyan chuckled softly and followed Waldros. Though the desire to bolt through the Shrine and snatch up Equinox had eased, nervous energy still filled Lyan, and he didn't want to stand still too long.

Waldros led him into a bathhouse. A large tub was set nearly level with the floor, just a single step to the lip and into the steaming water. Lyan looked toward it longingly, but wasn't sure he could actually sit still long enough to enjoy the promised bath.

"Let your new Spearbearer relax for a little while, Equinox," Waldros said firmly, a tone not unlike a parent gently reprimanding a child. "He's not going to run off without you."

"What? I...." Lyan began.

"Not all the anxiety you're feeling is your own, Lyan," the human said. "Venycia told me that the Spear tested you personally. Equinox has judged you and, apparently, approves. As the Spear is unlikely to be deceived by the same tricks twice, my concerns were unfounded. Now, relax, Lyan. When Equinox accepted you, and you agreed to bear the Spear, you became the Spearbearer. All traditions and celebrations aside, you are already Spearbearer. If you had to, you could call Equinox to you at this moment."

Lyan stared at him, mouth opening for a moment before he found words. "But...then...."

"There is a completion of the bond that you will only gain the first time you take up Equinox—that is what pulls at you now. But you, Lyan, are the Spearbearer, and no one can take it from you."

No one and nothing can take Equinox away from me. Not even Vynzent. "And Equinox is pulling at me?" Lyan asked.

Waldros snorted in amusement. "I have been a Guardian of the Spear for as long as there have been Guardians of the Spear. I have seen many Spearbearers before you, boy. I know what I'm talking about. Now get in that tub while the water's still hot."

Lyan stripped off muddy, ripped clothes and sank into the water. "I thought the Guardians consisted of those who tried to become Spearbearers and failed."

"Many are, but not all. Venycia, I, and a handful of others became Guardians by choice."

Lyan made generous use of the soap he found on the tub's rim. "What do you do when there is a Spearbearer?"

"Our guardianship becomes all the more vital when Equinox isn't here. The Spear provides protection to the shrine, but the Deceiver's minions are always searching for the Shrine. Equinox will return here when you die. Until then, we must keep it safe, lest only servants of the Mad God awaited the Spear."

"Oh." Lyan restrained questions to duck his head underwater and scrub his hair. As he blinked water from his eyes he asked, "The Deceiver is the Mad God, isn't he?"

"When he was still a mortal seeking the power of the Spears, he came here to take the Trials and claim Equinox. He had Equinox first, and Solstice he inherited by other means." Waldros collected Lyan's filthy clothes and set them in a basket, then set out towels.

"Solstice is passed through a family line, isn't it? Or was that started only after?" Lyan rinsed the soap from his face, then let himself relax in the warm water.

"It was passed through a family line in those days as well. A different family, however. Cailean Dev'gilla's ancestors weren't entrusted with Solstice until after the Mad God's defeat and imprisonment," Waldros answered.

Lyan nodded slowly in understanding. "So, did you separate me from Kithr and Cailean just so I could pester you with questions?"

Waldros actually chuckled. "All new Spearbearers have questions, whether they ask me 'How does the Spearbearer use the Spear?', or 'Are you and Venycia lovers?'"

Lyan stiffened, heat rushing through his face. He again remembered the argument he'd overheard. "Are you?"

"No." Waldros's wistful tone implied that he wished the answer were different. "We are very old friends who share a few unique traits."

"Unique traits? Do you shape-shift into some other form as well?"

"No. However, each of us who chose to become the original Guardians of the Spear is a child born of the union between a god and a mortal, each of us having abilities resulting from that."

"You're demigods," Lyan said in quiet awe.

"We are. Demigods do not become lovers with one another—such unions are forbidden. However, since mortals were good enough for our divine parents, why shouldn't they be good enough for us?" Waldros smiled. "And Venycia has a fondness for redheads."

The bright red blush Lyan felt ran all the way to his toes. Did *everyone* know he thought her the most beautiful woman he'd ever met? He changed the subject as quickly as possible, before his thoughts lingered any longer and he embarrassed himself more. "What about the other question? How do I use the Spear?"

Waldros's face grew more serious. "Each Spearbearer must learn that on their own. Equinox will guide you. As you've already discovered, the Spear can influence you. You must recognize when Equinox is telling you something, and when the impulse is your own. Equinox will guide you, but remember, it isn't always right. Don't follow blindly—think before you react. That will be the most important thing for you to do, Lyan—learn to control Equinox rather than be controlled by it."

Lyan nodded in understanding, though his thoughts tumbled over one another. He stood up to climb from the tub, then caught himself against the side as lightheadedness assailed him.

"Are you all right?" Waldros asked.

"Just dizzy for a moment. I stood up too fast," Lyan answered. Steady once again, he climbed from the tub and wrapped a towel around himself. "Are my bags somewhere close, for clean clothes?"

Waldros handed him a bundle of blue and gold cloth. "It's traditional for the new Spearbearer to wear this for the celebration."

Lyan shook wet hair from his eyes and unfolded the clothes. The blue cloth was a knee-length tunic with sleeves to his elbows. Tasseled cords fastened the slit down the chest. The gold cloth seemed to be a voluminous fringed cloak. Lyan looked at the outfit, then set it aside in favor of drying. Once his hair had stopped dripping, he pulled on the tunic. Elaborate, delicate embroidery caught the light in the bathhouse. He examined the sleeves, seeing runes stitched in the cloth.

Lyan picked up the cloak, looking at it, then at Waldros. "All right…how is this supposed to look?"

The demigod chuckled softly. "Give it to me."

Lyan gladly relinquished the massive piece of cloth, and watched Waldros fold it in two lengthwise, one side longer than the other to make two tiers of fringes. Waldros wrapped it around Lyan's waist like a skirt, produced a belt, and fastened it in place.

"That's one way to wear it—probably the most common.

The other style is more elaborate, and generally, Spearbearers haven't wanted to wait long enough." He handed Lyan a pair of sandals.

"This will be fine, I think," Lyan said distractedly. Anxiety pushed at him again, as if, now that he was washed and dressed, he should be getting Equinox immediately.

That's the Spear, not me. I must remember what Waldros said and not rush ahead blindly.

"Hungry?" Waldros asked.

In answer, Lyan's stomach growled. He flushed, then answered, "I guess I must be."

"Good. There will be plenty of food shortly. Put your shoes on."

"Shoes? Oh." Lyan looked at the sandals still in his hand, and slid them on his feet, awkward in the unfamiliar clothes. "I'm ready."

Waldros looked him over critically, then nodded in approval. "So you are. This way."

Outside again, and the light faded toward twilight. Lyan and Waldros walked toward the largest, central building. Inside, Equinox waited, tugging at Lyan impatiently. But in the courtyard between them and the building lay a gauntlet that Lyan didn't want to rush through. A bonfire burned in the fire pit, sending an uneasy shiver through Lyan, but tables laden with food and drink stood in rows along either side of the courtyard. What Lyan guessed to be nearly all the Guardians of the Spear, dressed in identical russet robes, milled around, setting the final touches on animals sculpted of fruits and vegetables, tuning instruments, arranging decorative plants, and talking in quiet voices.

At Lyan's entrance, everything grew still and a hush fell over the crowd. Waldros raised one hand and gestured to the musicians. They broke into a fanfare, as if anyone might have missed Lyan's arrival.

Waldros spoke. "Some among us have never before had

the opportunity to take part in the rite we celebrate tonight. This is a celebration of all we hold sacred. A celebration of our purpose, our goal, our continuing battle against the Deceiver. Tonight, we celebrate the birth of a new Spearbearer of Equinox. Lyan of Heartshrine Village has faced the Trials set before him, and he has been judged worthy by Equinox. Welcome him." The last was not a request, but an order.

As one, the Guardians of the Spear raised goblets to Lyan. "Welcome, Spearbearer." Some spoke with more enthusiasm than others, and Lyan remembered what Equinox had told him, that some would resent him for his success. He bowed to them all, accepting their welcome regardless of its sincerity, though his heart raced.

"Now, let the celebration begin!" Waldros ordered. The musicians struck up a tune, and the moment of tension passed.

"Where are my friends?" Lyan asked Waldros.

The man pointed to another path. "They are entering now. Custom dictates that the new Spearbearer arrive before any other guests."

It was no surprise to see Kithr first to enter the courtyard and make straight for Lyan. He did pause a moment and look askance at Lyan's outfit. Lyan shot him a scowl. "It's traditional for the new Spearbearer, or so I'm told."

"Well, it's different," Kithr replied. He'd bathed and dressed in fresh clothes—black hose and a dark green tunic with silver leaves around the cuffs. "I'm glad no one tried to get me to wear it. These do well enough. One of the Guardians gave them to me—said mine weren't fit for a festival."

Cailean and his men followed. Kithr stepped to one side as Shiolto ran up to Lyan. "Lyan! Lord Cailean told us you beat the tests! We were worried—six days waiting without knowing what was going on. But you're all right!"

Lyan embraced Shiolto briefly. "It didn't seem that long to me. Yes, I completed the Trials. It's good to see you again."

Dalrian followed his brother and slapped Lyan on the back with a grin. "Like there was any doubt you were going to succeed." He leaned close and whispered, "We had a wager going against Aikan. You won us both a full month's pay."

Lyan chuckled, reminding himself that they didn't know the consequences failing the Trials would have brought him. "Is that why Aikan's looking so sour?"

"Well, that and not having any idea what was happening with Lord Cailean during that time," Dalrian said.

Aikan, for his turn, scowled fiercely at Lyan. "You took your time. Do you think Lord Cailean has all the time in the world?"

"Cailean wasn't in any danger, Aikan. Just me."

"Hmmph. Then I suppose you are to be congratulated for not falling on your face."

Torqual studied Lyan long enough to make him uneasy. Finally the soldier said, "So, you're going to bear a Spear of the Stars. Who would have thought it?"

"Better than seeing it in the hands of a Tathren," Kithr countered.

"Ah, but isn't everything better if it isn't in the hands of a Tathren?" Torqual responded with a sly smile.

One of the Guardians approached. "The feast is ready, Spearbearer. Please begin."

"Thank you." Lyan took a plate from the closest table and accepted a healthy slice of roasted boar, adding a chunk of bread and helpings of the assorted, unidentified dishes, then a bowl of soup. The soup smelled like fish, though Lyan wasn't familiar with many fish large enough to make a decent soup.

Once he found a seat, everyone else descended on the food in a hungry, but orderly manner. Kithr, Cailean, and his men settled near Lyan to eat. Lyan didn't give much attention to anything beyond his plate until he felt someone watching him.

Looking up, he found an unfamiliar elf in the robes of a Guardian gazing at him with amber eyes. The other's hair had a green hue Lyan couldn't attribute to the bonfire's light, and his skin was brown and rough.

"So, you did find your way," the elf said. He plucked a piece of meat from his plate with long fingers that reminded Lyan of twigs on a tree.

Lyan recognized the voice as he did not the face. "Damasek. You left your forest."

Damasek made a dismissive gesture. "Some few events are worthy of returning to this limited body. A new Spearbearer is one such event. I did wonder if you would succeed in the Trial." He smirked. "You can see I failed in mine, but it's of no matter. The forest suits me well. We shall hope being Spearbearer suits you."

Damasek turned and strode away, giving the bonfire a wide berth. Cailean glanced at Lyan. "Who, or *what*, was that?"

"His name is Damasek, and he's a Guardian. He controls the forest that protects one of the runes. His magic is strong and directed toward plants."

"What did he mean about 'returning to a limited body'?" Dalrian asked.

"You know the forests in Tather that no Tathrens dare enter?" Kithr said. "Most of those are only influenced by someone with power. The forest that elf lives in is more than that. He's part of it, and every tree, every plant is his body. I think your word for it would be to say that he possesses the forest. That's also why his body is slowly transforming. Eventually, he will become a tree with the shape of an elf—a walking, speaking tree."

It was the longest explanation Lyan had heard Kithr give in answer to one of the Tathrens. He wondered if it was a sign that, despite himself, Kithr was starting to accept them.

The music changed tempo to a lively beat. A dozen

Guardians cast off their robes to reveal elaborate, colorful costumes and sprang to dance around the bonfire. One woman represented a bear, while another's slim, nearly naked body was painted with crashing waves. As the dancers gyrated past, Lyan saw one man carrying a lightning bolt carved of wood, his shirt a chaos of clouds and storms. He couldn't identify the costumes on all of them, and their chanting voices rose and fell with the music until Lyan couldn't distinguish words.

Venycia sat down beside him. "They represent the twelve original Guardians of the Spear, and the dance remembers the forming of this shrine on the ruins of an ancient city destroyed in the Devastation."

Lyan looked at her. "You don't dance your own part?"

She laughed. "A dancing bear is an awkward, clumsy creature, and I would only prove the truth of that. The dancers compete fiercely for the honor of a part in this particular dance. I wouldn't take that from any of them." Venycia sighed, watching the dance. "In any case, not all the original twelve remain. We are only seven now."

Lyan started. "But Waldros said all the first Guardians are the children of gods."

She nodded solemnly. "Yes. Five of our number were lost to break the Spears from the Deceiver when he warred against the gods."

Lyan looked back at the dance. *This is the heritage I will carry —the weight of souls who fought and died to protect Equinox and defy the Mad God.*

The dance spun to an end to thunderous applause. The dancers laughed, sagging against one another as they took their bows, and gratefully accepting goblets of wine. Venycia rose and walked to the woman in the bear costume, talking and laughing with her warmly. Waldros spoke to the man with the representation of the storm. Others separated from the crowd to speak to individual dancers. Seven of them in total.

Lyan felt a surge of sorrow for the five dancers who would never hear words of thanks from those they represented.

The music continued, and other dancers took the place of the first twelve. Lyan didn't see where Venycia went. As night covered the sky, the bonfire threw showers of sparks into the air, as if to cast the stars back into the shrouded heavens. Finally, Lyan quietly slipped away from the courtyard.

He found himself climbing the marble steps up to the building that housed Equinox. For a moment Lyan hesitated, then he continued climbing. The massive doors stood open, and inside, torches cast flickering light. Lyan stepped into the outer chamber, a room half the size of the massive courtyard below, where the festival continued. Weapons and armor hung on the walls. To his left, swords were set in semi-circles on the wall like the fanned tails of deadly peacocks. At the far end of the room stood a closed wooden door. Lyan slowly walked across the room.

He stopped abruptly, a chill running down his spine. Looking over his shoulder, Lyan saw figures in dark robes flow from the shadows. For a moment, he was sure they numbered twelve, but when he looked again, only seven stood gathered.

"Welcome, Spearbearer," one said. The hood hiding his face also distorted his voice, so Lyan couldn't guess who spoke. The others repeated the words, a disconcerting echo.

"My name is Lyan. I'd prefer to be called by it."

"Spearbearer, Lyan. We, the Guardians of the Spear, blessed by our gods, test those who seek the power of Equinox. But it is not we who chose the Spearbearer. Only Equinox has that right. Tell us, Lyan, why are you here?"

"I'm here because Equinox is calling me," Lyan answered.

The hooded Guardian waved at the wall, toward spears long and short like a deadly flower blooming on the stone. "Where is Equinox?"

Lyan blinked, surprised. He gave the spears only a glance, then said, "Beyond the door at the end of this room."

Drawing a deep breath, he continued. "I don't need your permission to take up Equinox. I'm already the Spearbearer; Equinox chose me. But I ask your permission all the same."

"It is given," answered a female voice. "Claim your destiny, Lyan, Spearbearer."

He bowed, then turned his back to them and continued to the door. It swung open even as he reached for the latch, and Lyan stepped into darkness.

3 2

But a step, leagues away
But a step, and one step more
But a moment within the day
But a moment, pass through the door

The door swung shut behind Lyan with a soft click. He'd closed his eyes as he stepped inside, and kept them closed now as he stood in the silence. A shiver ran down his spine as cool mist brushed over his skin.

He opened his eyes slowly. Faint light shone through the room, but mist hid the walls from sight. The room could have been large enough to fit all Heartshrine Village within, or it could have been no larger than the length of Equinox.

The Spear provided illumination, hanging in the air with no visible support. It was almost as long as Lyan was tall, the shaft gilt in gold. Serrations ran down the leaf-shaped head, ending in a pair of barbed wings. Runes edged the metal, and Lyan could only guess at their meaning. Equinox might never have seen battle for all the signs of wear it showed. Solstice carried the same air of perfection combined with deadly beauty.

Lyan let out a deep breath. "Well, here I am." He reached out with a hint of hesitation, and let his hands rest on the Spear's shaft.

Warmth rushed up his arm, then a burst of lights and colors erupted in his head, filled with sensations and chaotic emotions, as if an outside presence invaded his mind. For all its foreign nature, though, it felt as if it were a part of him. He thought he cried out, but the assault eased after a moment. Lyan panted for breath, finding himself on the floor, clutching Equinox against him.

"Maybe you could…warn me a little…before you do that again?" he asked.

In answer, restless impatience ran through him—a desire to get up, to act, to do… something. The sensation trailed away for lack direction or target.

Lyan smiled as he slowly picked himself up. "You want to do something, but you don't know what it is you want to do?"

The answer came—a sense not of impatience this time, but of long inactivity and a desire to stretch, to move, to leave this place of safety for one where they were needed. A question followed: where?

"Tather." The answer came easily. "If we're going to help Cailean and Solstice, we have to go to Tather." He looked at Equinox. "So is actually talking to me something you reserve for the Trials?"

"Taking a form and speaking in such a manner takes more strength. Within the Shrine, I can do so, but outside, it will be challenging." A vague shape formed in the mist, indistinct. "So if there is more you would ask, do so now."

"I'll always have questions," Lyan said. "But the one on my mind most right now is… the Trials. The two I went through here…they felt…too easy. Were they really the Trials?"

A soft laugh. "I let my Guardians test you as they saw fit, but their tests weren't your Trials. The first Trial, Vynzent

Col'renn, you endured alone and unaided. The second began with your choice of companions. You made two choices easily, but the third was the most important. Would you select one who would aid you, or one who would fail you when you needed them most? Would you select one who secretly wished you to fail? Would you select one who secretly serves a lord other than Cailean? Was that decision easy?"

"No," Lyan admitted.

"That choice determined the rest of your Trials as much as your skills did. You know Waldros accused Venycia of helping you on the second Trial, but she did nothing outside the adjustments the Guardians are permitted to make."

"How do you know—" Lyan stopped. "You woke me up and urged me to eavesdrop."

"Of course," Equinox agreed, unrepentant. "As far as companions went, I wondered if you would choose Shadowstar as the third."

Lyan started. "Shadowstar was an option?"

"Is he not your companion?" Equinox retorted. "Think outside the obvious, Lyan."

"What about the last Trial? Reading the stars?"

"I knew you could solve it, given enough time," Equinox said. "I didn't want to wait, so I nudged your thoughts in the right direction. Not that you needed much help once you had the right idea in your head. Then the Guardians were satisfied that they'd done their duty, and we could move on to *my* final Trial for you."

"You…." Lyan stared at the figure. "You mean… um… isn't that cheating?"

"No," Equinox said. "My bearer, my decision. I moved the preliminaries out of the way. Venycia or Waldros might have disagreed, and would probably have recognized that you were being influenced, so I insisted they remove themselves from monitoring that Trial. I wanted to test you myself. Have you ever touched Solstice, Lyan?"

"Yes," Lyan said. "Solstice made it very clear I wasn't to make a habit of doing so."

The figure nodded. "My brother knew that, given a chance, I would pick you. He could sense it about you. So he warned you against any aspirations toward trying to claim him. We have experienced the results of a mortal claiming both Spears once, in Murdo. We will not allow it to happen again."

Lyan licked dry lips. "Why me, though? Not that I would change this, but why did Solstice think I would be your bearer? He couldn't have known anything about me then. Neither did you. So how could you know?"

"Have you ever met someone, and on that first meeting known they were someone you could call a friend? Or, for that matter, an enemy?" Equinox asked. "Or, perhaps, have you felt certain you could trust someone, though you barely knew them?"

"Yes," Lyan said, thinking of Cailean and Yion.

"Can you explain it?"

"No," he admitted.

"Neither can we," Equinox said. "Only a sense that someone is suited to be a good partner to one of us. Now, I know Waldros and the others have given you many warnings. You should listen to them and remember what they tell you. Even I know I am impatient and sometimes too eager, perhaps not always as... subtle as the situation might require. Therefore, it is your job to temper action with wisdom. But don't think too long." A hint of humor touched the tone. "What else would you ask?"

"Is there a traitor among Cailean's men? If so, who?" Lyan asked.

The vision shook his head. "I cannot read minds, Lyan. I can sense impressions of their emotions, but not delve into their thoughts to learn their secrets. And every one of them holds secrets. I do believe that someone wishes Cailean ill, and

I wish that I could tell you who. But you and Cailean are like a pair of brilliant lights, throwing the rest of them into shadows that blur and run together. And more than that, there is the shadow of Murdo's touch on Cailean himself. More than that, I do not know." The ghostly image faded away, and the light emanating from Equinox softened to the faintest glow.

Lyan stood in silence. At any moment, he expected to wake and learn he had been only dreaming. Finally, he turned and reached out in search of the door. Fingers brushed wood and the door swung open.

Morning light flowed through the outer room, momentarily blinding Lyan. He raised an arm to shield his eyes with no clear sense of how much time had passed.

When his eyes cleared, he saw a table in the middle of the room set with a platter of fruits and another of smoked meats. Lyan popped a handful of blue berries into his mouth. When the sweet juice filled his mouth, his stomach woke with a growl of complaint. As he devoured the food, knowledge crept through his thoughts, supplied by the Spear. A new Spearbearer was often hungry, and needed to replenish the energy expended when calling on the Spear's power until he learned to find balance.

"Is that how Cailean's curse affects him?" Lyan asked. "Does it heighten that drain to prevent him from using Solstice? Would eating more when he uses the Spear help?"

Equinox didn't have an answer, but even if the idea didn't solve Cailean's problem, it might help.

Carrying Equinox like a walking staff, Lyan left the building and looked down on the courtyard. Remains of the festival still littered the ground. Smoldering coals from the bonfire spat up occasional burps of smoke. Most of the food had been cleared away, though half-finished plates still waited on some tables, and Lyan saw a few people sprawled out in sleep at the edges of the courtyard. He started down the steps when the sound of wings and a rush of air at his back made him turn in surprise.

A woman in the robes of a Guardian alighted on the steps. Lyan had noticed her at the festival when she spoke to one of the dancers after the first dance, but he'd somehow failed to take note of the wings she now folded against her back.

"Good morning, Lyan Spearbearer," she greeted cheerfully in a high-pitched voice.

"Um, good morning," he replied.

"We have not been properly introduced. I'm Ude, daughter of Fugol, a god of birds in Korlest."

"Lyan, astrologer of Heartshrine Village in Eilidh Wood."

"Yes. Venycia told me about you. She likes you."

Lyan flushed bright red and his answer tumbled out before he rethought it. "Venycia is one of the most beautiful women I've ever seen."

Ude continued in the same conversational tone, but her eyes glittered. "She's my oldest friend, and I want her to be happy. So know this, Lyan Stargazer: if you cause her pain, I'll tear you apart, Spearbearer or not. Just so we're clear."

Lyan swallowed hard. "Very clear."

She smiled warmly. "Good. Nothing to worry about, then!"

"Ude, are you *threatening* Lyan?" Venycia climbed the stairs. Lyan felt his face burn as he wondered how much she'd heard.

Ude smiled, unrepentant. "I'm not threatening. Simply stating a fact." With a smirk at Lyan, she sprang from the steps, wings spreading to catch the breeze.

Lyan glanced at Venycia and saw she was blushing, not meeting his eyes. "I'm sorry about that, Lyan…"

Lyan tried to hide his own embarrassment. "Don't worry about it. I'm… familiar with having protective friends."

The words drew a laugh from Venycia. "I imagine you are."

They walked down to the courtyard. Lyan carefully stepped over a snoring Guardian. He wondered how long had passed since the last time he'd slept. Weariness wasn't troubling him, but his ankle complained about too long spent moving, walking, climbing, and other abuse, and not enough time spent resting. He kicked a rock out of his sandal.

"Equinox is eager to go out into the world," Lyan said suddenly as they followed one of the paths from the courtyard. "And I don't really know how to wield the Spear."

"Nor do I, Lyan. Neither will any of the Guardians. You'll have to learn by doing."

"Are all the Guardians but the original ones bound to the shrine?" Lyan asked as that conversation seemed destined to die. "I know you can leave, and I assume the other six can…"

"We can, and we do when we need to. The rest of the Guardians have duties here that keep them occupied. Few, if any, have reason to leave." Venycia paused, expression serious as she considered her words. "However, as Spearbearer, you can call Guardians to your aid if you have need."

"I can? What if they don't want to?"

She shook her head. "They are Guardians of the Spear, bound to serve Equinox and the Spearbearer. They will obey. The only Guardians you cannot compel are those who joined willingly."

The thought raised a new question. "Any Spearbearer of Equinox? So even the Mad God?"

Her expression grew grim, and Venycia nodded. "He could and he did. He drew in all the Guardians of the Spear —all but the twelve of us, and used them to build his army. He forced us to fight our own comrades, former friends." She closed her eyes for a moment. "Some probably still live, wholly under the control of the Mad God and twisted to forms of his choosing. They're called demons now by those few who have survived an encounter with one. They were banished into the

Deceiver's prison with him, though I think that might have been a mistake, because they have bred, increasing their numbers. Sometimes, a fool summons one or two into our world, thinking to gain power from them. If we could have undone the Deceiver's corruption, we would have, but we had no means of purifying them. In the battle against the Mad God, many fell to them, and many more of us nearly did. I would have been killed had my father not broken from his own battle to protect me."

"Soldarr?" Lyan guessed.

She smiled then, and shook her head. "No, my father is not an elven god. My mother was an elf, and I respect Soldarr, but he's not my father. My father has never really forgiven Soldarr for having more of my loyalty than he does."

"Oh. I'm sorry, I just presumed...."

"It's fine, Lyan. As I said, I follow the elven gods, and it's no insult to me that you thought me one of their children." She paused before a small single-story building. "If you want to change clothes, yours have been washed and mended."

"Thank you." Lyan stepped toward the doorway. "Venycia? I'm sorry for prying into your personal matters, and for bringing up painful memories."

"You are forgiven, Lyan." She smiled gently. "I have made peace with the past. The future matters now."

Inside the building, Lyan found his clothes, neatly folded, along with a wash basin. A doorway led to a tub, but after a moment of consideration Lyan declined the bath. He washed his face and dressed, relieved to finally return to familiar clothes.

As he stepped outside once more, Lyan heard Yion's calm voice. "I am certain he is safe, and that we shall see him soon."

"And I should believe a mercenary," Kithr snapped.

"You will believe who and what you will," Yion said.

Lyan followed the sounds of their voices and found all his

companions gathered in a small courtyard ornamented with a fountain. Already certain he was once again the source of the argument, he said, "I'm sorry to keep everyone waiting."

He expected immediate reproach, not startled silence. Lyan shifted his weight self-consciously. "What?"

Shiolto smiled nervously. "Sorry Lyan. Knowing you beat all those Trials so you could carry a magical weapon is one thing, but actually *seeing* you with it…well…."

The reaction stung, but Lyan tried not to show it. Defying the sudden stillness, Cailean stepped around his men, walked up to Lyan, and threw an arm around his shoulder in an embrace of friendship.

"It's good to see you, Lyan. I don't think any of us had to wonder where you disappeared to last night." He cast an admiring look at Equinox. "So this is the elven Spear." Holding Solstice forward, he compared the two, finding them nearly identical. Subtle differences distinguished them visually, but Lyan knew with absolute conviction that even from the greatest distance, he could never mistake Solstice for Equinox. One Spear was his, the other was not, and he could never confuse one for the other.

An impulse struck Lyan, and he moved Equinox so the head of the Spear met that of Solstice. Both Spears glowed brightly for a moment, and heat ran up Lyan's arm. Cailean started, telling Lyan that the Tathren lord felt something similar.

The glow faded, and both Lyan and Cailean withdrew their Spears at the same time. Cailean smiled wryly. "Maybe warn me next time?"

"Sorry," Lyan apologized. "I think that was Equinox more than me." A sense of approval ran through him and with it, surprising Lyan, gratitude—Equinox thanking him.

This is going to take some getting used to.

"So, what are we to do now?" Aikan cut in. "We have

achieved your initial goal, Lord Cailean, if not in the manner we expected." For once, he did not glower at Lyan.

Cailean looked at Lyan seriously. "Lyan, my friend, will you and Kithr help me? Ewart still holds my home and threatens my people, and I cannot defeat him alone."

From the corner of his eyes, Lyan saw Kithr stiffen, whether at the thought of helping Cailean more or the thought of returning to Tather, Lyan didn't know. "I can't speak for Kithr, Cailean, but I will."

Cailean looked to Kithr, who spat in the dirt. "Yes, Tathren, I'm going with Lyan. I'm still not leaving him alone in your hands."

"Thank you." Cailean said it as genuinely as if Kithr had spoken words of praise.

"You'll be leaving us, then." Waldros's voice made them all start. Lyan wondered how long the Guardian had been listening.

Cailean recovered and bowed to Waldros. "Yes, I'm afraid we must. My home is in danger, and Lyan has agreed to help me."

"Can we have our gear and weapons back now?" Torqual demanded, tone sharp.

Waldros just fixed a long look on the guard, then gestured for all of them to follow him. "Come this way. There is a swifter way to go where you need to be."

The wording struck Lyan as odd. He followed Waldros along more twisting paths of the shrine. They came to the tall white wall and stopped before a gate. Sirex, the gatekeeper, stood beside it, and greeted Lyan with a smile and a nod.

Five Guardians led their horses in a solemn procession, Venycia at their head. The air was still and sounds muffled. A shiver ran down Lyan's spine. Only seven Guardians stood here. Seven demigods who served Equinox of their own will.

Shadowstar broke the stillness, snorting happily and

nuzzling Lyan's hair. Lyan chuckled softly and rubbed the stallion's nose. "Yes, I'm glad to see you as well, Shadowstar."

"The saddle is new, Lyan Spearbearer," said a Guardian whose name he didn't know. "You will find a resting place for Equinox, much as Lord Cailean has on his for Solstice."

"Thank you," Lyan said. He hadn't thought how he would carry the Spear while riding. He climbed into the saddle and settled into place, then looked to his companions.

Sirex returned weapons and gear to their owners. Torqual scowled and checked each item before setting it in place. Kithr smirked at the Tathren soldier, taking his own weapons as they were given to him and refusing to show any such concern.

Yion was the last to mount, and the one with the most weapons to put back in place. He went about the task with quiet efficiency, and everything found a spot, although Lyan wasn't sure exactly where Yion managed to hide all the blades and throwing stars. He did see the mercenary bow to Venycia.

"Lady, your uncle bids me give you his greetings and well-wishes."

She smiled. "Thank you. When next you speak with him, tell him that it was a delight to be host to one of his chosen champions."

Yion bowed more deeply. "I am honored, Lady, and I will bear your words to his ears."

Shadowstar pranced impatiently, and Lyan rubbed the stallion's ears, then looked around again. Sirex met his gaze.

"This gate will take you to where you must go. Travel with the blessings of Cantorelle of the Roads, and remember what you have learned here."

"Thank you." Lyan nodded, then looked to the rest of the Guardians, and especially to Venycia. "Thank you all. I... hope I will see you again soon."

Ude snorted. "You'd better, if you know what's good for you!"

Lyan chuckled nervously and nodded. "Of course."

He urged Shadowstar to a walk, and the stallion led the way. Sirex sketched the sign of Cantorelle, god of roads, in the air as they passed, and Lyan returned the gesture. Raising his hand in a final farewell to the Shrine and its Guardians, he rode through the arched gateway into swirling mist.

EXCERPT FROM THORNS IN
SHADOW, BOOK 2 OF THE CHOSEN
OF THE SPEARS

Chapter One

Cold, pale mist wrapped around Lyan, stealing him into its depths. The trees and stone arches of the Shrine of Equinox vanished behind him, swallowed in white. The songs of birds cut off. He saw only muted light with no source as his friends and companions disappeared. The mist thickened until he couldn't even see his stallion Shadowstar, though he could feel the horse's confident steps.

Where am I? Where are Kithr and the others? Fear gripped his chest and knotted his throat as he looked over his shoulder into gray haze. The doorway was gone.

"Peace, Lyan." The reassurance was more a sensation than actual words, like a soothing drink of clear water on a summer day.

The touch on his mind made him jump. Lyan was far from accustomed to not being alone in his thoughts. He felt down the stallion's shoulder, to the weapon strapped to the saddle, assuring himself that it, at least, remained close.

Another reassurance, tinged with amusement, brushed his mind, then withdrew. Lyan found a thin smile. "Thank you, Equinox." The mist muted his words and clung in his throat.

He raised his eyes, as if the mist might somehow reveal the sky while it hid the land. Assuming there was anything to see at all. His understanding of magical portals was limited at best. No stars glowed overhead, but Lyan did see shadows forming through the fog. They resolved into branches high overhead. Mist faded, and Lyan found himself gripping Shadowstar's mane with one hand, the other resting on Equinox.

The Spear stood nearly as tall as him, etched with arcane runes. The serrated head shone, flawless, as if it had not seen centuries of battle. Even lacking expertise with weapons, Lyan could admire its craftsmanship and deadly beauty.

From the Spear, a sensation brushed Lyan's mind, like a bird preening its feathers. He smiled faintly. Until a few days ago, he'd never thought Equinox, one of the two Spears of the Stars, most powerful magical weapons in the world, could be vain. Not until Lyan had taken the Trials and become bearer of the Spear had he even considered that the Spears might be aware and have thoughts of their own.

Shadowstar turned to look at Lyan and tossed his head, snorting as if to assure his rider that their method of travel was perfectly normal. Lyan let out a breath that became a soft laugh. Releasing the stallion's mane, he reached forward and stroked Shadowstar's neck. "Even my horse is more familiar with magic than I am."

Shadowstar snorted again, then lowered his head to investigate a patch of ferns. Lyan drew a deep breath, filling his nose with the scents of fir and pine. Cones littered the ground, and when he turned his gaze to the sky, he saw tangled and twined branches casting the forest floor in shadows. Despite the heavy shade, summer's heat pierced the air, stifling after the chill of the mist. Insects buzzed and whined in the still, heavy air, but no birds sang, and he heard none of the expected rustling of animals aside from Shadowstar's movements.

Much as Lyan wanted to rejoice to be under a forest's sheltering boughs, these trees loomed with malice rather than welcome. He instinctively tried to sense the spirit of the place, as he would have at home in the elven forest of Eilidh Wood. To his surprise, the wood reacted to his touch, pushing back with sharp warning. Branches shifted, dropping dry needles down on him. Lyan raised an arm to shield his head, but no larger missiles fell from above.

Raking fingers through red hair, Lyan shook out most of the needles and tucked straggling locks behind his long, pointed ears, careful not to tangle them on his ear cuff. He eyed the trees, wary of further reaction. "I'm not here to bother you. Just… passing through."

Branches rattled like dry bones, then settled. Lyan felt the forest watching him—just watching.

"Do you know where we are, Equinox?" Lyan asked in a low voice. "Are we still near your shrine? What about my friends?" At the Shrine of Equinox, the Guardian who opened the portal had told Lyan it would take him "where he needed to go," but offered no clues as to where that would be. Lyan had intended to accompany his human companions and help them retake their homeland. What part did this malevolent forest play in that goal?

Equinox responded with reassurance. Lyan's questions would be answered soon.

A jingle of tack and the heavy step of a horse made Lyan turn, gripping Equinox. His shoulders relaxed as a cloud of mist resolved into a grim elf in brown leathers astride a chestnut horse. Kithr had been Lyan's friend for nearly a hundred fifty years, since they were both children. Kithr was a study in brown—hair the color of acorns, well-traveled leather clothes, tanned skin. Like Lyan, he surveyed their surroundings. His brow furrowed in a frown that held more surprise than irritation, and he turned to Lyan.

"I don't suppose we've lost your Tathrens?" Kithr asked in a low voice.

"I hope not," Lyan said. "And I doubt it." He nodded at another mist cloud forming to Kithr's right.

"A pity." Kithr watched the mist, bow in hand.

The mists revealed the first of the humans: their leader, the Tathren lord Cailean Dev'gilla. His golden brown hair was trimmed short and his face clean-shaven. To Lyan's eye, Cailean looked close in age to him and Kithr, and he sometimes forgot the human had seen only twenty-six years, not one hundred and fifty. Cailean glanced around, then nodded to Lyan and Kithr. Lyan counted him as a friend. Kithr tolerated him, a vast improvement over Kithr's initial hostility, and nearly miraculous considering Cailean wielded Solstice, the second Spear of the Stars, and the impetus for the elven attack on Tather.

Trees shifted and swayed, spitting prickly pine cones at Cailean. He eyed the forest and shivered. His horse edged closer to Shadowstar without urging. "Hardly an auspicious greeting."

Lyan was less glad to see the next person who appeared. Cailean's steward, Aikan, was a stern man in his sixties who had never hidden his dislike of elves in general or Lyan in particular. The lines of his face told of a man more apt to frown than smile, and he fixed the familiar scowl on Lyan. "What gods-forsaken abomination have you whisked us into, elf?"

"I did not control the portal we entered, Aikan," Lyan answered tightly. "At a glance, though, I would say a forest."

Kithr snorted a laugh, earning a glare from Aikan. "Shade, shelter, and cover in one place. Why should we be anywhere else?" He and Aikan held each other in mutual disdain, though Kithr usually managed to restrain himself from needling Aikan too often.

"Bah. Just like an elf." Aikan's jaw tightened.

Cailean scanned the forest. "Aikan, the rest of my men followed you?"

"They should have, my lord," Aikan answered. He gave Lyan another suspicious look, not convinced he wasn't somehow responsible for the delay of the other four members of their group.

A mist swirled into existence beside Aikan, and the gray-haired man's horse drew back from it. Torqual and his mare appeared. The blond warrior rubbed at the perpetual stubble on his chin as he studied their new surroundings. When on foot, he stood equal height with Lyan, though on horseback he seemed shorter. Of all the Tathrens, he was the only one Kithr nominally respected, as one warrior to another. He was sparing with words, respectfully cautious of Kithr, and usually polite to Lyan.

After him came the brothers Dalrian and Shiolto, hunter and stable hand from Cailean's keep, respectively. Both greeted Lyan with nervous smiles. Shiolto was the youngest of the group, still in his teens, while Dalrian had several more years, just cresting twenty. Of all the Tathrens, they had been the most welcoming to Lyan when he joined Cailean's search for Equinox. At the same time, neither felt at ease amid quests for ancient magical weapons, meetings with demigods, magic portals, or actively hostile forests. Shiolto claimed such adventures were meant for men better than common peasants, but Lyan knew few he'd rather have at his back.

The final member of their group appeared moments after the brothers. Unlike the rest of the humans, Yion was not Tathren, but a mercenary who had attached himself to Cailean for reasons he'd never completely explained. He was shorter than the others, and his features flatter. His eyes seemed to slant slightly. When caught in the right light, the center of Yion's forehead had an odd oval divot he sometimes rubbed when thinking. At a glance, he drew little attention, carrying himself with calm ease, but Lyan knew that hidden under and in his plain, unrestrictive clothes, he bore an impressive arsenal of blades and throwing weapons to complement the short sword at his waist.

"We're all here," Lyan said. He paused. The forest had, if anything, grown darker and more threatening as his companions arrived. "Wherever here is."

Dalrian shivered, gripping his sword. "Can we leave? This place feels creepy."

"And if we leave this forest, perhaps we can find landmarks, or a village... something to help us determine where we are." Cailean walked his nervous horse in a tight circle. "And how far we have to go to reach my home."

Unexpectedly, Kithr laughed. "You mean to tell me you can't tell where we are? Tathrens, and you don't even recognize it?"

"Then enlighten us, if you are so much better informed," Aikan snapped.

Kithr smirked. "I know quite well where we are. I once lived here, plotting and raiding your people. This is Malgor Forest." He shook his head with another, softer laugh. "This, *this* is Tather."

APPENDIX: GODS OF NOTE

GODS OF EILIDH WOOD

Soldarr: The one male of the three gods of Eilidh Wood, Soldarr wields a battle axe in combat and is said to be a fierce warrior. In times of peace, he is lover to both Feyra and Tesseia. In the past, he has also engaged in trysts with mortal women; however, no such unions have been reported since Tesseia threatened to castrate him the next time he did so. Soldarr and the Tathren god Ahebban bear a grudge against one so old that few, if any, mortals know its origin.

Feyra and Tesseia: The goddesses are sisters, and both wield bows in combat. They are said to have a stronger connection to Eilidh Wood than Soldarr, understanding the forest and its whims more easily. Some Tathren priests claim that in addition to being lover to Feyra and Tesseia, Soldarr is also their brother, however, the gods vehemently dismiss this claim.

GODS OF TATHER (NOT ALL-INCLUSIVE)

Ahebban, Watcher on the Walls: Ahebban is the protector of fortresses. When a Tathren keep or stronghold is completed, the priests of Ahebban ask his blessing on it. One part of the ritual blessing calls for the god's protection on the fortress to prevent anyone outside the walls from using harmful magic against the keep or anyone inside it. He bears a fierce anger against Soldarr, and, by extension, the elves of Eilidh Wood. The bear is sacred to Ahebban.

Saiboti, god of warriors: Saiboti is brother to Ahebban. He doesn't share his brother's fanatical anger against the elves of Eilidh Wood. He is known to be a god of honor, and expects those who follow him to act accordingly. The hawk is sacred to Saiboti.

Erskine, god of the fields: Erskine is the god of the fields and harvest, venerated by farmers and all who work the land. His exact feelings toward the elves of Eilidh Wood are unknown, though it's doubtful that he looks very fondly on the invaders who burned, destroyed, and looted farms and fields. The cat is sacred to Erskine.

OTHER GODS

Veil: Veil is the god of divination. Said to live on the moon, Veil possesses the power to manipulate how the stars appear in the night sky. Astrologers interpret those signs to read fortunes and predict the future.

Toirni, the Thunderer: Toirini is the god of the weather, commonly called the Stormlord or the Thunderer. The nomads of the Apperet Plains revere him as a deity in their pantheon. He is the god they appeal to for rain. The power that Murdo has given to one of his minions, to cloud the sky, trespasses into Toirini's domain, but the Thunderer seems to be prevented from dispelling the clouds that hide the sky at night.

The Horselord: The Horselord is the god of horses on the Apperet Plains, and primarily worshipped by the nomads there. Most depictions of him show him as a centaur.

Nachyne, god of monsters: Even the monsters have a deity. Nachyne rules over the monsters, including but not limited to dragons, fairies, pooka, and sirens. He's not known to care much for mortals or to any great shows of benevolence, even to his own worshipers. He tends to take the form of a dragon or a man with draconic wings, claws, and a tail.

Cantorelle, god of roads: Cantorelle is the patron god of travelers, and takes special interest in the protection of refugees, women, and children. He is often invoked before a journey. Cantorelle does not have temples, though sometimes travelers will build a shrine in his honor after completing a particularly difficult stretch of their journey.

The god of roads has an order of priests/defenders of the roads, called Freewardens. As the god of roads practices neutrality in national disputes, so do the Freewardens, and they are allowed to travel across any border, through any land, without being attacked or detained by the denizens of that land. Any people who they place under their protection are equally exempt. No wise person would abuse this protection, nor interfere with a Freewarden—Cantorelle is fond of his Freewardens, and angering the god of roads promises to make any future travels fraught with peril.